I0729151

KENNETH BROWN

RESCUE
OF THE
STONE
WARRIORS

The Mountain King Series - Book 3

Adgitize Press

The Mountain King Series

By Kenneth Brown

Haskell –Orphan to King (Prequel)

Eclipse of the Triple Moons

Zita's Revenge

Rescue of the Stone Warriors

Copyright Page

Rescue of the Stone Warriors

Published by Adgitize Press

Copyright 2022 by Kenneth Brown

An Adgitize Press Book

Streamwood, IL

First Edition: January 2023

ISBN - 978-1-7322871-9-8

Library of Congress Control Number: 2022923696

ADGITIZE PRESS

Cover Art by

FXQuadro and backUp

Cover Design

Kenneth Brown

Editor

Red Adept Editing

CHAPTER 1

Zita stood in the antechamber of the Grand Wizard's office in the Velidred Castle. Would this man she loathed help her and her friends rescue the stone warriors in the mountains?

The castle seemed different in attitude from when her father was king. Back then, everybody roamed the halls in fear, and any wrong move resulted in a beating or time in the dungeon. Now the halls felt lively, and the servants were happy as they performed their tasks. Had Prince Krunal been able to change the feeling in the castle in such a short time? She hoped the Grand Wizard had changed too.

Zita wore the helmet of justice that she and her friends had seized on their trip to the Pit of Wretchedness. The helmet made her head itch, but it gave her insights into the people she spoke with, and she would need insights when speaking with the Grand Wizard, a wily, petty man.

Alpherge the Mighty, a six-foot-seven beanpole, stood next to her with his staff and said, "How long is this guy going to keep us waiting? We could have rescued the stone warriors and gotten back to Velidred by now. We have things to do."

"You can't rush the man. He's power hungry and knows tricks to manipulate a person, which is why he's making us wait."

"I can send a fireball and blast down the door."

"Please don't do that." Zita didn't need Al causing a ruckus. Her head hurt again this morning. Her stomach flip-flopped between feeling bad and feeling worse and not just from nervousness. She placed a hand on her stomach. The nausea came most mornings these last two weeks.

"Zita, are you okay?" Erik asked.

Erik and Al were two of the four teens that had arrived from planet Earth six months earlier through a strange portal that connected the mountains of Montana to the Village of the Stone Warriors on the planet Aloheno. Zita's life had been upside down ever since. She placed her hand in his. "Yeah, I'm okay." When they completed their meeting with the Grand Wizard and rescued the stone warriors, she would find someone to heal her. Just a few more days and they would be finished.

She had to keep the request to the Grand Wizard simple. Her father had taught her that. Ask for one thing and keep it simple. The more complicated the request, the harder it would be for the other side to grant. They were there to ask one question.

Alpherge said, "You don't think this guy will try to take our magical artifacts, do you?"

"No, because we will present ourselves as normal people with a simple, reasonable appeal. Don't offer any information. In fact, keep your mouth shut until we leave the castle." Al liked to run his mouth, and Zita would have preferred to have this conversation with the Grand Wizard without him, but Erik had insisted they both be involved.

"But we aren't normal people. We're great adventurers with awesome treasures. Shouldn't that get us some respect?"

"I know, but if you say too much, the Grand Wizard may very well trap us in the castle—or worse, take our magical items away from us and throw us in the dungeon."

Al said, "This room makes me nervous. In fact, the entire building makes me nervous. The last time I was here, the king threw me in the dungeon, and I'm not eager to go back."

Erik placed his hand on Al's shoulder. "Relax. Let Zita do the talking. She knows this guy, and she knows how to handle the situation. She'll use the Helmet of Justice to peer into his mind and manipulate him to tell us what we need to know."

"The helmet doesn't work like that. I can listen to his mind and determine if he's trying to cheat us, but I can't control him."

Al sighed.

She shook her head at Al. "Quit worrying. I've got this. We'll have a friendly chat with the Grand Wizard and walk out the castle doors with the information we need to rescue Erik's dad." Zita didn't believe any of that. No conversation with the Grand Master ended with a ruling in favor of the applicant. The Grand Master controlled everything about the meeting and would make sure he profited from the transaction, either in cash or political capital. The political capital he traded with the other wizards on the Council of Nine, a powerful and dangerous group in charge of wizardry throughout the region of Velidred and beyond.

Zita adjusted the helmet, pressing down in certain spots to scratch her head. Why did this thing irritate her this morning? She wondered if the Grand Wizard would penalize her now since her dad didn't control Velidred Castle anymore.

The door opened, and a servant girl, carrying a silver tray with two silver chalices, came out of the Grand Master's office. The girl saw Zita and stopped, frozen in place. A crimson flush crept across the girl's cheeks, extending to her ears, and she broke eye contact with Zita and smoothed down the front of her dress with one hand. Then the girl hurried off into the castle corridor.

Zita remembered the girl from the time when Zita lived here in the castle as a princess. The helmet led Zita to believe the girl was embarrassed for her. "Are you two ready?" A flutter of excitement went through her stomach, exacerbating the nausea already there. She knocked on the Grand Wizard's door.

The Grand Wizard called out, "Come."

CHAPTER 2

Zita led the boys into the man's office space. The décor hadn't changed since the first time she'd seen the room when she was in her early teens. A mahogany desk bearing two burning candles and three scrolls sat near the thin stone window. Next to one wall lay a chaise lounge covered in a red plush fabric with a couple of pillows thrown haphazardly on top. The large fifteen-candle candelabrum brightened the room.

The Grand Wizard sat behind the desk, where he studied a scroll. Without looking, he asked, "What do you want?"

Zita bowed. "Grand Wizard, we come for information."

"Yes, out with it."

She fingered a necklace her mom had given her many years before in this same castle. "Can we overturn the magic used to entrap the stone warriors and allow the warriors to return to their human selves?"

The Grand Wizard raised his head from the scroll and looked at the teens from underneath the cowl of his robe. A tentative smile built on his bearded face as he turned his gaze to Zita. The man removed the hood from his head, stood, and walked around the desk, his dark maroon robes swishing on the brick floor.

"Little Zita visits me. I thought you were dead, and what is that awful-looking thing on your head?"

Zita took a deep breath. She didn't want the Grand Wizard to know she wore the Helmet of Justice, known to everyone else as the magical but legendary golden crown. "We have a request about the stone warriors."

"Have you? Oh, and isn't this Alpherge the Great's grandson you brought with you? King Haskell expected you to die in the Velidred dungeon." The Grand Wizard smirked.

Al stood tall and held the staff straighter. Zita hoped the boy didn't get it in his head that he had to say something. If he ran his mouth, he would surely ruin the meeting and prevent them from gaining the information they needed.

"What is it you want?"

"We want to know what magic Dad used to entrap the warriors on the mountain. We"—Zita pointed at Erik and Alpherge with her hand—"want to release the stone warriors."

The Grand Master gave a moment's thought and then laughed heartily from deep within his belly. "You three think you have your father's magical capability?"

Alpherge said, "I defeated the king on the volcano."

The Grand Wizard gave an ugly twist to his mouth. "The boy wizard has one victory, which required others' help"—he nodded to Zita—"and you think you are all-powerful? That's not the way it works, *boy*."

Al opened his mouth to say something.

She sensed through the helmet that Al was getting riled, and the Grand Wizard was having fun manipulating him. Zita touched Al's arm. "Quiet."

Then she returned her attention to the Grand Wizard. "Maybe we won't be able to help them now, but you're pretty smart, and I thought you might know how my dad did it."

"May I examine that monstrosity on your head, the leather helmet with the golden dragon on top?"

The Grand Wizard reached out to Zita to touch it, but she drew back. "It's nothing more than a focusing tool like this necklace my mother gave me." She touched the necklace to move his attention away from the helmet.

"Are you coming back to the Velidred castle? I think the new inhabitant, Prince Krunal, will not be happy knowing you're here. Are you spying for someone?"

"I'm not spying. What can you tell us about the magic used in the mountains by my father?" Through the helmet, she sensed he was using his questions to make time, but time for what?

"Prince Krunal is a different ruler than your father. Not as much discipline and suffering. He's opening up the countryside and allowing the Kallurians to farm again. Each year, your dad would send wizards out into the harvest and burn the fields in hopes the Kallurians starved during the winter."

"I'm not here for a history lesson. Can we focus on the stone warriors?"

"A history lesson. Is that what you call it? I don't remember you being the best student in the castle."

Alpherge pounded his staff on the floor. "Come on, buddy, give us the information we want."

Al stood almost a foot taller than the Grand Wizard, but the Grand Wizard had a presence of superiority about him and a look that radiated supremacy.

The Grand Wizard said, "And what will you do if I don't give it to you?"

"Why, I—" Al sputtered.

"You won't do anything, Alpherge the Younger. I don't care who your grandfather was. The man never impressed me, and you don't have a tenth of his skill."

Al raised his staff.

"No, don't," Zita yelled. She placed her hand on Al's arms and helped lower them to his sides. "Relax, Al. We're civilized citizens of Velidred." She didn't feel civilized as the nausea and headaches increased each moment she was in the room. What thoughts did the helmet transmit from the Grand Wizard's mind? Right now, the greatest thought was contempt for her and Al.

Zita stared into the Grand Wizard's gray eyes and pressed forward with her questions. "Do you know an incantation that we can try on the stone warriors? Did you help my father create the magic?"

"Your father was a fool. I offered him my help on the matter, but he took the advice of someone else."

"Hah!" Al barked.

"And you, young man, are a bigger fool than the king. You three *children* are in way over your heads on this matter and need to think about other things. I suggest you, Zita, and definitely Al, should go back to wizard school. The king was in his fifties when he turned the warriors to stone. Why the sudden interest in the stone warriors? You've never been interested before."

"Haven't you ever wondered if they could be rescued? The Council of Nine should have the knowledge and power to release the warriors from their imprisonment."

"The Council of Nine has important matters to resolve and doesn't have the time to undo the effects of evil magic."

Zita smiled. "My father was stronger than all the members of the Council of Nine."

The Grand Wizard's nostrils flared, and he bared his teeth. "Were you saddened by your father's death? I heard rumors you sent the killing fireball."

She remembered sending the killing fireball and the months of anguish it had caused her. "My father's alive and at the Ice Castle," she blurted. She felt him react in shock, but he maintained facial integrity. If she wasn't wearing the helmet, she would think him dispassionate to the information.

"I'm not surprised that he could do that. Like I've been trying to tell you your father was—no, is a powerful wizard. The king had a strong connection to the old magic. He learned a lot from Gadiel, a man I suggest you spend time with."

Al pronounced, "Gadiel is dead. We killed him."

Zita rolled her eyes, pinched her lips, and shook her head. The boy couldn't keep his mouth shut. Gadiel had tried to kill the three of them after they returned with the magic treasures. They were forced to kill the man.

"You killed Gadiel? I would think you should have kept him alive. He could help with the stone warriors." Then his expression changed as if an idea came into his head. "The Corruption of Evil. Did that get transferred to one of you?" He spent a moment studying each party member's eyes.

"The corruption of evil—"

Erik interrupted Al. "He doesn't need to know everything. Remember, we're here for the stone warriors."

Zita shook her head. They had safely ensconced the Corruption of Evil into the Sword of Freedom. She wanted to scratch her scalp, but the leather prevented a good scratch. The itch only worsened the more she thought about scratching. Her headache pounded, and if she didn't get out of the room soon, she would vomit right there.

She turned toward Erik. "We need to go. It's apparent the Grand Wizard can't help us."

"No, stay for tonight's banquet. Members of the Council of Nine are at the castle, and I'm sure they would be interested in learning more about Gadiel and your father."

The helmet transmitted an urgent thought scurrying through the man's brain. He must keep them in the room for another few minutes. He had notified someone of their presence and hoped to capture them.

"If you found any magical items of interest, like that ugly helmet you're wearing, leave them for analysis by the Council of Nine. It's the law."

The Grand Wizard has figured it out. If wizard warriors capture us in the castle, then we won't leave with the helmet or the sword and will probably lose Al's staff.

"If we find anything of value, we will let you know, but we need to get back on the road now. It's been nice catching up with you." Zita grabbed Erik's hand and pulled him toward the door. "Al let's go."

The Grand Wizard's indifference changed into determination as his brow furrowed and he lowered his voice. "You three need to wait." He charged to get to the door before the teens, but they scurried past and into the antechamber.

Zita said, "Boys, follow me. I know this castle and its secrets better than anyone."

"We're right behind you."

The Grand Master yelled, "Stop. Guards, get them."

Zita led the chase through a hallway and headed down a set of stairs, which led to a tapestry-lined hallway.

Guards chasing them yelled, "Stop! Guards, at the ready."

That meant the next guards they encountered would be armed with bows and arrows ready and spears set to attack.

CHAPTER 3

Zita and the two boys raced down the hallway. Servants on the move with clothing and linen for wash contorted out of their way. One room up ahead contained a stairway for servants. One guard would be stationed at the bottom of the stairs. If they got to him before the guards sounded the alarm, they'd have free passage into the safety of the courtyard.

"In here." Zita flung open a door.

The boys followed her into a room with a bathtub occupied by a naked noblewoman. She and the servant washing her back screamed.

Zita chanted a spell, cutting off the sound of the screaming women. "Silence."

The boys had stopped. Erik looked at Zita as his face flushed, and he grabbed Al's arm. "Let's go."

Zita slipped behind a tapestry over the doorway and pounded down the circular stairs. She hoped few servants were in the stairway at the moment because those stairs were precarious at the speed she ran.

The next tapestry would be a hallway on the second floor, where Zita's room used to be. She thought back to her little music box and wondered where it might be now. Zita had hoped to look for it after the conference with the Grand Wizard, but that wouldn't be possible now.

She heard a commotion behind her as the guards entered the bathroom the teens had just vacated. Some nobleman would give Prince Krunal a tongue-lashing before sunset. The next set of stairs exited into three rooms—the washing room filled with hot water and dirty linens, the kitchen, or the exit into the courtyard gardens. She hurried into the courtyard.

This conference with the Grand Wizard couldn't have ended any worse. Guards were on the alert to their presence. The Kallurian warrior wizards were looking for them, and the Grand Wizard knew that Zita and Erik had magic objects of great power and mystery. He wouldn't be easy on them if they were captured.

Guards rushed toward them in the courtyard. The boys crashed into her, almost knocking her over. "Not this way." She turned them back toward the kitchen. "Follow the kitchen hall past the fireplace, turn right, and cross a small courtyard to the stables. Do you know how to ride a horse?"

"I can't ride a horse," Al yelled.

"You're about to learn." She pushed them forward.

At this time of day, the guard's morning practices should be complete, and a saddled horse or two might be available. As the group crossed the courtyard between the kitchen and stables, arrows flew from the castle walls.

"Watch out. This is serious." Al raised his staff over his head. "I placed a shield."

Zita barked out a command, "Into the stables. See if there are any horses."

The three ran into the stables. There were no available horses.

Zita pointed at a bale of hay by the stables. "Behind the gate, hurry. Hide in the hay."

"My allergies will kick in," Al said.

"Move." Zita pushed Al into the hay. "Be quiet and give me a moment's silence."

Erik breathed hard as he lay in the hay next to her. Concentrate. What animals would be found in a stable? Dogs, of course.

In the current situation, she had trouble relaxing her breathing to engage her shapeshifting ability. Gadiel had told her to practice more, but after he died, she spent her time kissing Erik and didn't practice like she should have.

Four guards entered the stables. "I saw them come in here. You two with the spears poke around in the hay but don't kill them. We'll check over by the horses. If I wanted to escape, I would try to steal a horse."

Zita raced through the relaxation and mind-emptying process as she prepared to shapeshift both herself and the two boys.

The guards raised their spears and approached the hay.

Zita took a deep breath and exhaled. The nausea rolled over her in deep waves as bile came up her throat. Her heart beat fast. She felt her necklace and closed her eyes. A dog barked next to her. Then a second dog barked, and she opened her eyes. Erik had changed to a black dog of mixed breed. Al had turned into a golden Labrador retriever. Zita looked at her four legs and figured that would be good enough.

One guard kicked at Erik, and Al growled at the man. Zita barked, and the boys followed her out of the stable. They raced through the castle's middle bailey, where townsfolk mingled, children played, people led horses to the stables, and chickens ran from the children.

Guards chased after them. "Stop those dogs."

The castle gate from the middle bailey to the outer bailey stood open, and the three dogs ran through the gate.

A guard yelled to the gatekeeper, "Close the outer gates! Thieves are trying to escape."

Another guard relayed the message further as the dogs raced toward the outer gate. Each step Zita took churned her stomach and made her head hurt even more.

The three dogs ran between the legs of nervous horses as goats bleated next to the wall.

Other dogs running in the yard chased the three. The barking caused a commotion. She heard the next guard saying words, but they came out garbled to her ears because of the noise from the barking dogs.

One of the larger dogs chasing them nipped at Zita's heels, and Erik intervened and growled at the larger dog.

Zita snapped at Erik's leg, and they raced out the open gate, followed by a pack of six barking and slobbering canines.

Guards chased them through the gates, but the dogs quickly outpaced them.

Zita and the boys ran into the nearby pine forest. By the time they reached a safe enough distance to stop, most of the other dogs had already halted, leaving only one dog to witness the three shapeshift back into humans.

The boys lay on the ground, laughing and gasping for breath. Zita went to a nearby tree and vomited. A stab of pain spiked through her brain.

Erik went to Zita and rubbed her back. "How are you doing?"

She was on her hands and knees, her head aching and sweat forming on her forehead. "I'm not doing well. The nausea is getting worse. I can't take much more." She removed the helmet and scratched her head.

Erik asked, "Do you want me to heal you again?"

The sickness numbed her feelings, and the running had left her weak. "Yeah." She gave a half-hearted shrug.

Erik took her head in his hands. They felt cool compared to Zita's fevered head. Just being out of the hot helmet without her head itching made her feel better. The fresh air and the forest pine scent boosted her spirits.

He shook his head. "Your brain looks different from what I've seen practicing healing with Cugbert. It's like something is trying to take over, but I can't see where it's coming from. I don't know what to do. I'm afraid I'll hurt you if I do something wrong."

Zita wondered if Erik doing something wrong would make her feel better or worse. "The Grand Wizard knew."

"What?" Erik asked.

"He knew we had a secret, and we gave him answers. It might have been better if Al could keep his mouth shut."

"Hey, you gave up as much information as I did. I'm surprised you didn't come right out and say, 'Here's the Helmet of Justice. Do you want it?'"

"I did the best I could, but you kept jumping in and giving him information, he didn't ask for. Before we met with him, I told you to keep your mouth shut." She picked up the Helmet of Justice and threw it at Al, hitting him in the upper arm.

"Hey, stop it." Al grabbed the leather helmet off the ground and heaved it back at her.

Zita picked it up again, but Erik stepped in and took it from her. "Why don't you let me carry the helmet for the next couple of days? I think it stresses you."

"It doesn't make me anything, but it causes my head to itch. That's all." She reached for the helmet, and he pulled it away. Fatigue washed over her, and she didn't feel like wrestling with Erik. "Fine, wear it for the day and see if your hair itches."

He plopped the helmet on his head, but it didn't really fit and leaned precariously to one side. "It has a bit of weight to it."

"When I put it on my head, I don't feel the weight at all. It's like it molds into my skull and becomes a part of me."

Al asked, "So, what do we do now?"

Erik pulled the helmet from his head. "I want to go up to see the stone warriors."

"We don't know how to rescue them and reverse the spell." Al used his staff to stand.

"I know, but I want to show my dad the sword and let him know what we're trying to do. There's nothing to stop us from trying a few things on our own." Erik drew the sword and brandished it. "We have the magical items."

Zita said, "The Grand Wizard knows that we have the Helmet of Justice and that we want to reverse the magic on the stone warriors. We can go up to the mountains and try one time, and then we need to find a place to hide until we get more information." She scratched her head and vomited.

CHAPTER 4

The three teens walked up the mountain to the Village of the Stone Warriors. A small village grew near where powerful magic struck the warriors and turned them into stone. The stone warriors' family members would stop and visit a few times a year. Erik had a personal reason to visit the stone warriors. His father had commanded the warriors on that fateful day.

Erik wondered what his father would say about the Sword of Freedom, a magical sword, but it only worked for healers and priests. Erik wasn't a full-fledged priest and healer, but he had used the sword once and felt its power.

They passed by the small mountain village and continued up to the battleground where the magic occurred. They crested a hill, and the soldiers stood solid where they had turned to stone. The interesting but sad part was that the warriors didn't die that day. They stood as stone statues, but they could talk to the people that visited them. They lived in bodies of stone, unable to move arms or legs, unable to get a fly off their face or hug a family member.

Erik adjusted the broadsword and walked to his father, Commander John Anderson.

The warrior who stood next to the commander said in a hollow voice, "The boy is back, Commander."

"I don't want to talk to him."

"Sir, he carries a sword."

"He has betrayed his family. He is dead to me."

Erik said, "Dad, I haven't betrayed my family. We're here to rescue you and all the stone warriors. I have friends with me, and we brought magical objects that may help reverse the magic that caused all this." Erik waved across the battlefield.

"What's the sword for? I thought you were becoming a priest."

"Yes, Dad," It felt strange calling this statue Dad. Erik had never known his dad until he and his friends went through a portal and ended up on this mountain on Aloheno. Erik's mom told him his dad had died in a military campaign on Earth, never revealing the planet Erik and his friends were born on. "I am still studying to be a priest, but Alpherge and I stopped our training so we could find some magic objects to reverse the magic that was used here."

"If you have turned your back on becoming a military man, why pretend to be a soldier carrying a sword?"

"The sword is the Sword of Freedom, and it can heal. Dad, we're here to help you and your soldiers."

"Help my men. You can leave me as stone. I don't want to live in a world without my wife and with my only son a priest instead of a soldier."

Erik's throat closed up, and he felt a tightness in his chest. Through clenched teeth, he said, "Dad, the portal will reopen in a few years, and then Mom can join us, you and me. There is peace in the land. We can live as a family and not lose people to wars." Why was the man so obstinate? How did Mom ever live with this guy? Mom was fun-loving, a live-and-let-live type of woman, and yet his dad seemed so closed-minded. Was Erik doing the right thing by releasing these people?

"Help my men, and then we'll talk."

"Maybe the magic we do here will open the portal and we can go get Mom right away."

"Don't make promises you can't keep. You've disappointed me enough."

Erik looked up into the sky and wanted to throw the helmet in his hand at the man. He showed the helmet to his father. "This is the Helmet of Justice, a powerful magical object that will release your men from their curse. Al and I risked our lives to seize the helmet and sword. We did it for you, Dad." He banged the gold dragon on the helmet against the statue's shoulder. "We did it for you."

He stalked back to Al and Zita.

Commander John Anderson asked, "Who's the girl?"

Erik wondered if he should tell his dad he was dating the daughter of the man who turned him into a statue.

Zita asked, "Well, Erik, are you going to introduce me to your father?"

"Maybe now's not the time for introductions."

Zita tilted her chin down and frowned. "And why not? Do you not love me?"

"It's not that, Zita."

Commander Anderson shouted, "Zita? The king's daughter? The man who turned us into stone. You brought his daughter here to make fun of us?"

And there it is. "It's not that." Erik shook his head. *How could this whole situation have blown up so badly?* He grabbed Zita's wrist.

"Stop, you're hurting me."

"Come here." He pulled her over to his dad.

"Dad, this is Zita. Zita, my father." This whole idea was bad. He had hoped not to introduce Zita to his father until after they had rescued all the warriors. Then his dad would be proud of him, and since Zita helped, he would realize that she wasn't like her father.

"I would turn my back on the girl if I could, but I can't."

"She's here to help. I love this girl."

"That was what you said about the blonde."

Zita flashed an angry look at Erik and made a slight growl in her throat.

He faced Zita. "You know we came to Aloheno to rescue Lily. So, don't pretend you didn't know I liked her."

She crossed her arms and turned her back on Erik.

Sweat built on Erik's forehead, and he wiped it with his sleeve. "Can we see if we can do this?"

Al said, "I'm ready. Where do you want to start?"

"As far away from this guy as we can." Erik pointed a thumb at his father and walked to the back of the formation of soldiers. The conversation with his father had made his jaw ache.

The other two arrived a few moments later, and Zita raised her hand. "Give me the helmet."

"He's just angry at me and trying to hurt me. Ignore my father."

"Give me the helmet and let's get this done. I want to go back and find some old friends of mine."

"Listen, about Lily."

She grabbed the helmet and stalked through the stone warriors.

Al held up his staff. "Let me check with the staff and see what it recommends. Callahan the Curious. Can you enlighten me on how to solve this riddle?"

"It's not a riddle." Erik rubbed a hand through his beard and tugged on it. "We need a magic spell to reverse the magic that King Haskell sent down on these men." He emphasized King Haskell and looked at Zita.

The staff spoke from one of its faces. "What is the problem to which you seek an answer?"

"The Mountain King turned these warriors into stone, and we need an incantation to reverse the magic and make them whole."

Another staff carving known as Isabel the Insidious said, "They created the stone warriors with extreme heat, and you will need to pour down fire from the sky to save them."

Callahan said, "Are you crazy, woman? Yes, they're created with tremendous heat, and that is why you have to use cold to transform them back into their former selves."

Erik asked, "Are we trying to reverse the spell, stop the curse, or heal them? I think that requires a different approach."

Zita strapped the helmet to her head.

Isabel responded to Callahan. "You're a crazy old fool. Alpherge the Great forced me into this staff, but you fell into it. Don't listen to him. The curse will require heat. You will melt the stone and then reform it into the shapes of the people, like a potter using clay."

Erik shook his head. "Are you saying we need heat so hot it melts rock? That would require the heat of a volcano. I think it's a healing touch, not like re-breaking a bone so it can heal, right? That's like having a car accident and then driving the car into something else to fix it. That logic makes little sense."

"But using cold on the statues allows them to become brittle. Then you whack them, and once they crack, you can remove the stone, like peeling a boiled egg."

Al said, "That sounds reasonable to me. How do we get them so cold the stone will crack?"

"If that is the answer, then we only need to whack them. They've already cooled into stone. How much colder do we have to get them?" Erik asked.

"It doesn't matter because I don't know how to increase the heat so much that it would melt stone or make it so cold the stone becomes brittle," Al said.

The remaining carved face on the staff said, "Did you ask the warriors how they were turned to stone in the first place?"

Erik looked at Al, and they both hunched their shoulders. "Nope."

They walked to the nearest soldier. "Can you tell us about the magic used on the day King Haskell turned you to stone?"

The soldier spoke in an old voice. "We stood on the battlefield. We had trapped the wizard, King Haskell, in front of the open cave, and we expected him to back into the cave and surrender. Instead, he raised his hands into the sky, gesturing at the Velidred moon. The moon was full, and he pulled lightning from the sky. A transparent dome covered us, and an intense, thick fog formed within the dome."

"Did you feel pressure within the dome?" Al asked.

"It's been so long. I don't remember exactly. I couldn't see my buddies next to me since the fog seemed like a gray sheet in front of my eyes. Then a lightning strike hit the dome, and the fog congealed around each of us like animal fat congeals in a bucket. At that point, I felt pressure around my body, like the fog had wrapped me in a blanket. Then I blacked out."

The man stopped talking, and he gasped for air.

Erik asked, "Are you all right, sir?"

"No, I'm not. I was already an old man when I first joined the service. The king frustrated many of us old-timers by keeping us from farming our fields. His warrior wizards burned our crops each year when the harvest moon rose in the fall."

"But you'll live forever as a stone warrior, right?" Erik felt the distress in the man's voice.

"Many of the families that visit don't realize that at some point their family member will die and they won't be able to visit with that stone warrior anymore. We lost Jonesy and Petroff this spring. They're nothing more than statues now."

Erik rubbed the palm of his hand against his chest and looked at his feet.

Silence covered the field.

Before too long, Al said, "It sounds like the fog and jelly stuff are important."

"Does that mean anything to you? Can you replicate it?"

"No, not a clue. How did the king create the dome? That's amazing magic." Al took a deep breath.

Zita said, "Which is why we probably shouldn't be helping these guys."

"I thought you wanted to help."

"I do, but these people might get injured and really die if we do something wrong."

Erik sent Zita a long, pained look and then broke eye contact. "They're already dying. You heard the man. If we don't find an answer on how to release them, they will die and forever be statues in a field."

"Don't you think that's better than blowing them into a million little pieces or using heat to turn them into liquid rock?"

"What does the helmet tell you?"

She looked at him with her green eyes. "The helmet tells me you love me."

"I already told you that." He reached out and held her hand.

"It also hints that a piece of the puzzle might be missing."

Al said, "What do you mean?"

"There's another object not in our possession that we need."

"Give me a break," Erik exclaimed. "We can't keep going after magical items, hoping the next one will be 'the one' that saves these guys. Can't we at least try something before we go traipsing off on another adventure?"

Zita said, "Okay, what do you want to try?"

Erik pulled out his sword. "I want to lay the sword on this guy right here. You will place your hands on my shoulders." Erik placed his sword on the stone man's right shoulder.

Zita placed her hands on Erik's shoulders. "Now what?"

"Al, shoot a little magic into the sword. Oh, and use the staff. Yeah, we need the staff."

"You're just making this up." Zita shook her head.

"Yes, I'm making this up. We can't just leave here today without trying something." *I need to prove to my father that I have the ability as a priest and healer.*

"What kind of magic am I supposed to shoot into this guy?"

"I don't know—magic healing juice."

"You're the healer. I'm more suited to blowing things up." Al placed his staff against the sword.

Erik felt the magic flow through the sword. The sword glowed blue, and Erik tried to divine the internals of the man they were healing. He searched through the stone, expecting to find flesh and blood underneath a layer of rock. He went deeper into the chest, careful not to puncture any internal organs. There must be a heart and lungs in the statue.

He paused. Nothing but rock. He closed his eyes and delved deeper. There must be life within, maybe an inch from where he was. He pursued further, and the sword glowed brighter.

Zita's grip on his shoulders weakened.

"Don't let go," Erik shouted.

"I can't hold on much longer. It's too painful."

What was Zita feeling, Erik wondered? The further he delved with his healing power, the more he found only stone. No feeling, no pain, and no suffering.

"I can't." Zita fell to the ground.

The sword vibrated in Erik's hands. He worked hard to control the quivering magic object as the sword's handle grew hotter.

Al asked, "Do you want me to release?"

"No, not yet."

"It isn't working, Erik. Give way."

"I have to back out slowly or it will trap the sword in the stone."

"Move fast because I don't like how that sword is glowing. You better not catch my staff on fire."

Erik worked backward from the way he came. He felt like he slogged through a field of deep mud, where each step required slow manipulation and precise foot placement. He moved the sword, and the handle grew brighter and warmer. They must hurry. He didn't want to burn out the sword as a healing device, and he especially didn't want the evil stored in the sword to attack him.

"We have only seconds. Once the staff catches on fire, I'm releasing. I don't care how it affects you."

"Wait."

The last few movements out of the man were slow and painful, but Erik exited the stone warrior. "I'm out."

Al moved his staff from the sword.

The sword handle heated to the point that Erik couldn't hold it anymore. He dropped the sword to the ground.

The soldier exploded into a thousand pieces of stone.

CHAPTER 5

Erik went to his knees as he tried to shield his face from the flying debris of the explosion. Hundreds of small stones bounced off his face, arms, and chest. He couldn't believe the stone warrior had exploded. What caused that? He had worked in slow, un-hurried movements within the warrior, and then, when he exited, everything was perfect. How did he kill this man?

Stones and rocks from the explosion rained from the sky and thudded against the stone warriors.

A buzz erupted from the soldiers as if they all spoke at the same time. "Dickerson is dead. The children killed Dickerson."

Erik had trouble catching his breath as the reality of his actions hit him in the chest. He had killed a man, one of his father's soldiers. He tried to do something without knowing how and ended up killing a man.

The buzz continued, "Dickerson is dead. The children killed Dickerson."

Erik planted his face on the ground.

The buzz from the stone warriors stopped, and silence filled the battlefield.

The sound started faintly, then built as the command grew closer to Erik. He couldn't make out the words at first, and then, as it got closer, the warriors shouted sharp commands to the next warrior in line.

"The commander wants to see his son." The nearest soldier commanded.

Erik's muscles tensed, and he felt nauseated. How could Erik stand before his father after killing one of his men? He swallowed hard and wanted to stay on the ground in this position until he died. He raised his head off the ground and looked around. A debris field of stones covered the area where Dickerson once stood. Small dust particles floated and sparkled in the sunshine.

Erik glanced behind him. Al lay face-first on the ground with his hands over his head. Zita huddled nearby, her knees shielding her face.

"Are you two okay?" Erik asked.

"What happened?" Al struggled to his feet.

"I don't know. I thought I had it under control, but when I removed the sword, the guy exploded."

Zita touched his shoulder. "It wasn't your fault."

"Yes, it was. I killed the man. He didn't deserve to die. What's his family going to say when they come to visit him, and he isn't here anymore? Even the warriors who die natural deaths are still statues for their family's visits. This guy has nothing." Erik ran his hands through his hair.

The warrior said, "The commander requests your presence."

"I can't go see my dad after this. He didn't like me before and—"

"We'll go with you." Al clapped him on the back.

Erik's stomach knotted, and he squeezed his eyes shut. The phrase "Dickerson is dead" rolled over and over in Erik's mind. How could he ever come back here, even if his friends figured out how to rescue the warriors? He looked at the warriors and then back at the ground. He couldn't face these soldiers, much less his father.

"The commander demands your presence."

"Yes, I heard you!" He bent and picked up the Sword of Freedom. It didn't offer freedom to Dickerson. As he turned the sword in his hands, the sun flashing off the blade as it turned, the explosion flashed in his mind. Every time he touched this sword, it would remind him of Dickerson. He wanted to throw it off the mountain but knew it might one day help the remaining warriors.

Al pushed Erik. "We should go see your dad."

The teens walked through the warriors toward the commander. In a soft voice, each warrior they passed said, "Dickerson, Dickerson, Dickerson." A hum filled the battleground. When they reached the commander, Erik faced his father.

"What did you do?" the commander asked.

Erik stammered, "We. . . um. . . tried to restore. . . um. . . one of your warriors."

"Dickerson. His name was Dickerson," the commander shouted.

"I know, I'm sorry. It's my fault."

"Is this how you repay me, by killing one of my men?"

A lump formed in Erik's throat; his head lowered as his eyes looked up at his father.

"His wife of forty years sees him three times a week since King Haskell turned him to stone. What do I tell her?"

"I'm sorry Dad. I was trying to help." Erik knew that was a lie. He didn't help but tried to make his dad like him. He didn't attempt the rescue for Dickerson's sake but for his own. Foolishness and pride.

"You killed a good man. I fought next to Dickerson when I was a young pup in the Velidred-Kallurian skirmish. He taught me how to hold a spear and how to set an arrow in a bow. I personally recruited him for this battle after he retired ten years earlier. I remember seeing his wife's face when I asked him to help us. She begged him not to go, but he agreed anyway because he was a good man that cared about others. I thought if I put him in the back lines and used him to teach the young men, he would be safe. Then King Haskell, her father," the commander said with contempt in his voice, "turned us all to stone."

He paused, and silence filled the battlefield.

Erik's arms hung loosely at his sides, though they trembled, and the sword's point touched the ground with the handle loose in his hands. What could he have done differently to save Dickerson? He replayed the process in his mind. He hadn't hurried as he exited the body.

"What do I tell Dickerson's wife when she returns? My son blew up your husband."

Erik said, "I'm sorry, Dad."

"Never call me Dad or Father ever again. You are dead to me. Address me as Commander Anderson."

In the silence, Erik's head drooped toward the ground. He couldn't even look at the stone statue, but he felt his father's presence.

"Leave this place and never return. You and that girl."

CHAPTER 6

With weakness in his legs, Erik trudged up the hill to the Village of the Stone Warriors. His friends followed to the tavern where Erik first met Zita. The dark tavern sported a stone fireplace with a roaring fire, which kept the high mountain chill out of the air. The bar that separated the dining area from the kitchen contained vertical slats of wood with three missing slats. A large, round man worked the kitchen and the dining room.

They ate a meal in silence. Erik looked at his bowl and avoided eye contact with his friends. He ate nothing. He only moved the food around in the bowl.

After Al wolfed down two bowls of stew, he asked, "What do we do now?"

"I don't know." Erik stared at the wooden table.

Al's staff lay at an angle against the table. The topmost figure in the staff said, "You need to talk to Finn."

"Who's Finn?" Al picked up the staff.

"Finn is a former member of the Council of Nine."

Zita spoke, "If he's a"—she swallowed the food in her mouth and continued—"member of the Council of Nine, then they won't be willing to help us. In fact, they will try to confiscate our magical items. We already saw that with the Grand Wizard."

The staff said, "She's right. You have to be wary of any members of the Council of Nine, but Finn was secretly on our side. Right before the war, the Grand Wizard waged a political campaign against Finn. He brought trumped-up charges against him, and they kicked Finn out of the Council of Nine. He went into hiding."

"Why should we trust him? He might want to get back into the Council of Nine's good graces and may turn on us for his own political gain." Al said.

"Finn was a good man, and he will help you. That's assuming you can find him."

Al adjusted his body on the bench. "Assuming we can find him? You don't know where he is?"

"The last we heard of Finn, he lived in a little mountain hut as a hermit. He didn't communicate with the rest of the wizarding world. He's considered an outcast."

"What were the charges leveled against him?" Al started on his third bowl of stew.

"Well, this part is true. He brought a number of young wizards to Velidred for training. He thought he could create a spell that would turn other people to stone."

"Like shape-shifting?" Zita asked.

"Yes, but as a defensive matter, like arresting wizards for destructive behavior. The plan was to turn them to stone, remove their weapons, and then secure them for proper penalties."

"Was that the same spell Zita's dad used on the warriors?" Al asked.

"Yes."

Al's eyes sparkled, and a wide grin spread across his face. "Then yes, he's the one that can help us. We gotta find this guy."

"Slow down, big fella," the staff interrupted Al.

"You just told us he was the one that invented the spell. Doesn't that mean he'll know how to release the spell? We find him and we're good as gold." Al drummed his fingers on the table.

"Finn did not perfect the skill. In fact, Finn went on a trip for a couple of months and left the students to study on their own. King Haskell came to them one day and asked about their studies. One student showed their progress and turned an animal to stone. The king found that interesting and wanted to know how to do it. The students showed him. Then the king turned the students to stone and left."

Al asked, "Are you telling us Finn doesn't know how to reverse the spell?"

"Nobody does. But he will know more about this process than any living wizard. Maybe by now, he's figured out how to reverse the magic."

"We need to search for Finn and find out if he's resolved the issue."

Erik shook his head, a painful lump in his throat. "I've done enough damage for now." He took Zita's hand in his, enjoying its warmth. "I think it's time I found Cugbert and returned to my studies. And I want to see if Cugbert can cure Zita's physical problems because I can't help her."

Zita brushed her long hair out of her eyes. She looked at Erik with eyes of large, liquid pools of green and smiled. "Do you think he will heal me?"

Erik shrugged. A darkness had encapsulated his thinking.

"You guys aren't coming back to Tanuku and seeing Sherry and Lily?"

Sherry came to the planet Aloheno with her friends Al and Erik to rescue their friend Lily from kidnappers. The portal that made it possible to come to Aloheno from Earth closed a few hours after reaching the planet, and they couldn't return to Earth. They had tried to talk Al and Erik from going to the Ice Castle for a great quest for a golden crown. "I don't think I can see Sherry right now. After killing"—Erik's voice hitched—"Dickerson. She'll just disapprove of our actions."

Al pressed his lips tight. "You'll make me take the brunt of their anger by myself."

Erik broke eye contact with Al. "Cugbert is always wandering from village to village. We'll get back to Tanuku and see the girls in due time. Plus, I plan to give Cugbert the Sword of Freedom because I'm not worthy of using it."

Al rubbed the back of his neck and sighed. He looked at the staff. "Where do I find Finn?"

"In the mountains."

"Which ones? There are a lot of mountains."

The long-bearded face on the staff said, "You might have to ask around a little. Your mouth still seems to work."

The tavern owner came to collect the bowls and Al asked, "Sir, have you ever heard of a wizard named Finn?"

The man scratched his arm and looked up at the ceiling.

Erik gazed at the wooden beams with strands of spider webs reflecting the light from the fire.

The man shifted his gaze to the two large barrels high on the wall behind the bar. "Well, I don't know for sure. But I thought I heard that name years ago. A wizard expelled from the Council of Nine. I think he lives in the mountains north of here, past the Velidred Volcano."

Al rolled his eyes and shook his head. "Did you hear that, Erik? The wizard's on the other side of the Velidred Volcano. I hate this planet with all this walking, and it's always uphill."

"Stop and see Sherry, and maybe she'll be ready to come with you." Erik wondered if Sherry and Lily were still alive. He had focused so much on retrieving the helmet and handling the mastodons on their trip to the Ice Castle that he had thought little about their friends still back in Tanuku. "I bet they're bored with village life and are ready for an adventure."

CHAPTER 7

Sherry sat on a bench at the Crossroads city council meeting, waiting her turn to state her case before the mayor and the councilmen. It was all a staid, boring affair, and she hoped to increase the excitement in the room.

The boys, Al and Erik, had left months ago to capture a magical golden crown, and she didn't know or care if they were dead or alive. Her blood boiled when she thought about how they ran from responsibility to have an adventure and excitement in their life.

She and Lily spent the time finding work as seamstresses in the village of Crossroads, taking in sewing from the local village people. Lily wasn't very good at it, and Sherry did a lot of extra work to correct Lily's shoddy stitching. Tonight, she would present a new project to the city council that would help Sherry realize a childhood dream. She hadn't realized how difficult it would be to get this project off the ground.

The speaker at the front of the village council complained about the lack of fresh water. The man claimed the well was running out of water and turned muddy after a rain. They needed to find a fresh supply.

Sherry couldn't have agreed more with the man. She hated taking her once-weekly bath in boiled muddy water. She cringed every morning trying to wash her face and brush her teeth in the vile brownish liquid.

Only about twenty villagers were at the meeting. Five old men, the councilmen, sat on a bench behind a table, while the mayor had a chair with a back and sat on a dais one step above and behind the councilmen. He had to have some kind of Napoleon complex.

She rubbed her sweaty hands on her dress as her nerves flared before her chance to speak. Butterflies danced in her stomach. It was the same as getting stage fright before a school play; she knew once she started speaking, she would forget the nervousness and concentrate on what she wanted to say.

The man who spoke about the water issue droned on and on, repeating himself every three sentences. Finally, he completed his speech, and the councilmen spoke.

Councilman one, a thin man, the local tailor, thanked the man for saying his piece and then said, "We understand the water quality has deteriorated over the last few months, and we are studying the issue and looking for solutions."

The petitioner asked, "But what are you doing about it?"

The tailor looked at his peers on the bench and shook his head. "You may sit now. We will study the matter and let you know what we find at the next meeting."

"That was what you said the last two meetings, and yet you've done nothing."

The presider, a dark-haired man with a trimmed beard, spoke. "Sit down. Your time to speak is over."

"How many times do I have to come back to you before you do something about the water quality in this village? It will be winter soon enough, and then what will you do? Wait till next summer?"

The presider's nostrils flared, and he bared his teeth. "Sit." He banged a gavel on the table and nodded to a couple of guards in the back of the room.

"What are you doing to help the village? Nothing."

The guards grabbed the petitioner's arms and dragged him out of the building.

A slight murmur rose in the room from the villagers that agreed with the petitioner.

Sherry shook her head. That wasn't the lead-in to her request she had hoped for. She wanted the person before her to ask a banal question and the councilmen to approve, and then she could make her request. Now that they were angry, it would be more difficult to get them to accept it.

The presider banged his gavel. "Who's next?"

Sherry rose, brushed off her dress, and took a deep breath. "I have been a member of this village for a few months now, and I think the village needs a school for the children."

The tailor laughed. "Why would we need a school?"

"The children just run around the village all day. Just two days ago, a horse and wagon trampled a young eight-year-old. The child died a senseless death. If she had been in a classroom learning to read and write, she'd still be alive."

The presider spoke. "That's what I call an education. The other children learned not to run in front of a wagon."

The people in the room murmured.

Sherry shook her head. "You can't be serious to laugh at a child's unnecessary death." The councilmen already had her off her prepared speech. "The children can learn math, science, and how to write."

A man in the audience yelled, "Why do they need to learn math and science?"

An agreement rose from the other meeting attendees.

Sherry hardened her stomach and pinched her lips together. "An educated workforce will be happier, work harder, and be more efficient. It'll help you grow the village."

A woman called out, "Bill, your two boys can do math while they're plowing the fields."

The room erupted with laughter.

Sherry let the laughter die down. "Mr. Mooney, you're a tailor. That requires math to measure the fabric and geometry to ensure the pattern uses the least amount of fabric." Sherry pointed at Vishaan, the blacksmith. "A blacksmith needs to know how much metal he needs to make a knife or shoe a horse."

The tailor spoke. "That's why we have apprentices."

The crowd murmured agreement with the tailor.

"What if you didn't have to teach numbers to the kids when they become your apprentices? Wouldn't that make it easier to train them?"

"We take the boys at age eleven. They won't become full-fledged tailors until they're twenty-two. That's plenty of time to teach them their numbers. Otherwise, they'll desire to go on their own at eighteen, and I'll lose four years of service. Do you want me to starve?"

The crowd chuckled.

How can these people be so stubborn and obstinate? What can I say to make them understand the actual need for a school?

A second councilman said, "Who's going to be teaching at this school? Most of the men have jobs already, and the others don't know how to read or write."

A couple of people laughed.

Sherry said, "I plan to teach them how to read and write, and I have a good science background."

A village member said, "Look at her, a woman that knows how to read and write."

The people jeered.

The presider said, "You're a woman. No boy wants to be taught by a woman."

Sherry's fists tightened into balls as her fingernails dug deep into her palms. "I don't want to teach just boys. Girls need to be educated too."

A woman yelled out, "Yohannan, you got a couple of boys nearing marrying age, don't you? You think they can wrangle a wild, red-haired woman like this one?"

The meeting erupted in laughter again.

The presider banged his gavel on the table. "I think you can see that the consensus is we don't need a school for the boys. We have an apprentice system that teaches the boys what they need to know when they're ready for that position."

"Give me a break." Sherry let her frustration bleed into her voice. "We all know that the only boys that will serve an apprenticeship are boys that are connected politically in the village. There are many boys smarter than your sons that could be apprentices, but this outdated feudal system is crippling their ambitions and reducing their opportunities in life."

"Jack, didn't you just hire a young boy to feed and take care of your animals?"

Sherry decided it was time to tell them her actual purpose, to educate the girls and give them a chance to grow up with opportunities beyond being simple stay-at-home parents. "It's time to provide women with better opportunities."

"Our girls have a wonderful education in learning to sew, grow vegetables, raise their kids, and cook meals. That's enough for them."

Sherry sighed. "I came here to request a building to teach the kids."

"Denied."

"But you haven't heard all my arguments."

"We heard enough. Denied." The presider nodded to the back of the room, where the guards stood.

"Come on. Are you going to drag me out of the room instead of hearing my reasons for educating your children?" She glanced at the people around her. "Don't any of you want to educate your boys and girls so they don't have to settle for a lifetime of hard labor?"

One guard grabbed Sherry's elbow.

She shook her arm loose. "Don't touch me. I can walk out of here on my own." She turned and stomped out the door.

CHAPTER 8

Sherry ground her teeth as her muscles quivered. She wanted to hit something, specifically the men in that room. "How can men be such obstinate creatures?"

Lily said, "Did you really think they would approve your request the first time?"

"Yes, I did. There's a genuine need in this village to make people aware of their circumstances." She swept her arms wide to encompass the entire village as they walked back to their cabin. "Did you hear that man? 'Our girls have a wonderful education in learning to sew and raise babies?'"

"What can we do? These people have been doing it this way their entire lives and their parents' lives and *their* parents' lives before that."

"There must be something we can do to get these people to see reason." The night took its time releasing the day's summer heat, and Sherry wiped sweat from her forehead. It would be another sleepless night in the stifling small cabin. If only these people had electricity for fans and air conditioners. Instead, this culture would indeed do exactly what their forebears did, nothing new.

They walked a few steps in silence as a million thoughts raced through Sherry's mind.

Sherry said, "We need to find people that will support our plan and bring them to the next village council meeting. We need to arouse passion in a group that agrees with us."

"How would you do that?" Lily brushed back her long blonde hair with a hand. "Send out brochures?"

Sherry stopped in the street. "Can't really send out a mailing since very few people in the village can read, but we can talk with the people. We canvas door to door, asking people to support us."

"There didn't seem to be a lot of support in the village."

"We saw mob control in the room tonight. You remember those psychology lessons in high school? People will join a mob. We just have to get the mob on our side."

"The people don't want that kind of change."

"We don't talk to a group of people. I'm not running for mayor or the village council, though I might. We talk to individuals. The Village of Crossroads doesn't want a school, but Mrs. Smith and Mrs. Brown might want their children educated. We need them on our side so we can teach them to think for themselves. Teach them not to fear it or run to superstitious old wives' tales when they don't feel well."

"Do you think we can convince them as women?"

That was a brilliant question. Will these people listen to educated women like Lily and me? In a culture controlled by men and stupidity, will they embrace new ideas and logic?

Lily said, "It would be easier if the boys were here and could talk with the people too."

"I don't think the boys are coming back."

"What do you mean?" Lily placed her hand on her breast, and her eyes widened.

"They've been gone for months. We don't know where they went or how safe the conditions were. This is a strange land, and Alpherge doesn't always make good decisions. He's smart, but common sense eludes him. Wild beasts could eat them, or they might break an arm and leg. Who knows? Maybe a confrontation with a wizard that didn't like the way the boys talked."

"I believe they're still alive."

"I want to believe that, but I'm not sure it's true." After tonight's failure, she could use one of Al's hugs. The tall boy's embrace always made her feel better. "Look, we believe in strong, confident women, right? To convince the populace here in this village, we have to act assertive and resilient."

CHAPTER 9

Sherry woke the next morning and ate her normal breakfast, bland oatmeal. They had run out of honey a couple of days ago and had no money to get more. The breakfast wasn't fulfilling or invigorating, and it didn't give her the confidence she needed to convince the villagers they needed to educate their children.

She brushed her teeth with a frayed stick and rinsed using dirty water from the well. *This is so disgusting.* Her mom had instilled in Sherry the habit of brushing her teeth and the daily hygiene necessary to keep her body healthy, but no one could stay fresh and pretty on this planet.

Lily agreed to go with Sherry on this first day, which turned out to be a mixed blessing. Crossroads contained about three hundred homes. Sherry did not know the number of children in the village. What age should she target for her school? Below six was too young. She had no intention of starting a babysitting service. She wanted the kids to be teachable and behaved enough to sit still for a few hours each day. On this planet, people were self-sufficient and often got married by the time they were sixteen.

Lily and Sherry discussed options and split the village into four quadrants. They would try to do a quadrant a day. They walked to the southwestern side of town and began knocking on doors. The homes stood close together, some sharing a common wall.

The first door opened, and a woman with a child on one hip and another holding her hand asked, "Can I help you?"

These kids were too young, but Sherry thought she should make sure the woman had no older children—not in the house but running around with friends. "Hi. I'm Sherry, and I'm starting a school in Crossroads. Do you have children in the house older than six?"

"We don't have any boys, just three girls. My oldest is playing with her friend somewhere in the village."

"What's the age of your eldest?"

"She's not marrying age yet."

Sherry thought that was good—older than these two, old enough to play with friends on her own but not old enough to marry. She might fit into the demographic. "Would you like your daughter to be educated?"

"What for? I can teach her how to birth children and take care of them. She's been helping me take care of the little ones, and I'm showing her how to cook. I don't think she needs any more education than that."

The girl holding her mom's hand, let go, wiped her nose with the hand, then placed her hand back in her mother's.

Sherry cringed but continued, "We can teach girls the sciences, math, reading, and writing."

"Why would a female need to read?" She bounced the baby on her hip as it got restless.

"You could read a storybook to your children before they go to sleep. Or your daughter could work with numbers and be an accountant for one of the village's businesses. There are lots of things an educated woman could do. Maybe she would like to be a teacher."

"I don't think my daughters are interested in going to school." The woman stepped back into her home and closed her door.

"Okay, then," Sherry said to the closed door. She headed to the next home.

She knocked, and a teenage boy opened the door. He looked at Sherry, and his eyes got big when he saw Lily. The boy's hands and face were dirty.

"Is your mom home?" Sherry asked.

"No, but Dad's out back with the chickens."

"Can you ask him to come to the door so we can talk?"

He stared at Lily for a few moments. "What did you say you wanted?"

Sherry shook her head. "We need to speak with your dad."

He broke eye contact with Lily and stepped to the back door. These cabins were like studio apartments without running water or bathrooms. A single wooden table with two chairs, no stove or sink, and a simple mattress, probably filled with straw, lay on the floor.

The boy came back with a medium-sized man with long dirty brown hair. A curved scar ran from his ear to the corner of his mouth, jagged like someone cut him with a broken bottle. There was no attempt at reconstruction surgery to hide the scar.

"What do you want?" the man drawled in a long breath.

Sherry said, "We're wondering if your son here would be interested in going to school and getting an education."

"Why would he want to do that?"

"To teach him about math and science. Does he know how to read and write?"

"Hah, few folks can in this village."

"I'm well aware of that, sir, but if we started a school, we could teach your son these necessary skills."

"Not much need of him learning that stuff."

Sherry wanted to scream.

The boy tugged on his father's shirt sleeve.

"Whatta you want, son?"

"I want to marry that girl with the blonde hair. She's pretty." He smiled, showing a mouthful of crooked teeth.

"Well, we might arrange that." He pointed at Lily. "Who's your daddy, little girl?"

"My father is dead," Lily answered.

He leaned toward Lily. "That'll make you cheaper."

Lily raised one eyebrow. "I'm not for sale."

Sherry pushed Lily toward the next house. "Okay, we're done here. Thanks for your time."

"You give me a price for the girl, and I can raise some money."

"No thanks, not for sale."

"And the redhead?"

Sherry shook her head. "No, not interested."

Lily was laughing by the time they reached the next house. "You don't need Al anymore; you can get yourself some local hunk."

"I'll pass, thank you very much."

No one was at home at the next two homes, though Sherry couldn't think of where the residents could have gone. It wasn't like these people had a mall to shop at or a local salon where they got their hair cut and fingernails polished. There were so many conveniences that Sherry and her friends had given up when they got trapped on Aloheno. Sherry missed fast-food hamburgers, driving to the theater, and other entertainment possibilities.

The next home contained an eleven-year-old girl and a boy that Sherry estimated to be about nine. Sherry gave her pitch to the mother. "Would your children like to go to school?" Three other children, all under five years old, came to the door.

"You mean my son?"

"Yes, your son, but your daughter too. Females can learn and study, just like the males."

"No, they can't. Boys are smarter than girls."

How much more of this ignorant culture would Sherry have to endure? "No, boys are not smarter than girls. It's just that boys have more opportunities to learn than girls do. And I promise if you send your son *and daughter* to our school, your daughter will be twice as smart as any boy in this village."

"But what are they going to do with an education? An education doesn't put food on the table. Just hard work does that."

Sherry stared down at her hands. "Smarter people with strong logic skills will help you put food on the table. That might mean smarter crop rotation or learning a trade skill or being able to bargain your education for money."

"Where is this school you're talking about?"

"It's not active yet. We're trying to get support for it."

"Well, we can't give you any money to educate my kids. We barely can feed this one." She pointed at her son, who looked like he had missed five meals in the last two days.

"Money isn't an issue, at least not yet. Right now, we need your support at the next village council meeting. We need to show the council that there is an interest in the village for a school. I'm hoping to have the village council pay for it."

"I don't know if I can make it to a meeting. Maybe I can send my husband."

Sherry and Lily slogged to the next household. The process was frustrating. How could she break through thousands of years of cultural behavior?

An ache formed in the front of her head, a sign that the Anticletus moon was rising. She didn't need this extra stress today. How could she handle these bull-headed, ignorant people? Their lack of knowledge, common sense, and decent courtesy baffled her.

Sherry muttered, "One more. If this person doesn't give us a sympathetic response, then I'm giving up on the idea altogether."

The next door opened to a sad woman with an eight-year-old son standing next to her. "What do you want?" she asked.

"We want to talk about educating your son."

She parted her lips, made eye contact with Sherry for a moment, and then said, "My husband is dead, and I can't pay you anything. If little Joey was older, I would send him to the mines to help the laborers with the stone."

"We won't charge your son any money to educate him. We'll teach him math and science and how to read and write."

"Do you want to come in for some tea?"

Sherry looked at Lily, and they both smiled. "Yes, we would like that."

The lady's name was Iris, and her husband had died in the stone pit less than a month before. The family struggled to make ends meet. She didn't have any skills, and her son was too young for the trades.

"I understand how difficult this can be for you. Do you know how to sew?"

"Yes, I can do mending."

Sherry said, "We mend clothes for some of the local villagers. You can help us mend clothes, and I will teach your son for free. Then you will receive the money earned for the sewing."

The woman gave Sherry a watery gaze. "How can I thank you?"

"We need villagers to come to the next village council meeting and support us when we ask for a school building. For now, we will teach your son in our little cabin." Sherry reached out to Lily and grasped her hand.

Sherry and Lily slogged through the entire southwestern quadrant of the village, achieving poor results. The pain in Sherry's head worsened at every home that said no. For every twenty homes they visited, nineteen either wanted to marry Lily to one of their children, brothers, uncles, or neighbors or couldn't see a need to educate their children. Most didn't think females should be educated.

Early afternoon, Sherry and Lily finished their task and walked back to their cabin. Clothes needing mending lay on the table, but Sherry's head pounded in discomfort. They needed to keep on top of their clothes-mending if they wanted to survive in this village. Twice this month, they'd had to go without food because they ran out of money. Some people paid them in eggs, and one gave them a chicken, which they traded for some more of the oatmeal-like mush.

Today's pain made it difficult to concentrate on the sewing. Sherry said, "I can't do this."

"Should we visit Forest River Blossom? She said she could help you."

Sherry felt her blood pressure rise as she snorted a laugh. "Hah, that woman is as bad as the uneducated women in this village." Forest River Blossom represented all the problems on this planet. She carried the respect of her village residents, local mayors, and kings but only because she was a palm-reading, runes-throwing, moon-watching fraud.

"She said she could heal your headaches."

Sherry wondered if Forest River Blossom could do anything for her headaches or if the woman only wanted to study her or gain some power by associating with her. "Forest River Blossom wanted us to go home and leave you to die as a sacrifice at the volcano."

"I thought she was a pleasant woman, and her people were happy. All the girls dance, and they have music."

Sherry squeezed her forehead with her fingers. Nothing she had tried on her own to ward off the headaches had worked. Pain forked like lightning bolts pinging inside her head. She tried a couple of foul-tasting local remedies that didn't work. This world worked differently than Earth. Magic worked on this planet, and logic and medicines didn't always perform the same way. She had seen their friend Cugbert, a priest-healer like Erik, heal with a touch. Should she trust Forest River Blossom to heal the headaches torturing her each week? The spiritualist said she had predicted these moon-induced headaches.

Sherry said, "We would have to walk for an hour and a half to get to the village."

"That's okay. I don't feel like sewing today," Lily replied.

CHAPTER 10

Two hours later, Sherry and Lily stood in Forest River Blossom's home. She was one of the fortunate or rich people that had a wooden floor in their homes. As they waited for the spiritualist to finish up with a client in another room of the house, Sherry realized by all indications Forest River Blossom fit the picture as a successful businesswoman. *How can I help women see they can have what Forest River Blossom has if they had an education? I should appreciate that aspect of her.*

Forest River Blossom opened a door, and a young couple, near Sherry's age, walked out holding hands. Were they married? Sherry couldn't imagine getting married at her current age. She wanted a college education and maybe a master's degree or even a doctorate before settling down.

Forest River Blossom invited Lily and Sherry into her office. "I was expecting you."

Sherry rolled her eyes. "I bet you were."

The spiritualist said, "The headaches are back, and today's pain is worse than normal."

"Yes," Sherry bit her lip. *This woman takes the obvious and makes it look like a precognition event occurred. Why else would we be here?*

Forest River Blossom always wore jewelry, and today she wore long, metal earrings shaped like dancers. She wore a simple leather strap fastened tight around her neck and a large emerald ring around one finger. The spiritualist walked around Sherry and then took Sherry's head in her hands. "Close your eyes." Then she whispered words in a soothing singsong voice. The woman had a lovely voice, and the melody of the words sounded like a song.

"Tell me about the pain. Where is it located? When does it start, and how does it feel?"

"It starts in my forehead where it meets the hairline. Then as the moon rises higher in the sky, it radiates along my skull." Sherry ran her hand from the front of her head to the back, just above her ear.

"And the pain?"

"Is excruciating. Once it reaches my jawline, it explodes into a thousand shards of glass that bounce back and forth through my brain."

"When does it start?"

"When the moon rises and until it sets."

"Any difference whether it's day or night?"

Sherry hadn't analyzed that aspect of the pain. She tried to push through the pain once it started and had never paid a lot of attention to whether it increased during the day or night.

"I don't know if there is a difference." She knew she didn't sleep well at night because of the sharp pain in her skull during the new moon, which happened once every six days. The Anticletus moon was a blue moon and one of three moons circling the planet.

"And tell me, child." The spiritualist touched Sherry's arm and checked her pulse. "Have you used the Crown of Anticletus recently?"

The Crown of Anticletus allowed Sherry the ability to influence others during Anticletus's new-moon phase. Sherry would glow and then force others' thoughts to her point of view. "No, I haven't had need of it."

Lily stood in the corner. "You should use that to influence those creeps on the village council. Sherry spoke with the village council yesterday, trying to gain support for her school. I suggested she use the Crown of Anticletus to manipulate those old men."

"I will not use my power to manipulate others for political gain. There will be times when I use it to prevent my friends, like you, from dying. We should be able to convince others with strong, well-thought-out logic, and not have to resort to magic or whatever this is to manipulate others. I won't do it."

"Maybe you should allow the crown to present itself, and that might release some of the pressure in your brain."

"Might be worth a try." She folded her arms across her chest, hating to concede a point to Forest River Blossom. What would the neighbors think if the building next to them glowed blue? Plus, she couldn't walk through the village glowing like a lightbulb. That would never do.

"Did you try the herbs I gave you?"

"Yes, and they did not help at all."

"Hmmm," the spiritualist mused. "Should they be the same herbs, only stronger or different altogether?"

"How about something that doesn't make me gag? Those last herbs stunk up the house for a week after we boiled them."

"I see."

Sherry figured the spiritualist would double the batch of the same herb just to make her smell the stench. Then nobody would allow her to teach in the village.

"Are there any other frustrations in your life that might aggravate the situation?"

A snort escaped Sherry. *Were there other frustrations? Yes, everything about this planet frustrates me. Not being able to go home to the comforts of Earth and to hug my mother. The lack of fresh clean water in the village. There are no hot showers or cars on this planet.*

"What was that about, child?"

"I want to go back to Earth."

"You'll have to wait until the portal opens."

"Is there no way to make the portal open sooner?"

"No." Forest River Blossom looked down at her emerald ring and rolled it back and forth on her finger.

"Have you ever been to Earth?" Sherry asked.

"No, dear. We sent you and your moms to make a life on the planet to save you from certain death on Aloheno."

"I wish I had never come here. Life here can be easier." She waved her hand around the room. "Just clean running water would be nice."

"I see. Have you found boys to teach in the village?"

"A couple, but not nearly enough. And I'm looking for girls too. Not just boys."

"Girls? Why?"

"Females can be educated."

"There isn't a lot for females to learn, and they aren't as smart as boys."

Sherry's blood pulsed through her pounding heart. It infuriated Sherry when people said things like that. She raised her voice as she felt color rise into her freckled face. "Girls are just as smart as boys. Some are even smarter than boys." She wanted to slap Forest River Blossom across the face for saying what she had just said. "You of all people should know that. Look how successful you are."

"Are the headaches causing you to feel this way, dear?"

If she calls me dear one more time... Sherry sucked on her cheeks as she blinked multiple times. *This woman is as bad as the men. But maybe an educated populace would devalue her skills.*

Sherry said, "Listen, educated girls lead to intelligent women, who lead to better health care, business decisions, and care of the village." She wagged her finger at Forest River Blossom. "You don't have to worry about someone taking your place as a spiritualist. An educated person will recognize your mumbo-jumbo as the nonsense it is. And they will put you out of business."

Forest River Blossom rotated the green ring on her finger and dragged it to the end of her finger and back and flashed a wintry smile. "I see dear. Would you like to take home some of these mumbo-jumbo herbs for your pain?"

CHAPTER 11

Sherry hurried down the path to Crossroads so she could finish up the mending work. If they didn't do some every day, they wouldn't make enough money for the month to pay their rent and have food. They strode through an oak forest, the tight canopy-filtered sunlight throwing late afternoon shadows across the ground. It was summer, and the days were long, so there was no concern about reaching the village before the sun set.

Forest River Blossom had given Sherry three bags of herbs she thought might help. Two of the three cloth bags smelled okay, but the third reminded Sherry of boxwood bushes from Earth, and she didn't like that smell. The instructions were to take a small portion of lavender from the first bag, dried honeysuckle flowers from the second, and a larger portion from the vile-smelling third pouch. Then Sherry had to mix them all together in a pot of boiling water, strain the mixture, and then drink it like tea.

The Anticletus moon raced across the sky as it circled the planet every six days, which limited its time as a new moon to just a few hours at a time. Sherry could already feel a reduction in the pain coursing through her brain. *Good, I won't have to take this vile mixture today.*

Lily said, "Are you expecting the children we talked to today to come over tomorrow for lessons?"

Sherry, engrossed in her thoughts, stopped. "What?"

"Do you need a lesson plan for tomorrow?"

"Oh no. You're right. I have to plan a lesson for tomorrow." Three parents had agreed to send five boys, not girls, to her house tomorrow for their first lessons. At least she hoped they would be there to learn.

"There are a lot of different ages," Lily said.

"Yeah, but age doesn't matter because none of them know the basics of reading or math. Most of my lessons will be simple, teaching them basics like first graders get on Earth."

A shadow passed over Sherry, and she looked skyward as a large, dark creature flew above the canopy. She couldn't make out what it was, but it seemed larger than a normal bird.

"Did you see that?" Sherry asked.

"Yeah, was it a bird?"

Sherry's scalp prickled, and she felt a quiver in her stomach. "I'm not sure." She increased her pace and looked left and right in the forest. *Just when I think this planet is safe and I'm aware of its dangers, some other strange animal literally flies by.*

They weren't far from the village, maybe ten minutes in the forest with another three minutes of open grasses once they got close. She had seen large birds before and remembered Al shot fireballs at a bird big and strong enough to carry off a young child.

"Will we be safe?" Lily asked.

"I believe the forest canopy will protect us for now, but we might have to run between the forest and the village gates." Sherry's heart beat harder. Was she overreacting?

They walked for another five minutes and didn't see the shadow or the bird again. Without knowing what it was, Sherry couldn't accurately access the danger, so she continued forward, still watching the forest to her left and right with an occasional glance behind.

A bird fluttered in the trees above them, causing another bird to cry out, "Ca-caw."

Squirrels raced through the leaves on the forest floor and jumped onto nearby trees.

Lily jumped at the sound. A nervous laugh escaped her lips.

Sherry exhaled, not realizing she was holding her breath. *Relax*, she told herself, *it's nothing to be concerned about.* She remembered their first encounter with the stegox, a bearlike creature, and she hoped she never encountered another one of them.

"Come on, we have nothing to fear. We're strong women," Sherry said out loud, more to bolster her own spirits. She strained, listening for any strange sounds or unusual movements. They neared the end of the forest and could see the village walls from their location.

At the edge of the forest, Sherry searched the sky. "I don't see any large birds, do you?"

Lily stood closer to Sherry than normal, looked up, and shook her head. "Should we make a dash for the wall?"

Sherry didn't want them to run to the village like a couple of scared school-children. The villagers would laugh at them. The guards would tell the village council, and they could never convince them to let her teach their children. She just needed to be firm and brave, like an adult.

She grabbed Lily's hand. "We will walk like the adults we are."

A voice called out from the forest, "Ladies."

Lily screamed.

Sherry held back a scream as she felt the blood drain from her face.

A man dressed in black with a touch of red at the collar walked up to them.

Lily cried out, "It's Kestrel, the Falcon Prince. Of course, he was the one that flew overhead."

Indeed, Sherry thought, Kestrel could fly, another irregularity on this planet. Sherry didn't know if anyone else on the planet had the ability. She wasn't happy to see Kestrel since he was the teenager that kidnapped Lily and drew the others through the portal to Aloheno. She could lay this whole horrible life at his feet.

Kestrel bowed and flourished a black cape. "Hello, Lily."

Sherry's muscles quivered, and she felt a vein in her neck throb. She would not allow this to happen. Sherry had given up too much to live on this planet, and she wouldn't let Kestrel force them into further trouble. "Stay away from us."

Kestrel said, "I've changed."

"What do you want?" Sherry shook her head. This couldn't be happening—though she wondered what she could do to stop Kestrel. The problem was Kestrel had wizard abilities close to their friend Al's wizarding skills. He had worked hard to kill Lily, Sherry, Al, and Erik during the eclipse of the triple moons. She only heard about the battle Al and the student wizards had in the Velidred dungeon against Kestrel. He wasn't a good person.

"I want Lily."

"You can't have her. She's helping me start a school. She's busy, now go away."

"Why should I go?"

"Erik, Lily, Al, and me. You know the people you tried to kill? That's enough for me to tell you to stay away from us."

He swaggered up to Sherry. "I want Lily, and I get what I want."

Sherry stood toe to toe with Kestrel the Falcon Prince. The Anticletus Moon hadn't set yet, and Sherry sensed the blue glow forming about her body, a manifestation of the Crown of Anticletus. She thought back to when she told Forest River Blossom that she used the power only for good. Keeping Kestrel away from Lily was good. He was a dangerous man, and she wouldn't allow him to take advantage of Lily.

"Why are you here, Kestrel?"

"I've been healing after your friend, Erik, stuck a pike through my gut. I've been out flying and saw you two walking, and I thought I would say hi."

"Hi, now go away." She had developed a little control over the power she had, though the first time she found out about the power, it all happened without her doing anything. This time she felt the power, but she didn't want to use it yet.

Lily touched Sherry's arm. "Don't send him away. Invite him to dinner."

Heat rose in Sherry's body, and she crossed her arms. "We can't let him get close to you. Have you forgotten what he did to you? To all of us?"

"Dinner would be fun," Kestrel said.

"No, it wouldn't be fun, and we don't want you to come for dinner." She scrunched her face and released, trying to regain control. She couldn't have Kestrel come for dinner. They had work to do. Instead of doing the work, they would visit, and the mending wouldn't get done. She needed to think about what to teach the kids. Plus, they didn't have enough food for another person. "We don't have enough food."

"I can bring food from the Kallurian Castle."

"Aren't you an opponent of the Kallurians?" Sherry asked.

"I was, but my father got involved with Prince Krunal, and now I'm staying in the castle. You should come to the castle for dinner."

Lily clapped her hands. "Wouldn't that be more fun than eating that horrible soup you make every night?"

Sherry swallowed hard. *Lily doesn't like the food I serve? I don't have any spices or potatoes or anything that tastes good.* "We can't go tonight. I'm not even sure how far away it is, and we have work to do."

"For me, it's an hour of easy flying, but I understand you can't reach the castle that fast. It would take a couple of days. It doesn't matter. I'm not allowed in Crossroads yet. They're still angry about the fireballs I pitched into the village during a raid. I might have burned down some homes and buildings."

Sherry breathed a sigh of relief.

Kestrel walked near Lily. "But you'll join me for dinner at the castle soon, won't you, my princess?"

Lily brushed her hair from her eyes and smiled at Kestrel. "Yes, my prince."

"Give me a break." Sherry closed her eyes.

Kestrel walked to the edge of the forest and turned into a falcon. He took a few steps and lifted into the sky. He flew up above the treetops, looped three times around their position, climbed into the sky, and flew east toward the Kallurian castle.

Lily walked over to Sherry and pounded on her upper arm with her fist. "How dare you use your powers to talk to Kestrel? You told me you only used the Crown of Anticletus for good. The first chance you have, you use your influence against Kestrel."

"I didn't use—"

Lily's nostrils flared. "Liar, I saw you glow blue."

"Yes, I—"

"I saw the crown on your head, and then Kestrel left. I like Kestrel, and the only reason he did what he did in the past was because King Haskell controlled him. Now you're no better than the Mountain King controlling people with your blue, glowing crown thingy."

Lily stormed off to the village, watching the sky as she walked.

Sherry's face felt hot as heat flushed through her body. She was filled with anger at Forest River Blossom, Kestrel, Lily, Erik, and Al. They all made her angry. She ground her teeth until her jaw hurt. She didn't use her powers against Kestrel, and she needed to keep Lily from seeing him. Though if she could get a hot bath and a good meal at the castle, that would be nice.

"Lily, wait."

CHAPTER 12

The next day, Sherry held her first class in her house. Five boys sat on the dirt floor of her little one-room cabin. Three boys came from the same family, ages seven, eight, and fifteen. The other two boys were the eldest children of two different homes. At age nine, they weren't old enough to work in the mines or to apprentice for a trade.

The boys' hygiene skills were horrendous. She watched them pick their noses, lick their fingers, and engage in all kinds of other nasty habits. She would work on those soft skills but wanted to get them learning the alphabet so she could teach them to read.

The fifteen-year-old boy, Travis, walked in and said hello to Lily.

She was polite and welcomed him to the class.

Then, as Sherry began working on the first lesson, teaching the alphabet, she noticed Travis looked at Lily instead of her. "Travis, watch over here to learn this. Focus on the lesson, please."

Sherry fell back to talking about the difference between the letter *B* and the letter *A*. When she looked at Travis, his attention had shifted back to Lily. "Travis, are you paying attention?"

"Yes." His head still faced Lily.

"Please look this way."

Sherry worked with the students one on one, letting them write their letters on the dirt floor with a stick. When she reached Travis, she said, "Let me see you write the letter *A*."

Travis looked up at her. "Do what, Miss Sherry?"

"Write the letter *A* in the dirt with the stick, like I was showing the other kids."

"I don't know how."

"That's why we're practicing, so you can learn."

He glanced over at Lily and smiled.

Lily didn't see him since she worked on mending a tunic.

Sherry said, "Okay, that's enough, Travis."

She walked over to Lily and whispered, "Can you go for a walk in the village for an hour?"

"Why?"

"You're distracting the students."

"What do you mean, I'm distracting the students? I'm mending this tunic." She raised the cloth to show Sherry.

Sherry looked at the sewing job Lily did and thought she would have to re-work this sewing later. "I know you're not doing anything but sewing. You distract Travis, and he isn't paying attention."

"Tell him to concentrate on what you're teaching."

"He seems to be here to look at you. He doesn't seem interested in learning his letters while you're in the room."

Lily folded her arms across her chest. "It's my fault he doesn't want to learn his letters? I thought you were a great teacher. You can teach anyone anything."

Sherry glanced at the ceiling and opened her mouth to criticize Lily's snippy behavior and stopped. Lily had been angry since she had sent Kestrel away, and she was sure that drove this conversation. She couldn't argue with Lily in front of the children. That wouldn't do. How could she get Lily to leave, and would she have to send Lily out of the room every day?

Lily stared at Sherry in defiance.

Sherry changed tactics. "Travis, come with me." Sherry stepped outside the door of the cabin.

Travis followed.

Sherry said, "Listen, do you want to learn your letters?"

"Yes, Momma wants me to."

"Do you understand the advantages you'll have over your peers if you get an education?"

"What are peers? Is that a fruit? I think my Uncle Franklin has a pear tree."

Sherry took a deep breath, let out a long sigh, and shook her head. "You need a formal education. There's a difference between your peers and a pear tree. If you pay attention to the lessons, then you'll learn what that difference is." She struggled to find something that might make him listen to her.

"You seem to have an eye for Lily."

"She's pretty. Momma wants me to get to know her and ask her to marry me."

Sherry smiled and wanted to laugh, but she imagined she found the trick to keep Travis interested. "Lily is smart and educated. She will not marry you for your good looks because she'll want to marry an educated man. This class will help educate you and give you a better chance to marry her."

Travis mused for a moment like he was deciding if Sherry was lying to him. "I guess you're right."

"Are you going to come in, listen to the lesson, and practice your letters like the other kids?"

The door opened, and Lily stepped out. "I'm going for a walk."

Travis kept his eye on her as she walked down the dirt road toward the center of the village.

Sherry touched Travis on the shoulder. "Let's go in and practice our lessons."

Travis looked down the road, watching Lily.

"Come on Travis. Lessons?"

"I'm done for today, Miss Sherry." He followed Lily.

"Travis, she's looking for an educated man." She shook her head, realizing that Travis wasn't interested in learning. With a sigh, she returned to the kids in her little classroom.

CHAPTER 13

Two days later, the room felt crowded as Sherry taught four of the original five students. Travis didn't return for more lessons. Three other boys had joined the group. The kids seemed to enjoy being taught, and Sherry brought different objects into the room to help the children visualize the math lessons. Two boys were brighter than the others in the group, and Sherry worked hard to keep them interested while getting the others up to speed.

She still wanted to get girls involved in this school. What would the mayor and village council do if they found out she was running this school in her home? She hoped if the kids went home each day and told their parents what they learned, then the parents would support her at the next village council meeting.

One eight-year-old student, named Kabir asked, "How come there aren't any girls in the class, Miss Sherry?"

Sherry thought about the best way to answer the question. Should she share the political and cultural reasons for these decisions? She understood the importance of keeping the local political class happy.

An older boy shouted, "Because girls are stupid."

Sherry said, "No, they aren't. Girls are just as smart as boys."

"That's not what my daddy says."

She clenched her hands into fists. *That, my friend, is the problem.* "Girls can learn just as well as boys, but society dictates some social rules that prevent girls from having opportunities that are given to boys."

Kabir raised his hand. "My little sister wants to go to school. Yesterday, I showed her what we learned, and she wants to come."

"How old is your sister?"

"Seven."

Sherry felt a tightness in her chest and pulled an earlobe as she wondered if she should pursue the next move. Could she ask Kabir to bring his sister into the class? Would she come? Would her parents let her come? She remembered meeting Kabir's parents, and they seemed a little less socially regressive than others in the village.

"What's your sister's name?"

"Misha."

What's the right thing to do here? "Kabir, can you bring Misha to class with you tomorrow?"

"Yes." The boy's eyes lit up as a smile stretched from ear to ear.

The older boy said, "My daddy doesn't want me studying with girls."

"Misha should learn the same as you, so we will invite her to our class."

Tension built between Sherry's shoulder blades all day. They finished the lessons that day by early afternoon, and she sent the children home. She grabbed Kabir's shoulder before he left. "You tell Misha that we would like to see her tomorrow."

"Okay, Miss Sherry, she'll be really excited."

Sherry wasn't so sure the entire class would share that enthusiasm.

* * * *

Three days later, the class grew by another five students. Another older girl, Gabriella, joined Misha. Sherry had recruited all the students except Gabriella. She didn't know who Gabriella's parents were, but the girl picked up on the lessons fast and helped Misha after she finished her own work.

The students sat on the dirt floor in a semi-circle, crowded around Sherry. Lily would leave the cabin shortly after the students arrived. She wouldn't return until an hour or two after the class ended. Lily was quiet about what she did during those times, but Sherry didn't care. Teaching the kids and working hard on the mending after school kept her too busy to be nosy.

"Who can tell me what three plus two is?" Sherry asked.

Gabriella and two boys raised their hands.

"Gabriella?"

"Three plus two equals five."

"Very good."

"And what is three plus five?"

The same three raised their hands.

"Kabir?"

"Eight."

A knock sounded on the door.

"Wait just a moment, kids." Sherry's pulse increased as she wondered who was knocking. She hoped it wasn't another child wanting to be educated because the room had reached its limit in class size. Sherry worried it might be the mayor, but she didn't think she had been teaching long enough for him to get wind of the news.

She cracked open the door, and the mayor pulled it from her hands and opened it wide. The mayor and Mr. Mooney from the village council walked into the room, pushing Sherry out of the way.

Mr. Mooney said, "Gabriella, what are you doing here?"

A sudden coldness struck Sherry in the core of her body as she placed her hand on her chest. Gabriella, one of her best students, was the tailor's daughter? Was Mr. Mooney really surprised that his daughter was here, or was she a plant, a trick of the mayor to upset Sherry's plans?

"I'm authorized by the village council to shut this school down. All you children go on home." The mayor helped the little children to their feet.

Sherry stood in front of the mayor. "You can't send them home. We need to educate them so they can be good citizens."

"The village council denied your request, and here you are flouting our laws."

"You have laws that children have to be left stupid."

The mayor rocked on his heels and took on a posture of superiority. "Our laws clearly stipulate a woman can't teach them."

Her body temperature rose, and Sherry rubbed the back of her neck. "Give me a break."

"We gave you a break when we heard you were teaching boys. Now we find you're teaching girls too. That is absolutely illegal, and we will hold you accountable." He marched to the cabin door and opened it. "Men, come in here and secure her."

"Secure me for what?"

"We're locking you up. This is serious business, and we won't let you get away with defying our laws."

"Do you realize how stupid you sound? 'We won't let you get away with educating our children and making them smarter, more responsible citizens.'"

Two guards came in and secured Sherry's wrists behind her back with shackles.

Sherry had trouble swallowing, and she struggled, but the men were stronger.

"What will you do with me?"

"We have a place out in the woods to keep you from doing this again. Prince Krunal will come to the village in a couple of days and will hear your plea. He will provide the decision for your punishment."

Sherry ran at the mayor, but the guards hauled hard on the chains around her wrist, and she fell hard to the floor.

The kids ran out of the room screaming.

The mayor laughed. "We know you're not from here, but you will learn about our village and follow our laws."

Pain pounded between her ears. Her vision clouded. She wanted to scream but didn't want to give these bullies the satisfaction. "Why do you let women be wizards and go to wizard school?"

"Wizards are a privileged class and have to be educated to prevent them from doing harm to the village and to themselves. We told you and your friends to leave the village a couple of months ago, and yet you came back. We told you not to teach the children because girls weren't smart enough to teach, and yet you did it anyway. If you won't listen to reason, then we have to take matters into our own hands."

"Reason?" Sherry yelled. "You know nothing about reason. I was born with a brain, just like a man. I have logic skills, and I know science and math. And I know how to read and write, just like you."

"It doesn't matter how smart you think you are. You can't teach in your home. You can't teach our children because you're a woman, and you can't teach in our village because we say so. The sooner you accept the facts we tell you, the more enjoyable your stay. We don't allow troublemakers into our homes, and the village is our home. Take her away."

CHAPTER 14

The men secured Sherry's legs and threw her into a small wooden cage. The men lifted the cage and placed it on a wagon. The wagon moved with a shake when the cage landed on the rickety wood.

She bounced off the floor of the cage and pain rushed through her shoulders. She kicked at the cage's bars, but they didn't move. She screamed at the men to let her go, but they just laughed. This wasn't good, and her extremities shook. What would these crazed, power-hungry men do to her?

The wagon meandered through the village, and she heard shouts from the people.

Really? They're driving me through the village as a sign of what not to do? "We can't have our populace educated. That will never do."

Then the first object hit her. She didn't know how it made it through the bars, but an egg exploded against her head, and the yolk streamed over her red hair. Some soft fruit, she guessed something like a tomato, hit her in the eye, forcing her to lower her head.

She heard her student, Travis. "Miss Sherry isn't supposed to be teaching girls."

A large rock smacked her in the upper arm, and she cried out in pain.

These people are monsters.

People yelled at her as small rocks hit her body from three sides, and three more eggs smashed into her head. She raised her hands to protect her face. Objects pounded against the bars of the cage but didn't strike her. She was thankful for that. The wagon rattled on down the road. A rock struck her along the side of the head, and Sherry saw black spots cross her vision.

Sherry flinched every time she heard something hit the cage or her body. She didn't know if her head was bleeding or if it was egg yolk or tomato juice dripping between her fingers. She curled into a fetal position to make her body a smaller target, but rocks continued to bruise her back and legs. Sherry gasped for air between sobs and whimpers.

After what seemed like an eternity, the pummeling stopped, and the cart cleared the village gates. Then what would they do to her? She tilted her head from side to side, watching and listening to changes in the road or what the guards might be saying. She felt thirsty from teaching all day and from fear of what the guards might do to her. Where were they taking her? Would they leave her tied to a tree in the woods for wild animals to consume? Could she somehow escape her captors?

They traveled for ten minutes along the road toward the next mountain village. Then the cart turned off the main road, and the cart and cage sloped upward. They were heading toward the mountains.

After half an hour of travel, the wagon reached a small cabin in the woods. The wagon stopped, and one guard said, "Do we leave her in the cage?"

Another guard said, "No, this cabin has floor anchors you can attach the chains to. We dump her out, rearrange the chains, and secure her to the building."

Sherry watched the men take a break as the smell of tobacco smoke from cigars drifted in her direction. She moved a little to rearrange her clothing and loosen her cramping extremities, and a slight shiver went up her neck as she felt someone watching her. Did she need to be concerned about these guards? She only heard two voices, but that didn't mean there weren't more of them. She worried about their activities with other women prisoners that they know they could get away with in what she assumed was a secluded location.

A guard said, "Okay, let's finish this. The mayor's going to be expecting us back soon."

Sherry braced for the movement of the cage. Since she didn't have to worry about being pummeled with rocks, she held onto the side cage slats as the guards pulled and shoved the cage off the wagon. They lifted the cage and carried it across the ground. They dropped it hard, hurting her bottom as it landed.

She yelped.

One guard laughed.

Padlocks were unbolted, chains unleashed, and a door with a squeaky hinge opened.

"Okay, little lady. Be nice now and we won't hurt you."

The guards pulled the cage into the dark building, and the temperature cooled. One of them opened the cage door.

Sherry faced the opposite direction and held onto the slats as the guards rotated the cage ninety degrees. She felt if she didn't hold on, she would fall.

"Let go, you little wench." A guard smacked her fingers with a stick, and Sherry fell to the floor on her back, her tunic rolled up to her belly.

"Grab the chains and hook her up."

Sherry struggled to arrange her clothing and pulled on her tunic to cover her exposed skin.

Chains ran through brackets and padlocks snapped around them. She felt the chains tighten and then loosen. One guard pushed her, and she put her hands back, ready for a hard fall against the floor, but the other guard caught her and held tight. "Ugh. She's a gooey mess."

"Let go."

Another chain pulled tight, which yanked her leg.

"Woah, you dropped her to the floor."

The other guard said, "She's secured."

The man released her. It was dark in the cabin, and it took her a second for her eyes to adjust to the light. She looked around the small room, which was only five strides wide by five strides long. A door on one side and a single window boarded closed.

"Okay, hold her for a second so we can get her clothes off."

"Don't you dare. Leave me alone." Sherry struggled against the man holding her.

The other guard took a knife and sliced her tunic from bottom to top. As he neared her head, he said, "I recommend you stop struggling about now or you might find your neck accidentally sliced."

Sherry stiffened her body, her neck straining away from the knife and her eyes watery. What were these men going to do with her? This was such a cruel, rotten planet. Once she got off Aloheno, she would never return.

The man with the knife had black hair and calloused hands, and the man holding her smelled of sweat and testosterone.

She jerked.

"Whoa, careful." Another slice with the knife and her tunic fell to the floor, leaving her in her smallclothes.

Sherry whimpered.

"Take that messy thing outside. That'll attract animals and help secure the building for us."

The man picked up the tunic and walked outside with it.

The other guard put the knife into its sheave and stood back from Sherry. "Woo boy, they bruised you up good. Okay, here's what's gonna happen. I'll bring some water in here so you can clean some of that"—he waved his hand in a circular motion—"junk off you. Hopefully, you can clean up the eggs and fruit before it dries.

"You'll get three meals a day, and a lady will come in once a day to take your piss pot. Be nice to her and she'll take good care of you. You're lucky because men don't get treatment this nice."

Sherry's pulse raced, and the sound of her heartbeat thundered in her ears. Sweat poured off her, and her hair felt matted and sticky to her head. She whimpered. "I only want to educate your children."

"Yeah, I don't judge the cases, lady." He left the room and shut the door, and she heard chains rattling as they secured the door.

She felt numb and empty standing in her smallclothes, chained to the wall and floor. Sherry collapsed into a heap on the floor and sobbed.

* * * *

A few hours later, she woke to a darkening cabin. She could still see, so she knew the sun hadn't set yet.

Her bruised body ached, and she had injured her right shoulder from all the twisting. The shackles rubbed against her wrists and made them bleed. She worked hard to keep her hands steady to prevent further damage.

What choices did she have? The chains ran through a bracket on the wall and another on the floor. She had some space to move in the cabin, to the piss pot and a corner of the room. She couldn't reach the window or the door. There were no chairs or beds in the room, which meant she would sleep on the floor at night.

The guard left a bucket of dirty water within reach, and she went to it and splashed her face. She felt gashes on her cheek, and it hurt sloshing water on them. The egg yolks had dried on her hair, leaving a single, yellow mass like a shower curtain. Shards of eggshell littered her hair and face, and the tomato juice burned the cuts on her face.

At no point in the process did she believe that trying to teach children their ABCs would cause her to be stoned and layered with egg. This planet was a backwater group of ignorant troglodytes. She renewed her commitment to leave this planet as soon as possible, assuming she escaped this mess with her life.

She didn't know if the guards were guarding the cabin or not. An evaluation of the chain and bracket system didn't lead to any obvious ways to escape. If she got out of the chains and shackles, she would still need some way to get through the door or a window. The guards locked the door from the outside.

She didn't have a tunic anymore and would be considered a disreputable woman in any village she entered. She would have to wait for an audience with Prince Krunal. She had met him once when he imprisoned Erik and her. That seemed so many lifetimes ago. They'd escaped from his grasp, and she wondered if he would remember her.

Sherry would plead not guilty at her trial. The prince couldn't charge her for educating young people.

She didn't want to guess what the justice system in this province entailed. No lawyers came to the cabin, so she figured she'd have to represent herself. She thought eleven years of school on Earth made her ten times smarter than the average person here. But did intelligence even matter? Did wizardry, political power, and strength count more than an education in math, logic, sciences, and languages?

Had she miscalculated her opponent, the mayor, and the city council members? Did Mr. Mooney force his daughter, Gabriella, to take her class just so they could arrest Sherry for trumped-up charges? That would be a shame because Gabriella was smart and funny. So many of these kids seemed to crave the knowledge she wanted to impart, and yet here she was.

A commotion outside the cabin door interrupted her pondering. She heard the crack of a whip against flesh, and a woman screamed.

"Stop struggling."

"Get your hands off me," A woman yelled.

Sherry yelled, "Lily!"

"Sherry?"

The whip cracked again but didn't make contact.

A voice whimpered.

Sherry yelled, "It's okay, Lily. I'm here."

The padlocks were unbolted, chains pulled through brackets, and the door opened.

Lily stood on the other side of the doorway, chained like Sherry but without the egg wash on her body. One crack of the whip had sliced open a slash across Lily's face.

Sherry opened her arms in welcome, her eyes wide and shining.

Lily looked up, and her mouth fell open. She stared dazed and confused at her friend. "What did they do to you?"

"Shut up." A guard cracked a whip but didn't hit her.

Lily whimpered.

A second guard pushed Lily into the room. "Get in there and don't cause any more trouble."

They worked quickly in securing Lily across the room from Sherry, giving Lily the same play in her chains as Sherry. The men left Lily in her smallclothes after ripping her torn tunic from her body.

The taller guard said, "Let's go. We've got work to do."

They left the room and secured the door.

CHAPTER 15

Erik and Zita had walked for three days in their search for Cugbert. It seemed they were always a day behind, or they had just missed him. On the third day of their search, Zita became severely ill, forcing them to stop and rest.

Zita asked, "Will I die?"

They were in a tiny cabin in a small village of only twelve cabins, far from Tanuku and Crossroads.

Erik didn't have the energy to pursue Cugbert and take care of Zita. Every step seemed hard and unnatural. The foods he ate had no flavor, and sleep was difficult and irregular. He did his best to help Zita, but he couldn't focus on his healing because of his lack of sleep.

What would he tell Cugbert? *I killed a stone warrior with my hubris. I should have gotten more information about the process instead of acting like a spoiled five-year-old.* It would be difficult to tell Cugbert what he had done. He wondered if Cugbert would kick him out of the healing priest group and not let him study anymore.

Zita moaned from the straw mattress on the floor of the cabin. The Helmet of Justice lay near her head on the floor.

Erik went to her. "How are you doing?"

She murmured, but Erik couldn't understand what she said.

Zita's pallid face and vomiting every hour concerned Erik. The only time she looked comfortable was when she slept. He tried to heal her again that day, but something in her body didn't react as expected. He didn't know how many days of this she had left. Cugbert had the skills to heal Zita, but he couldn't move her in this state.

He lifted her head to give her water. "Drink this."

"No. It just comes back up."

"You're becoming dehydrated. You need to drink something, and even a little will help." He held the cup to her mouth until she relented. Then he kissed her cheek.

The last people they'd spoken to had said that Cugbert passed through their little village the day before and then proceeded east. He planned to stop in the next village three miles away. Erik thought they could catch up to Cugbert this day, but then Zita's health turned worse, and they had to stop. She collapsed right on the dirt path. A local farmer had helped him carry her to the village, where someone had offered a deserted cabin for her to rest.

He thought about going to find Cugbert, but Zita's health was such that he didn't think he could leave her. He couldn't let her die alone. What was causing this problem? Was it the helmet or something else?

The next day, Erik asked, "Can you travel?"

Zita said, "No."

"Do you want me to go find Cugbert and leave you here to rest?"

She grabbed his arm, digging fingernails deep into his skin. "Stay with me."

"Cugbert can heal you." His stomach tensed as he stared at her pale body. He didn't know if that was true or not, but he had to give her hope. Six weeks they'd been together, and Erik couldn't think about losing her to illness.

He dipped a rag in the bucket of water and mopped sweat from her forehead. She went between bursts of fever and waves of chills. Right now, she was hot. Erik rubbed his hand through her hair, and a handful of it just came off in his hand. A thought tugged at his memory.

She fell into a restless sleep.

Maybe I can sneak out while she's sleeping and run to the next village. If it's only three miles away, I could be back in an hour or two. He didn't know how fast he could run, but the mountain topography in this area would make it slower. And even if he found Cugbert, would the priest come to help Zita, or say he could come in a day or two? Two or three days might be too late.

Flashes of lightning and peals of thunder shook the tiny cabin. The rain started falling a few minutes later. Then hail pummeled the cabin roof. A drip of water soon formed into a puddle on the dirt floor inches from Zita's head. The cabin walls seemed to move closer together in the gloom.

A feeling of heaviness tightened his chest as he stared down at Zita. He could never forgive himself if he snuck away and Zita died before he returned. He was her only friend, and he refused to let her die alone.

A knock sounded at the door.

Who would be crazy enough to be outside in this weather? Erik unwound his body from the floor beside Zita and opened the door. A woman and her twelve-year-old son, Brit, from the cabin next door brought food into the house.

"You must eat. Feed the girl." The heavyset woman had kind eyes when she smiled.

"Thank you." Erik ran his hand through his hair.

"How is the girl?" The woman bent and checked on Zita, who continued to sleep. She felt Zita's forehead and pinched her cheeks. Zita didn't rouse. "There might not be enough time."

"I tried to heal her." His pulse raced as pressure built behind his eyes.

"You need Cugbert."

Erik pointed at Zita. "She can't travel, and I don't want to leave her here by herself."

The boy said, "I'll go get the priest."

Lightning struck nearby, causing a flash of light in the room followed by a loud boom that shook the cabin walls.

Shaking his head, Erik said, "I can't let you do that. The weather is horrendous. Maybe you can find Cugbert after the storm." Rain continued to pound on the cabin roof.

The woman placed a wet rag on Zita's head. "Brit, it's too dangerous. Stay for a few more minutes."

"I'm strong and faster than lightning," Brit said.

"No, not in this storm."

"I agree with your mom," Erik said. "It's too dangerous."

Zita coughed in her sleep but didn't awaken.

A quiver of pain wobbled through Erik's stomach as he tightened his hands and loosed them. Yeah, he wanted the boy to run and find Cugbert. Yes, even in this rain. Erik knew he was a horrible person to allow a boy not even in his teens, to do what he wouldn't even do.

With the other people in the room, Erik felt claustrophobic. The dark, humid room tightened.

Brit picked up the sword, which lay beside the helmet on the floor. "Are you a soldier?"

"No."

Brit waved the sword in the air. "I want to be a soldier someday. My grandfather was a great warrior." He dropped the point of the sword to the dirt floor. "They encased him in stone at the mountain top."

Erik swallowed hard and sat on the floor as his knees felt weak. The memory of killing Dickerson flooded into his brain. Could he have been this boy's grandfather? No. Erik was too ashamed to ask the boy's name.

"If I run and get Cugbert, will you give me the sword?"

"No, Brit, I can't let you have the sword." Erik wanted the boy to have the sword. Anybody but Erik could take the sword and he wouldn't care, but as long as there was hope of rescuing the warriors, he couldn't part with it. Not yet. He hoped Cugbert would want it for its healing power and offer to take part in rescuing the stone warriors. Was the Sword of Freedom even important to the process?

"The storm is passing," Brit said.

Sure enough, lightning and thunder sounded in the distance even as rain pounded the roof.

"I can go get Cugbert now."

"It's still raining like crazy. Wait." Erik listened to the rain.

"I'll run faster than the wind, Mom. Can I go?"

"No, wait, son."

Zita mumbled something unintelligible.

Erik thought, *Yes, boy, go. Don't listen to your mother. Leave now and sprint until you find him.* But he said nothing.

Brit dropped the sword on the cabin floor. "I'll be back soon." Then he swooshed across the room and out the door.

Erik didn't know if it was possible, but the raindrops sounded as though they were growing bigger and faster. *Run, little Brit. I hope you don't die for me like Dickerson did.*

CHAPTER 16

Erik didn't know how much time had passed. The storm swelled in intensity, with another round of lightning, thunder, and hail. Zita slept the whole time with fits of mumbling about her father, and sometimes she yelled, "Watch out, Mom."

Brit's mother stayed with Erik and Zita. She would look at Zita then at the cabin door, her gaze never fixed on one spot for long. Erik could see her biting her lower lip.

What chance did a young boy have against a storm of this magnitude? The winds increased their fury throughout the day. Erik paced across the small room and opened the door, only for the wind to blow at him mercilessly. He imagined Brit blowing down the mountainside, unable to maintain his footing with his negligible weight.

Erik stopped his pacing. "Was the soldier Brit mentioned your father?"

"Yes. We visit him a few times a year. Brit adores him."

He feared to ask the woman her father's name. What would he say or do if she said, "Dickerson?" Would he be able to tell her there was no reason to go back to the mountaintop because her father was no longer there?

"My father is a stone warrior too."

"Do you visit him?"

"Well, I did." There was so much to the story about Erik and his dad that he didn't know where to start. It just seemed so pointless at the moment. He sat in silence.

"My family name is Weaver."

Erik perked up from his reverie. "Weaver?"

"He was on the front lines next to the commander."

The door blew open, and Brit stood at the entrance, waving down the street. "Come on, hurry."

Brit entered the cabin. Water dripped everywhere, causing puddles of mud to form on every step. Erik noticed for the first time the boy wasn't even wearing shoes.

Brit's mom ran to him and hugged him, not worrying about how wet she became.

Cugbert followed close behind, and the room felt tiny when the large Third-Braid priest of the Pankratios entered the room.

Cugbert boomed, "Madam, you have a brave and persistent boy here. He will be an influential leader someday. A boy that size who convinces me to put down my bread and ale to plod through fast-moving waters during a legendary storm like this is worthy of applause."

The mother tightened her hold until Brit squirmed and griped, "Mom, you're crushing me."

Though she loosened her grip, she didn't release him altogether. "I'm so glad you're safe. I was so worried. . ."

Erik's breath temporarily bottled up in his throat as he gazed at Zita's last hope—Cugbert, healer and friend.

Cugbert went to one knee to examine Zita. Wet hair clung to her cheek and forehead from her sweating in her sleep.

He touched her forehead and murmured some words. His brow wrinkled. Then he clasped her face with both hands.

"I haven't seen this sickness in a long time."

"Can you heal her?" Erik dropped to one knee next to Cugbert. His knee landed in a small stream of water that had formed from the rain.

Cugbert removed his hands from her forehead. "Have you acquired any new objects? You searched for a golden crown, did you not?"

"Yes, we found the Helmet of Justice. It's over there."

Cugbert picked up the helmet and examined it. "It radiates sickness. This was supposed to be buried and never found. Where did you get it?"

"That's it. The golden crown, only it wasn't a golden crown like we thought but this helmet with a gold dragon on top. We also found a sword, the Sword of Freedom."

Brit exclaimed, "The Sword of Freedom! I held the Sword of Freedom. Wait till I tell Vanesh."

Cugbert stared at Erik with blue eyes beneath his bushy red hair. "Where's the sword?"

"Right behind you." Brit rushed over and picked it off the floor.

Cugbert examined the sword, following the same process he had employed when studying the helmet.

Erik said, "There is a healing component to it. Not as strong as the golden frog in the temple."

"Golden frog?" Brit asked. "Are you a mighty adventurer?"

"No," Erik said, the word sharp and full of rebuke. He didn't feel like a mighty adventurer. He felt like a fraud. Half the time, he was just trying to stay alive while he made stupid mistake after stupid mistake.

"You and Alpherge went into the Pit of Wretchedness, then?" Cugbert asked.

"Yes, and Zita too. We used the sword, the helmet, and Al's staff to remove the corruption of evil from Gadiel." *Zita almost died that day, and if we don't stop talking, she will die today.* "Can you help her?"

"For this type of sickness, there isn't much I can do." Cugbert weighed the sword in his hand, examining the handle and guard. He ran a finger down the blade and stroked the diamond on the handle.

"Even for someone with your third-braid healing knowledge? You have the touch." Erik stroked Zita's hair with his hand, and when he raised his hand, more of Zita's hair clung to his fingers. "Look at this. It's coming out in clumps."

Cugbert was silent as he focused on the sword.

Zita moaned.

Erik's knees trembled, and his fingers felt numb. He sighed, and his shoulders slumped. "Cugbert, please?"

"The sword has a healing component that radiates potency. Let me try with the sword." He took the sword and laid the point in the middle of Zita's chest while he held on to the handle. "It lets me see deeper into the body, better detail."

Erik had noticed the same thing about the sword when he used it.

"The sword wants to draw the sickness out." He shifted the sword in his hand, placing the blade point on Zita's forehead.

Erik had seen this done when they helped Gadiel. The sickness or evil withdrew through the point of the sword. In Erik's case, he had to place the point on Gadiel's eye without breaking it. He realized he had been using it wrong with the stone warriors. He treated the sword like a king knighting someone when he should have been using it as a focusing point.

Brit asked, "Is it working?"

"Quiet," his mom said.

Cugbert chanted a song or words in a language Erik didn't understand, something Erik hoped to learn someday. The sword handle and blade appeared as if flames encircled it.

Zita thrashed in the bed.

"Hold her so I don't injure her." Cugbert continued to concentrate on Zita, the flames from the sword licking at his hands.

Mrs. Weaver held Zita's legs while Erik held Zita's shoulders. Cugbert continued his chanting. Her body was wet with sweat, and she had lost weight these last two weeks. The skin tightened around her skull.

Erik raised his eyebrows and gave Cugbert a questioning look, and then Zita convulsed. Heaviness weighed on Erik's mind as her body shook, and he increased pressure to contain her shaking. *She's not going to make it. The sword isn't enough.*

"Hold, we're almost done."

"I can't believe how strong she is." Erik worked hard to keep her still.

Cugbert went back to the chanting.

As Erik held Zita, he delved into her body. The sickness leaked from her bones to the sword. He could see it in his mind. What was this?

Suddenly, Zita relaxed.

Cugbert pulled the sword from her forehead.

"I watched the discharge from her bones."

"Yes, people with this disease don't live long after they reach this point. The sword helps, and ideally, this will comfort her."

Erik felt a sinking sensation in his stomach. His brows pinched together. "Comfort her? Are you saying it won't last?"

"I'm saying she won't be in as much pain now."

"Why have we done all this work if the healing is temporary?" Erik's chest tightened, and he wondered what else he could do to save Zita.

"She's experiencing a very aggressive disease. I've pulled all the negative energy out of her." Cugbert took Erik's arm. "Let her rest and we'll examine her again in a couple of days. The sword helped."

Erik took a deep breath and scowled. "What caused it?"

"The Helmet of Justice."

"What? She's been wearing that for two months."

Cugbert sat on the cabin's dirt floor. "The Helmet of Justice provides great insight for the people that wear it, but all the literature describes the people that have worn it to develop a wasting disease and die. Some died faster than others, and it seemed related to the amount of time they wear it."

All this triggered the thought that had eluded Erik for the last twenty-four hours. "Of course. Why didn't I see this before? Her hair falling out and a wasting disease. Cancer. On Earth, it's known as radiation poisoning. They must have made the helmet of radioactive material, probably the dragon."

Cugbert laid the sword on the dirt floor. "You need to bury the helmet and never use it again."

"We want to use it to rescue the stone warriors."

Brit's mother gasped.

CHAPTER 17

Erik walked to the village blacksmith carrying the helmet. Every village had a blacksmith, though he didn't see horses or a need for ironwork in this small village. The pounding of metal against metal sounded in the still morning air. He needed to talk with the guy about a lead box for the helmet to prevent the radiation poisoning from leaching out when they carried it.

He found the blacksmith heating a piece of metal in a forge made of stone and brick. The blacksmith worked the bellows and watched as the metal turned a bright yellow-orange color then pulled it out of the fire and pounded it with a giant hammer. Striking the hot metal with the hammer again and again, the blacksmith widened the metal as he reduced its thickness.

The blacksmith looked up and saw Erik but said nothing. He didn't even ask him to wait but just kept working. He handled the heavy hammer like it was a child's toy as he continued the re-shaping process until the metal's color and malleability reached the point that it needed re-heating. Then he threw the metal back into the fire.

"What do you want?" the blacksmith asked.

"I need a metal box to fit this helmet."

"When?"

"I don't know. Can I get it today?"

"Nope." The blacksmith rubbed his forearm across his sweaty brow, leaving dirty tracks of ash on his forehead. His long blond beard looked singed on the lower edges.

"It has to be made of lead."

"Why?" He adjusted his leather apron, spotted with burn marks from the forge.

"Safety reasons."

"A lead box will be heavy. How thick do you need it?"

Erik didn't know the answer to that question. "I don't know. Let's go with an inch thick. And I need a hinge on it so I can take the helmet out when I need it."

"Okay, let's measure it. Hand it here." The blacksmith examined the helmet and caressed the gold dragon. "Nice dragon. What is this?"

Erik hadn't considered that the blacksmith might find the object valuable. Was the dragon solid gold? The man could whack Erik with the hammer and steal it. He placed his hand on his sword.

The blacksmith coughed, took out a measuring stick, and measured the helmet as he made plans for the lead box. "The leather flaps can fold up underneath?"

"What? Oh yeah, that'll be fine."

"It's gonna be heavy. Are you planning on carrying it anywhere?"

Erik hadn't considered how to transport the box afterward. "How much weight?"

The blacksmith looked at the measurements he had scrawled with chalk on a piece of metal. "I estimate somewhere between fifty pounds to seventy pounds. Empty."

"It will weigh that much empty?" Adding the helmet and dragon wouldn't mean a lot of extra weight. Zita had been wearing it on her head nonstop for six weeks, but who would haul it once they put it in the box? Could they store the box and helmet someplace?

"Do you have an animal?"

"For what?"

"To carry the box."

Erik grunted. "No."

The blacksmith used a pair of pliers to grip the hot metal in the fire and pulled it out of the fire, plopped it on the anvil, and started pounding. He pounded, rotated the metal, and pounded some more. Then he shoved it back in the fire. "Can you leave the helmet here so I can get a good fit?"

Erik had an empty feeling in his stomach. He was no match for this guy, and even if he drew his sword, he didn't really know how to use it, but he fingered the sword handle anyway. "No, my lady needs it." He thought if he referred to Zita as "lady," it would make the man believe an army was traveling with her.

The blacksmith lifted the helmet. "Did you steal this boy? Maybe I should hold it till I can get the local constable involved."

Erik drew his sword.

The blacksmith rubbed his sweaty hands down his pants leg. "Hey, there's no need for that." He threw the helmet at Erik.

Erik caught the helmet with his left hand, still holding the sword with his right.

"When will you have it ready?"

"Give me a week." He picked up his hammer.

Erik backed out of the smithy.

When he arrived back at the cabin, Cugbert sat on the floor, talking with Zita, "Your dad is alive?"

"Yes. I couldn't believe it when they introduced him at the castle. I never suspected he lived. Burn marks dotted his face and arms where the fireball hit him and an injured shoulder. I took away his magic."

"Using the helmet?"

"Yes, it gives me insights. I feel naked without it now."

"What insights?" Cugbert asked.

"I can't describe it. I know I'm not reading people's minds, but from the way they sit, their eye movements, and their facial expressions, the helmet can tell me what they're thinking."

Erik broke the conversation when he handed the helmet to Zita. "He'll have it ready in a week. But it'll weigh up to seventy pounds. How will we transport all that weight?"

Zita set the helmet on the floor. "I used to have a little music box that would allow me to carry something that heavy, but I left it at the Velidred Castle. I wanted to stop and get it while we were there, but then the guards chased us."

"You can put a cubic foot of metal into a little music box?"

"I put Al's staff into it."

"Really?" Erik did a slow, disbelieving shake of his head. The life he lived growing up on Earth was at odds with Zita's life here on Aloheno.

* * * *

Five days later, Erik and Cugbert took the helmet to the blacksmith's shop to pick up the lead box. He carried his sword in the sheath on his hip and had unhooked the clasp in case he needed it in a hurry.

The blacksmith's blond curls were damp with sweat even though the shed of his smithy stood in the late afternoon shade. When Erik entered the building, the man looked up. He held his hammer like a weapon.

The blacksmith turned to the back of the shed and wrestled with a box. He eventually got a handle on the metal container and walked it over to Erik. "Your lead box, sir."

Erik looked at the blacksmith. The laborer had arms the size of a crocodile's body, and he had strained to carry the heavy lead box. *How will I lift that box?*

The blacksmith showed them how the lid worked. They maneuvered the helmet and the dragon into the box. Closing the box left the enclosed helmet with a little wriggle room.

"Did you want a lock for the door?"

Erik nodded. "Yes, we need to lock it."

Cugbert paid the man.

Erik bent down to the box and lifted. It didn't budge. He squatted next to the object, put his hands beneath the metal edges, and tried to stand. With a loud grunt, Erik stood, his legs shaking.

Sweat beaded on his forehead as he struggled to frog walk it back to the cabin. How would they transport this box? The radiation needed to be contained, but this wouldn't work.

Cugbert nudged Erik. "Let me try."

The priest squatted, carefully fitted his fingers beneath the box, and then drove his hips upward. The box came off the floor. Cugbert headed down the road back to the cabin.

Erik's eyes widened, and he shook his head. "How can you make that box look so light? What does it weigh?"

The blacksmith rubbed a cloth across his forehead. "Near one hundred pounds."

When Erik had worked with the mastodons on the trip to the Ice Castle, he thought he could handle one hundred pounds.

Cugbert walked with the lead box in his hands all the way back to the cabin. The large man breathed hard but exerted little more effort than it would take to carry a heavy bag of garbage to the trash.

* * * *

Zita waited in the cabin for the men to return. She had something to say to Erik but feared his reaction to the news. She had spent the last three days deciding on a course of action that would answer questions she had about the stone warriors.

Her condition had improved, and she felt capable of journeying by herself. She had an idea about the stone warriors but wanted to speak with Finn. Now that Cugbert had healed her, she worried about Erik's reaction to her leaving him to pursue this course of action.

Cugbert brought the lead box into the cabin and dropped it on the floor.

Erik approached Zita. She adored his smile when he entered the room. "How are you feeling? Will you be ready to travel tomorrow?"

Zita fingered her necklace as her breathing accelerated. "Yes, I feel much better. Not back to normal but not nauseated today."

"We have a problem. The box weighs over a hundred pounds. I'm not able to lift it."

Her chest tightened as she walked to the box. "What are we going to do?"

"I'm thinking Cugbert could carry it." Erik looked at the priest with raised eyebrows.

"No, I have to attend to my people, and I can't do that while keeping track of the box. Find some other way to transport it."

"Should I buy a horse or mule or another domesticated animal? Will I need a wagon?"

Zita thought about the weight of the box. She wanted the helmet to be near her the entire time but didn't want the added burden of taking care of an animal and a cart.

Cugbert said, "It'll never do for us to wander around the mountainside with an ox and cart. You've seen the trails we travel."

Erik replied, "We can use the cart for other things. We can take more supplies with us to serve the people."

"No, you haven't learned your lessons yet, have you?" Cugbert crossed his arms over his massive chest. "We travel light, we visit the villages, and we work with what we have, trusting the people to help those less fortunate. We aren't building a caravan for our duties."

Erik spluttered. "We have to use an animal. It's a hundred pounds of lead."

"That's what you ordered." Cugbert's eyes narrowed. "Are you ready to resume your studies for the Second Braid? You aren't wearing your First Braid. Why not?"

A flush crept across Erik's face, and his shoulder slumped. "Well, uh, I, uh. . ."

"You don't know how to braid your hair, do you?" Zita snorted a laugh.

Erik looked sheepishly at Zita. "No."

Cugbert laughed a big, booming laugh that filled the small cabin with sound. Three long red braids flipped and flopped across his shoulders as he laughed. His beard bounced up and down on his chest.

"Come here." Zita patted the floor in front of her. "Let me show you."

Erik sat and Zita brushed out his hair. Heat radiated from her chest. She loved touching his long hair and strong shoulders. Zita hummed a quiet childhood tune that reminded her of her mother. She admired Erik for choosing to become a healer priest like Cugbert. This world needed more people like Cugbert and Erik, good-hearted people that cared about others.

Cugbert walked out of the cabin to check on the needs of the village.

Zita stopped humming. "Do you remember your mom?"

"Uh, sure, it's only been a few months since I saw her last. Why?"

"Doing your hair reminds me of times when my mom did mine. She didn't have to, being queen and all, and I had a nanny that took care of me. But when Mom took the time to comb out my hair, those were special moments to me."

"Tell me more."

Zita went back into her memories, not even knowing where to start. She had been so young when her mom died. She wished they had had more time together. "My birthday when Mom gave me the music box was memorable. My grandfather had died the previous day, and though Mom was distressed, she made sure I had a nice birthday. The music box was my favorite gift. She and I sang the song that the music box played. It seemed to comfort her."

"Will you sing it for me?"

Zita touched the necklace she wore. She didn't know if she felt sadness or happiness at the memories.

She sang,

Touch my hand when you are near.

You'll be close all the year.

I feel you by my side when you are gone.

When your heart longs for me,

Sing this song.

Distance and time draw us apart.

Know that you are in my heart.

When I can't be by your side,

I'll think of times together,

Loving memories you supplied.

"You have a beautiful voice."

Zita couldn't speak. Her eyes filled with tears. Pleasant memories of her mother warmed her. Unfortunately, every wonderful memory soon exploded into that night of violence when her father killed her mother. Zita dropped her hands from Erik's hair and covered her eyes.

Erik rotated on the floor and wrapped his arms around her shoulders. "It's okay, Zita, I'm here for you."

She jumped as he first touched her, clenching her jaw tight, then relaxed into his embrace. A jolt of joy raced through her body at his touch. She had a task that she wanted to attempt. It could help solve the stone warrior problem, but she needed to go into the mountains for answers. Separate from Erik for a while. Would she be able to give this up, even for a few days or weeks? She yearned for him. The world always felt safer and better when Erik stood beside her. "I love you."

"I love you too." Erik squeezed her closer.

She leaned her head into his shoulder, enjoying his body's warmth. She pushed against his chest and created a small separation.

"What's wrong?" He drew back from her, relaxing his embrace, and he held her hands.

"Nothing."

"Come on, Zita. I'm not wearing the helmet, but something's on your mind."

Zita looked Erik in the eyes and then looked down.

He touched her chin and lifted. "What is it?"

She opened and closed her mouth then pinched her lips together. *What is the best way to say this without worrying him?* "What are your plans?"

"I'm going with Cugbert to resume training."

"Where?"

"Cugbert doesn't have a set schedule or follow a plan. He follows the needs of the people, feeding, healing, and counseling them." Erik tilted his head to the side and pursed his lips. "What do you mean 'my plans'?"

Zita's abdomen tightened as a sour taste formed in her mouth, the nausea on the verge of returning to her stomach. She had considered slipping out of the cabin and disappearing at night without a word.

"Zita?"

She looked down, and her hair fell over her eyes like a wall to shield her from Erik's reaction. She leaned away from Erik, her fingers sliding from his grasp. "I'm not going with you and Cugbert."

Erik swallowed hard, and he gave his head a slow shake. "Why would you not go with us?"

"I need to go back to the castle for my music box," she lied.

"You can't be serious? Velidred Castle is the last place you need to go. Why?"

"Memories of my mother. I don't want them to destroy my music box. It's already damaged, and I'm afraid they'll throw it away."

"Let me come with you."

"No."

"The helmet?"

"I'll take it with me." She glanced at the heavy lead box and shook her head.

"You can't lift it. I can't even lift it."

"You know I can do magic, right?"

"Yeah, but what are you going to do? Who will protect you?"

Zita worried that being sick might influence her magic. She felt weak, though better than before. She searched for the magic and thought about the shapeshifting skills Gadiel had taught her. Zita concentrated on the lead box and saw movement as she initiated the magic to change the object's shape. The process stopped, and she felt a moment of concern when nothing happened. Then her magic and shapeshifting skills clicked, the box changed, and a dog barked. A large black mastiff raced into Zita's arms, knocking her to the floor and licking her face.

"Where did… what?" Erik moved toward Zita and the dog.

The dog turned toward Erik and growled.

"It's the lead box, silly. He's going to protect me, aren't you, Jackson?" The dog licked tears from Zita's face.

CHAPTER 18

Alpherge the Mighty walked down the mountain path from the Village of the Stone Warriors with staff in hand. He would search for the wizard named Finn, but first, he had to catch up with Sherry. Who knew? Maybe she would like to help Al find the wizard.

It would be nice to hold her hand and hug and kiss her. Al and Erik had traveled for twelve weeks with the caravan. He wondered if Sherry would even recognize him. He figured she and Lily had stayed in Tanuku after they had been banished from Crossroads. Al walked faster in anticipation of seeing her.

Al entered Tanuku on a hot day. Sweat poured from his head while he swatted at gnats and mosquitos. Forest River Blossom had promised to help Sherry with her headaches, so Al knew it would be important for her to stay close to the spiritualist.

Al walked through the Village of Tanuku, where homes painted bright cheerful colors made the village seem more optimistic than the depressing and dusty homes of Crossroads. He passed residents sitting in the shade on their homes' porches, some waving multi-hued hand fans to keep cool in the mid-afternoon heat.

Should Al go straight to Forest River Blossom, or should he ask the residents? Asking the residents if Sherry was in town could save time. Surely, the locals would know.

He stopped at a home along the dirt road he walked. Two elderly ladies sat on wooden chairs facing each other.

Alpherge said, "Hi."

The women looked at him, their postures relaxed and friendly. "Ah, the young wizard is back from his travels," one woman said.

Good, they remember me. They'll know where I can find Sherry. "Do you know where I can find my friend, Sherry? She's a redheaded girl about so high." Al raised his hand to about shoulder height, though he didn't think she was really that tall.

The woman with her gray hair in a bun said, "The redhead and the blonde, you can't miss them."

Her friend, the other woman with darker skin and long, flowing black hair with a touch of gray at the temple, said, "Weren't those young women cute?"

The bun woman said, "That blonde could dance better than I've seen since you were young, Maggie."

Maggie beamed. "The joy of nature's energy flowing through our bodies." The woman closed her eyes as she moved her arms as if imaginary music played in her head.

"Richard used to watch you dance for hours, like a dog waiting for a bone."

Maggie giggled. "I enjoyed teasing him. I miss those days."

Al placed his hands on his hips and scowled. He said, "I'm sorry to interrupt, but can you tell me where I can find the girls?"

"I think this boy is as eager as Richard was."

Both women giggled as Al felt the heat rise in his cheeks. He didn't want to be rude, but he didn't want to spend hours chit-chatting with a couple of old women either.

The bun woman stared at Al. "Slow down and relax a little. Spend more time with the redhead and less time thinking about magic. She's going to be angry when she sees you. You were gone a long time. Seems she's angry both when you're here and when you're not."

Maggie said, "Boys are always hurrying to do nothing."

Al looked to the skies as he clenched his fists. Should he leave and find someone else to tell him about Sherry? The girls were probably across the street, staring out the window and laughing at him. He turned his head and checked the house across the street, where two people stared through the window, but they were not Sherry and Lily.

Maggie said, "Our lives could have been different if Richard and Carlson hadn't run off to fight the battles against the Mountain King's forces."

"Why didn't they listen to us, Maggie? I miss Carlson."

The two women sat in contemplation.

Al walked on, figuring he would just stop at Forest River Blossom's place. He had hoped to avoid the woman, but maybe she could give insight into Finn's location too. He hadn't made it halfway through the village before he heard the drums, flutes, and cymbals that always accompanied Forest River Blossom when the teens traveled through her village.

The woman led a congregation of about thirty men and women on the dirt road. Eight women clad in short white dresses danced around the congregation, spinning and leaping in the air.

Al stopped, figuring he would give the congregation more time to play their music. He didn't know how many strangers entered the village needing a welcoming committee. Forest River Blossom wore a thin green material that flowed around her shapely body. She was a tiny woman whose presence commanded attention and respect.

It took the group about a minute to reach Al. Then Forest River Blossom stopped in front of him and let the music play for another minute before raising her hand to stop the musicians.

Oh brother. Talking about someone needing attention. He knew Sherry despised the spiritualist for all the pomp and pageantry the woman displayed. It made him think of the Napoleon complex.

"You have returned?"

Al couldn't tell if she asked him a question or made a statement. "Yes," he answered.

"Did you find the golden crown?"

He hesitated, not sure how much information he should share with the spiritualist. He should tell the entire story but decided against sharing the fact that the crown wasn't golden, just a dirty old helmet with a gold dragon on top.

"Yes, we found the crown."

"And you don't have it with you? I expected you to return with your friend Erik."

Three drummers tapped out a rapid set of beats.

Al imagined the drummers adding mystery and a tone of intrigue and danger. His stomach felt like it was doing flip-flops. He closed his eyes and drew a deep breath. "Erik's fine. He returned to study and work with Cugbert. Zita's with him."

"And what happened with the stone warriors? I heard of an accident there."

Al rubbed the back of his neck and then ran his fingers through his beard. How did the woman learn about the accident with the Stone Warriors? His throat tightened. Should he try to downplay their role in the accident? No, the woman must know what happened. Not because she was a spiritualist but because she was a busybody.

"Yes, we"—*really, the stone warrior debacle fell on Erik*—"tried to heal one stone warrior." *We should have listened to Zita and not attempted anything.* "And the warrior…" *How can I say this politely around all these people?*

"You killed Dickerson." Forest River Blossom didn't beat around the bush, but she blurted out the words.

The congregation gasped. Some raised their hands to their mouths. Others placed their hands on their chests. All moaned in agony. One drummer beat his drum in a slow dirge.

The thickness in Al's throat tightened, and his heart beat three times harder than normal. He dropped his chin to his chest and couldn't meet Forest River Blossom's gaze. Al had no answer for the woman. They didn't mean to hurt Dickerson. They'd hoped only to help, and something went wrong. Al had no idea what had happened. Erik had everything under control, and then the stone man exploded.

"It was an accident; we didn't mean it."

"I have tried to educate you and your friends from Earth, but you go about this planet like you know what you're doing. I'm telling you, stop it. Listen to me. Listen to other elders in our world."

Al didn't know how the tiny woman did it, but she made him feel like a little boy being chastised for misdeeds. Was now a good time to ask about Finn? She had encouraged him to listen to the elders, and the wizard, Finn, was supposed to be an old guy. "Could you tell me where I can find a wizard named Finn?"

The congregation gasped again.

Now what?

This time Forest River Blossom frowned, stepped back a step, and pushed her long black hair out of her face. "No one has seen Finn in a while. What do you want with him?" She twisted a large emerald ring around her finger.

"The stone warriors—"

"Leave the stone warriors alone. You're not experienced enough to help them now."

"But Erik wants to rescue his dad. I thought you could tell me where to find Finn?"

"The wizard isn't interested in being located."

Al rubbed the back of his neck and sighed. "Why not?"

"It's not your business."

"He can train me."

"Finn doesn't tutor wizards anymore."

"Why not?"

"Leave it." Forest River Blossom's nostrils flared, and she swept her arm in a large circle about her chest.

Al wondered how hard he could push this woman to give him the answers he sought. If he continued to push, maybe she wouldn't tell him where to find Sherry. Couldn't she say Finn was somewhere in the mountains and point him in the right direction? That was what everyone else did.

He softened his voice. "How about my friend Sherry? Do you know where she is?"

"Sherry doesn't want to see you either."

"Why not?"

"You abandoned her."

Al raised his free hand toward the woman. "What do you mean? You told us to go and to leave Sherry and Lily here."

"It doesn't matter."

"We're trying to save the stone warriors," Al said in a louder voice.

"You're killing the stone warriors." Forest River Blossom's voice grew softer.

"Dickerson was an accident. We want to learn how to do it right. That's why we need to find Finn." Al shouted.

Forest River Blossom raised her hand, and the drums started a cadence. The cymbals and tambourines took up the beat, and soon the flutes joined in with high-pitched trills.

"Leave Finn alone. He can't help you," Forest River Blossom said. The spiritualist turned and walked through her congregation, and the parade of musicians and dancers followed.

"How about Sherry?" Al yelled but got no response.

CHAPTER 19

Al stood in the street for a few minutes, baffled by the exchange he'd had with the crazy woman Forest River Blossom and her cult followers. He needed more information about Finn to see why the people were so shocked when he mentioned his name. He decided he needed to find Sherry and get some feedback from her. With all the shouting, Al figured if Sherry lived in Tanuku, she would have heard him and come out to check on the noise generated every time he entered the village. Well, if she wasn't in Tanuku, then Crossroads was the next logical choice.

He walked toward Crossroads. As he got closer, a gigantic shadow flew across the ground in front of him. He recalled his previous awful experience with the kids and the giant bird. It didn't matter; three months had passed, and they wouldn't even remember him. *What kind of reception will I get in Crossroads?*

Two guards wearing the same-colored garments stopped him at the village wall gates. "What's your business here?"

"I'm looking for someone, a woman with red hair."

"Are you a wizard?"

Al nodded to the staff in his right hand.

"Be out of the village by nightfall."

"Why?"

"Village laws. The Village Council doesn't like wizards lately. They cause trouble."

Al didn't think it would take that long to find Sherry, so he agreed he would leave the village before sundown.

He proceeded into the village, not sure exactly where to start. There weren't a lot of redheads in the village, and he didn't think it would be hard to find people who had seen Sherry.

The first person he encountered was a thin man with greasy brown hair and a smudge of dirt along the side of his nose.

"Sir, I'm looking for a redheaded woman named Sherry."

"Don't know any red-haired women," the man drawled.

He met a woman with a young boy less than five years old at her side. She carried an empty bucket, heading to the village well.

"Excuse me, do you know any redheaded women in the village?"

"Yeah, a woman meeting that description tried to start up a school. Walking around bothering people."

"Yes." Al cheered at the recognition. "Where does she live?"

"How do I know?" The woman walked away.

Al interviewed three more people with no luck.

A man's face lit up in acknowledgment of Sherry's existence. "Yeah, she has a cute blonde friend."

"Yes, that's them. Those are my friends. Can you tell me where they live?"

"Maybe, if you have coin."

Al sighed and closed his eyes. He pulled out his money pouch, which jiggled with coins from payment from his work with the caravan. Al turned his back, picked a couple of coins from the pouch, and handed the coins to the man.

"Their house is over that way." The man waved his hand in a general direction and then said, "Take this road to the next block, turn right, walk a block and a half, and their house will be on the left, a white cabin with blue shutters. The foolish girls tried to start a school in their home. Can you believe that? A female teacher. Totally improper."

Excitement built in Al at the prospect of finding Sherry, though his thoughts were tempered with concern. Al thanked the man. *These people don't allow women to be teachers?*

He followed the man's instructions and saw the store sign for the Magic Shoppe. He remembered the place fondly since the owner had hooked him up with Master Ishwa. Al would have to stop in and ask the owner about Finn.

After a turn and a block-and-a-half walk, Al stood in front of the white cabin. Should he knock or just walk in and surprise the girls? Would Sherry rush to greet him, or would she slap him? Would she be so upset with him that she'd ask him to leave and never see him again?

His stomach did flip-flops as he stood in front of the door. He raised his right hand to knock. *I wonder if she will be happy to see me.* Al dropped his hand. He tilted his head back and forth as he tried to decide whether he should or shouldn't.

A person tapped him on the shoulder.

Al jumped. "What?"

A woman held a toddler's hand and balanced a baby on her hip. "They aren't there."

"Who?"

"The blonde and the red-haired woman. They aren't there anymore."

"Where did they go?"

"You need to see the mayor."

A slight shiver went down Al's spine. He had met the mayor. The man ran Al and his friends out of town three months previous, and Al didn't like him.

"Tell him Bonnie sent you."

"Bonnie? Why?"

"The kids need food. That's why."

Al headed to the village council building near the center of town. He didn't know where the mayor lived, but maybe the man would be at the office. In the center of the village stood a post office, bank, and tailor shop all around a small park where the Kallurian flag waved in the slight breeze.

He entered the village council building, where stuffy air greeted him. The wood building had a simple wood floor. The boards weren't tongue and groove, and they squeaked as Al walked through the hallway. A door on the right had a sign that read, Village Council Meetings. On the left side of the hallway, the door's sign read Mayor's Office.

Al didn't know the protocol for a little village hall. Did the mayor have an antechamber where he could just walk right in and talk to a receptionist, or did this door open directly into the mayor's office? He couldn't decide, so he knocked.

A man's voice responded, "Come in."

Al opened the door to find three men in the room. The mayor sat behind a small table. Al didn't recognize the other two.

"Ah, the young wizard decided to visit us." The mayor turned to the man on his right. "Justin, you can leave now. Shut the door."

"Shouldn't I stay, Your Honor?"

The mayor's lips hardened.

Justin stepped out of the room and shut the door.

Okay, it's just the three of us, then.

The mayor said, "What can I do for you, young fella?" He waved a cigar in the air as he motioned for Al to sit.

Something didn't feel right, but he wasn't sure what it was. "Bonnie sent me."

"Well, good for her. Make a note Mr. Mooney."

Al towered over the shorter mayor, and he knew magic, yet he still didn't feel comfortable. He looked hard into the mayor's eyes.

"What do you want, boy?" Mr. Mooney asked.

"Bonnie told me you could help me find my friend."

"We like to monitor the wizards in this village, ever since you almost killed those children in a fire."

"I told those children to go home, and they didn't listen." Al felt tired suddenly, and he didn't feel like arguing with these men.

"We have witnesses that saw you entice them out of the safety of the village walls, which we erected for their safety from wild animals."

"Nope, that wasn't the way it happened. But it doesn't matter because I'm not here to lure your children away from their mothers. I'm looking for two people, a redheaded woman named Sherry and a blonde woman named Lily. Bonnie told me to talk with you."

"Yeah, they ran into some problems here in the village. We had to send them away for a while."

"Okay. Where did you send them?"

"Away. They were troublemakers. Just like you. We don't normally allow wizards in the village."

"You used to have a warrior wizard training school in the village, and you have a Magic Shoppe near the gates. Is it wizards you don't allow or just me?" Al moved his staff to his side with his right hand.

"Don't give us trouble, boy. If you want trouble, I can get a battalion of guards down here in a flash."

Did the mayor send Justin to round up some guards to lay the groundwork for a trap? It didn't matter. He didn't plan on staying around much longer. While he held the staff, he placed a spell around the room to warn himself if magic was being used.

"Since the mayor doesn't know, Mr. Mooney, can you tell me where my friends Sherry and Lily are?"

Mr. Mooney didn't have the mayor's practiced skill of lying. He stammered a little as his eyes shifted back and forth between Al and the mayor, "They are. . . Well, they went. . . I mean, they. . ."

The mayor interrupted Mr. Mooney. "What he's trying to say is your friends went to see Prince Krunal at Velidred Castle."

"Why would they want to do that?"

"She's trying to start a school in the village and is looking for funding for a building. She said something about the prince owing her a favor for something she did for him." He hunched his shoulders and showed his palms.

Mr. Mooney chimed in, "Yeah, she made a presentation at the last village council meeting, and the village council rejected her request because of lack of funding."

Al watched them both. His muscles were tense, ready for the fight-or-flight response to kick in. They were lying to him. He knew it but couldn't prove it. "Anybody else can corroborate your story?"

The mayor responded, "Every member of the village council. I'll be happy to send Mr. Mooney out to round them all up, and you can ask each one separately if you so desire."

Al looked at the mayor, who stared back at him, a smile almost crossing his lips. Mr. Mooney deliberately lowered his head and studied the floor. "Okay, I'll be on my way." Al watched for visual cues of their deceit as he rose slowly from the chair. His spell held firm, and he let it pulse out from the building a few yards, checking for traps.

The mayor stood and said, "Don't come back to our village. We don't like you."

Al snorted in agreement. He exited the room into an empty corridor. He erected a magic shield in case he walked out of the building into a hailstorm of arrows. When he reached the door, he opened it slowly, prepared to defend and attack as needed.

He peeked out the door and saw a normal flow of traffic through the village. No guards stood in the streets or hid behind barrels. People weren't running for cover like they did on those old TV Westerns back on Earth. He marched through the street, still wary about the people he encountered.

Al grabbed a man coming out of the post office. "Sir, I'm looking for two girls, a blonde and a redhead. They were in the village starting a school; do you know where I can find them?"

The man sent a quick glance at the village council building. "Ask the mayor."

"I've already asked him."

He frowned, looked down at the ground, and then pinched his lower lip. "Can't help." The man walked away.

"This is ridiculous," Al mumbled. "This village is nothing but a bunch of lunatics."

CHAPTER 20

Al wanted to make one more stop before he left the village—the Magic Shoppe. He knew where to go but made a couple of different turns in case someone followed him. *That's crazy. No one would think I was worth following.*

He found the building and walked through the front door. The smell of leather from old books and scrolls of magic spells filled his nostrils. There were a couple of windows, and most of the light came from candles burning on tables and mirrored wall sconces that reflected candlelight back into the room.

Would the proprietor recognize Al from those many months ago when Al had first stopped in here from Earth?

An elderly man shuffled from a back corner of the building. "Ah, young man, is there a need to be throwing up a shield in my shop?"

"What? Oh, the shield. Sorry. I thought I was going to be ambushed."

"I'm supposed to report you to the mayor if I feel magic in the village."

"Well, I just came from the mayor's office, so you can save your time."

The shop owner studied Al's staff. "The staff of Ishwa. I wondered who had possession of the staff after Ishwa was killed."

One member of the staff, Callahan the Curious, asked, "How's she cutting, Tobias?"

"Just fine, Callahan, and you, my friend?"

Callahan said, "Have you figured out a way for me to get out of this blasted stick?"

"I'm still trying to figure out how you got into the staff. Didn't I warn you not to do things you didn't know how to do?"

"Yeah, that's a problem of mine."

Tobias asked, "How can I help, young fella?"

"The staff recommended I find a wizard named Finn."

"Don't blame me," Callahan said. "It was Alpherge the Great's idea."

Tobias raised his eyebrows as his stooped posture perked up. "Now, why would you want to look for Finn?"

"We're trying to rescue the stone warriors, and my staff thought Finn could help."

"He's a dangerous man. You don't want to find him, and I assure you, he doesn't want to be found."

"I just want to ask him a couple of questions." Al wondered if the entire village would irritate him today. "Why wouldn't he want to see me?"

"You are about the age of the young wizards that betrayed him to King Haskell. Might bring back memories." He rubbed his chin. "Yeah, Finn doesn't want to revisit those."

"Can't you just wave your hand in a general direction?"

"No. Trust me, kid, he doesn't want to see you."

The top image on the staff, the grandfatherly carved figure, said, "Tobias, tell him what you know. It's important."

"Alpherge, you know Finn doesn't want to be bothered. Not by this wizard that's still wet behind the ears."

"He's my grandson, and I want to visit with Finn too."

"Are you sure, Alpherge? You know the dangers; the boy may become one of them stone statues."

Alpherge the Great said, "The boy will be okay. He's got a good head on his shoulders."

Tobias pinched the bridge of his nose. "Maybe I should send him to the Council of Nine or the Grand Wizard."

Al's stomach clenched at the mention of the Grand Wizard. *No, that won't work at all. I've seen him and don't want to see him again.*

Alpherge the Great lowered his voice. "The boy needs to see Finn. It'll be okay."

Tobias shook his head and muttered something unintelligible as he walked to the shelving in the back of the store. He brought out a scroll and opened it on a table in the room. He pulled a candle holder with three candles over to the table. The scroll showed a map of the region near Crossroads. He ran his hand up and down the map, getting his bearings, and then said, "Yes, near here."

Al studied the map, asking questions about roads and crossing rivers and the best mountain trails to take.

Tobias said, "I don't know exactly where he is, but three years ago I knew he was in that general area." He pointed at a village on the map. "Your best bet is to stop in this village, Oakwood. Someone there will send you to a smaller village until you meet the three people on the mountain who know where to find him. I hope you live through it."

Al stared into Tobias's gray eyes. *How dangerous is this trip going to be?*

* * * *

Al left the village ruminating about Sherry. Did she really run off to Velidred Castle to visit with Prince Krunal? She was doing important things, helping teach the children. She was always doing good and helping others.

He was bummed he'd missed her. Would she want him to stay? If her trip would take only a couple of days, then he could wait for her to return. It should take a maximum of four, maybe five days to travel there and back. Give it a day for her audience with the prince. *I can stay in Tanuku for a few days until she returns.* The mayor didn't want him staying in Crossroads.

He imagined what standing in front of the king asking for money to build a school for children might be like. If he were king, then he'd say yes.

The map showed a trip of three or four days to find Finn. Ask the dude a couple of questions. He would give Al the answers, and then he could return to Sherry in less than a week. She wouldn't even know that he had returned already.

A shadow passed overhead, and he looked skyward, where a gigantic bird circled.

They needed to find out how to save the stone warriors, and it would be great if Finn could help. Long-term, maybe the dude would coach Al in wizardry. He desperately needed training, but would Finn force him to stay in the mountains instead of being back here with Sherry?

Maybe he should stay local until Sherry gets back. He hated these life problems and preferred studying science and math. *Two plus two is four. The rate of an object falling because of gravity is nine point eight meters per second. Factual, no need to make a decision. It is what it is. Add people to an equation, and everything goes awry. Will she criticize what I'm wearing, or is it okay to wear this to an event?*

A nearby swoosh sounded over the trees, and Al stopped. Was that a dangerous bird? Should he shield in case the crazy bird wanted to eat him?

Al felt adrenaline rush through his body, and the fight-or-flight instinct kicked in. He probed the forest for signs of the beast. He prepared a fireball to vanquish the animal before it ate him.

"There is no need for magic here."

Al jumped as the sound came from his right. He tensed his muscles for an altercation.

"It's Alpherge, isn't it?" A man dressed in black with a touch of red at the collar advanced.

Al made slow, cautious movements as the man approached. The man looked familiar. Kestrel. Al didn't wait. He created a shield.

Kestrel said, "Relax, I come as a friend. I'm not here to battle you."

"What do you want?" Al knew Kestrel was no friend of theirs. He held tight to his staff for fear Kestrel would try to use magic to steal it from him.

"I'm looking for Lily."

"Well, she isn't with me."

"I can see that." Kestrel bit his lip and wrinkled his brow. "I don't know how to ask this because we've been keeping it a secret."

"What game are you playing?" Al pulled back a bit and took cautious glances at the surrounding forest.

"No game. I'm your friend."

"Four months ago, you tried to kill my friends and me, and now suddenly you're my friend?" Al's breath increased in speed. He kept his shield up.

Kestrel held up his hand. "I don't blame you for not trusting me, but I'm really not going to hurt you."

Al stood, legs apart, staff ready to attack.

Clouds covered the late afternoon sun, and the forest grew darker. A squirrel ran through the underbrush, making a crinkling sound on last fall's dead leaves.

In his heightened state of alertness, Al almost shot a fireball at the squirrel as it scurried up a tree.

"Listen, I've been seeing Lily."

"What?"

"Yes, she's been sneaking out of the village while Sherry teaches, and we've been"—he hesitated and looked off into the woods—"well, you know, talking and kissing."

The man had to be lying. "Sherry wouldn't let Lily do that after all the trouble you've caused us."

"Sherry doesn't know. I think that makes it more exciting for Lily, knowing that she's getting away with something. Sherry's been concentrating on her teaching, and Lily hasn't told her of our rendezvous."

Al smirked and exhaled a snort. "Why should I believe you?"

"I think they're in danger."

This was another of Kestrel's tricks. "Lily is in danger. Come follow me through this galaxial portal to another planet even worse than Aloheno." No thanks. Kestrel the Falcon Prince wouldn't fool him again. He hoped Kestrel hadn't already convinced Erik, and it was only Al remaining to be snookered.

"I don't believe you," Al said.

"I haven't seen her for a week."

"Sherry probably found out and stopped it. Doesn't matter. They're not in town at the moment."

"Where are they?"

"None of your business." Al wasn't giving this man information that he could use to bamboozle Lily or Sherry.

"I tell you they're in danger. I've been flying over the village, and I haven't seen them. They have to get water from the well. Right?"

"Have you tried just walking into the village and checking on them?"

"I can't." He rubbed his hands multiple times through his hair.

A squirrel skittered in the forest. Kestrel sent a fireball at the animal but missed.

"Easy, man. No reason to be killing little animals over this."

Kestrel shouted, "There is something wrong. The girls are missing."

Al didn't want to get into a fireball fight with this dude. Not now, not here.

Kestrel paced back and forth, sometimes looking at Al and other times just staring at the ground.

How good of an actor was Kestrel? Could he be putting on a show for Al's benefit? Al believed the girls weren't in danger. The mayor told him specifically where they were. *And I thought he was lying.* Al hoped they were safe at the Velidred Castle requesting a presence with the prince. Would Lily be safe if Kestrel knew where she was?

Kestrel shot another fireball at the forest floor.

"Easy on the fireballs, man. You're gonna set the entire forest on fire."

"Help me find the girls."

"And there it is. You want me to go with you, get ambushed, and be placed in the dungeon."

"No, it's not that. I'm truly concerned about Lily's safety."

"Listen, I know where they are, and they're safe."

"Where?"

Al hesitated before he said these next words. How would Kestrel react? Al prepared for battle. "I'm not telling you."

"I'm pleading with you, tell me. Just to keep me from worrying."

"All I'll say is they are safe and are expected back in a couple of days. That was what the mayor told me. Okay?"

"Can't you tell me more?"

Al crossed his arms over his chest, the staff pressed up against his body. "That's all you need to know."

Kestrel appeared to be considering what Al had said.

The forest was quiet, the squirrels smart enough not to move until the two men left the area.

"Okay, I'll wait a couple of days." He grabbed his cape, wrapped it around his shoulders, and walked off into the forest.

Al wondered if the mayor had lied. Were the girls in danger, as Kestrel said, or were they at the Velidred Castle? He lingered a moment, pondering his path, then headed to find Finn.

CHAPTER 21

Sherry's wrists were red and raw from the shackles the men had placed on her. Something had to be done to relax the chains' tightness. Lily lay on the floor in the fetal position with her back striped red from the whipping she'd endured the day before. Sherry knew they had to get out of this cabin. Even though the mayor had told her they would get an audience with Prince Krunal, she didn't believe the wily political hack.

When Lily roused, Sherry called out to her, "Are you okay?" Her friend had cried the whole night and wouldn't talk with Sherry. She wanted to embrace her friend in a hug. Sherry never realized the dangers she had put them both in by starting the school. How could Lily ever forgive her?

Lily unwound herself from her fetal position and moaned. "Ahh. I'm sorry, Sherry. It's my fault." Lily didn't look at Sherry.

Heat rushed into Sherry's face. "No, it's not. It's my fault for starting the school." The little cabin smelled of sweat and fear.

Lily had an uncertain look on her face. "Kestrel told me it was dangerous for us."

"What are you talking about?"

"You know. Kestrel and me."

"This is about the school. The mayor and Mooney dragged me out of the cabin and rode me through the town while people threw rocks and eggs at me."

Lily turned away as if gathering her thoughts. "Kestrel warned me that seeing him would be dangerous."

"When did he warn you? We only saw him that one time." *What is Lily talking about? How could Kestrel warn her?*

A flush of red crept across Lily's face, and her ears turned red. "I didn't want to tell you about us."

Sherry waited while Lily coughed.

Lily pulled her knees to her chest. "When you told me to leave the cabin each day, I searched for Kestrel."

"No."

"I left the village and headed back into the forest where we first saw him."

Sherry gasped. "Are you serious?"

Lily swallowed as tears formed in her eyes. "He's cute."

"No, he's dangerous."

"I knew you would react this way. You don't know him the way I do. He's gentle and sweet."

Sherry shook her head. "He tried to sacrifice you."

"Kestrel wanted to marry me and tried to talk King Haskell out of sacrificing me."

"He almost killed Al trying to get the staff. And multiple times, he threw fireballs at us on the volcano. He's not a nice guy."

Lily sat quietly as she gazed at Sherry with a haunted pale face.

"Don't see him—" *Who am I kidding? I have no control over Lily and her actions. If she wants to see Kestrel, I don't care. Let her, and this time I won't try to rescue her. It doesn't really matter since we're trapped in this cabin with no way out.* "Listen, I'm sorry. If you want to see him—" Sherry couldn't say it. *I hate this planet.*

They sat in silence for a few minutes.

Sherry said, "I'm sure the reason we're both trapped is my school. The tailor's daughter was a plant, and they arrested me because I educated the girls."

"Why did they have to shackle us?" Lily rattled her chains.

"Do you have a bobby pin or something we can use to escape?"

"No."

* * * *

Sherry spent the next week mulling over ways to escape. They could try to attack the lady that showed up to clean the cabin. She was late today. Sherry doubted the woman would have the means to help them.

The mayor said they would be tried in a couple of days and those days had already stretched to a week. Could they handle waiting more days? Would the authorities release them from their chains to attend the trial? They wouldn't put Lily and Sherry on trial shackled and looking like this. Would they?

If they escaped, where would they go? She knew they were in the forest somewhere. They couldn't go back to the village. But it didn't matter because they had to escape first. She felt thirsty and tired since she had trouble sleeping with the shackles on her, and when she did sleep, bad dreams tormented her.

Lily took a deep breath. "Is this something you're willing to use your blue Crown of Anticletus power to help save us?" Lily asked.

"Yes, I will use the crown to save us from this, if I can. It's not like magic. I can't use it all the time. It's only once every six days, and I think it's limited to the visibility of the moon. I don't think it'll work if the cabin is all closed like it is now."

"You still get the headaches?"

"Yes, those don't go away. When—if—the cleaning lady comes I will see if I can stand someplace near the door, and if the moon is visible, or anything that might help."

"These people are so backward."

"Quiet, I hear voices."

There was a knock on the door. Sherry didn't know whether she was supposed to tell the person to come in or something. It wasn't like she could get to the door and open it.

The locks on the door rattled as the person unlocked the door.

Sherry couldn't figure out why their captors were so worried about the girls escaping. They were in the village the whole time, and the chains and shackles were on so tight that she and Lily couldn't reach the door to escape.

The door swung open slowly and a woman said, "Hello?"

Sherry sighed. "Come in." Did the woman think Sherry would have to put a frock on or something before she entered?

"Good morning. My name is Ciara." A different woman than the normal lady that cleaned and brought food stood by the door. This woman was full-bodied and had her hair covered with a scarf.

Sherry looked for some kind of bobby pin in the woman's dark hair.

"Oh." Ciara wrinkled her nose. "I will leave the door open while I work, if you don't mind."

Two guards stood outside the door.

Ciara brought in a bucket of fresh water. She emptied the chamber pot fifty feet from the cabin and cleansed it with a splash of water from a bucket. When she brought it back, she looked at Sherry.

"How are you holding out?" Ciara asked.

"My wrists are scraped and bleeding from the metal cuffs. Is there any way to loosen the shackles?"

Ciara approached Sherry but stayed outside of Sherry's reach.

Sherry held her wrists up for inspection.

"Those look bad. Do you want me to tell someone?"

"Yes," Sherry demanded.

Ciara pressed her lips together in a slight grimace. "I know you're in pain, but sometimes it's better to accept the pain you're in now than opt for a possibly greater pain in the future."

Sherry paced back and forth within the limitations of her chains. "I don't see why we're in these shackles. We aren't hardened criminals. You can tell whoever is holding us that if they take the shackles off, we won't try to escape."

The cleaning lady smiled. "Okay, dear, I'll let them know. I hope it doesn't make matters worse."

"How could things get worse for asking for a little comfort? We didn't kill anyone. We tried to educate your children. What are you people afraid of?"

Ciara turned her back on Sherry and spoke with Lily. "And you? Do you have concerns?"

Lily said, "I would like some cream for my back."

Sherry noticed the guards peeking through the door. She didn't trust them.

"Okay, ladies, I will share your concerns." Ciara took one more look at the room and left. The guards locked the door.

CHAPTER 22

Three days and three nights came and went, and no changes occurred in Lily and Sherry's imprisonment. Whenever the cleaning lady left, they would work on breaking their shackles. Sherry banged her wrists together and whacked the shackles against the floor. She broke a couple of fingernails trying to get into the lock. Her wrists bled and caused her pain. Nothing worked.

Late in the afternoon, the door locks rattled. Ciara had already cleaned that day. Sherry didn't know who this could be.

Lily looked at Sherry with a questioning look. "Is it Kestrel?"

Sherry shrugged and mouthed, "Don't know." She hoped Prince Krunal had come to town, and they could have their trial and be done with this pain and humiliation. Sherry worried about Lily's back, which looked red and infected in a couple of places.

If Kestrel entered, would she accept his help? Yes, of course she would. She might not be happy about it, but she would do almost anything to be free of this imprisonment.

They waited for the mystery person to finish the door locks, and then the door opened.

A man stood at the door, the man that had shackled Sherry to the walls of the cabin that first day. This wasn't the nice man of the two. This guy's hair was greasy and mussed. He carried a long pole in the shape of a cross. He slammed the door shut.

What's he going to do with that? Sherry wondered.

The man asked, "Who's having problems with the shackles too tight on her wrists?"

Sherry felt the tension in her gut. Should she raise her hand and tell this guy she was the one that made the request? She stared at the man for a long time, saying nothing.

The man looked at Lily and whistled. "You must be the one with the back problems. Well, I might help you out. Let me work with your friend first."

He turned to Sherry.

Sherry swallowed hard and shuffled back toward the wall.

He approached her like a person who needed to capture a wild animal might. He stood back a moment then used the metal cross to poke Sherry in the chest.

She pushed it back at him. "Stay away from me."

"I'm instructed to make the pain in your wrist go away." He moved to the right.

Sherry moved as far as she could to the left and shook her chains at him. "Stay away."

He jerked to the left, and Sherry scurried right.

The man laughed. "I like wild animals. They're more fun to play with."

He moved closer, trapping Sherry in the corner. With tremendous force, he threw the iron cross against the wall near Sherry's right. Then he pounced to the left, timing his jump with Sherry's expected move in that direction. He hit her hard in the chest, knocking her breath away.

Sherry went to the floor, eyes bulging, trying to catch her breath. She felt pain in her chest.

The man sat on her body, put his knee over her left arm, and reached for the iron cross. He worked fast, setting the iron cross across Sherry's chest and placing her right hand at the end of the cross. He unshackled her hand, placed the iron cross shackle in her hand, and tightened hard.

Sherry still tried to catch her breath, panic hiding in the shadows of her mind. If she didn't breathe soon, she would pass out or die. With the man sitting on her, she couldn't pull in a breath.

Just as fast, he grabbed her other arm, stretched it as far as it could go, unclasped the shackle, and re-shackled the wrist to the iron cross.

The man's breath felt hot and reeked of alcohol as sweat poured off his long, greasy hair. Sherry had to do something, anything, to get him off her.

He rose to grab a chain that dangled under his leg.

Sherry sucked in a huge gasp of air and bucked her body.

"Whoa, girl," the man laughed. He pushed hard on her face, driving her head back to the floor. With the other hand, he manipulated a collar around Sherry's throat and shackled it tight.

Sherry tried to say something, but the collar was so tight she could barely breathe. "Stop it," she wheezed.

The man laughed again as he ran the wall chains through the iron cross. Then he attached the chains from her left leg to the iron cross where her left arm was secured.

She screamed as the man pulled her leg toward her arms.

With a quick movement, the man maneuvered her right leg and arm the same way, and she cried out in pain.

He checked the shackles and verified everything was secured.

The sound of her heartbeat thrashed in her ears. She tried to calm her body and catch her breath.

The man slapped her across the face.

She lay on her back, staring at the ceiling. Her jaw hurt, and blood flowed from her nose.

The man laughed and moved over to Lily. "Aren't you a cutie?"

Lily shuffled back.

He pulled out a small jar and screwed open the lid. "I won't hurt you. See, I brought cream for your back. Here, smell it. Lavender, I think."

Lily moved close and sniffed the air. She nodded.

"This will make your back feel better and keep you from getting infected. The mayor doesn't want your back infected before the prince hears your case. This will be real easy. Lift your linen top, just a little. I'll rub my hands on your sores with this cream, and then we're done."

Lily looked at Sherry.

Sherry tried to shake her head, but the neck shackle was too tight, and she feared moving her head too much.

Lily grimaced and shook her head no. "That's okay, I'll be fine."

"Listen, lady, cooperate and I won't smack you in the mouth. And, if you give me trouble, I'll have the blacksmith create another iron cross just for you."

Lily stepped back and held her hands in front. The chains rattled as she moved her hands. "No, please, leave me alone."

"Come on, honey. A couple of swipes of the cream, and I'll leave you and your friend alone."

Sherry wanted to scream at Lily, "Don't do it—it's a trick—fight back," but nothing came from her mouth.

"You promise?"

"Yes, ma'am." He made a strange circle in the air. "I swear by the moon of Velidred and all my family." He beat his chest three times.

Lily said, "Okay." She turned her back and lifted her linen shift up a couple of inches.

"That's a good girl. I won't have to put no iron cross on you." He rubbed his fingers in the jar and applied it to Lily's back. "Doesn't that feel better?"

She nodded.

"I'm gonna lift your shift up just a little more, okay? Don't panic or anything. Then I can finish applying the rest of this cream."

Lily nodded her assent.

The man placed the jar on the floor, grabbed the bottom of the shift, and shoved the garment up over her shoulders, trapping her arms. The chains dangled from the shackles high above her head.

Lily screamed and tried to lash out but couldn't because the shift trapped her arms. She rotated toward the man and tried to kick him, but he blocked her.

Sherry screamed and tried to stand, but the odd angle of the iron cross made it almost impossible for her to move. She wriggled and squirmed on the floor, trying to get closer to Lily.

The man pulled a knife from his waist.

"Watch out, Lily. He has a knife."

Lily moved back.

"Shut up, redhead, or I'll use the knife on your throat."

He pulled Lily toward him and grabbed the linens around her waist.

"No, please don't."

He bent down to cut the linen, and Lily kneed him hard in the face. Something cracked in his face, and the man fell backward to the floor, out cold.

Lily struggled with her shift around her shoulders, trying to wiggle through the fabric to bring the shift back over her chest.

Sherry continued contorting her body, secured to the iron cross, toward the man. Sweat poured off her body, and slivers from the wood floor sliced into her legs. She ignored the pain and kept sliding toward the man. She needed to reach him before he regained consciousness, or neither she nor Lily would live.

Lily got the shift off her shoulders and used her hands to pull it down over her body.

The man's head had landed on Sherry's side of the room, and she wrapped the chain between her leg and arm and pinned the man's neck to the floor. She placed her right leg on the man's shoulder and brought the shackle down hard.

The man moaned.

Sherry said, "Quick, grab the keys."

Lily could reach his knees, but the keys jangled from his waist.

"I can't reach them."

"Pull him toward you."

The man was deadweight, but Lily dragged him toward her side. Sherry's chain across his throat tightened, and she could tell he struggled to breathe.

Lily reached for the keys. The man woke, grabbing at the chain around his neck. He kicked for purchase, and Lily stepped back.

"Get the keys," Sherry shouted.

Her friend hesitated as the man's legs pounded up and down. He moved closer to Sherry.

"Get them before they're out of reach."

Lily dove into the man, driving her fist into his scrotum.

He screamed and stopped struggling.

After a quick maneuver to grab the keys, Lily pulled free.

"Hurry, undo your shackles before he moves. I don't know how long I can secure him."

Lily worked fast and released the shackles. She grabbed the man's legs and placed the shackles on him. Then she pulled him toward her.

"Release his neck."

"Are you sure?"

"Yes, I got him."

CHAPTER 23

Sherry rubbed the cream into Lily's back, her hand riding the ridges where some of the skin had healed.

Lily asked, "What's our next move?"

Sherry held her hand up with her index finger poking up and mouthed, "One second." She nudged the door a little and peeked outside. The sun hadn't set, but the trees threw long shadows. She didn't see any other guards. Sherry breathed in the fresh air of freedom.

She opened the door and let the air freshen the room.

"Mr. Mooney will skin you alive when he finds out you escaped." The guard had awoken.

"Shut your mouth before I put this knife through your gut," Sherry said.

"What's he gonna do to you when he finds out a couple of girls captured you?" Lily asked.

Sherry smiled.

"He'll never know because you're both dead when I get free."

Sherry had placed the iron cross on the man's arms but didn't run his legs through the device. She felt it was too cruel.

She grabbed the rag they used to wash the sweat off their bodies and moved toward the man.

He jerked toward her, and she scurried back.

Lily went to the other side of the man and approached.

The man feinted toward Lily.

Sherry jumped on him and jammed the rag into his mouth.

He spun, trying for a hold on Sherry, and she pushed off the floor. The girls backed away.

"Should we put his legs into the iron cross?" Lily asked.

"I don't know. Let's ask. Should we shackle your legs to the iron cross too?"

He backed to the wall and shook his head. He mumbled something they couldn't understand because of the gag.

Sherry said, "It's almost dark, and I'm not interested in going back to the village in the dark. I don't really know where we are, and we don't want to chance running into a hungry stegox in the dark."

"Then what do we do?"

"Do you think anyone will miss this guy overnight?" Sherry rubbed the cream on her wrists, which caused both more discomfort and some relief from the pain.

"Hard to say. Can't believe he has a wife or family, but some other guards might miss him and come here."

"I wish I knew where we were in relation to other villages in the area. We could be a quarter mile from another village and not even know it."

"We can wait until Ciara comes in the morning and ask her."

"She always comes with guards. We don't have the resources to fight three of them."

Lily was right. They had taken their attacker's tunic and the shirt he wore underneath it. The clothing smelled of sweat and a man's body odor. The plan was to wear them to escape the cabin, but the smell convinced them to wait until they needed them before putting them on.

"I think we need to be out of the cabin before Ciara and the guards get here."

"Do we just leave this guy here?"

Sherry thought about that. "We could take him up the mountain away from the path they brought us and tie him to a tree. Keep him gagged, and they won't know where we put him."

The man moaned, trying to say something.

"Do we go to the trial after Prince Krunal arrives?"

Lily shook her head. "We can't do that. They'll charge us for escaping and throw us back into this—" She circled her hand around the cabin.

Sherry knew Lily was right, but she needed an audience with the prince. She had to tell him what these people, these men, were doing to their citizens.

"You know, if we escape and go back to the village, we might meet Ciara and her guards on the way back down the mountain. Should we go to another village instead? We can lie low and do something else." Lily's eyes watered. "I can't get whipped again."

Sherry hugged her friend. They had an open door beckoning them to leave and were afraid to go and afraid to stay.

Lily raised her hands in surrender. "I can't get captured again. We should try to find Kestrel."

"Why hasn't he looked for you?"

"Maybe he has."

"Do you think he's been flying over these woods or over the village?"

Lily's eyes sparkled, and a smile lit her face. She ran outside.

Sherry and Lily stood in the pine-scented forest, searching the sky for Kestrel. If he could come to their help, Sherry might forgive Lily for bringing him back into their life.

Birds flickered among the trees, and squirrels skittered around the forest floor, looking for seeds, nuts, fruits, and insects. A slight breeze took the heat out of the air.

They locked the cabin door on the off chance their captive figured out a way to escape.

The air felt pleasant, and the shadows cooled the hot day. Sherry didn't mind standing outside in her smallclothes. Even if someone came, she and her friend could quickly put on the man's clothing and would be okay. Sherry looked at her red and swollen wrists. Bruises the color of eggplant dotted her legs and arms, and she feared to examine the ones on her belly, back, and chest.

If Kestrel didn't show, then they would be forced to sleep in the cabin overnight. That wasn't something she desired, but it was the right thing to do. Even now, in this strange forest, who knew what animals might think of them as an evening meal? How difficult might it be to tie their captive to a tree farther up the mountain? He wouldn't go easily and might use his superior size and strength to overtake them.

Shadows lengthened as the sun fell from its perch on the horizon. Sherry imagined things moving in the shadows.

Sherry put her arm around Lily's waist. "I'm sorry. He isn't coming. We should go inside."

"Just a few more minutes."

A mosquito bit Sherry's arm, and she whacked it hard and screamed. "Ow, I shouldn't have done that." Pain reverberated from the bruises throughout her body.

Lily asked, "What was that? I thought I saw a large bird."

Sherry searched the sky. "Where?"

"Over there." She pointed in the direction Sherry thought Crossroads might be.

Lily yelled into the dusk, "Kestrel! Help us."

How did Lily even think it could be Kestrel? It might be a large bat—a rabid, human-eating bat. She wondered if the large vultures they encountered on Velidred Volcano would fly this far for food. She grabbed Lily's arm. "We should go back to the cabin and make sure we're secure before darkness makes it too hard to see our prisoner."

"You go back in. I'm staying outside. I saw Kestrel. I know it."

"Come on, Lily. It could have been anything. In this dusk, it could have been a dragonfly that was close and looked bigger than normal."

"Help," Lily yelled into the darkening sky.

Sherry hoped there weren't guards near enough to the cabin to hear Lily's shouts.

The first evening stars flickered in the twilight.

Sherry heard a flapping of wings behind her. She turned as a flock of birds scattered out of the canopy.

Lily shouted Kestrel's name again.

"I'm getting nervous out here. I don't know if the noises I'm hearing are friend or foe." Sherry grabbed Lily's arm. "Come on, let's go inside."

Lily shook Sherry's grip loose from her arm and yelled, "Kestrel!"

"What are you doing out here?" a man asked behind them.

Sherry felt adrenaline spike into her body as the blood drained from her face and the hair raised on her neck. She wanted to turn toward the voice, but her legs stayed rooted to the ground.

Lily screamed.

CHAPTER 24

Adrenaline rushed through Sherry's body. The man came up behind them so fast that Sherry didn't have time to protect herself.

Lily launched her body at the man.

He caught her in a tight embrace.

She wrapped her legs around his body.

They kissed. Between kisses, Lily said, "I knew you would come. Sherry didn't believe you would find us, but I believed."

"What are you two doing way out here in this cabin?" Kestrel asked.

Sherry said, "The Crossroads mayor held us captive."

"I told Al they might have kidnapped you, but he said you went to Velidred Castle to meet with Prince Krunal."

Sherry's stomach fluttered as she leaned toward Kestrel. "Al's back?"

Lily settled down enough for Kestrel to put her on the ground. "He was."

"What do you mean, he *was*?" Sherry's shoulders slumped, and she wrapped her arms around her stomach.

"I don't know where he was heading, but he didn't seem happy to see me."

Lily spoke up. "He doesn't know you're with us now."

Sherry opened her mouth to tell Kestrel he wasn't *with* them, but then decided not to. "It's getting dark. Can you recommend someplace for us to be safe?"

Kestrel grabbed Lily's hand. "Yeah, come with me. I have friends nearby, and we can find you clothes."

I can't believe Al came to town and didn't try to find us and rescue me. He was gone three months, and he couldn't stay in town for one night? Where did he run off to? Sherry wanted to smack Al and hug him at the same time.

* * * *

They walked half a mile in the forest, found a road, and walked three more miles to a little village Kestrel called Triponca. The village contained a tavern and a small inn in the center of town, but they walked past the village and then turned to the right. After another half mile, they came upon a large farm. The farm home was larger than the town's inn.

The night had grown late, and only two windows showed candles burning in the rooms.

Sherry shivered in the cool night air. She asked, "Who lives here?"

"Family friends. These people have known my parents for years. My parents would vacation here during the summer months. It's cooler in the mountains."

Sherry was impressed and never realized that Kestrel came from money. Oh, he called himself the Falcon Prince, but she thought that was a nickname, like Al calling himself Alpherge the Mighty. It meant little. Was this where Kestrel planned to take Lily and Sherry for dinner, though he had talked about dinner at a castle, not a farm?

Kestrel roused the household servants, who found fresh clothing for the girls. The servants fed Sherry and Lily fresh fish, breads, and sweets, the best food they had eaten since coming to Aloheno. The staff also offered the women sparkling, clean water to drink.

Servants heated water for a bath, but Sherry had difficulty stepping into the tub and submersing into the water because of the pain from the bruising over every inch of her body. The water hurt the raw skin on her wrist and ankles. While soaking in the hot bath, she thought about her next move. She needed to talk with Prince Krunal and clear her name in Crossroads.

* * * *

They woke the next day to a lavish breakfast with honey, breads, nuts, and fruit. After the struggle to earn enough for food and their little one-room cabin, this felt wonderful. To be pampered with a hot bath, fresh food, and a bed on a wood frame with a straw mattress was too much. She didn't realize anybody lived like this on the planet.

Lily asked, "Do you think they'll come after us?"

The two girls and Kestrel sat on a large, covered porch at the back of the house. A spectacular view opened to them. In the distance, snow-covered mountain peaks climbed into the sky. To their right, the land fell off to a view of a distant valley. Before them, a large, clear lake sparkled in the sunlight. Gigantic trees of pine and oak dotted the landscape around the lake.

Sherry didn't want to think about being on the run at the moment. "Why do they call this village Triponca?"

Kestrel answered, "Triponca is the Kallurian word for three lakes. This is one lake, all on the farm owner's property. Then there are two more surrounding the village. The fishing in all three is outstanding."

"How far are we from Crossroads?"

"We are one mile in elevation change above Crossroads, but the road extends about eight miles because of all the switchbacks to change elevation. We sit on a plateau that is difficult to get to. The path that we took from the cabin last night to the road is the only way to go. About a quarter mile from the cabin, the mountain turns into a granite cliff. Because of the arduous path, we get little traffic."

Lily asked, "Does that mean we don't have to worry about guards from Crossroads coming after us?"

"Yes, they will come up here. But this building has been a wayward stop for soldiers and spies over the years. Our people will notify us if guards approach the village, and we'll hide you in hidden safe rooms. They won't find you."

Sherry took slow breaths, and despite a good night's sleep, she felt drowsy and comfortable. She looked across the calm lake. "I'm going back to Crossroads."

"What do you mean, you're going back?" Lily asked.

"You don't have to go with me."

"It's not about me going with you. Why do you have to go at all? Do you not remember the treatment you received the last few days?"

She remembered the treatment. Her wrist and ankles still hurt, and it was difficult to sit down because of the bruises on her buttocks. "We have to clear our names."

"What if they convict us and say we have to serve sentences of three months, three years, or more? We'll never survive in a jail that long."

Sherry figured Lily wouldn't be happy with her decision to attend the trial, but Sherry still wanted to start a school in that village. They needed it. In Crossroads and all over the planet, and Sherry would be the one to get it started. That was something she could do in the four years they had to wait for the portal to re-open.

"No. We won't survive if they sentence us to prison."

Kestrel said, "Prince Krunal will side with the mayor and his cronies."

"Why? I thought he was the seat of justice. Won't he listen to both sides of the argument and judge fairly based on the evidence presented?"

"That's how people hope it will work, but think about Prince Krunal's position. He's just been crowned king. He has the whole Velidred Kingdom to manage. This early in the takeover of Velidred Castle, the prince is in a precarious role, where only half of the people in the kingdom are happy that he is king. When he comes to Crossroads, he doesn't want to make enemies. Unless the current structure is really broken and bad—"

"Which it is," Sherry interrupted.

"That may be, but he'll wait a year to make those changes. This trip will serve three purposes for the new king. Give him a chance to see what his base is like, check the villages for weapons and people who are opposed to the new king, and show the people that King Haskell isn't in charge anymore."

Lily stared at Kestrel, and as she watched him talk, she smiled and nodded.

After the pain and suffering over the last few weeks, it's nice to be among intelligent people and just relax.

Kestrel's cousin, Paxton, who owned the property, came onto the porch. "Beautiful country, isn't it?" The man had a full but trimmed red beard and long, curly strawberry-blond hair that flowed to his collar. He wore a pressed sky-blue tunic.

Kestrel stood and clasped Paxton's forearm in greeting. "Cousin, have you any word on when Prince Krunal will visit the villages?"

"I'm waiting for word from one of my ambassadors in Velidred to notify me. Should be any day now."

"Our redheaded friend here wants to engage Prince Krunal in a debate about educating children in the villages."

"The boys have their apprenticeship programs," Paxton answered.

Sherry said, "The children run around the village like a pack of hungry wolves. The time they spend playing, doing nothing, and getting in people's way can be better served by educating them. And not just the boys. We should educate girls too."

Paxton raised his head and stared intently at Sherry. "Educating girls will never fly."

Another man in this backward society that needs to open his eyes to the power of women. "That was why they arrested us, because two girls showed up in my classroom. I think the mayor wouldn't have cared, but when Mooney heard the news, he sent his daughter into the class to verify."

Paxton mused, "Hmm."

"It's a shame because his daughter was really smart, and I could have taught her a lot."

Kestrel said, "Prince Krunal will not side with you."

"I don't care. The people of Crossroads are bullies, and I detest bullies. I'm going to confront them."

A bell sounded at the front of the house.

Paxton touched Sherry's shoulder. "Would you all be so kind as to follow me? It seems we have guards coming up from the village."

CHAPTER 25

Alpherge the Mighty used his staff to trudge up the last hill to the mountain village. This was the first village Tobias had asked him to inquire about Finn. He crested the hill to see homes, shops, and taverns crowd a narrow street. Oakwood was a busy village, with residents hauling buckets of water, children playing games in the dirt road, the sound of the blacksmith pounding out metal, and boisterous conversations emanating from the taverns.

Three days of travel and Al had made it. He hoped to ask someone here about Finn and get an answer like, "Oh yeah. Finn has a small cabin over the next hill. Come on, I'll show you where it is."

He didn't expect it to take so long to reach Oakwood, and Al found the journey difficult. The villages he encountered were perched on hills or nestled in cozy green valleys. The entire trip, he walked either uphill or downhill. His calves and knees hurt most from the downhill treks.

Al stopped in the middle of the dirt road. *Where do I go to find another wizard?*

The sound of a blacksmith punishing hot metal clanged nearby, and Al walked the short distance to the shop. The short, muscular blacksmith wore a leather apron and black smears smudged his face.

"What ya want?" the blacksmith asked.

"Looking for a wizard named Finn. I was told I could find him in this village."

The man shook his head and waved Al off. "Check the taverns or the inn."

That made sense to Al. The tavern owners encountered travelers who visited the town and locals wanting a brew. The small village had three taverns.

He walked into the first tavern, where two old men perched on benches, leaning their elbows on a wooden table. An old man with a salt-and-pepper beard that ran to his chest yelled over to Al, "Young wizard, what brings you to Oakwood?"

The question sounded promising. Al ventured closer, "Looking for a wizard named Finn."

"My name's Einar. Buy me an ale and I'll tell you of Finn's dangerous shenanigans."

"Get one for me too." The other man, a tired, sad-looking fellow, raised his hand.

Al figured these guys knew something, and he brought two wooden mugs of ale over to the table.

"Where's yours?"

"Oh, I don't need an ale."

"Becca, bring this boy an ale," Einar yelled to the serving girl sweeping the tavern floor, "Sit, boy. Let's talk about a wizard named Finn."

Al leaned in closer to the men, excited about the opportunity to find the wizard's location and resume his travels. "Do you know where he lives?"

"No. No one knows where he lives, but I have stories about Finn you should listen to before you search further." Crumbs of bread perched on the man's scraggy black and gray beard. The long stripe of male-pattern baldness disappeared as he took a long pull on his ale.

Becca placed an ale in front of Al. She eyed Al's staff, which lay against the bench where he sat. "Are you a real wizard?"

Al smiled at the thirty-something woman. He didn't know why it surprised people when he claimed to be a wizard, but they would request magic to prove his worth. "Yes, I am."

"Can you do a trick?"

Al glanced at the stonework surrounding the untended fireplace. People who asked these questions required little proof, just a little dazzle to prove they had encountered a wizard. Candles burned in the dark tavern, providing minimal light. Al raised his right hand, palm extended, and waved his left hand over the right, concentrating on magic. He said words, unnecessary for the trick, but they provided showmanship and glamour. He touched his raised hand with his index finger and a blue globe lit the girl's face.

Becca clapped and said, "Are you famous?"

"Alpherge the Mighty at your service." Al bowed his head slightly.

Becca and the two men stared back at Al with blank faces.

"It doesn't matter." Al drank a bit of ale, which tasted wonderful after the morning's hike to this village. "Can you tell me about Finn? Is there anyone in the village who knows where he lives?"

"Let me tell you a story, young man." Einar drank more ale, which leaked to the sides of his beard. With a flourishing wipe, he said, "I would say three years ago." He glanced at his friend for verification.

His sad-looking friend nodded. "Sounds about right."

"There was this young man, a wizard, kinda like you. He said he was searching for Finn." He tugged another drink. "You appear older than the young wizard in our story, and I'm sure you're more experienced."

"Becca, how tall was that young boy?"

She giggled and said, "He was smaller than me." Al estimated Becca's size at just over five feet.

The man said, "Yep. How old?"

"Said he was twenty-eight." Becca giggled again.

"I didn't believe he was that old, but I didn't push him on it."

"And Finn? Does he play a part in this story?" Al asked.

"Easy, boy." The man drained the mug. "Becca, I need a refill. Wizard-Boy is paying." He stared at Al as if daring him to say different.

Al rolled his eyes and nodded.

The man said nothing until Becca returned with a drink for him.

Al placed a couple of coins in her hand.

The storyteller continued, "The young wizard asked about Finn, the same as you. 'Where can I find the great wizard named Finn?' he asked. Someone at the next tavern directed him higher up the mountain." The man smiled at Becca and winked at her.

She smiled back.

"So, we didn't hear from this boy for two, three months. Nobody sees him. We don't know if he's dead or alive."

Becca leaned toward the storyteller.

The storyteller stopped talking for a moment and stared into Al's eyes.

The man's speech picked up speed. "Then a wild mountain goat comes down from the mountain. This goat is huge, with horns the size of my legs." The man raised a leg onto the table and pointed at his leg. "It terrorizes the village, crashing through windows, knocking down doors, chasing children, and causing destruction and mayhem. Old Lady Myrtle broke her hip trying to dodge the beast."

The storyteller paused and took another long swig of ale.

Al hoped the man would finish his story before his ale so he didn't have to spend all his money buying the man drinks.

After taking another drink, Einar stared into Al's eyes. A yellowish hue colored the whites of Einar's bloodshot eyes.

"This beast of a mountain goat was terrorizing the village. No villager was safe. We sent out our best archer to calm this beast." The storyteller clapped his friend on the shoulder. "This man right here. Herman."

Herman looked like he was two ticks away from falling asleep, and he opened his eyes when the storyteller touched him.

"Three days and nights Herman stalked after the mountain goat, horns the size of my leg." He plopped his leg back on the table.

Al took a sip of his ale.

The storyteller grabbed Herman's shoulder, "Here's the best part. Herman. Stay awake."

Herman opened his eyes and sat up straight.

"The goat stood in a meadow on the side of the mountain eating flowers. Herman, standing above the goat, stared at the beast two hundred yards away. The wind direction was favorable."

Becca said, "I thought the beast was three hundred yards away."

"Who's telling this tale?"

"Sorry, Dad, you are."

"Where was I? Yes, the beast stood"—he eyed Becca—"three hundred yards away"—he winked at her—"and the wind was favorable to the archer."

The storyteller lifted the wooden mug to his lips and drank until the mug was empty. He burped and wiped his sleeve across his lips. He looked at Al then at Herman, let his gaze linger on Becca, and smiled.

No more drinks to finish the tale, Al thought.

Einar moved his mug to the middle of the table. "This mug represents the beast." Then he emptied Herman's mug of ale with a long swallow and placed it on the other side of the table. "Here stood Herman, tired from chasing the beast for three days and nights. Herman aimed his bow and arrow at the animal, wondering if he could reach it from three hundred yards away."

Finish the story, old man. I have to find Finn.

"Herman released the arrow. This man was Oakwood's best archer, known far and wide." He slapped Herman's shoulder and woke him. "The arrow flew straight, but before striking the beast, the arrow dodged off at a strange angle.

'What is this?' wondered Herman. 'What strange beast is this that controls arrows?'

He knocked another arrow." The storyteller grabbed Al's drink. "Can I have this, boy?"

"Sure, just finish the story."

The man smiled. "Herman blamed the miss on a fluke of the wind, so he recalibrated distance, wind, and speed. He didn't dare move closer on account of possibly spooking the animal. He thought it strange the arrow that whizzed over the animal's head hadn't spooked it."

The storyteller took a drink of Al's ale.

Al looked at Becca. "Should you cut him off?"

She smiled at Al. "Oh, he's fine. He's just getting started."

"Herman has it all lined up. The animal is grazing the wildflowers in the meadow. Herman releases the arrow and notices the animal changing its shape. It's too late. Herman can't bring it back. The arrow flies high with the perfect parabolic arc to strike the beast. Only it isn't a beast anymore. It looks like a little boy, but Herman recognizes him right away. It's the young wizard who passed through town a few months previous.

What do you think Herman does? He shouts at the wizard, 'Move!'"

Al leaned toward Einar. *The wizard can place a shield up if he knows the arrow is coming.*

"Herman is watching the arrow and shouting at the boy. The arrow reaches the highest point of the arc and starts its descent. The wizard still looks like he's eating flowers and doesn't even realize he's changed back into a human."

Becca must have heard this story a hundred times, but she was enthralled, leaning toward the storyteller, fixated on the story.

"Herman doesn't know if the boy hears the arrow or hears Herman's shout, but the boy looks up the hill as Herman waves his hands."

The storyteller finished Al's mug of ale, and Al didn't care.

"Through the boy's chest and right into his heart, the arrow lands true. The boy-wizard grimaces at Herman with a question on his lips. Herman races down the mountain, barely able to keep from falling as the momentum carries him forward. He arrives and finds the boy on his side clutching the arrow. The archer is too late."

The room went silent except for Herman's gentle breathing as he slept.

The story was dumb, and Al figured he was out at the cost of four ales.

Al stood. "Thanks for the story."

The storyteller said, "Wait. Don't go to see Finn. He hates young wizards. He'll turn you into a goat, monkey, or even stone." Einar tried to stand, but the ale altered his balance enough that his legs got caught up with the bench, and he fell awkwardly to the floor.

Al helped Becca place her father back on the bench. Then Al walked down the dirt road to the next tavern.

CHAPTER 26

The atmosphere at the Hound and Chicken differed completely from the previous tavern. In the room's corner, a man sat on a chair on a small stage playing a zither, which lay on a table in front of him. A plump woman sang a bawdy ballad about the romance between a princess and a stable hand.

Al liked the music and hoped he could find an answer about Finn here. The people here were younger. A sizeable crowd filled the tavern despite it being still a bell away from lunchtime.

The music competed with discussions between men and women at the tables. A dice game held the attention at one table and a card game at another.

A buxom woman wearing an apron squeezed Al's elbow and planted a little kiss on his cheek.

Al tried to pull away, but a man loomed between him and the door.

The large man carried a stick shaped like a baseball bat. "You can't get a kiss without paying the fee."

"What?"

"Kisses aren't free."

"I'm not here for a kiss."

"Nellie just kissed you. That's worth a bronze coin."

"I didn't ask her to kiss me."

The man bounced the bat's business end in his left hand. "Doesn't matter. If you get a kiss, you pay the price." He narrowed his eyes and moved closer.

"I didn't see her next to me, and I didn't want a kiss." Al pushed his arm away from the woman and stood toe to toe with the bouncer. Al raised his voice. "I'm not paying for the kiss; it wasn't even a friendly kiss." Al stood seven inches taller than the bouncer but at least a hundred pounds lighter.

"Do you plan to end up on tonight's menu?"

Al said, "You might end up like a mountain goat before the day's over." Al menaced him with the staff. *Two can play this game.*

Quick as lightning, the bouncer unfurled his sizeable arm muscles, moved the bat handle into both hands, and swung at Al like a home-run king aiming for the fences.

Alpherge the Mighty expected the reaction.

A swing like that would have crashed Al to the floor, except his shield stopped the swing in mid-air.

The bouncer screamed in pain and dropped the bat.

The room went quiet.

With nostrils flaring and a reddening of his face, the bouncer cracked his knuckles and threw a hard, roundhouse punch at Al. A blow like that could pulverize an average man.

The sound of bones cracking preceded the man's screams as he flopped to the floor.

Al surveyed the room for anyone else that might want to take a swipe at him.

The music had stopped. The patrons at the tables stared at Al with open mouths. A man the size of a football player rose from his chair, but his friend sitting next to him grabbed his arm and said, "Not now."

Al shouted, "Any of you know a wizard named Finn? I'm looking for him."

A guy sat in a corner of the room with a relaxed posture as if he saw this every day. The guy wore a faded blue felt hat with a slight brim turned down in front, which made it difficult to see his eyes. A white and gray feather decorated the right side of the hat. He raised his head, made eye contact with Al, and shook his head.

"Okay, then. Thanks." Al walked out the door.

* * * *

This village contained its share of charlatans and thieves, Al thought, and he was no closer to finding Finn. The sun stood at midday, heat building in the street even in a village high in the mountains. Al sweated in his tunic, the rush of adrenaline pumping through his body.

He wrinkled his forehead and weighed his next move. Should he go across the road to the last tavern or just move on to the next village? He couldn't stay in the village for too long. The bouncer probably had friends, and they wouldn't be happy that a wizard had hurt him. One of the bouncer's friends might even be a wizard.

Al longed for those times on Earth when he could just search the internet and find the information he needed. All this wandering around the mountainside talking to people was too difficult.

Would the next village be better or worse? He rubbed the back of his neck and sighed.

"Young wizard, can we talk?" The man with the felt hat approached from the direction of the Hound and Chicken.

Al stiffened and searched the road and buildings behind the man. "Maybe."

"Follow me." The man in the hat headed toward the next tavern but turned into an alley between the tavern and a tailor's shop instead.

Should I keep following?

The man didn't look back but kept on down the alley.

After a glance around the village, Al followed into the shadowed space between the buildings, setting his shield up as he walked. Al assumed the man would stop and talk right there, but he moved on behind the buildings and into the forested area onto a small, well-traveled path between bushes and trees.

Al hurried to catch up, watching left and right as he moved into the forest. A short while later, the path opened into a wide field of grass where a couple of goats grazed. The man stopped next to a goat.

"Listen, I need to talk fast." The man lowered his voice to a whisper. "My name's Tice. It's not wise making enemies in this town. This is the only way to get from the upper mountains to the lowlands and Velidred. Whether or not you find Finn, you'll have to come back this way."

"It's not my fault."

"These brain-dead mopes will blame you. As a wizard, you're a responsible citizen."

"But I didn't even throw a punch or anything. I just protected myself."

"A wizard isn't supposed to use his magic on us normal folks. People get upset about things like that. Weren't you taught that in wizard school?"

Heat rose in Al's face, and he stammered, "Well. . . I came to this wizard thing late in life."

Tice grabbed Al's tunic. "It doesn't matter. This village follows rules, and you have to know those rules."

Al raised his hands in surrender. "Okay, I'm sorry, I didn't know. Do you know Finn and where I can find him?"

"Not exactly."

Al slowly shook his head. *Great.*

"Why are you searching for Finn?"

Al looked at his staff. Should he tell this man that his staff told him to find Finn? Considering the way Tice talked about wizards, he figured a lie was better. "Someone told me Finn could train me in magic."

Tice harrumphed. "That wizard is dangerous, especially to young wizards. He had a batch of young wizards he taught, and then one day he turned them to stone."

"Finn didn't do that," Al said.

"I've heard many stories about whose fault it is. I blame Finn. He shouldn't have been playing with that kind of magic. Be careful going near his hut. I've heard it's guarded by magic traps."

Al knew spells that identified magic traps, so the knowledge about the traps didn't sound too problematic to Al.

Tice pointed east of the village. "Head toward the mountain peak. Keep on the path to Stone Bokken and speak with Jolene."

"Stone Bokken and speak with Jolene."

Al heard voices coming from the village.

"Now, hurry on your way." Tice pushed Al toward a path that led near the edge of the mountain.

CHAPTER 27

Al hurried along the ledge, skirting a long drop to the curved mountainside below. The path flowed in and out of sections of large rocks interspersed with pine and aspen. Sometimes the summer growth of the forest made the trail hard to find. Stacked cairns along the windswept ledge guided him to the next opening. Twice he chose wrong, forcing him to double back to the last track.

Every mile or so, Al stopped and listened for people that might have followed him through the forest. He wondered if Tice had fooled him. Everybody else in the village seemed to have a scam going on. Why not Tice? Maybe this Jolene person was the Hound and Chicken bouncer's brother.

Al continued up the mountain path, but by midafternoon, fatigué settled in his body. He stopped by a clear mountain creek feeding from the melting snow higher up the mountain. His breathing came in gasps in the thin air. He guessed he was at an altitude of five thousand feet or higher. Was the planet Aloheno nothing but mountains?

To the south, Velidred Volcano stood strong, sending out a puff of ash every few minutes. Deciduous tree leaves blew in the wind. Al rested while he gazed out over a majestic view. He hoped Stone Bokken wasn't far from his current location because he didn't want to have to spend the night in the forest.

After his rest, he continued walking, and two hours later, he heard voices nearby and slowed. The voices emanated from a distance in front of him, which Al thought helpful. He advanced cautiously and peered around a tree at a man feeding chickens.

Al said, "Good afternoon."

The man seemed startled for a moment. "Hello." He looked at Al as if he'd never seen someone so tall. "Welcome to Stone Bokken."

Al decided not to share information with the locals. Tice didn't say to avoid telling anyone he was looking for Jolene, but Al acted as if he wasn't looking for anyone.

"Are there inns in the village? I'm looking for a place to stay."

The man didn't answer right away. He looked down at his chickens and raked some of the grass. "Only one inn, a quarter mile, just around the corner." He pointed toward some buildings peeking out above the trees in the distance.

Al thanked the man and walked to the main road, turned the corner, and saw a sign dangling from a bracket. The sign, colored bright green, had a wooden sword drawn on it. The larger-than-life sword hung over a man sleeping on a mattress.

"This must be the place." Al walked into the two-story wood building and noticed it served as an inn and a tavern. He hoped he received better treatment here than he did in Oakwood.

A tall, handsome woman with gray hair pulled into a tight bun greeted him. "How may I help?"

"Can I get a room for the night?" Al clutched the staff tight as he studied the tavern dining room, looking for familiar faces from the altercation in Oakwood. He felt the release of the tightness in his neck and shoulders when he didn't recognize anyone.

"Are you meeting up with friends?" she asked.

"What? Uh, oh no. Just looking at the clientele you serve."

"Don't get many visitors this far north. These guys are all locals. First floor or second floor?"

Did Al have to worry about what floor he was on? If he was on the second floor, there was less chance of someone breaking in without him knowing, but the first floor offered a quicker and easier escape. He shouldn't have to worry about the guys from Oakwood. He had walked at least ten miles. Surely, they didn't care about him that much, and if Tice was right, they would just wait for him to show on the return trip.

"Second floor, please."

"I have to charge you extra since you're a wizard."

He barked out a laugh and shook his head. "What? Why?"

"Village rules. I don't make them, just follow them."

Al snorted. "Okay." *This place is as bad as Oakwood, looking to take advantage of strangers.*

She handed Al a key to the room. "There's wood in the room if you want to warm up the fireplace. Gets cold when the sun goes down. If you need more wood, it'll cost you extra."

Twelve wooden swords hung against one wall. Al pointed at them. "The village name, Stone Bokken, is rather strange. How can someone make a wooden sword of stone?"

"We host the Festival of Stone Bokken every summer. It's a great festival with hundreds of visitors seeking to win the prize of the stone bokken."

"I thought bokkens were wooden practice swords."

"Twelve years ago, a wizard used magic to turn a bokken into a stone sword. We remember the event and host a festival that lasts for many days. The best swordsman on the mountain gets a wooden sword with his name painted on it and hung on our wall." She pointed at the row of swords.

"What was that wizard's name?" Al figured it was worth a try to dig up a little information. Then he could naturally ask if she knew where he could find Finn the wizard.

"His name is—" She stopped. Then she looked at her customers and rubbed her hands nervously on a dishcloth in her hands. "Now that I think about it, I don't remember his name. I'm sorry. One of the serving girls needs my attention. Your room's on the second floor, third door on the right." The innkeeper disappeared into the tavern.

* * * *

An hour later, Al dug into his second bowl of stew as he listened to an elderly man playing the flute. The man had a long gray mustache that he waxed and twirled on both ends.

Al still hadn't figured out the best way to find out who Jolene was. He didn't want to come right out and ask in case she didn't want that kind of attention.

The flutist finished up an extensive set of music and took a break. He went and spoke with the innkeeper. Occasionally, the musician turned to look at Al.

The hair on Al's back raised. *What does the flutist want with me?* Al reached for a staff that wasn't there. He had left his staff in the room upstairs in hopes few people would recognize him as a wizard.

After finishing his conversation with the innkeeper, the flutist came to Al's table, stared intently at Al, and then sat down across from him.

"Innkeeper tells me you're a wizard."

Al's heartbeat increased, and his muscles tensed as he looked at the exit to see if he could flee. He prepared a shield, just in case. He had tried to keep a low profile, and yet, by now, everyone in the village probably knew there was a wizard in town.

"Yes, sir."

The flutist studied Al. "You look familiar."

A serving girl brought him a drink.

Al tried to stay calm. "This is my first time in Stone Bokken. Great stew." He raised the bowl. "You're terrific with the flute. My girlfriend would love to hear you play someday. Do you always play around here?"

"Oh, heavens no." He leaned in close to Al and whispered, "These mountain people don't appreciate elegant music. They're always asking for modern music, no appreciation for the classics. I have performed for kings and queens around the world." He looked at the small crowd in the room, and a bitter smile crossed his face. "Today, I'm as far away from civilization as a man can get."

Al nodded.

"I used to play at the court of Alpherge the Great, at the Greystone Castle in the Province of Ron-Salem."

Al's eyebrows shot up, and his eyes widened.

"Thought you looked familiar. How's your mother?"

Suddenly, the stew wasn't sitting well on his stomach. Al took deep breaths to settle the rising nausea. *I don't know who this man is. He already knows my family, my history. Good grief, even my mom.*

"I can tell you don't trust everyone you meet." The flutist winked at him and tilted his face close. "Answer me this, kid. Did your mom travel back through the portal with you?"

The fireplace was burning a single log with a low flame, but Al's body heat increased. He glanced around the room, looking for answers. Friend or foe? He didn't know. The flutist knew his mother went through the portal, but Kestrel and King Haskell knew it, too, or at least figured it out.

The man fingered his mustache, curling the ends around his fingers. "I guess I'll have to earn your trust before asking you all these questions. My name's Rollie."

"Hello."

"Like I said, I didn't always play up here in the mountains. I played for your dad and your mom, Patricia. I enjoyed spending time with your family. Your grandfather entertained us for hours by telling stories of magic, wizards, and horrendous mistakes. He may have been known as Alpherge the Great, but let me tell you, he was one of the humblest men I've ever met."

The serving girl took Al's empty bowl.

Al stared into Rollie's steel-blue eyes. He tried to picture Greystone Castle, his family's home. He must have been a little baby there, but he remembered nothing about it.

"I comforted your mother when your grandfather died. She was heartbroken by her father-in-law's death. Your father was attending meetings about the Triad's reaction to King Haskell's ambitions."

"The Triad?" Al asked.

"A council of kingdoms seeking to stop Haskell before he killed more people. The Triad comprised the Goodwins, Torkels, and Greystones."

Al ticked the names off on his fingers. His friends, Sherry Torkel, Lily, whose mother's maiden name was Goodwin, and Al, Alpherge Greystone. Three kingdoms and three friends sent to Earth out of King Haskell's touch.

"Know those names, boy? Is the portal open?"

Al felt a tightness in his chest and opened his mouth to answer. Then he closed his mouth and rubbed his hand over his chest. If he wasn't honest with this man, would he lose out on knowing his family better?

"Boy?"

"The portal opened for one day that I'm aware of. Then it closed again on the same day. It's currently closed, and no, Mom didn't make it through. She's still on Earth."

Rollie dropped his gaze to his hands. "Oh. I'm sorry."

"She's still alive. Just on Earth." Al hoped she was still alive. Why wouldn't she be?

"I always liked your mom. When I heard about your father's death, I learned about the portal. I reached the castle two weeks after your mom left the planet. Shame, I'd love to see her again." He wiped moisture from his eyes.

So would I.

They sat in silence, each reviewing his catalog of memories.

The fire died down, and Rollie said, "What brings you to Stone Bokken?"

Al examined the people in the room. The low ceiling made it feel crowded. No one was near their table, as Al had sat far from the flutist when he first arrived.

"I'm here to get information from Jolene," Al whispered.

Rollie scanned the room and then leaned close to Al. "Looking for Finn?"

Al nodded.

Men from a nearby table yelled, "Rollie, are you playing anymore tonight? Let's get some music going." They banged their hands on the table.

Rollie waved at the men. "Just a minute." Then he whispered to Al, "See the innkeeper before the twelfth bell rings but after this room empties. Most of these guys are local, and I see them every night, so they'll leave after my last set. Tell your mom I said hi." He walked to the stage.

Numbness engulfed Al. All the confidence he felt on Earth was useless here. He had a ton of questions he wanted to ask Rollie.

Rollie tuned up and then played a catchy little tune that had Al humming and clapping with the other patrons.

After the eleventh bell, Rollie walked off the stage, winked at Al, and drifted up the stairs. The room's patrons retired for the evening, and Al was left by himself.

The serving girl came around to Al. "Can I get you anything more, sir?"

Al glanced around the room, looking for the innkeeper. She stood with a dishrag in her hand, keeping watch on the two serving girls as they cleaned up. "No, I'm good."

He got up from the bench and walked to the innkeeper.

She looked at him, her face devoid of emotion.

He whispered, "Can you tell me where to find Jolene?"

The innkeeper looked at the serving girls as they wiped tables and gathered napkins and mugs. "Follow me to the back door."

Al stayed close, and they both exited the inn.

An animal howled in the distance, and the woman looked in the sound's direction.

"Are you looking for Finn?"

He stiffened. "No, I'm looking for Jolene."

"I'm Jolene, you fool boy. Finn?"

Al sighed with relief. The tension in his shoulders relaxed. "Yes, I'm sorry. I didn't know."

"Shssh." An animal scurried in the darkness, red eyes reflecting light from one window. Jolene waited a moment. "Tomorrow, go to the village called Svero Garden."

"Okay."

"There is a woman you need to see. The arrow maker. Her name is Ylfa."

Al strained to hear Jolene's every word. The woman spoke as if the mere mention of this person's name would get her killed.

"Lose the staff."

Coldness hit him in the core. "What?"

"You heard me. If the locals see you with a staff, they'll know you're a wizard. Hide in the woods until dark. Then go to Ylfa and ask about the wizard. She'll know."

A twig cracked thirty feet away.

"Whatever you do, don't let Ylfa know you're a wizard." Jolene watched the yard.

"Why not?"

"Quick, inside." She pushed Al back into the kitchen and slammed the door.

Three arrows thwacked into the wooden door.

CHAPTER 28

Al lay in bed, afraid to close his eyes. Who had fired the arrows? If they were the guys from Oakwood, then he needed to stay hidden. The attempt on his life hadn't worked, and now he needed to be alert that someone may try to kill him tonight. That meant searching Svero Garden the next day for Ylfa without revealing his ability to do magic just became more difficult.

At least twice, he heard footsteps in the hallway. Both times, his heartbeat increased, and he prepared to jump out of bed and run or confront his attackers.

Anxiety and fear kept him from getting comfortable. It didn't help that the covers were too short for his size. He twisted in the bed, and the covers came off his feet. He lay on his belly and then switched to his side. After a few moments on his side, he rolled onto his back and had to re-adjust the covers again. The blanket was four inches too short, and either his feet or his shoulders were cold. Fatigue from many hours walking in the mountains brought on a fitful sleep.

Al woke in a dark room. The fire had burned out. Muffled voices sounded in the hallway.

His scalp prickled as he tightened and loosened his fists over and over. *What can I do to prevent these guys from hurting me and make the least noise possible?* Tossing a fireball was too noisy, and though he had some ability with wind, knocking the men over that way would cause a noise when they hit the floor. Maybe a shield and then they would walk away, knowing they couldn't hurt him. A shield wouldn't require much power, and it would prevent notice from other wizards, though the last village said it was improper to use magic shields against commoners.

The latch lifted, and Al heard metal scraping metal.

"Don't go in there."

"Stay in the hallway."

The door squeaked, and Al saw a glint of steel. He formed a shield over his body, afraid to move.

The guy moved toward him, though Al didn't really see him in the darkness. He just felt his presence in the room.

A hand came toward him and stopped over his head.

"Aren't you going to wake him?" a man whispered.

"I can't get close to his body."

"Why not?"

Al's throat was too dry to swallow, his neck muscles tight as he strained to find out what was happening. Should he light a candle? He expected one man to bring a hammer, axe, or knife down on his head. He hoped the shield would hold. Would it be better if he could see them and they could see him, or did he have an advantage in the dark?

"Wake him."

"I can't touch him. There's a shield."

"Told you he was a wizard."

"I knew he was a wizard. I told you."

"No, you didn't. I told you first."

Who were these guys? Their conversation sounded to him like a bad comedy routine. Al couldn't take it any longer and used magic to light the candles and torch the log in the fireplace to blaze red.

One of the two men stood near Al, his hand touching the shield. The guy jerked away when the lights came on.

Al rolled to the other side of the bed and stood. "What do you guys want?"

One man with a patchy beard raised his hand up and down, palm side down. He whispered, "Keep your voice down."

Al's heartbeat thumped in his chest, and he cocked his head at the men.

Patchy Beard said, "We need to warn you about Svero Garden."

"What about it?" Al narrowed his eyes.

"Don't go there."

"Who said I was going there?"

"Doesn't matter. Stay away."

"Why?" These guys irritated him. He thought maybe he should just light them on fire and see what they would do.

Patchy Beard lowered his gaze and ran his fingers through his hair. He looked at the other guy, a younger man, a mouth breather with big lips.

Al waited.

Patchy Beard said, "We know you're looking for Finn. You're a wizard, and the only reason wizards come this far into the mountains is to find Finn."

"So what? Wizards like to learn things from other wizards," Al said in a raised voice.

The guy raised and lowered his hands to tell Al to keep it down. "Finn's not popular around here. He's mean to the locals and steals our goats and chickens. Our children go missing for days and then return and tell us Finn ran experiments on them."

Al's fight-or-flight response mechanisms were slowing down, and he began breathing a little more easily. "Okay."

"Finn turned some of his own apprentice wizards into stone statues."

Lips said, "I saw them with my own eyes, seven stone statues."

"What if I can help Finn solve that problem?" Al strode to the fireplace.

"You can't. He's a crazy man. You can't get close to him."

The night chill and short blankets had driven the cold deeply into Al's inner core. He tried to warm his hands by the fire. "How did you see the stone apprentices if you couldn't get close?"

Patchy Beard said, "We saw him walk down the mountain and knew it was safe to check on his place. We were kids ourselves and were curious."

"I was told there were magic traps. How did you get through the traps?"

Lips stuttered, "We, ah, we, that is, we saw."

Al crossed his arms and tapped his foot. "The truth. You've never seen his place, have you?"

"We've heard stories."

Al snorted. "Stories. You woke me for stories."

"Finn hurts children."

Al thought back to his own experience with children following him in the village and then getting into trouble for no other reason than getting near a wizard when they shouldn't be. "Maybe it was an accident."

"It was no accident."

"Don't go to Svero Garden. They outlawed wizards in that village because they've lost several children. They'll lock you up."

"I won't have to go to Svero Garden if you tell me where Finn's place is."

Patchy Beard lowered his head and shook it. "We've never been."

Al shooed the two men away with his hand. "Go away, I need sleep."

"We warned you."

Al shoved them out the door and closed the latch again.

* * * *

The next morning, Al slept late then had breakfast composed of bread with a jelly-like spread and goat cheese. He washed it down with goat's milk. Jolene was in the kitchen, and he noticed she was watching him. He thought about asking her about the men but decided to let it go. No need to make more trouble.

After breakfast, he washed, grabbed his staff, and headed down the stairs.

Jolene waved him toward her. "Go this way." She took him through the kitchen and toward the same door they stood at when the arrows flew.

"You want me to go through the same door where someone shot arrows at us last night?"

"It's the safest route. There's a trail over there. Take it around the village and head east toward the mountain. When you get back to the stream, you can cut over to the road. Svero Garden is a three-quarters-day journey. When you reach two stone huts without rooftops, then you're less than a mile away. You must enter the forest at that point, or someone from the village will see you. If you hear anyone on the road, hide. They mustn't know you're coming."

Al thanked Jolene and then went through the backyard. When he turned back toward Jolene, she had already reentered the inn. No arrows protruded from the door or the wall.

After a few minutes up the path, Al didn't hear the village anymore. No hammering blacksmith, no voices of workers feeding animals, and no children playing in the square.

He found the stream and used his hands to slurp up a drink. He studied the woods to see if anyone followed and saw nothing but birds and squirrels. With a quick walk to the road, he turned back east to Svero Garden.

An hour after midday, Al moved into the forest and found a place where he could sit and watch the road to see if people were following him. No one passed in either direction. He rested for an hour and then continued his journey.

The wizard on the staff, Callahan the Curious, had taken to singing songs as they traveled, and Al welcomed the distraction. Callahan had a beautiful tenor voice, but he tended toward sad songs of lost loves, which made Al think of Sherry.

Al said, "Callahan, you should have sung on stage with Rollie. He might have appreciated the accompaniment."

"He wouldn't have been able to match my outstanding perfect pitch, and I would have been left singing all by myself while he cried in the corner."

Al laughed. "Hey, Callahan, if I used my magic shield while in the next village, would the villagers know? Are there people on Aloheno that can determine if a person has magic capabilities but wouldn't be classified as wizards themselves?"

Callahan fell silent for a moment. "Yes, someone with low-level skills like Gadiel. They recognize magic and can sense it in others but can't compete against trained wizards or wizard warriors."

"Interesting," Al said. "Why wouldn't the village condemn them?"

"They hide the skill. Maybe they don't show any capabilities when others are around or have specifically muzzled the ability, never using it. If they have untrained wizard skills, they would fear their skills could hurt others or themselves. I've known people who did something when they were young using magic, hurt a sibling or a friend, and were too frightened by it to continue becoming a wizard."

Isabel the Insidious, another former wizard carved into the staff, said, "Finn was a cantankerous old cuss."

Callahan laughed, "You're a cantankerous old cuss."

Isabel replied, "He really doesn't like children. If you're younger than fifty, he doesn't want to talk to you."

"Well, I need to talk to him," Al said. "Nobody said he had to like it."

* * * *

The shadows of the day were long when Al reached the two stone huts. The road curved up ahead and continued up the mountain. A meadow lay just past the curve. Maybe that was what Jolene warned him about. Once he reached the meadow, he might be visible to the village.

He headed into the forest, trying to pick his steps so he didn't make too much noise. He scurried through the trees and brush, staying out of sight of people who might be in the meadow.

A wild animal roared somewhere in the distance.

The forest darkened a little more each quarter hour, but Al kept silently plodding. He stopped behind three large spruce trees and peeked through the forest. Sun shone through the trees, throwing a combination of shadows and light on village buildings.

This must be Svero Garden. How do I find Ylfa, the arrow maker, if I have to hide from the villagers and can't ask questions? First, I need to find somewhere to stash my staff.

Al decided on his next course of action as he stood behind an enormous tree trunk. If he was going to hide the staff, the best location was beyond the village. That way, if he needed to make a fast getaway, he wouldn't have to backtrack to find it.

As he walked through the forest, he studied the buildings he passed. Many looked the same, with a single window looking out the back. A couple of buildings were larger, obviously businesses, maybe inns, taverns, or smithies. What would an arrow maker's business look like from the back? The business should be near the blacksmith's place for the metal to make arrowheads. He imagined she would have her own furnace to keep the metal hot, maybe dip the arrowhead into the hot metal and then pull it and let it cool.

He listened to the village sounds and then heard the pounding of metal against metal. *Ah, the smithy shop is close.* He moved closer to the buildings to get a better look. The village seemed larger than Al thought it should be this far from real civilization.

Al heard voices. Then someone said, "Quiet." A moment later, an arrow thwacked against a tree ten feet from Al.

CHAPTER 29

Al ducked behind bushes to prevent another arrow from hitting him.

"Clive, what are you shooting at? The targets are over here. You missed big time."

"Thought I saw an animal in the forest. Stop a moment while I retrieve my arrow." A large man stomped through the forest, not making any attempt to be quiet.

Al watched between leaves on a bush as a man came to the tree and worked the arrow loose. After grabbing the arrow, he glanced at the forest and the bush Al hid behind. Al recognized the man as someone he saw in the Hound and Chicken. Clive moved back to the buildings, and the two men went back to practicing their archery.

What do I do now? Are these guys at the arrow maker's shop? That's the only thing that makes sense.

Surely, a potential buyer might ask, "Are the arrows true? Do they have a good point?"

Then the arrow maker could respond, "Here, go try a few of them. There's a range out back."

He made a mental note of the building's location so he could find it again. Now the hard part—getting out of this area until nightfall.

Clive sent three arrows in rapid fire, which thwacked against the straw-filled target.

His friend said, "Wow, all three in the bullseye."

"That wizard boy is as good as dead when we see him again."

"You should have shot him last night at the inn."

"Yeah, but this gets me out of the house for a few days. My wife has been asking me to go ask the stonecutter for a job. I think this bit of work will be just fine."

"Are we supposed to bring back his head?"

Al's shoulders tightened as he held his breath. He imagined an arrow sticking through his chest while he remained alive as Clive used an axe to decapitate him.

Clive released another three arrows. *Thwack. Thwack. Thwack.* "No, Blackstone only wants the staff. We get that and we're golden."

"What's your wife gonna say if you don't come back with any money?"

"I don't care what she thinks. If I see the wizard, he dies."

A tall blonde woman came out of the building and stood with the men. "What do you boys think of the arrows?"

"They'll do just fine for our purposes," Clive said.

"One of you is talented."

"Clive's the man." His friend pointed.

"We have a contest during the fall festival in two weeks. Winner gets fifty silver pieces."

Clive smiled. "That sounds like easy money."

"Don't know how easy it is. There're a lot of talented archers in the area. Brings out the best every year."

Clive held his bow in his left hand and wrapped his right arm around the woman. "You're looking at the best right here, baby. Do you want to have a drink with me tonight? I'm staying at the village inn, and we can drink all night long."

"You have a drink, and I'll be over later. I need to finish a project." She patted his bottom and walked back into the building.

Was that woman Ylfa? Al wasn't sure how to assess her. If she was going to meet up with Clive, then Al needed to stash his staff and get back to her for information before she left the shop. He was supposed to wait until dark, and that wouldn't be for at least another hour. How long would she wait at the shop before heading to her meetup?

After speaking with the woman, Clive and his friend took their bows and arrows and walked away from the practice field.

Al rose from his hiding place and moved with caution through the forest. He hoped he would be less visible as the summer sun poured out its last rays for the day. The last village building came into view, and he started counting his steps while looking for a landmark that he might recognize in the dark. He walked five hundred steps and studied the surrounding area.

Wolves howled in the distance, followed by a roar that was definitely not from a wolf. Then Al realized he didn't have anywhere to sleep tonight. No safe, warm inn with a nice dinner and some food in the morning before he left for the day. After his discussion with Ylfa, he would have to trek through the night or sleep out here with the wild animals.

He found a strange rock formation that formed a little hill in the forest. *That will do as a marker.* Then he wondered if he should put the staff under some leaves or in a tree. In a tree would work. He almost used magic to lift it high before remembering not to use magic. He found a crook of a tree that he could reach on tiptoe and was sure no one else could get to it. This late in the day, no one would be here to see it.

Al hurried back to the arrow maker's shop. He didn't want to come crashing out of the forest. He hid in the forest, waiting a little longer for nighttime. The colors had disappeared from the building rooftops, but he couldn't risk exposure by walking in too soon, especially if Clive and his friend saw him.

Nightfall descended on Al's location in the woods. The woman had no visitors practicing their archery. A candle still burned in the building as Al saw light shining through the one window.

It was time to make his move. Al peered into the shop from a window that was high on the building.

The woman he saw with Clive earlier sat on a bench next to a pile of sticks. In front of her, steam rose over a large black kettle heating over a yellow fire. A liquid in the pot simmered red and yellow. She had a handful of sticks and would take one stick and dip its pointed end into the liquid. Then she set the stick on a rack with two wooden rungs, one of which was set an inch higher than the other. The woman laid the metal portion on the rack with the dripping metal facing away from her. Any drips landed in a metal pan so she could re-heat and reuse the waste.

Al felt his stomach tense. With one last check of the yard and practice field, Al reached the door and walked in. "Uh, hello."

The woman gasped and held out one of the pointed sticks at Al.

"Oh, sorry, didn't mean to scare you." Al raised his hands like he was surrendering to the police.

"Don't get many visitors at this time of night. Best time to get work done. Cooler and no one bothers me." She smirked. "What can I help you with?"

Al could feel her gaze running up and down his body. He hadn't come up with a plan for what he would say to her, so he hesitated and stammered to get his mind working. "I'm Al. I'm here for, uh, you know, like I might need a—" He spied a bow nearby. "Bow or something."

The woman laughed. "Might need a bow or something." She stood and walked over to Al.

Al had noticed her height when she was outside but was still surprised to find she stood a minimum of six feet two inches. She was a beautiful woman with nice cheekbones and full lips.

She placed her hand on Al's chest. "I'm Ylfa, and you, my friend, look delicious."

Al's heart pounded a rat-a-tat-tat that he was sure Ylfa could hear. He got lost in her big blue eyes. Her smile showed straight, white teeth.

Ylfa said, "I thought Clive might be the catch of the day, but I'm going to throw him back into the lake." A gleam of amusement flashed in her eyes.

Al laughed, a little louder than he should, a little higher-pitched than normal, and longer than the situation called for.

"Now, what are you here for, just to stare into my eyes like a lost puppy dog?" She ran her hand across Al's jaw, traced a line down his neck and chest, and stopped near his belly button.

Al's mouth went dry, and he took short, quick breaths. He stepped back into a rack of bows. "I'm, uh, looking for information."

"Maybe you won't be so nervous if we have this conversation with an ale or two."

The woman kept him off-balance and distracted him from remembering what he was there for and what he planned to say. "No ale." His voice choked from the tightness in his throat.

"I understand. Business before pleasure. You know, sometimes I get wizards in here, and they always do a magic trick for me. Please do a magic trick for me, please, please?" She smiled while her eyes bounced light like diamonds.

Al giggled and knew just what trick to do. The lighting in the room was perfect for the glowing globe trick, and the girls ate it up. And he really wanted Ylfa to like him. A lot. "Watch this." Al put his palm up and traced a line along his palm with his other hand. Then he stopped.

She looked at him, blinking twice and her smile relaxing.

"Wait, this will be better. Give me your hand." He took her hand in his and placed her palm up. He was shaking so much it caused her hand to shake. With a wave of his other hand, he traced a line on her palm, following one of its natural lines. He was about to say the words and do the magic when he remembered Jolene's warning. Then he looked into Ylfa's eyes.

She looked back, but her smile was turning into a grimace.

Al opened his hand to expose all his fingers and raced them along hers. Then he turned her hand, bowed slightly, raised the back of her hand to his lips, and kissed her hand.

When he stood again, her smile returned. "That's nice magic."

Al waggled his eyebrows at her the way he remembered Wagner doing with the cooking girls on the caravan months ago when he and Erik had traveled to the Ice Castle for the Helmet of Justice.

She giggled.

Sweat from both nervousness and the heat in the room streamed in large drops down his back. "I need to ask you a favor."

"Yes?"

"I'm looking for a wizard named Finn. Can you tell me where to find him?"

The smile disappeared. "Are you a wizard?"

"I'm not. But I have a rather clumsy friend." He paused. "She drank a potion and…" Al didn't know how to finish this story.

"She, uh, like, turned into a frog. We were in Oakwood, and they told me to check out this guy up in the mountains. Finn."

"A girlfriend?" Ylfa crossed her chest with her hands.

Al looked sheepish. "Yep."

"I should have known because you look like a keeper." She stroked his chest and looked disappointed.

Al smiled and waggled his eyebrows again.

Ylfa stared into Al's eyes as if she was sucking his very soul from his body. "Finn is my stepbrother. Other wizards have taken advantage of him in the past. Young wizards your age have a habit of getting Finn in trouble. I have to take care of my older brother, you know."

Every muscle and ingrained habit in Al's body wanted him to look away, break contact, and run from the room. But he stood toe to toe with Ylfa and made himself believe he wasn't a wizard.

She touched his arm and flipped her hair. "Where are you staying tonight? We have time for dinner together."

Despite the heat from the metallic sludge used for the arrowheads, Al felt chilled to the bone. He didn't have a quick lie to tell Ylfa. Of course, he hadn't thought about where he planned to stay tonight. He hoped to run as far as possible from Ylfa, Clive, and this village. His chest tightened as he wondered how to answer the question.

A smile didn't quite touch Ylfa's eyes. "Frankly, Finn might make things worse for your girlfriend."

Al feared offending Ylfa by saying the wrong thing or even moving his arm, so she no longer touched him.

"Listen. Do you promise me you aren't a wizard?"

If she finds out I'm a wizard, what will she do to me? As Finn's stepsister, is she imbued with special magical abilities? Heat rose to his cheeks as he lied to her. He nodded.

"Do you promise not to tell anyone else how to find Finn?" She bit her lower lip.

Al nodded.

"Promise me you'll stop and see me on your way back down the mountain?"

He took a deep breath, and the heat in his face made him wonder if his head was in flames. Saying the wrong thing now could ruin his chances of finding Finn. He whispered, "Yes."

She gave him instructions on how to find the wizard, which included several ladders up the side of a mountain on his way to Stökkar Klettar.

The back door opened, and Clive and his friend walked into the room.

Al felt the blood drain from his face.

Clive stumbled into the room staring at Ylfa. He'd obviously been drinking heavily and slurred, "I thought you were coming to the inn."

Ylfa glanced at Clive.

The room spun, and Al wobbled on unsteady legs.

Clive yelled, "It's the wizard."

CHAPTER 30

The area around the Crossroads village council building swarmed with villagers seeking an audience with or just wanting to gawk at Prince Krunal. This was the day the new Velidred king visited Crossroads and provided justice to its people in the form of public court. Sherry sat on a bench within the village council's main room, awaiting her audience with the king. She hoped to receive a favorable ruling on her crimes against the village.

Sherry didn't hide her presence, but Kestrel, who sat beside her, wore a black hood over his head, hiding his face. Kestrel's cousin, Paxton, sat on Sherry's other side, holding her hand. They all felt it was safer to leave Lily back at the farm in Triponca. They didn't want to risk her getting caught up in this trial.

Paxton patted her hand. "It's going to be fine. They accused you unjustly and imprisoned you without a trial. The king will take those facts into consideration and be lenient with you."

She couldn't eat breakfast this morning because of a loss of appetite, and her stomach felt tied in knots. Sherry bit her lip and looked around the room at the numerous people that had thrown food and rocks at her. She squeezed Paxton's hand.

The prince hadn't arrived yet, though they expected him to appear any minute. The mayor must have been with the prince, which explained his absence.

"How will this work?" Sherry asked.

"They'll call your name. The mayor will present his case against you. You will explain your account of the facts. Then the prince decides who's in the right and the proper retribution."

"Am I allowed to ask questions of the mayor?"

"No, it doesn't really work that way."

"How can I get all the information out if I can't ask questions?"

"You get to make your statements. You don't get to ask questions."

Sherry wrapped her arms around her belly. Last night she felt confident that she could plead her case and win, but now, with the village crowd sitting on benches and many standing in the aisles and against the back wall, her confidence slipped. The people on the benches seemed better dressed than the standing villagers, and she wondered if there was a class system to this process.

Who was she kidding? She knew nothing of the legal system in this society. She hoped Paxton was right, that they would give her a slap on the wrist, tell her not to do it again, and set her free. Anything would be better than more prison time. She suspected she wouldn't survive imprisonment by these people.

The doors in the back opened, and Prince Krunal entered the room. Everyone bowed to the new ruling power of Velidred.

The prince looked different from the last time she had seen him. Back then, the prince had suffered a tremendous loss during his battle with King Haskell's forces, and she saw him in a moment of despair, a defeated commander that had taken to drink over his failures.

Now the prince walked victoriously into the room. He wore a crown of gold marked with a handful of green and red gems over a full head of curly black hair. A knee-length red silk cape ringed in white with black dots fell over his navy tunic, which had his family crest emblazoned on the chest. The man wore a wide leather belt with a golden buckle cinched around his waist, while leather boots came up near his knees. He held his head high as he walked to the mayor's stage and sat on the mayor's chair.

The herald, one of the prince's men, read from a scroll, "Hear ye, hear ye, hear ye. The royal justice of the kingdom of Velidred, Prince Krunal Kalluri, will now deliver impartial justice to the village of Crossroads. You may be seated."

A scuffle of boots and benches filled the room with noise as people settled back into their places.

The room felt hot to Sherry as the people closed in more tightly.

Paxton had added Sherry's name to a list when they had arrived and told her she would be the fifth case called to the court. The prince's courier sat at a bench and small table, taking notes on the trial. The mayor sat in the front row in front of the prince.

With a straight back and loud, confident voice, the herald stood and announced, "The first case before the prince, the landowner dispute between Mr. Mooney and Mr. Zimmerman. Please bring in Mr. Zimmerman."

Doors opened in the back, and Justin the jailer brought in a man dressed only in his smallclothes with whip marks across his back. Justin hauled the man to the left side of the room, just to the herald's right. Mr. Zimmerman looked malnourished and beaten.

The herald said, "Mr. Mooney, please present your case."

Mr. Mooney stood from his spot on the first bench next to the mayor. "Mr. Zimmerman was squatting on land that I owned. I purchased the land two weeks before and asked him to remove himself from the land, but he refused. Village guards accompanied me on the next visit, and we again asked him to vacate the land. He refused. I apologize for his condition. We had to use force to remove him from the property."

The herald said, "Mr. Zimmerman, please state your case."

Mr. Zimmerman wavered on his feet as he tried to talk through swollen and cracked lips. The man tried to be royal and proper but dressed as he was and looking like a bum, he did not express confidence. "Prince Krunal, two of my sons served for you in the war."

The prince nodded at Mr. Zimmerman. "Thank you."

Mr. Zimmerman swallowed, though it looked difficult. "I did not sell the property in question to Mr. Mooney. My family has owned the property for the last seventy years. My grandfather first farmed that land as a child. At no point did I agree to sell my land and home to Mr. Mooney. It's a lie if Mr. Mooney thinks he has an agreement that the land is his."

The mayor stood. "Prince Krunal, the reason Mr. Zimmerman didn't have ownership of the property is because of failure to pay taxes."

"What taxes? I live over a mile outside the village—"

The herald cried out, "Quiet. Mr. Zimmerman, you've had your chance to state your case."

"But this is new information."

"Quiet."

The room fell silent.

Prince Krunal said, "Thank you for your testimony."

The mayor sat.

The prince nodded at the herald.

"Prince Krunal will rule on the case," said the herald.

Prince Krunal stood and said, "Based on the villager failing to pay the village tax, I approve the property sale. Mr. Mooney is the owner of the property. Since the criminal did not leave at the proper time, he will spend a year in prison."

Mr. Zimmerman cried out, "Robbers and thieves. You're all robbers and thieves."

Justin hit the accused with a short stick that took him to his knees. A couple of guards grabbed Mr. Zimmerman under the arms and hauled him out of the room.

The next case involved a man who robbed a distillery of a barrel of ale. The ale shop owner presented his case for the missing barrel, identifying the robber seen running down the road with the barrel in the middle of the day.

A working-class man with rough dirty hands, wearing a leather apron, made his case, which comprised a half-hearted attempt to say it was okay because it was for his sister's wedding.

The mayor stood and confirmed the distiller's story.

The prince announced a quick ruling in favor of the distiller and sentenced the man to three months in jail. He would be required to pay the distiller for a barrel of ale.

Sherry didn't like this process, and the next case proved true to what she was seeing. The victim talked about the issue. Then the suspect stated their case, but then no matter what the suspect said, the mayor stood and confirmed what the plaintiff said or offered additional information in the plaintiff's favor.

Each time before the herald announced the ruling, the prince looked at the mayor, who nodded, and then the prince ruled in the mayor's favor.

The herald stood and announced, "The next case before the prince. We charge a woman for educating children without a license, setting up a school in her home, and educating girls."

People in the council hall whispered among themselves about the idea of educating girls.

"Quiet!" the herald called out.

The conversation died down slowly.

The herald raised his voice and returned to his list. "For educating girls, for resisting arrest, for attacking the jailer, for escaping from jail, and for hiding a known convict."

The herald waited a moment, then said, "Bring in Miss Torkel."

CHAPTER 31

Sherry stood in Crossroad's village council chambers, which were being used as a courtroom. "No one is bringing in Miss Torkel. I'm a free woman, and I will walk in myself."

Sherry went to the spot reserved for suspects and criminals and stared at the prince. She wondered if the man recognized her from a previous meeting during the first week she and Erik had reached Aloheno. She hoped not since that would just add to the charges being filed against her.

The herald said, "Mr. Mooney, what do you have to say?"

Mr. Mooney stood and stared at Sherry with cold, hard, flinty eyes. "Your majesty, this woman came to the village council to request to teach our children. The village council's decision on the matter forbade her to teach."

Sherry rolled her eyes and shook her head.

"The next day, we found that the woman had visited homes in the village and invited their children to come to her house for schooling." He turned to the audience and raised his voice. "To her house."

The audience mumbled amongst themselves.

"A few days later, the mayor and I found she was running a school out of her home and educating"—he stopped and scanned the room—"both boys and girls." He put his shoulders back and chest out and held up a sheet of paper. "We have a list of all the boys and girls whose parents sent them to this woman's house for an education. Your Majesty, we request you not charge these parents since they didn't know about the ruling we had made at the village council meeting."

The prince nodded.

"To verify that the suspect really included girls in her school, I sent my daughter."

The amazed audience became rather loud.

Sherry felt overheated and light-headed as her face reddened and sweat formed on her forehead. She glanced at the audience, looking for a friendly face, one that didn't believe educating girls was akin to skinning cats. No one was on her side.

Mr. Mooney continued, "When the mayor and I showed up, there was my daughter, sitting with twenty students, half of them girls."

Sherry felt her heart freeze, and her hand went to her chest. For a moment, she thought she might lose consciousness. Then she regained control and shouted, "That's a lie."

The room erupted in conversation.

The herald shouted, "Quiet." When the people kept talking, he looked at the prince. Again, the herald shouted, "Quiet."

The prince stood and raised his hands. "Please take your conversations outside. This is not the place for talking. This woman is on trial. Quiet." He had to raise his voice a little to get everyone's attention, but soon the room went silent.

Mr. Mooney said, "The mayor and I arrested the woman and took her to the women's prison."

Sherry harrumphed. "That wasn't a prison. That was a torture chamber."

The herald said, "Miss Torkel, you may not talk until it's your turn to speak. We are a civilized society here."

"This isn't a civilized society. This is a kangaroo court." Sherry didn't know if anyone in the room even knew what a kangaroo court was, nor did she care.

The herald asked, "Is that your testimony, Mr. Mooney?"

"Yes, sir."

Mr. Mooney sat.

The herald called out, "Justin Archambeau, do you have testimony against this suspect?"

Justin, the jailer, walked by Sherry and threatened her with the baton he held in his hand.

Sherry's eyes narrowed as she backed away from him.

Justin stood in front of the prince. "I took this woman prisoner to the women's prison outside of town. She was a difficult and feisty woman." He stared at Sherry and smiled. "We tried to treat her with dignity and respect, but she fought every step of the way."

"Dignity and respect?" Sherry yelled. "You treated me like an animal."

He squinted at her and gave her a hard smile. "We wrestled her into the cabin and shackled her in the room like we do for every criminal, your majesty. She bit and scratched and fought like a stegox."

A tall man who stood in the back yelled out, "Just the type of woman you like, Justin."

Everybody in the room laughed.

Sherry shook her head. *I hate this planet.*

Justin continued his testimony. "We sent Ciara, the mayor's wife, in to check on the woman three times a day."

"No, you didn't," Sherry shouted.

The jailer shouted back, "Three times a day."

The prince looked at the mayor's wife, who sat next to her husband. "Can you corroborate that, Ciara?"

Ciara didn't flinch, color or blink. "Yes, Your Majesty. Three times a day, food, water, and a walk in the sunshine."

Sherry took a deep breath.

Justin cracked his neck. "Like I was saying, we gave this woman the best care anyone could give. Ciara told me that our suspect requested we loosen her shackles because they hurt her arms."

Sherry said nothing. She just raised her arms into the air, showing the blisters and bruise marks that still appeared on her wrist.

"That witch and her blonde friend attacked me when I came in to loosen her shackles. I even brought a cream for the blonde woman to soothe her sores, and yet they attacked."

"You didn't loosen my shackles. You put me on an iron cross, and then you tried to molest my friend Lily."

One guard hit Sherry over the back of her neck with a baton. "You're supposed to be quiet."

She saw a moment of blackness but didn't fall.

"These women had planned an escape. The blonde lifted her shift, and when I looked, the redhead threw her chains over my neck. It was my fault, Your Majesty. I should have been expecting these wily witches to attempt an escape." He showed the prince the welts where Lily had gotten the chains over his neck. "They subdued me, almost killed me, and then grabbed the key and escaped."

He looked at Sherry with a smirk and a look of superiority, his chin high in the air.

She shook her head in disbelief.

After Justin, the herald called three guards who corroborated Justin's story.

Finally, Sherry figured it was her turn to talk, but how could she dispute so many witnesses with false testimony against her?

The prince stood and said, "I would like to add another charge to this woman's long list of crimes against this village."

Sherry's chest tightened. This was an unusual move by the prince, and she tugged on an ear. *What is this?*

"During the war, we held this woman and a friend of hers captive."

Sherry rolled her eyes. "Oh brother."

Justin stood by her with the other guards and whacked her on the back of the head with his baton.

She rolled to her knees as stars danced in her head.

The prince continued his testimony. "In the middle of the night, the two prisoners jumped out of a third-story window and ran away in the dark. The guards reported witchcraft being involved since they saw her talk with a stegox and force it to chase the guards."

The crowd gasped.

This was so ridiculous that Sherry stayed on her knees. She was going to die. How could they have the person judging her give testimony against her? That made no sense at all. They had built a mountain of lies, and she knew it didn't matter what she said. They had all lied, and she would be sentenced back to jail.

The prince sat back on the throne, or at least the mayor's throne.

The herald said, "Miss Torkel can now give testimony."

She snorted and rose from her knees.

Justin stood beside her, baton at the ready.

Sherry looked at the crowded council chamber. Two faces on her side, Kestrel and Paxton. The mayor and his cronies had already convinced the rest of the people in the room of her guilt. "There are many charges against me today. Three are true. The rest are false testimony."

Justin went to smack her with the baton.

She saw it coming and caught it in her hand. A shock wave of pain shot down her arm. She stared at Justin.

Justin stared back.

Sherry released her grip on the baton.

Justin brought it to his side.

"Everything this man beside me said is a lie."

She didn't react fast enough.

The baton crashed against the side of her head. She fell to her knees, bringing her hand to her ear. Blood dripped over her fingers.

Sherry worked to keep the tears out of her eyes. "Prince Krunal, was this what you meant when you said you were here to provide just and impartial decisions to the village of Crossroads? You beat your suspects as they give their testimony. Is that the just part or the impartial part?"

Adrenaline rushed through Sherry's body. The pounding in both ears and all the pain she felt needed to wait. No matter what, she was determined to let these bullies know she wouldn't go down without a fight. She knew it was coming this time and caught the baton with both hands. She pulled hard. Justin wasn't expecting her to resist, and the baton came out of his grasp.

"You little witch," he yelled.

She grabbed the baton and jumped to her feet. Sherry pounded Justin over and over on the arm, shoulders, and face. She hit him so hard that she didn't feel the blows raining on her body from the other guards. They had four hundred pounds on her five-foot body, but she had anger and adrenaline on her side.

People piled on the confrontation. Some tried to pull people off her, and others wanted a crack at her.

The herald kept saying over and over, "Quiet. To your seats. Everyone. The prince is in the building."

Sherry smelled the men's sweat. When the guards grabbed her arms, she kicked at Justin and landed a solid foot in his ribs.

The guards pulled her into the air and threw her to the floor, knocking the breath from her lungs. She quit struggling as her body screamed for that first solid breath of air. It didn't come.

Sherry looked at the guards holding her to the floor, one on each limb. They would not rescue her.

Justin stood over her. Blood streamed over his face, his nose broken and one eye closed.

She smiled at him.

He kicked her in the side.

CHAPTER 32

The room spun above Sherry. She heard muffled voices. No emotion was left in her body. She'd spent less than six months on this planet, and all she had to show for it was a premature death. Where was Al? She would have liked to see him once more before she died. Still, her lungs failed to start.

Justin kicked her twice more.

The kick jumpstarted her lungs, allowing her to breathe again. She sucked in vast quantities of air.

The room was in pandemonium. People yelled at the prince, at the guards, at Sherry, and at the mayor. No one was happy. Women screamed and cried. Somebody let a barking dog into the building.

The herald continued to ask for quiet.

The prince stood on the mayor's stage with hands raised to the sky for silence.

The king's guards paraded into the room, and the noise and confusion slowed.

Four strong village guards held Sherry's spread-eagled limbs to the floor. She thought of her mother on Earth. How would she react when she heard the news four years from now? Did she think Sherry would fit into life on this planet, a homecoming of sorts? Aloheno was the Dark Age to Earth's current enlightened age.

The noise diminished to where Sherry could make out distinct voices. The mayor called for quiet. Prince Krunal yelled for the guards to bring peace. The herald still asked for silence.

Guards brought Sherry to her feet and shackled her hands behind her. They couldn't have a suspect more brutal than the thugs they called guards.

She stood straight and defiant as if nothing had happened. Pain ripped her side where Justin kicked her, and she thought he might have broken one of her ribs. Blood streamed down the top of her head into her eyes. She couldn't hear out of one ear.

Sherry took in slow, shallow breaths as she worked to calm her pulse and heartbeat. Despite the pain crying through her body, she smiled, contented in not sitting idly by as they railroaded her into death. She closed her eyes.

Prince Krunal asked, "Is the suspect secured?"

The four men surrounding her nodded. One said, "Yes, Your Majesty."

Prince Krunal looked into the crowd and the guards who had pushed into the room. "Are we going to finish this trial?"

People looked at one another, at the prince, and at Sherry. It seemed everyone agreed they could go ahead.

The prince nodded to the herald.

The herald said, "Miss Torkel, please continue your testimony."

She looked at the guards, who were still holding her. She shook her shoulders, but they didn't let go. Sherry looked for Justin and noticed the other guards were holding him along the wall. She didn't even know where she had left off before they had attacked her. Her brain didn't want to work. Sherry worked her jaw. It didn't feel quite right.

"Let me start at the beginning." She took a calming breath and explained about coming to the council meeting and how she was told not to start a school. She had complied but thought if she brought concerned citizens to the next meeting, citizens of Crossroads that thought it was important to have their children educated, that the next meeting might be different, and the village council would approve her desire.

The prince looked unimpressed.

The mayor looked angry.

"Kids came to my house the next day, and I started teaching them. Reading and writing. Where I come from, we teach all children to read and write. I've been reading and writing since I was six years old. You all want your kids to read and write, don't you?"

The crowd just sat there, but she could see in the eyes of some women that yes, they would like a chance for their children to read and write.

"A sister of one child came the next day, and soon Mr. Mooney sent his own daughter, Gabriella. She is very smart, by the way."

Mr. Mooney scowled at Sherry.

"At no point did we have twenty children in my small cabin. And only two of the children were girls."

Sherry took a deep breath and stared around the room, trying to collect her thoughts.

"Later that day, these thugs shackled me and carted me around the village as the people in this room threw eggs, vegetables, and stones at me."

The people had different reactions to that comment. A few looked at their feet. Color rose in their faces. They pulled their hats lower on the head, unable to meet Sherry's gaze, or tears leaked down their cheeks. Other people's reactions were more defiant. Yes, this woman deserved everything she got.

She looked at Justin and wondered if this next part of her testimony would be the part that killed her. "At the women's *prison*, they shackled me to the wall. That woman"—Sherry nodded her head at Ciara—"came *once* a day."

Ciara stared at Sherry but didn't deny the comment.

"Ciara was nice, and I asked for help with the shackles. You saw my wrists. I didn't think it was that important that a woman who wanted to teach children their A B Cs would need to be shackled to a wall, miles from town.

"That jailer, Justin, is not a nice person, and he didn't loosen my shackles the afternoon he came into the cabin. He placed me on an iron cross. I would show you what that looks like, but these guys don't want me to move."

"Then Justin. . ." Sherry looked at the man.

Justin's nostrils flared, and he bared his teeth.

Sherry took a deep breath, reliving the experience with Justin in the cabin. "He pretended to want to place cream on my friend Lily's back. Lily never taught at my school. She didn't have any desire to teach or really to spend much time with children. Each day, she left our little cabin so I could work with the children without interruption.

"When Justin arrived at the cabin, he planned to hurt her psychologically and physically. She fought back, and we escaped and secured Justin in his own shackles.

"We didn't leave town per se, and I even showed up for my trial. See, here I am. I didn't have to. I could have run far enough away to see none of you ever again. That's not my style. I'll take the blame for things I do wrong and credit for things I do right. I was trying to help the residents of this community."

Sherry was quiet for a few moments.

The herald asked, "Have you finished your testimony, Miss Torkel?"

"I have." Tears welled in her eyes.

"Does the mayor have any comments?"

The mayor stood facing the prince. "As you heard from her own lips, Your Majesty, she has admitted her guilt for the crimes we have charged her with. What say you?"

The mayor sat.

The prince placed his chin in his hands and stared at the floor.

Sherry's neck muscles felt stiff. Her head hurt, and each breath she took caused pain in her side. After what seemed an eternity, the prince looked at the herald and nodded.

"Prince Krunal will now rule on the case."

The prince stood.

Sherry wobbled on unsteady legs.

"I have given this case much thought. I can see that Miss Torkel is very passionate about her desire to teach your children."

A murmur of anger rose in the crowd.

The prince raised his hands. "I know, I know. This village isn't ready for that yet. I understand." He looked at the mayor.

The mayor nodded at the prince.

Sherry's shoulders slumped as she realized the inevitability of the case's outcome. Death would come slowly or quickly, but her time was up. It didn't matter.

"I sentence Miss Sherry Torkel to a beating with a leather strap of ten strokes, a day in the stocks, and a sentence of one year in a women's prison."

Sherry stared over the crowd, seeing but not seeing, as numbness encapsulated her body.

CHAPTER 33

Alpherge the Mighty, standing in the arrow shop, looked for an exit to escape from Clive. Ylfa's posture stiffened, and she gasped at the realization that Al was a wizard. Then she reached for Al.

Al leaned back from Ylfa. Her fingernails grazed his tunic but didn't hold.

Clive picked up a bow and bull-rushed toward a quiver of arrows.

Ylfa asked in a soft voice, "Why did you lie?"

He couldn't say anything through the thickness in his throat. A fire and cauldron of hot metal stood between Al and the back door. Al shook his head and headed toward the door.

Clive yelled, "Stop him."

With a quick and fluid motion, Ylfa grabbed a bow and reached for one still-cooling arrow from the rack.

Al raced out of the shop. An arrow thwacked the wall next to the open door, and he sprinted across the open practice field. He had to reach the cover of the forest before Clive and his buddy from the Hound and Chicken found arrows and began firing.

Ten steps into the safety of the forest, Al heard the first arrow thump against a tree. Al didn't believe that was a warning shot, and he dove for the forest ground. Three more arrows whizzed over his head and thwacked into trees in the forest.

Al wanted to use magic to shield his body, but something told him not to use magic near this village. He crawled on all fours, keeping his body low but moving fast.

A voice yelled out, "Come back here, wizard. We're not finished with you!"

Clive said, "He's running. Go after him."

Al veered to the left and zig-zagged through large spruce trees. The limbs smacked his face and arms. Being tall was not an advantage in the forest. He understood the need for silence to escape his assailants at night, but fear forced him to run. He had to get out of this area and pick up his staff.

Clive made just as much noise as Al, yet Clive gained on him. Every few yards, Clive would stop and let loose an arrow.

What could Al do to escape these guys? If he refused to use magic, what could he do? He didn't have the arm strength to climb a tree, and he didn't know the forest well enough to find a hiding spot. He thought about his staff and moved in the direction the staff relayed to him like a GPS homing device.

A nearby animal's roar stopped Al in his tracks.

Clive and his buddy also stopped running.

Al stepped in a direction away from the animal's sound.

An arrow whizzed over Al's head but hit nothing.

Suddenly, the animal charged at Al, came within ten feet, and stopped. It roared and rose onto its hind legs.

Al froze, the sound of his heartbeat thundering in his ears. This animal acted like a Montana bear, launching a fake attack to intimidate its competitors. If Al didn't move, then it might not fake the next attack. Did it see Al as a competitor or as dinner? The black animal had the size of a bear, a long muzzle, and a white stripe down its snout. It snarled and dropped back onto all four legs.

All Al could see were the large teeth and slobbering spit coming from its mouth.

Clive said, "No, don't shoot the stegox. Let it eat the guy or drive him back toward us."

"I don't want to get eaten by it," the other guy said.

"Don't worry, it'll eat the wizard, and we can go back to the tavern with Ylfa."

"Are you sure?"

"We don't want to waste all our arrows on the stegox."

The animal roared.

Al clapped his hands to his ears, and he wanted to fall to the ground and curl into a fetal position. He retreated from the animal.

The stegox backed away. Then it snarled, roared, and charged at Al again.

He gasped for air and tried to reason. No way could he go into hand-to-hand combat with the creature. Growing up in the Montana mountains, he knew there were two ways to handle bears. A black bear you might intimidate by looking big. A party of two or more hikers might raise their hands, make a lot of noise, and scare off the black bear. For a grizzly bear, you may save yourself by lying on the ground and covering your head. Was the stegox like either of those bears?

Treat it like a black bear and try to intimidate it. Despite his trembling body, Al raised his arms, waved, and yelled at the creature. "Hey, stegox."

The creature stopped charging ten feet away.

Al moved perpendicular to the animal. He couldn't afford to back up toward Clive. Maybe he could get the animal between himself and Clive. He shouted again, still waving his arms.

The animal snarled.

Al walked backward now, still targeting the staff but keeping his eyes on the stegox. He opened a distance of twenty-five feet.

The stegox roared and charged toward Al.

Al felt his blood pounding through his brain as his breathing came in deep rasps. Despite a strong desire to flee and his inner angst arguing to get out of the dangerous animal's way, he stood firm, waved his arms, and shouted at it again.

It might have been Al intimidating the stegox, or maybe it was just a false charge, but the animal stopped. The beast roared from ten feet away, showing a mouthful of sharp teeth.

Al felt the wind from its stinky breath.

He looked at the stegox, and it roared back at him.

He heard his attackers move. One of them stepped on a twig, cracking it. The stegox's earlier roars had caused every nocturnal animal to find shelter and stay silent, so the sound of the twig breaking carried through the quiet forest.

The stegox looked back at the men.

Al stood still, afraid to move a muscle.

The men from the Hound and Chicken weren't being stealthy. At least one of them shuffled his feet on the forest floor, causing leaves to rustle.

The stegox turned its attention in Clive's direction and charged at the two men.

Clive's buddy said, "Shoot it. It's coming toward us."

Al heard the twang of the arrow releasing, the whiz as it flew to its destination, and then the thump into the stegox's body.

The stegox screamed.

Everything stopped for a second.

Then leaves rustled, and bushes slapped against a moving body and each other. The animal charged through the forest toward Clive.

"Shoot it again."

"Run!" Clive shouted.

Al ran in the opposite direction, away from the stegox, from Clive, and from Svero Garden. He retrieved his staff and hurried to the road.

A human screamed in the forest.

Al felt a prickling on his scalp, and a shiver ran down his back. He clutched his staff and held it as a shield between himself and the scream.

CHAPTER 34

Al slept through the night and woke when a wet snout nuzzled his face. Startled awake, he rolled from the animal to the edge of the outcrop, almost falling from his little perch.

Fully awake, he noticed the animal was a bighorn sheep. Large horns curled off the top of its head. It had brown fur and a white muzzle, which highlighted its black nostrils and black lips. Al rolled farther from the bighorn.

Al screamed when he noticed he had rolled inches from a drop-off to a valley meadow a hundred feet below. He scurried back toward the bighorn sheep on the rock outcrop.

He scooted as far from the drop-off as he could get without irritating the ram. Once he felt safe, he surveyed the land below. The villages of Oakwood, Stone Bokken, and Svero Garden squatted in meadows in the distance. He didn't realize how far he had traveled and how far up into the mountains the path climbed. An icy breeze blew down from the mountaintop, and Al saw little lakes of blue with patches of snow dotting the landscape.

He also saw a figure walking up the path but still half the distance between where Al had slept and Svero Garden. He couldn't make out the figure in the distance and wondered if Clive had survived and still followed. It didn't matter who it was—Al needed to move in case the person presented a danger.

Al edged off the rock outcrop to the firm ground below, where he found the road. The bighorn sheep had moved to a precarious ledge and munched on a plant sticking from the wall.

This next part that Ylfa had told him about worried him most of all. He was to climb up rocks, a thin mountain path, and then a ladder of two hundred steps to reach Groft Kyrtill. There would be a meadow and a mountain lake, and somewhere in that area was Finn's hut.

The walk up the road warmed him, and the road had turned into a trail that contained more rocks than dirt. The trail became a series of cutbacks on the mountain's side, with Al having to take high steps over boulders to reach the next level of the path. Fine pebbles littered the trail, causing him to slip.

As he walked, the path of rock became thinner and thinner until he stood on a foot-wide ledge with a drop of ten feet to a rock below. A mountain wall stood on his left. The trail ended a few steps later, where Al saw a set of four iron steps pounded into the mountainside. Al looked down to a twelve-to-fifteen-foot drop and up to a small landing above if he could master the steps.

He tossed his staff onto the ledge above, placed his foot on the first rung, and grabbed the third rung with his hand. He looked down, shook his head, took a deep breath, and reached for the next handhold. After the three steps, his body was mostly over the ledge, but he found himself stuck. If he had something to pull on, the task would be easy, but one slip of his feet would send him tumbling off the mountainside.

Al tried to reach a handhold but couldn't since they were just out of his reach. He thought about launching his back foot and pushing himself but worried about what might happen if he didn't secure his landing. Adrenaline trickled into his body, and his heart beat faster—not because of the exertion but from fear.

He was stuck. Al couldn't go higher or back down, and he examined the rocks in front of him, desperate for a handhold.

Placing his palm flat on the rock ahead, he pushed up with his hand and his foot simultaneously, which took him to the next level, and he crawled to safety.

Deep breaths of relief washed over him as he lay on the rock. Why did this crazy wizard live way up here, anyway?

For the next few minutes, the trail ascended the rocks, going back and forth as it climbed. Every so often, the figures on the staff, Callahan and Isabel, made disparaging comments on how poorly he traversed the steps, breaking his concentration.

Then the next set of metal rungs presented itself—a set of twelve, except the seventh step had broken, and only a single piece of metal stuck from the rock. Al's height and long limbs allowed him to navigate the missing section, and he was happy to find a handhold at the top to propel him to the new level.

Trying to hold on to the staff the whole time became a serious concern for Al. It made it difficult to navigate the ladders. The next set of steps again ended in a section of rock on which it was difficult to find a place to put his hand, but Al figured out a way to position the staff between a couple of rocks. He pulled on the staff to lift himself off the rocks, and it slipped out of its position. He flung himself onto the rock outcrop.

Callahan said, "Are you trying to kill us?"

Isabel asked, "Isn't there another way up this blasted mountain? We're all going to die. We would have been safer in that last village, where the people disliked wizards."

"Quiet, all of you. It's a difficult path. We'll find a way, and I won't use you as a handhold next time."

They traveled in silence for the next few bends until Al reached a rock bridge. A large, flat section of rock, thirty-five feet long and two feet wide, connected the ends of two mountain paths. Two hundred feet below the bridge, a green lake lay surrounded by piles of snow.

Just looking at the distance, Al's chest constricted, and his insides quivered. He rubbed the back of his neck.

There are no handholds or side railings, and there's no way I'm going to the other side. This is the end of my journey. I can't go any farther. Even if I want to save everyone on this planet, I can't go across this bridge.

He sat on the path, his legs weak.

Wind swirled up and around the bridge. Off in the distance, birds flew in wide circles.

Coldness gripped him and he pulled his arms around his body for warmth. The distance looked insurmountable. He didn't know how or when he had become scared of heights, but this would be the moment that no matter how great a wizard he was, the bridge would break him.

If he created a magic shield and fell, would that cushion his fall? He couldn't imagine how tightrope walkers could walk over a small canyon or Niagara Falls on a single rope when he couldn't even picture himself walking over a bridge that was two feet wide.

Would the bridge hold his weight? Finn didn't need magic traps when he had a bridge that would crumble under any weight heavier than him.

A man called out from the other side of the bridge. "Hello."

Al looked to the other side as adrenaline rushed through his body.

The man wore a red robe over chain mail and carried a sword in his hands. "Are you coming over or not?"

Al shook his head adamantly. "No, I'm staying here. Come on over."

The man began to walk over the bridge. He probably weighed the same as or more than Al. Although not as tall as Al, the stranger was solid, with large thighs. And Al figured the sword and chain mail would bring up any missing difference.

The man stopped halfway.

Al waved at him. "Come on, I'll make room." He backed away to allow the man to pass him unobstructed.

The man didn't move. Instead, he said, "Okay, come across so we can duel, and let me ram this sword through your heart."

"I already told you I'm not coming across, and I'd rather pass on the sword-through-the-heart portion."

"You must."

"No, I don't think so." Al looked out over the edge and felt queasy. He was too afraid to cross the bridge with no one on it, and he would definitely not try with someone guarding the path.

"I am here to slay any troublemakers who try to cross this bridge."

"Well, I'm not planning on crossing."

Al noticed movement below him, but he couldn't tell whether it was human or animal as the shape disappeared into a spot below some rocks. Was that the person he saw earlier in the day? He decided someone was following him.

Al stood to get a better look but saw nothing. If it was Clive, then Al had to move. Clive didn't need to be too close to hurt or even kill him with a well-placed arrow.

The sword-wielding guy on the bridge waved his free arm in a come-here gesture. "Are you ready for me to smite you? No human has ever breached this bridge since I have been guarding it."

Maybe Al could hide in some other place until Clive went by. Let the guy with the sword kill Clive. It might be another wizard, someone that might not be happy to see Al there. It didn't matter. Al was out of options, and he had to get across the bridge.

He shook his head. What did he need to do to this guy? He didn't want to watch the guy fall to his death. The man might have a wife and family, while Al just wanted to get to the other side. He threw a fireball over the guy's head and let it burst into the air like fireworks, hoping the loud boom would distract his opponent.

The man ducked as the fireball passed overhead, even though Al knew he wasn't in danger. "Come on, then. A real man wouldn't use magic. They would use a sword like a true gentleman."

"That may be true, but I didn't bring a sword. All I know is magic."

"Okay, then, I was wrong to bring my sword." The man's clothing seemed to change colors; it was hard to tell since he had the sun at his back. Then the man said, "We are both wizards now. It is a fair fight." The man's clothing had changed to a black robe with red trim, and a black hood hid his face. The sword had become a staff with a crystal ball that made the light sparkle and shine in Al's eyes.

Al shuffled back a couple of steps and stared at the wizard. Was this one of Finn's magic traps? Was it Finn? What if he went into fatal combat with Finn and killed the guy? How would Al be able to know if this was Finn?

"I seek Finn, the wizard," Al said.

"Finn is dead. Turn around and go home."

"Are you Finn?"

"No, I'm the ghost of Groft Kyrtill, spirit of elusiveness, chosen by the ancients to guard this pass."

How does someone kill a ghost? *If the guy is a ghost, I should be able to walk by safely, without being injured.*

A fireball hit the mountain wall next to Al, shattering shards of rock that fell on Al's head.

Al ducked and backed to a safer location. Now what? He peeked over the side of the rock he hid behind, and the wizard maintained his position on the bridge. Well, he said he wasn't Finn. Al sent a fireball right at the wizard's chest. It went through the specter.

"Nice try, but you missed," the ghost-wizard said.

He returned fire, and Al ducked to stay alive. The fireball exploded against the rocks behind him. Al knew he hadn't missed his shot at the ghost. He sent a strong, concentrated gust of air at the ghost, hoping to knock it backward. It had no effect.

The apparition mimicked Al's spell and sent a powerful gust of wind at Al, forcing him back behind the rock. When the wind died, Al said to his staff, "Do you guys know how to kill a ghost?"

Callahan asked, "What kind of ghost?"

"I don't know. Just a ghost guarding the path to Finn's place. He claims to be the ghost of Groft Kyrtill."

Alpherge the Great within the staff said, "Finn has the ghost of Groft Kyrtill?" The character on the staff laughed.

"Do you know it?" Al asked.

"Yes. He's the mimicker ghost."

"The mimicker ghost?"

"Yes, whatever you do, he does. Whatever spell you send toward it, he'll send back at you."

The ghost of Groft Kyrtill signaled for Al to approach him on the bridge. "Come on, let's get it on. I'm ready to defend the bridge."

"I'm not coming across. Maybe I don't have to see Finn," Al shouted.

"Finn will be disappointed that I didn't kill you."

Al took a deep breath and thought of ways to cross the narrow path. *A mimicker ghost. If I fling a fireball, he fires back. If I shoot a shaft of air, he mimics my action.* His stomach churned as he thought of a solution. He closed his eyes, thinking of the possible ramifications if he chose this action. "Okay, I'm coming across."

"Ah, finally a chance to banish you to the depths of the mountain lake." The ghost pointed at the green mountain lake below.

He stared at the two-hundred-foot drop to the lake below. The best solution to defeat the ghost of Groft Kyrtill was to walk backward across the bridge. Theoretically, the ghost would imitate Al's behavior and walk backward away from him. *I hope the ghost doesn't shoot a fireball into my back.*

Al was going to vomit, right over the edge of the bridge. He closed his eyes and sighed. Then he opened his eyes, turned, and walked backward to the bridge.

The ghost of Groft Kyrtill watched Al but didn't move.

Al ran his hand through his hair. He wasn't actually on the bridge yet. *Sure, wait until I'm on the bridge and can't defend myself and then let the ghost shoot me with a fireball.* Al walked backward and took a tentative step onto the bridge. A quick glance over his shoulder to look at his adversary threw him off-balance, making him wobble right along the edge of the bridge. His heart pounded in his chest as he glanced at the lake below and steadied his quivering legs.

"Small baby steps." Al shuffled backwards. He kept his focus on the mountain in front. Twice, he looked at his feet on the bridge, but the distance to the ground below was too much, forcing Al to stop. His blood pounded in his ears. He concentrated on the far side and hoped he stayed on the bridge.

CHAPTER 35

A l continued sliding backward across the bridge. Each step filled him with dread since he couldn't look down but had to make sure he was walking straight back. He crossed the halfway point and didn't see the ghost, so he assumed the strategy was working.

He saw movement from the side of the bridge he had just left. A person had ducked back behind some rocks when Al glanced. The movement caused Al to lose his concentration and stumble. He wobbled to the right and corrected, overcorrected, and swayed back to the left. *Easy.* He wanted to close his eyes and center his body, but that just made him feel he would fall to his death. *Keep moving and let the next person encounter the ghost.*

Al hurried, not enough to make him think he might fall but to get to the other side faster. He reached the end and almost tumbled to the ground since the stone bridge stood on top of the path, causing a half-foot drop.

He turned away from the bridge expecting to see the ghost of Groft Kyrtill, but no one was there. As Al waited to catch his breath, he watched the other side of the bridge for movement. Not seeing anyone, he hurried along the mountain path.

He came across another set of metal rungs, got the hang of them, and easily managed over the ledge. Then he came to the last ladder. Two hundred rungs ran straight up a cliff face and exposed Al to dangers above, dangers below, and his fear of heights. His heart pounded as he stared at his destination high above him.

After the first ten rungs, he got into a rhythm and made good time to the thirtieth rung. Then his arms got tired, and his legs, already tired from the other challenges, shook. His hands became sweaty, and he wondered if he would drop the staff. He was supposed to leave the staff at the bottom and call it to come at the top, but he forgot, and now it seemed to get in the way with each rung.

He looked at the cliff top, but as he gazed at the rungs, the mountain cliff seemed to edge out as he went up. Would he be climbing the last few rungs at an angle that might make him fall if his hands became sweaty, or if he slipped? Would he hang over the countryside with his legs loose from the rungs and only his arms holding him to the side of the mountain?

Al was too high up and had worked too hard to get to this point to go back. He continued up past the fiftieth rung. He lost count and thought that it was the fiftieth. Another hundred and fifty to go.

At the hundredth rung, Al needed water. He needed a breather, someplace he could get off the rungs and rest. His arms burned. His legs shook, and it became more difficult to bring his foot to the next rung. No way could he do another hundred. He had to be the worst wizard to visit Finn. He wondered if there might be an easier way to the wizard's hut. Did Ylfa and Finn have a sense of humor and want to see who might make it this far? One hundred more rungs to go, and Al wondered if he would make it.

After another twenty rungs, Al grabbed with his left hand and moved his right foot at the same time. Sweat dripped in his eye, and he almost used his right hand to rub it. For a moment, he only had one foot on a rung, while his other limbs remained suspended in the air.

The experience made him go light-headed as he crashed against the rungs. He steadied himself while pain charged through his lungs, heart, and throat. He was thirsty, hungry, and tired, and his hands were scraped raw from grasping the rungs too tight. Blisters formed on his palms. His fingers were cramping.

He wrapped his arms around one rung and put the staff on a rung between his body and the wall. Al pushed back on the tips of his fingers to take out the cramping. He tried to leave the staff where it was, go up a rung, then grab the staff and go up again. That worked for a handful of rungs, but Al realized that would take forever. He just had to force himself up the mountain.

Suddenly, an enormous bird with a six-foot wingspan, white belly, and gray and black feathers brushed past him, screaming like a bird of prey. *Yikes, eagles and kestrels build their nests on mountain ledges.* Al watched the bird fly away from the edge of the cliff and then circle back at him.

Al huddled close to the rungs, and the bird grabbed a flap of his tunic and ripped the cloth with its claws. He rushed up two more rungs before the bird returned and clawed a six-inch scratch across his back. Al screamed in pain, and his legs went weak. Black spots floated in front of his eyes.

I can't let go. That'll be certain death. He scrambled up a few more rungs before the bird returned. Al waved the staff at it, not wanting to hurt it, but he had to keep it away from his body. The bird had a sharp beak. Traces of white feathers underneath the wing showed as it hovered for a moment in the air and circled back around. With deep gasping breaths, Al rushed up another seven steps. The bird didn't attack but continued to fly near his head every few seconds.

With ten more rungs to reach the top, the bird had stopped its attacks, and Al could see it in a nest where three baby birds chirped about food.

Al was done. He couldn't take another step. His legs shook. Like he imagined, the cliff bowed out at the top, which made it difficult to hold on to the rungs with his feet. He pushed down hard, but the shaking in his legs was too much. He couldn't deadlift his body with only his hands.

Even if he made it to the top, he didn't know if he had the physical or mental capability to crawl over the lip of the ledge. *Have I come this far just to die?* He would hold on until his body couldn't hold anymore and then just let go.

Al started a mantra. "One more rung," he chanted.

Then, using all his strength and mental toughness, he struggled up one rung.

"One more rung."

Another rung mastered.

He continued until the last rung. With a gasp and a quick movement, he threw the staff over the lip of the cliff onto the ledge. He held on with his hands and moved his feet another rung. The top of the cliff came into view. A meadow stretched out over the landscape.

This was the part that confused him—getting his body over the ledge. Did he put his hands on the plateau or one hand and one foot? He got a little rhythm going as he moved up and down on the rung and then threw an arm and a foot over the edge. Fear held his other hand to the rung. He tried to push off the rung and raise his leg higher to gain more purchase on the land. There was loose gravel there, and his leg slipped. His hand couldn't find a handle. His leg slid on the gravel.

Al screamed, "Stay up there." His hand on the rung grew tired. He couldn't go back down. He had to make it now. With a mighty effort, he kicked out his foot, trying to find a hold while reaching farther with his hand. He flattened his fingers and arm to the ground to give his body more surface area. Then he pushed with the leg still on the rungs and stopped sliding.

There was no time to rest. He was afraid to let go with his hand on the rung, but he didn't feel like he could move his body farther up the cliff, so he just hung suspended in that position for a moment. He knew that most people could do a task like this in a few seconds. Fear left him frozen on the side of the cliff two hundred feet from death.

CHAPTER 36

I *will not die on the side of this mountain today. I must survive today so I can see Sherry one more time.* He imagined Sherry standing on the other side of this last struggle. If he could get over the ledge, then he could give her a big kiss. *Do it for Sherry.*

With a deep breath and a mighty scream, Al hurled his body over the ledge, where he rolled three times away from the cliff, panting and sucking dirt into his parched mouth. He really hoped this was Stökkar Klettar, where Ylfa had told him Finn lived. There was no way he could do any more climbing.

Brushing himself off, Al found a log to sit on and dug into his travel bag for water while he examined the meadow. To his left stood a mountain wall that extended forty feet into the air. Before him, many-colored flowers waved across the meadow. On the right lay a lake, and beyond the lake, more mountain peaks rose in the distance. The food made Al feel better, but fatigue still closed in on him.

No mountain huts showed in the immediate area, though a trail led through the meadow. *Where does a crazy wizard put a hut to live in?* The thin air and lower levels of oxygen at this altitude made it difficult to breathe as he grabbed the staff and lumbered through the meadow path.

He kept the mountain wall on his left and the pond on his right and searched for intersecting trails that ran in either direction, but he found nothing and continued moving forward at his sluggish pace.

Twenty minutes later, a path crossed his. It ran from the mountain wall to the lake. *A ha! I've found him. The wizard must have a hut near the wall.* He turned toward the wall, which was a two-minute walk from his current location.

When he reached the wall, the trail stopped. There were no steps to go higher. No path along the wall to continue following. It just stopped. It looked like an area where someone could live. Two large boulders, taller than Al, stood a few steps from the wall. A large tree rose majestically above the boulders, which Al thought provided a pleasant shade for someone living there.

He touched the wall to make sure it was real. Assured at its permanence, he turned to leave. He paused when he saw a small, thin man with a ragged white beard walking in the meadow. Al raised his hand and called out, "Finn!"

A spider's web sprung from the boulders and tree and encapsulated Al in seconds. It wound itself around him, pinning him next to the wall.

Al had forgotten about the magic traps. He didn't remember who had warned him, but here it was. Al should have remembered after the battle with the ghost on the bridge, but he had forgotten to check for traps. "Arrggh."

He moved his right hand a few inches, and it became more entangled in the web. Did the web include a spider, or was the web itself the trap? His left arm held his staff pinned to the wall, unmovable in its position.

Al yelled, "Finn, come on, help. Let me go."

No one came to Al's rescue. He didn't see the man anymore and wondered if that person was a ghost too. Al struggled, which caused him to become more entangled. He tried to remember his times playing D&D back at home. Had he ever encountered a web trap? *How do I get out of something like this?*

Every time he moved, the web tightened until only his eyes were moveable. He suspected fire could burn the web, but what might happen to him? Would the whole web go up in flames and engulf him? A stick would clean up a real spider's web, but he couldn't move his left arm and therefore use the staff to clean the web.

A sudden coldness grasped at his core. He had worried about the cliff, and now he imagined several large spiders or one huge one coming to have him for dinner. His eyes widened, and he shrieked in a soprano voice, "Finn, help me!"

What did he have in his arsenal of magic to counteract a web? He thought he could create a sword of flames, which might cut the web but also catch the entire structure on fire. Could Al do anything to prevent his own death in case the flaming blade turned the web into an inferno? He remembered a magic command for a Fire Suit that allowed the wearer to withstand burning flames.

A light-hearted optimism sprang into his body as he took deep breaths to steady his panic.

Al chanted a few words, and his clothing became encased in a fire-retardant material. Then he created a flaming blade that emitted from his right hand as a sword. As the sword grew to its full three-foot-long size, the web burned and sizzled where the blade touched it.

A few strikes with the blade, and Al created a path through the web and detached himself from the wall. He walked out of the web trap, and when he passed the tree, he turned off the flame and removed the fire-retardant suit. He brushed his face and tunic to remove the remaining strands of web still sticking to his body.

His fingers trembled as he fell to his knees. He struggled to control his emotions while deep, gasping, panic-stricken breaths violently heaved through his body.

After cleaning off his body as best he could, he regained control and headed back to the path that ran through the meadow. The next intersection also sent a path to the wall. Would this be another trap? This time, Al used magic to sense the trap before he reached the wall, but he identified no traps.

The path ended at a hut next to the wall, and Al was sure he had found Finn's mountain hut. He knocked on the door and waited. No one answered. After several knocks with no response, he found a window and peered inside. No one lived here. The room was empty, with no clothing, food, tables, or beds. He opened the door and stepped inside, searching with magic for a trap door or secret that would tell him how to find Finn. Nothing.

Ready to leave the small hut, Al opened the door and found a wall of thorns between him and the trail. His throat tightened, and he slapped the doorframe in frustration. Did Finn test the wizards that came to him to compare their wizarding ability, or use these as training runs for the students he once educated?

Al didn't panic since he felt he could get through a wall of thorns. He tried a regular magic sword and hacked at the thorns, but they grew back faster than he could hack. Then he tried a cursing spell to see if he could get the thorns to wither, but they held. Again, they grew more and entered the little cabin.

His next choice would have been a magic fire—controlled, of course—but he stood in a wood hut and worried about that choice. He considered placing his asbestos suit back on, but he didn't want to burn down Finn's hut.

As he thought about the best option for removing the danger, the thorns continued to grow and form in the hut, pushing Al closer to the back wall. "Staff, do you have any ideas for stopping the growth of these vines and thorns?"

"Burn it," Callahan the Curious said.

"Use an axe," Isabel said.

"An axe might work." Al created a magical axe and began striking at the fast-growing thorns. He couldn't keep pace with their growth and finally tired of the exercise without making significant progress against the threat.

Isabel said, "Why are you using the axe with your hands? You know you can create many small axes that will do the work for you?"

Al smiled. He knew his tool bag of magic skills was lacking, since he grew up on Earth. He created ten small axes, not thinking it safe to create any more than that. Then he watched them hack at the threat.

It looked like a battle to Al. The axes made inroads into the thorns, but the thorns fought back, growing thick and fast. The axes chopped in a flurry of activity and opened a clear area around Al.

"Hey, it's working."

Then the thorns grew back, reclaiming the lost ground.

Alpherge the Great said, "Have you tried to spray a flame retardant on the hut and burn the thorns?"

"That's it. Let me try that." He didn't really spray flame retardant but said the magic words while he imagined the desired result. Not even a liquid, really. Al saw the hut covered in a large retardant blanket. "Here goes."

Isabel said, "I hope I don't get burned again."

"Me too." Al recited the words for magical fire, and the thorns began burning. For a couple of minutes, Al wondered if this idea might fail. Smoke filled the hut as the thorns in the room smoldered. Then a whoosh sounded outside the hut, and a large flame burned, the thorns sizzling where fresh growth touched the flame.

Al stayed low near the hut floor, coughing in smoke as his eyes teared.

It took ten minutes for the burn to clear enough space for Al to exit the hut, but once it died, Al jumped back onto the trail. He looked back at the hut, and the thorns unwound their twisted selves and disappeared. No harm to the hut at all.

When he returned to the path, he wondered if he should skip the next intersecting trail. How many of these tests did Finn create? Al could fight these things for the next week, and what would happen if he encountered an obstacle he couldn't beat?

The main trail wound through the meadow, but he saw in the distance a section with no flowers on it. A small granite dome separated the meadow. The dome looked to be about fifty feet high, and Al considered it an opportunity to scope out the meadow for a hut, a small village, or possibly views of Finn.

When he reached the dome, he probed the rocks with the staff five times to see if he could trigger a trap. Nothing happened. He stepped on the dome with only one foot in case the trap needed a human's touch. He waited.

Nothing.

Al stepped with both feet and stayed near the edge so he could jump off at a moment's notice.

Nothing.

He used his detect-magic spell on the dome, reaching out over a hundred yards, which was his maximum capability for that spell.

Nothing.

"Okay, let's go to the top and see what we can see." Al crept up the slight slope, watching for traps and concerned about finding a precipitous drop, preparing for the worst. Everything was okay. Nothing exploded, grew, pounced, or tackled him, and he continued to the top of the mound.

Al saw a small village a half-mile away, containing five buildings. There was a good-sized cavern next to the wall on his left, a lake to his right, and another hut near the lake. He heard a minor explosion and a woman's scream from his original path and looked back at the area where the web had exploded over him. He couldn't make out any faces but saw someone struggling and entangled in the web.

A woman's voice? Did Ylfa follow me? Maybe the noise was nothing more than another trap by Finn. He could make it sound like someone needed rescuing, and then when I attempted to help, the wizard would spring another snare entrapping me.

Where should I start, the cavern, the hut, or the village? Where would I live if I were a recluse wizard? The village would be nice, but everyone he'd spoken with had mentioned Finn living in a hut. Then the hut by the pond would be the logical choice.

The dome curved slightly down to a path through the meadow that headed to the hut. *I'm searching the hut.* Al took five steps on the granite dome, which suddenly turned to ice. Al tried to maintain his balance but slipped. He splayed his arms out to stay upright but ended up falling on his butt. He began to slide down the slippery dome gaining speed as he went.

CHAPTER 37

The staff slid down the hill. Al accelerated as the dome's steepness increased. He tried to find something to hold on to but failed. He screamed, not sure whether to enjoy the ride or fear a bad outcome. What would happen when he reached the bottom?

His skin tingled, which showed magic occurring nearby. He looked at the surrounding countryside but didn't see any wizards. So far, the situation looked okay. Maybe he could expect a hard bump at the bottom, but the ride was enjoyable overall.

The tingling increased, and Al's breath caught. Lying at the bottom of the dome in Al's current direction, the rocks weren't smooth and icy. Al hurtled toward pointed spikes. He recognized them for a magic spell called Spiky Swarm. They weren't there when he began his descent, but the dome had transformed, and Al was going to get hurt.

Finn had used an undetectable spell to create these traps. Spiky Swarm was visible to the naked eye only when close, and once you entered the area, you couldn't get out of the spiky stones without walking over them. Al wouldn't be able to get back up the icy dome, anyway. It was the Spiky Swarm or nothing.

Al thought of a spell that he thought might work against the spikes. "Disable Undetected Trap," he shouted.

The spikes looked more dangerous as he got closer.

A second spell came to mind as time slowed the nearer he came to the treacherous spikes. He shouted, "Disintegrate."

The air between Al and the spikes seemed to grow soupy, but the spikes didn't disappear. Time was running out.

Al's staff beat him to the spikes and bounced up and down, making a sound like wood bouncing off concrete. He heard Callahan and Isabel curse.

He had time for one more spell before his body would rip to shreds on the spiky rocks. Which should he try, Transform Rock to Mud or Stop Body in Motion? Al ran out of time and commanded, "Transform Rock to Mud."

The dome leveled, slowing Al's progress, and the spiked rocks turned to mud. He splattered into the muck.

The meadow trail was only about twenty feet away, but he was stuck in mud up to his chest. His staff had stuck upside down, and Al worried about its inhabitants. He plowed through the mire toward the staff.

He pulled the staff from the mud, which made a loud sucking sound when it released its grip.

"Was your intent to suffocate us?" Callahan the Curious asked.

Isabel said, "Was it not enough to drown and burn us? Do you spend every waking moment thinking of ways to torture us? I think the rocks might have marred my natural beauty."

Al examined the staff. Mud filled the crevices that formed the shapes of the faces, making all the staff's wizards unrecognizable. He would have to wash them in the pond. They would not like that.

It wasn't easy slogging through the thick quagmire, and it took nearly half an hour to reach dry land. He sat on the meadow trail and reversed the magic spell with a Dispel Magic chant that turned the mud back to rock. The icy section and the spiked rocks had resumed the shape of their normal granite dome.

He walked through the meadow, by the hut, and to the lake. He sat on a boulder by the water and gently washed the mud out of the staff's inhabitants. Isabel the Insidious gave him a mouthful of hateful words, and he noticed a slight gash in the wood right below her carved image.

"How long did you have this staff, Alpherge the Great?" Callahan asked.

"Fifty-seven years," the staff answered.

"And at no time in those fifty plus years did you burn us, drown us, or suffocate us in mud, right?"

Alpherge the Great said, "The boy is new at this stuff. Most wizards can't use a staff like this until they're in their forties. Give him a break."

"We might not live long enough for him to reach forty."

"He learns fast. We'll be all right."

"But will we?"

Al rubbed his forehead and grimaced. Was Finn in the hut, cavern, or the village? Al was tired of the games the wizard made for people that searched for him. *Just come out of hiding. Tell me you don't want to help and let me go home.*

He thought of Sherry. She had probably talked with the prince in Velidred and received his approval and a grant to build a large building to educate the kids. She probably was right now taking a hot bath after a full day's work as a teacher, enjoying life and not even thinking of Al.

He returned his attention to the problem at hand. He had a thirty-three percent chance of picking the right location to find the man on the first try. Was there any way to improve the odds? He could look through the hut's window and see if Finn was there. If not, then he could check out the cavern. If he went straight to the village, he would have to check each building. Maybe other students lived in the village. Why would Finn need an entire village all to himself? The village might have been useful in the past, but after he'd turned his apprentices to stone, were the buildings empty?

He got as much mud as possible off the staff without a brush that could dig deep into the crags and crevices. Al felt an ache in the front of his head, right behind his eyes. He held his head in his hands and groaned.

A whooping sound of joy echoed off the wall, and Al looked at the dome. A woman slid down the dome like he had. She acted like she enjoyed the experience, whooping and hollering like a kid with a toboggan after a snowstorm.

Al watched the woman for a few moments. The bottom section turned into the Spiky Swarm. Al needed a friend, and he switched the spikes to mud. The woman splashed into it. He hauled himself to his feet and walked back to the dome. He wanted to see this person who had followed him.

The woman came out of the mud, her hair and face caked in the stuff. She was smaller than Al, and she struggled to keep her mouth above the mud.

He waited for the woman to reach him on the trail.

When she got within ten feet of Al, she said, "What did you do that for?"

"I thought it would be easier than going through the rocky spikes."

She shook her head. "When you turned it to mud, you reversed the spell I threw moments before yours. My spell should have turned it into snow. I would still slide but not as fast as on ice. Now, I'm a stinking glob of muck."

That was the kind of day Al was having. Even when helping people, he did it wrong. He recognized the voice, but with all the mud, he didn't recognize her face. "Zita?"

The woman slabbed huge slobs of mud from her face, exposing one green eye.

"What are you doing here? Where's Erik?"

"Erik is studying healing and priestly things. I need to see Finn. There's something on my mind."

Al was about to turn the dome back to rock when he saw movement in the mud. An animal's head poked out of it.

A dog barked.

"Jackson, come on, boy."

A big black dog bounded out of the mud. It licked Zita's face, and then, with a long black tail wagging a mile a minute, it jumped up on Al and knocked him over. He fell to the ground, and the animal licked his face.

"Off, Jackson."

Jackson didn't move until Zita dragged him off.

The staff figure, Alpherge the Great, said, "The dog radiates energy and a little magic. What kind of dog is he?"

Zita giggled. "Oh, that." She flicked her wrist and shapeshifted Jackson back into the original lead box. "Jackson holds the Helmet of Justice." She turned Jackson back into a dog.

"How did you get the dog up two hundred steps?" Al asked.

"The question is, why did it take you so long to get up the ladder? I thought for sure you wouldn't make it and either step your way back down or fall. I was afraid to even start until you were all the way to the top."

"I went slow to enjoy the spectacular view."

"Hah, you were scared like a child."

Color rose in Al's cheeks.

"Have you checked the hut by the lake?"

"No, I'm tired of all the magic traps."

"I think they're great fun. Each one is a challenge, and I have to ask, how do I get out of this predicament? I was doing pretty well until someone dumped me into a hill of muck. I'm going down to the lake and washing off. Come on, Jackson." Zita strolled to the lake while Jackson scampered through the flowers.

How did she get Jackson up the ladder?

By the time Al got back to the lake, Zita had washed the mud off her body and was submerged in lake water to her shoulders. Her black hair looked mud free. She had her tunic off and was scrubbing it and wringing the mud from it. Jackson ran back and forth in the lake, chasing fish.

"Are you going to wash the mud out?"

Al stood next to the lake. "The water's cold."

"You baby. You can't walk around with mud all over you."

Al walked into the lake up to his knees, but the water was too cold, and he stopped there and cleaned his hair and face by splashing water up and over.

Zita said, "Turn around a second."

Al complied, and in a moment, Zita walked past him, the wet tunic fitted to her body and her hair dripping water. When she reached the shore, she used magic to dry her hair and tunic, and a magic brush combed out her hair.

Al stepped out, tunic still muddy, a patch of mud on his cheek, and with wet boots. The chilly mountain air cooled him. Shadows stood long on the meadow.

"Are you ready to check this hut?" Zita asked.

"No."

"Come on. I'll go with you and hold your hand." She giggled.

"Was Cugbert able to heal you?"

"Not completely. I get sick most mornings, but by noon I feel pretty good."

They checked the hut. The one-room hut contained a thin mattress on the floor, a table, one wooden chair, and a fireplace.

Nothing bad happened to them, and Al felt relieved when they left the building without incident.

Al asked, "Where do you think Finn is?"

"I'm betting the cavern."

"Why not the buildings? He had students, and they would need a classroom or a room to practice their magic. I bet that's where the stone statues are."

"Let's check the cavern first."

"No, I don't want to check the cavern."

"What could go wrong?"

"Anything. Everything. The guy likes to harass wizards."

Zita tramped off toward the cavern. Jackson ran through the meadow, its nose close to the ground but nowhere near the path. The dog poked its head above the flowers occasionally to check Zita's position then scurried through the flowers some more.

Al felt a weakness in his muscles. He stared at Zita and the dog. Fatigue washed over his body, and he wanted to lie down in the meadow and sleep. Instead, he took a deep breath and followed. "I don't want to get trapped in the cavern."

CHAPTER 38

After Prince Krunal's courtroom decision, the guards escorted Sherry toward the courtroom door, but before they reached it, she remembered her final defense. She didn't want to get whipped. She didn't want to be put in the stocks for twenty-four hours, and she definitely didn't want to be sent back to the prison where she knew she would be abused and die. She hoped this last proposal would help.

Sherry yelled out, "Prince Krunal!"

A guard slapped her.

She didn't care. "Prince Krunal. Why haven't you thanked me?"

The prince stood and raised his hand. "Wait."

The guards still pulled her to the door.

"Guards stand down."

Three guards stopped, but one kept pushing Sherry.

The mayor said, "Prince Krunal, there is no need to listen to a desperate woman that you found guilty."

He ignored the mayor. "What do you mean, why haven't I thanked you?"

One guard continued pushing her to the door.

Sherry resisted.

Prince Krunal commanded, "Stand down."

The guard stopped.

"Tell me what you mean."

Sherry looked at the prince. She looked at the guards, the mayor, and the people in the council room.

She had one chance to make her argument, and she reviewed different strategies in her head. The case had to be logical and make the prince feel guilty.

Sherry took a deep breath. "Why didn't King Haskell return to Velidred Castle?"

"I heard he died at the volcano."

"Do you think you should reward someone for his death?"

"I didn't care. My men defeated the castle guards, and we claimed the castle as our own."

"The warrior wizards didn't return?" Sherry's neck muscles felt tense, but she didn't dare move the chains and remind the prince he was having a conversation with a prisoner rather than a competent woman.

"We had wizards too."

"The mountain king trapped many of your warrior wizards in a dungeon until my friend rescued them. King Haskell was alive and well until my friends, Al, Erik, and I killed him."

The room took a collective gasp.

The mayor said, "You can't believe this nonsense, Your Majesty. She's trying to trick you."

"We are the reason you now have possession of the castle, and yet you haven't thanked us. Is this how you treat your friends, by putting them in prison and beating them? That sounds like something King Haskell would do."

"Stop this nonsense. Take her away," the mayor yelled.

A murmur rose in the crowd.

The herald said, "Quiet."

The prince waved a hand at the guards. "Bring her back to the front of the room."

As the guards dragged her back to the front of the room, the crowd talked amongst themselves. Sherry heard people who approved of her and others saying to forget prison and take her to the gallows. She knew she wasn't out of the woods. Removing the chains from her arms would give her a better position of power, but she couldn't see a path to that yet.

She needed an alternative strategy to going to prison. She could live after a whipping, and she thought sitting in the stocks for twenty-four hours wouldn't be too bad. Justin would kill her if she went to prison.

The herald quieted the room.

The mayor stood with a stiff posture, his muscles rigid and his neck muscles corded tight. Through clenched teeth, he said, "She's playing you, Your Majesty. She and her friends had no involvement in anything that happened at the volcano. It's a lie. That's what she does. Lies and manipulates people."

The prince stared hard at the mayor.

Sherry didn't wait for the prince to think about the mayor's comment. "When we first met you, Your Majesty, your forces were losing the war. My friend Erik offered critical suggestions for you to take the castle. Did you use his suggestions?"

The prince thought for a moment and nodded. "They proved valuable to our commanders."

He nodded for Sherry to continue, but she could tell by his tight expression he hadn't committed to her story.

"The king's warrior wizards killed Master Ishwa, right here in this village. That day they defeated and killed most of your magical defense team and captured the remaining students. My friend Alpherge was a member of your warrior wizards, and the king's men hauled them to the Velidred Castle dungeon. Al spearheaded the drive to help those captured escape the dungeon."

The mayor shouted, "Nothing but lies!"

"No! I've heard this story from the wizard Blaze," the prince replied. "We have confirmed it from other sources."

Sherry waited for the prince's words to register with the crowd.

Then she continued. "Al almost died in that dungeon. When he came out, he couldn't breathe because of the Marugotapa, a dangerous mold that grew in the dungeon chambers. Despite incredible odds, he kept going to the volcano and the solar eclipse. Al, Erik, and I defeated the mountain king. None of us could have done it alone. Before you sentence me to death, Your Majesty, please say a word of thanks for our service to you and"—Sherry gestured with one hand with a small rattle of the chains—"your loyal subjects."

The prince smiled a little, which turned into more of a smirk. "Thank you for your service. The kingdom thanks you for placing your life in danger to save my people from misery and starvation."

Sherry smiled and nodded to the prince.

Then the prince continued. "That doesn't absolve you of your crimes against the village of Crossroads. Doing a good deed and then blatantly disobeying orders doesn't relieve you of your duty to the village's citizens."

The mayor's smile spread from ear to ear. He sneered at Sherry.

"I understand completely, Your Majesty." *Let's see how much of this outrageous sentence I can remove.* "I ask a favor from you."

This would be the hard part. Sherry realized now that the prince wouldn't commute her sentence. He might lessen the sentence if she made the right appeal. Maybe less time in the stocks and fewer strokes with the whip.

The mayor's smile changed as he waited for Sherry's comments. He placed his hands on his hips and narrowed his eyes.

She was sure the man had a comeback to throw at the prince, but she had to make a play. *I can win nothing by holding back. I will ask for the best possible outcome, but I'm willing to accept a lesser agreement if it's better than going to prison.*

"Your Majesty, my crimes against the people of Crossroads were serious but not dangerous. If I were to walk the streets of this fine village, no one's life would be in danger. I'm not a hardened criminal or murderer."

The mayor rolled his eyes. "She's a prison escapee. We can't have her running loose in our community with her wild ideas."

A couple of members of the community voiced their agreement.

"Instead of prison time, I request community service."

"What is this community service?" Prince Krunal asked.

"I will help the people by improving the village in some fashion. I've heard it helps reform criminals in other. . . communities." She didn't think telling them it worked in a country on Earth would apply to the conversation.

"Do you have a proposal for us, or is this something that you request the village mayor to address?"

Heavens no. The mayor is the last person I can count on to make this fair. "I would like to make a suggestion and would like the mayor's agreement on it." She had to accept the fact that he would want a say in the service.

"Okay." The prince took a drink from a chalice next to his chair.

Sherry did not know what to propose up to this point. Here in the village of Crossroads, she couldn't pick up fast-food wrappers from the side of the road or sand-blast graffiti off buildings. The prince put down his cup, and a servant refilled it from a bottle of wine. Then a thought struck her.

"I propose—" She thought as fast as her mind could think if her idea would be possible. "I propose to create an aqueduct to bring in fresh water to Crossroads."

The mayor blustered, "That's preposterous."

The murmurs running through the crowd indicated they didn't think it was such a bad idea.

"Where would the water come from?" the mayor snorted.

Sherry glanced at Paxton and Kestrel. "From Triponca."

Paxton raised his eyebrows and smiled.

Kestrel shook his head.

The prince's opinion was the only one that mattered at the moment. He sat deep in thought.

The mayor yelled out, "Triponca is eight miles away! It'll never work."

"I guarantee I can bring fresh water from Triponca to Crossroads."

"Your Majesty, she's looking for a way to be free of prison so she can run away. A task like that will take years. The geography in the area is such that the idea has never been seriously considered."

"I can do it in three months. Before the winter snow falls."

Women in the crowd clapped.

"It's an outrageous trick to escape punishment for her crimes."

The prince was deep in thought. Sherry could only imagine what he might be thinking. The prince had to keep the mayor happy. What kind of precedent would this decision make in the future? Any criminal might make this request. How could he decide in each case?

A woman near the back of the room shouted, "The water in this village is dirty and smells of rotten eggs. We need fresh water."

A couple of men said, "Yeah."

"I can't keep the mayor's clothes clean with the village's dirty water," Ciara said.

The crowd laughed.

The mayor's face reddened, and a vein pulsed in his neck. "Shut up, Ciara."

The prince cleared his throat, and the crowd quieted.

Sherry's breath felt bottled up in her chest. She looked toward Paxton and Kestrel for assurance her plan might work.

They both shrugged in response.

"You have committed a crime against the people of Crossroads. We can't deny that or pretend it didn't happen."

Sherry chewed the inside of her lip.

"We also can't deny the service you have given the prince, the Kallurian nation, and the people of the Velidred Kingdom."

He gazed at Sherry. "Considering your crime and your service, I will adjust my ruling." He eyeballed the crowd, who all set on the edges of the benches, waiting for the prince's decree.

Hope bloomed in Sherry's chest.

CHAPTER 39

Sherry knew the prince was worried about the long-term consequences of his decision.

"I can't allow the defendant to go unpunished for her crimes. Therefore, I amend my decision. Give her five lashes with the whip."

The mayor groaned, "Your Majesty."

"Instead of twenty-four hours in the stocks, place her in the stocks till nightfall and then send her home."

Sherry hadn't realized she was holding her breath, but she released it. The sentencing wasn't complete, but she had hope.

"I regret that the village of Crossroads has dirty, smelly water. Foul water in a village this size leads to sickness." The prince looked at the mayor's wife. "The defendant will build an aqueduct to deliver fresh water to the village. She will have three months to complete the project, and if she cannot deliver on time, the mayor is free to place her in prison or the gallows."

Some people clapped, a couple cheered, and the murmur of conversation grew. The herald worked hard to bring the crowd back under control.

The prince waved his hand at the guards, and they moved her to the door.

Sherry looked back at the prince and mouthed, "Thank you."

The prince grimaced. "Wait, one more thing."

Sherry stopped. What else did the prince think of? She thought this was okay so far.

"You must report your progress to the mayor's office once a week. If you cannot appear each week, then we will consider you a prison escapee, and we will hire men to hunt you down and bring you back dead or alive. Agreed?"

"Yes, Your Majesty." *Yes. I can live with that request.*

The guards dragged her forcefully out of the room, and Sherry knew the punishment was just beginning. She hoped she could handle the pain from the whipping and the resulting scarring.

They marched her outside, where a couple of hundred people stood in the village square near the council building. A short, squirrelly-looking guy said, "You got what you deserved."

She wondered if everyone outside knew the full sequence of events yet. In a village this size, news would travel fast, but would it get shared the same way in every household? Each person would spin the tale differently based on the people's point of view of the sentence.

Could she complete an aqueduct in three months? That was an unknown that could still cost her life.

The guards led her to an open area in the village square.

A woman with a friendly smile and rosy cheeks came up to Sherry. "We're going to tie this rope around your waist."

Sherry wondered what that was all about.

The woman tied the rope around her waist, and when finished with the rope, she said, "Now sweetie, don't complain too much about this. The village wants a show, but you control yourself and keep your honor." Her eyes looked sad.

Sherry had no clue what the woman was saying. *Keep my honor?*

Then, with quick hands, she unclasped the buttons on the back of Sherry's tunic.

Sherry gasped as she realized what was about to happen.

When the woman finished with the buttons, she said, "Okay, get them off."

The guards wrestled the shackles off Sherry's wrist and held tight to her arms.

"Right arm first," the woman said.

The guards allowed the woman to slip the tunic over Sherry's arm, and it fell to her waist.

By instinct, Sherry tried to cover herself, but the guard's strong arms held firm. She still had her shift on. It would be okay.

They ran through the same process on the left side, and Sherry stood there with a shift on and her tunic top around her waist.

Sherry sweated through her shift as the noon sun beat hard on the village square. She felt a sense of vertigo, and her bottom lip trembled.

The woman touched Sherry's back. "I'm sorry, honey."

The crowd jeered, and a couple of guys whistled.

Sherry's eyes and cheeks felt hot. Her nose dripped as sobs trapped in her throat.

The woman touched Sherry's shoulder and whispered, "I'll put some cream on you after the whipping."

Despite the woman's gentle nature and apologetic words, Sherry stood in the town square in front of hundreds in only her smallclothes above her waist. They hadn't even hit her with the whip, yet she already felt broken. Sobs got trapped in her throat as she tried to maintain her dignity when every instinct told her to run and hide. She bowed her head and let her shoulders curl over her chest.

Justin stood in front of her, holding a whip. He flicked it at the ground, just missing her foot and causing a loud crack.

She couldn't breathe. She tried to hold her head up to look at Justin with defiance, but she couldn't manipulate her head in that direction.

"Let's get this started," Justin announced to the villagers.

The crowd cheered and jeered.

Justin stood to her left and practiced additional snaps against the ground.

Sherry jumped at the sound.

The crowd laughed.

The first whip tore through her linen shift and drew blood from her flesh, and Sherry screamed in pain. Her knees went weak and buckled, but she stayed firm. She stood back up as best she could.

Justin laughed. "That was just a practice one, right?" He came around in front of her and kissed her on the cheek. He whispered, "I'm not finished with you."

Kestrel pulled Justin away from Sherry. "Finish the whipping. I'm counting."

Would Kestrel expose himself to the rulers of Crossroads and the prince's guards to rescue her?

Justin cracked the whip at Kestrel.

Kestrel sidestepped the whip and pulled Justin close. "Just the woman. You can have a crack at me later when your friends, the guards, aren't around." He pushed Justin back.

Justin found his position next to Sherry and snapped the whip, which exploded across Sherry's freckled skin.

How could I have allowed this desire to educate these worthless peasants to lead me to this humiliation and pain? She bit her lip and tried not to cry out.

"Two."

Three more times, Justin made contact while Kestrel counted to five.

The crowd jeered.

"Barbarians," Sherry screamed.

Justin cracked the whip across her back once more until Kestrel wrestled the whip from him.

The guards threatened Kestrel, who stepped back from Justin and threw the whip to the ground.

The guards led her to the stocks. A wooden contraption to lock up criminals and shame them, hoping their embarrassment would prevent them from committing a crime in the future.

There were two stocks in the village square, one taller than the other. The guards escorted her to the smaller of the two. Sherry expected to see a bench to sit on, but there wasn't one. The guards forced her to bend over and manipulated her arms and head into the stocks. They shackled her arms to the wood.

Sherry stood the rest of the day in a hunched-over position. Her back ached with no way to reposition or stretch her muscles. The sun blazed across her fair skin, causing flames of sunburn to scorch her body.

The woman who had unbuttoned her shift came and spread a cream on Sherry's back where the whip had flayed her. Before she left, she bent down next to Sherry's face. "You did right nice, my lady. I hope you can bring us fresh water." She squeezed Sherry's shoulders.

As the shadows lengthened, Sherry felt emotionally numb despite the physical pain. Her back hurt, her shoulders burned, and her neck ached, and she stopped noticing the people who had abused her.

The prince left town and never stopped to check on her or to chide the community for their behavior toward the prisoner.

They're all barbarians.

CHAPTER 40

The trip back to Triponca in Paxton's coach was painful for Sherry. She had so many bruises, and bouncing on the hardwood benches caused her more pain. Her back screamed for pain medicine that could relieve the whip's sharp bites into her flesh and the fire that burned along each opened channel of skin. Muscles ached from bending over all afternoon. She felt broken.

Sherry leaned her head on Paxton's shoulder. She wanted to wallow in pity but knew her promise to build an aqueduct to bring fresh water from Triponca to Crossroads in three months would be a monumental task. Despite the pain she felt, she knew it was important to start the project immediately.

Sherry whispered, "What do you guys think about the aqueduct?"

Kestrel shook his head and rubbed his beard. "Three months? There's no way you can finish a project that size in three months, not even in three years."

"I promised."

"Who's going to help you?"

"I don't know."

"Where will you get the materials?"

"I haven't given it any thought."

"Why did you make that promise? Even with my father's help, it will take more time than you gave the prince."

Fatigue and pain wracked Sherry's body. She wrapped her arms tight around her chest. *Why did I make that promise?* She didn't know what materials they needed for this project. In a dull monotone voice, she said, "I just wanted to keep out of prison. I would have promised anything."

Kestrel said, "But—"

Paxton touched Kestrel's arm and shook his head. "We'll talk about the project tomorrow. For now, just heal." He pulled Sherry close to him.

* * * *

The next morning, Sherry sat on the porch eating breakfast and looking at the lake. The view offered a peaceful moment after all the stress and worry from the previous day.

Kestrel, Sherry, Lily, and Paxton studied maps Paxton had found in the house. The maps offered only a two-dimensional view.

Sherry rummaged through the maps. "We need a topographic map."

"What's that?" Paxton asked.

"It shows the heights and peaks of the surrounding area. How high is this hill? How does the land flow? Where are the steep cliffs and more gentle elevation changes? Which hill is higher, and if we run water from this point in Triponca to this point near Crossroads, will water flow in that direction?" She ran her finger across the map.

"I have nothing like that. Can't say I've ever seen one."

Sherry thought about the problem. Were there any topographic maps of this area on the planet? Had the people ever created one? Most of the people couldn't read, so they didn't have a local library. An internet search engine was obviously out of the question.

What did primitive people use to determine the altitude or height of a mountain? From junior high school science class, she remembered a project to figure out the height of a small mountaintop near the school. It required using a barometer to measure the barometric pressure of the mountaintop compared to the barometric pressure at sea level.

She looked at the people at the table and guessed they didn't have a barometer. Sherry remembered creating a homemade barometer with water, a bottle, and a jar one summer with Al. He would be a big help right now, with his math skills and creativity.

She needed other ways to measure the height of a mountain. Did she need to know the exact height of the location or just that it was higher or lower than the surrounding area and the village of Crossroads?

"Kestrel, can you do me a favor?"

He cocked his head and raised his right eyebrow. "Maybe."

"Can you fly over the area between one of the Triponca lakes and Crossroads and determine a rough estimate of a downward slope path?"

"What?"

Sherry pointed at the map. "Let's say you started at this lake. Then you followed the mountainside down to Crossroads as if you were riding Paxton's coach down the hill. But not just tumbling down uncontrolled. Stay close to the mountainside."

She pointed at Paxton. "Do you have a marble or a ball?"

"Let me see." He went back into the house and came back a few seconds later with a marble.

"Perfect." Sherry took the marble, placed it on one of the porch boards, and watched it roll to a point and then stop. "We need to create a path that allows the marble to roll all the way to Crossroads. Notice how it stopped in the dip in the wood."

"I guess I need to fix that, don't I?" Paxton smiled.

"Don't worry about it. The mountainside is perfect for our needs," Sherry said. "If the Triponca lakes were below Crossroads, we would have a problem. Our only concern is, can we control the flow of water from the lake to the village?"

Kestrel asked, "Why control it? Just let it flow down the hill."

"If it's uncontrolled, it'll just blast down the mountainside, and we'll end up wasting gallons of water every minute."

Sherry touched Kestrel on the shoulder. "As you fly over the mountain, look for sections where we can work without ropes to hold us to the mountain. A gentle descent rather than a cliff face."

"What plans do you have about labor, tools, wood, and whatever else you need?" Paxton asked.

Sherry scrubbed her hand through her hair. She loved the opportunity to work on a project to take her mind off the pain in her body, but she had no clue how to build an aqueduct.

They worked through the project for the rest of the day. Kestrel flew over the mountain for reconnaissance work, and then they would update their map to reflect what he found. Sherry, Lily, and Paxton talked about building methodology.

They would need lumber, a milling process, a resin, pitch, or tar to seal the wood, and a way to move lumber from where it was harvested to the mill. It might take three months to figure out all the plans and build the infrastructure.

She needed wood for burning, to harvest resin, and the ability to hold water. Could she make a concrete, metal, or ceramic pipe and forget the wood completely? She thought there could be areas to create a gravel creek to run the water, but she didn't know where to find the amount of gravel she needed.

By the end of the day, all her aches, pains, and bruises cried for attention, and she had to stop. *Why did I say three months? I need ten years to finish this project. The mayor knew from the moment I said it, he had won.*

CHAPTER 41

Al watched Zita enter the cavern. He stood outside and waited for the inevitable magic trap to spring, but nothing happened. She walked more deeply into the cavern until Al could no longer see her.

He searched the area for any sign of life as Jackson bounded into the cavern. Al shook his head. *I warned her not to go into the cavern. I hope she didn't expect me to rescue her.*

Zita said, "Hey, look at this."

"What is it?"

"Come in here. You gotta see it."

"Just tell me what it is."

"Don't be a baby. Nothing will happen."

"Why can't you tell me?" Al crossed his arms in front of his chest.

"Get in here."

"How do you know the magic trap doesn't require two people to be in the cavern at the same time?"

"Do you want to see this or not?"

"No. Really, I don't. Bring it out here so I can look at it."

"It's not something I can pick up."

Al sighed loudly and wrinkled his nose like the cavern had emitted a foul smell. He couldn't imagine what might be so important that it required him to come to Zita. Al licked his lips and shook his head. Then, against his better judgment, he headed into the cavern.

The cavern's interior smelled of dampness and mossy rock. Streaks of dark veins of rock were interspersed with lighter hues along the walls. The only light came from the front of the cave, which didn't reach Zita's location. He allowed his eyes to adjust and found Zita ten feet deeper in the cavern. Dripping water pinged into a pool. "You brought me in here to see a puddle?"

"Look at this. It's amazing."

Al looked at the water and saw an image of a man walking through the meadow. It looked like the man was walking from the buildings. *This is pretty cool.* The image in the water reminded Al of a television screen or a security system. The picture was in color.

"Is that Finn?"

Zita said, "I think so. I met him once at a castle party, but I was pretty young."

Jackson bounded out of the cavern into the fading sunlight.

Zita and Al ambled toward the cave entrance, but they didn't make it out before a wall grew up in front of them, blocking their exit.

Zita backed away from the wall and screamed.

The wall was composed of writhing, crawling insects, spiders, vermin, centipedes, and scorpions. A mass of creepy-crawlies crawled in the air from one side of the cavern to the other. They crawled and buzzed over and around one another, preventing the two wizards from exiting the cave.

Al tensed his muscles as his pulse quickened. He made an audible noise through his nose. "I told you, but you wouldn't listen. Do you think we can dash through it?"

"I'm not dashing through that. I'm not going anywhere near it." Zita backed from the wall of creepy-crawlies to the pool of water, hugging her waist.

Al laughed. "This is what you're afraid of?"

"Said the man who can't go up a flight of stairs without closing his eyes."

"It wasn't a flight of stairs. Two hundred rungs up a cliff face. That's a lot worse than this."

"Show me how it's done, then."

Al went to put his arm through the swirling mass and came within an inch but drew his arm back. There were too many bugs, and were those scorpions? Heat crept up his face. "I can't."

"See."

"If there weren't any scorpions, then I could."

A voice called out from the other side. "Are you kids comfortable in there?"

Al crossed his arms as a twitchy feeling sank into his toes. "Are you Finn?"

"Who's asking?"

"Alpherge the Mighty."

"The old wizard Alpherge is dead."

"Alpherge the Great is dead, but I'm his grandson, Alpherge the Mighty. Can you let us out?"

"You may call yourself Alpherge the Mighty, but I don't have to believe that's who you are. If you're so mighty, then let yourself out."

"Come on, we're here to see the wizard, Finn. We have questions to ask him."

"Finn's not here."

Zita snuck closer to the wall of creepy-crawlies. Through clenched teeth, forcing the sound out, she said, "I recognize you, Finn."

"Who's that with you, young Alpherge?"

"I'm Zita. King Haskell's daughter and I demand you release us immediately."

"No, I don't believe it. Alpherge's grandson and Haskell's daughter. Too bizarre to be true."

Al paced back and forth by the wall. His patience failed him. He looked at the ceiling and sighed. The day had been too long for this nonsense.

The man standing outside the cavern said, "Send out the staff. I want to examine it."

"Are you Finn?"

"Might be. Might be someone else."

Zita shouted, "Finn, I know it's you! Let us out."

"Haskell's daughter should be able to figure a magic way out of this trap. You've done better than others at solving the previous traps."

Zita's face reddened, and a sheen of sweat built on her forehead. "Enough! I'm going to send a fireball through the wall and scorch you."

"Poor decision. There is a slight rebound effect for some magic attempts."

Zita didn't listen and shot a fireball at the wall. The fireball grew big, hit the wall, and in slow motion, collapsed against the wall and rebounded toward Zita.

"Duck!"

Al hit the floor as the fireball flew past and exploded in the cavern behind him. Rocks fell from the ceiling and walls where the fireball hit.

"Told you," Finn said. "That's why the cavern gets a little bigger every time a wizard comes to see me. Throw the staff through the wall and I'll set you two free."

Zita said, "Go ahead. Give it to him."

"No. If he wants to look at it, then he can remove the wall, and we can talk like adults."

Zita stepped back from the crawling bugs.

Al tried to calm the tension rising in his muscles. *Why is this guy wasting our time?*

He walked back to the pool and saw Finn's image standing in front of the cavern. Jackson stood next to Finn as he rubbed behind Jackson's ears.

"Why are you being so difficult?" Zita asked.

"I'm not the one being difficult. The boy is the one with the problem. Give me two minutes with the staff, and I'll release you. The longer you wait to decide, the wider the wall of vermin will spread, leaving you with less room in the cavern."

The wall grew bigger and closer to Al and Zita.

Zita said, "Give him the staff."

"I'm not gonna let the guy bully me."

"The wall is getting bigger. Unless you have some way to stop it growing, then give Finn the staff."

"No one gives it back when I let them look at it," Al said, "It's mine."

"Do you ever listen to yourself? You sound like a five-year-old."

"Okay, I'll throw it out. Stop the growing wall."

"Agreed," Finn said.

Al tossed the staff through the insects and saw Finn in the reflecting pool catch the staff.

The wall kept growing.

Zita stomped her foot on the cavern floor. "You promised to stop the wall."

"You two are smart. Figure it out yourself. This is easy."

Al felt a tenseness in his stomach as he stalked close to the wall. "Don't do this to us."

"Oh, wow. Who do we have on this staff? Callahan and Isabel? What in the world?"

Callahan said, "It's Alpherge's fault."

Alpherge the Great said, "No one asked you to examine the staff. In fact, I purposely left it in my room out of your sight. And yet, you let yourself into my room, and look, here you are."

"You can let me out of here anytime. Or your grandson can."

"Alpherge, is that really your grandson?"

Zita screamed, "The wall is still growing!"

Alpherge the Great said, "He's wet behind the ears. They don't have magic schools on Earth."

"Right. That was where you sent the babies. I miss the daily news and gossip out here in the mountains."

Al's jaw hurt from the frustration building in his body. He grabbed a clump of his hair and pulled. "We had an agreement."

"Should I let them out?"

Alpherge the Great laughed. "They should be able to find a solution."

Al shook his head in disbelief. Even his grandfather was against him. "Zita, do you have any ideas?"

"Let me try fire against it." Zita closed her eyes, held up her palms toward the wall, and chanted. Fire burned from her hands. Though insects died, others quickly filled the void.

Zita said, "You try it too. If we kill enough of them at once, then we can kill them faster than they can refresh the void."

Finn yelled, "Nope, they'll fill in too fast. You need something else."

Al looked at Zita.

The buzzing of the insects grew, and Al's stomach tightened as the cavern's space decreased.

"We're running out of time." Zita continued to bombard the insect wall with fire.

Al joined the fight as he and Zita emitted fire at the wall, but like before, the insects replicated faster than the magic could kill them.

Finn looked up from studying the staff. "Told you."

Al said, "Let me try the command Prevent Chaos." He chanted at the wall, but it continued to close in on the young wizards.

"Come on, Finn. Give us a break," Zita yelled.

"Keep trying."

Al asked, "What if we tried a magical energy attack?" That kind of magic spell acted like touching a metal pole against an electric fence.

Zita shook her head, walked back to the wall, and then returned to stand next to Al. "I've only seen that used once. Can you control it?"

"Do we have other choices?" Al furrowed his eyebrows and waited for an answer from Zita. He had never actually tried the magical energy attack spell. He remembered reading about it once. Could he say the right words and handle the power from the attack?

"You won't kill us, will you?" Zita rubbed the back of her neck. "I'm sure Finn has other methods to escape this trap. Maybe we should look at alternatives."

"I'm tired of looking for alternatives." Al bit his lower lip. He wished he had the staff right now. He always felt more powerful with the staff, even if it did nothing since he hadn't learned all its secrets. *Wait. I can retrieve the staff right now.* "Come, staff."

Additional buzzing ensued, and Al felt the staff moving, but it slowed through the mass of insects. Isabel sputtered and mumbled about insects in her eyes.

The staff cleared the insect wall with a few scorpions, centipedes, and spiders clinging to it. Al caught the staff and brushed the insects off as Zita stomped them.

The buzzing, writhing wall of insects had pushed the teens to the back of the cavern.

Al pointed the staff head at the wall.

"Wait. There's a simple solution. We don't have to do this." Zita pleaded.

"Stoova tofrandi orku." The staff head glowed bluish-green, and Al jammed the staff into the mass of insects and arachnids. Nothing happened.

Then the wall exploded with a whoosh into a million pieces of dead arthropods, splattering Al, Zita, and Finn with their remains.

CHAPTER 42

They dined that night at Finn's cottage home in the village. Al ate three bowls of a tasty stew filled with vegetables and meat. The conversation lagged early in the meal since Al and Zita were still angry about all the traps.

Al asked, "I didn't see any animals here on the mountain. Where did the meat come from for tonight's stew?"

"One of the great mysteries in life that I will explain to you another day."

It irritated Al that Finn never gave direct answers. The team always had to make multiple requests for every piece of information they retrieved. They needed advice on the stone warriors, but Al wondered if Finn would tell them anything.

"What's the real reason you two have come?" Finn asked.

Al looked at Zita. Did she come here for the same reason as Al, or did she have a different mission?

Zita nodded at Al.

Al said, "I'm here to see if you have knowledge about how to release the stone warriors."

Finn didn't answer but stared off into the distance. He sighed.

"We want to rescue them. My friends and me. We have magic objects that we believe might help."

"Like what?" Finn's brows drew closer, and his face tightened.

"We have the Helmet of Justice and the Sword of Freedom."

Finn's steel-blue eyes lit with animation. "Exciting to know you have these magical objects, but the artifacts themselves won't release the stone warriors. You have to know how the warriors turned to stone." He began cleaning the table.

"That's why we're here. We want your advice. How were they turned to stone?"

"My advice is to leave it. The quest you seek is impossible. I've tried many spells over the years, and nothing changes." He stopped with a dish in his hands and looked at Al. "Having additional magic objects isn't enough. It's not extra magic that is needed. We need a paradigm shift."

Zita said, "That's why I'm here."

Finn stopped and stared at Zita. Silence filled the room. "Well, are you going to sit there all night?" he asked. "What is it?"

"Can I see your students?" Zita stood.

"I don't like to show them to visitors. Everyone knows they're here, but—" His face turned crimson, and he sank into a chair.

"Please, let me look, and we can talk." Zita softened her voice and touched his hand. "Please?"

The old wizard smiled at Zita and closed his hand over hers. His eyes crinkled at the corners, and he sighed. "I'm not proud of what happened to these poor souls. It's a terrible reminder of the power I hold in my hands."

He rose from the chair and led the group to the largest of the village buildings, a three-story structure with windows on the second and third floors.

Finn said, "This was the wizard schoolhouse. We used the upper floors for classes, discussions, potions, and dormitories."

He opened one of three doors on the building, and they entered an open room, that had large wooden posts the size of telephone poles holding up the floors above. A rough wooden floor covered the entire room.

Al thought it might be a big enough place to hold a school dance or some sporting event if the poles weren't in the way. Looking closer at one pole, he noticed charring blemished its base.

"The first floor we used for experimentation and spellcasting."

"And the students?" Zita asked.

Finn's face tightened. He pointed at the back of the room. "This way."

They walked through the large room, opened a door, and entered a kitchen containing a fireplace, a long wooden table with twelve chairs, and a wood-burning stove. A black kettle hung from a metal rod over the fireplace. There was no door to the next area, just an open arch that led to a patio and greenhouse.

"This is the conservatory. Our garden." Finn waved his hand to take in the room.

Green plants grew around the room in large ceramic pots. Un-ripened tomatoes hung heavy on green foliage. Flowers of red, yellow, purple, and white bloomed along a wall. Green beans grew in a six-foot tray in the middle of the room.

Something was wrong with the greenhouse. It had beams as if the room should support windows, but the windows were missing. The room was warmer than the outside temperature as if invisible windows held heat in the room. Al would have to ask how Finn achieved that effect. Al stopped short when he saw seven stone statues standing in single file in one aisle.

Finn walked to the statues. "I had to move them. He cast the spell turning them to stone when they were busy harvesting plants for a potion. I couldn't do my farming because they were in the way. We harvested most of my plants for potions from this building."

Then Finn moved closer to the stone students. The spell had turned one student to stone as he bent over gardening. Now he would spend eternity in that state. Finn walked over to a female statue, and he leaned in close and kissed its cheek.

She seemed older than the others.

Al and Zita walked around the statues. Zita thumped them with her fingernail and rubbed her hand up and down a cheek. She spent a minute with her hands on one student's shoulders as if trying to delve into the mystery of its creation.

Zita nodded at the statues. "Did my father do this?"

"Yes." He looked at Zita with distrust.

"Who concocted the spell?"

"I did. I taught the students the spell as we experimented on different carbon creatures. We knew how to turn them to stone, but we hadn't figured out how to bring them back to their original forms."

Al touched one statue and pulled his hand back quickly at its coldness. "Can you teach us how to perform this spell?"

"No. Never."

"I just thought—"

"Never ask again. I've done enough damage."

Al rubbed his hand through his hair. "If we know how to create the spell, that may help us determine a solution. You want to bring these kids back, don't you?"

Finn looked at the stone woman and rubbed his hand across her cheek; a look of longing and desire filled his eyes.

Al continued to talk. "Can you tell us parts of the spell, key indicators, talismans, or charms used?"

"No."

Zita stood next to Finn. "What's her name?"

"Ursula."

"Friend or lover?"

"My wife. We were married for a year before this happened. She didn't want me to go, to leave the mountain top. She sensed danger on the horizon, but an emergency meeting was called for the Council of Nine. The only reason I went was to resign from my position on the council. The meeting was out of cycle from the normal meetings, and Ursula felt it was unusual, especially with King Haskell conquering kingdoms and killing kings and queens. She begged me to stay."

Finn was silent for a few beats as he stroked Ursula's chin.

"Ursula and I had planned to travel and visit friends after I resigned."

Finn paused.

Al opened his mouth.

Zita touched his arm and shook her head. She mouthed, "Another time."

* * * *

Later that night, Al and Zita discussed the day's events as they sat by the fireplace. The wood had burned to coals, and their red glow provided the only light in the room. Finn had gone to bed.

Al was reading a book he found in a classroom. "We have to find out how the spell works if we want to correct it."

"He doesn't want to talk about it."

"What if we can convince him we'll bring Ursula back? If he gives us a bit of knowledge, then maybe we can solve the problem."

"What happens if she suffers the same fate as Dickerson?"

Al bowed his head as heat rushed to his face. "I don't want that to happen. But if we have more information, then we might have the knowledge to help."

"Give him time. He's lost a loved one."

"How many years ago? Five, eight, twenty?"

"It doesn't matter. Some of us take years to mourn those we lose." Zita fingered her mother's necklace and stared into the fire.

"So, tell me." Al tapped his foot on the floor. "What was your great idea?"

"Now that I've spoken with Finn, I don't know if it'll work."

"What was it? Maybe I can offer an opinion."

Zita stood from the chair and turned her back to Al. "No, it was stupid."

Al sighed. *Why won't these people just tell me things?* "Maybe it's something Finn hasn't thought to try yet. Did you notice these statues didn't talk the way the stone warriors did?"

"Yeah, it might take a little of the pain away from Finn if he could talk to Ursula."

"So?"

Zita turned to Al and tightened her jaw. "Are you going to pester me until I tell you?"

"Yeah."

Zita turned to the fire and wet her lips. She shook her head as if arguing with someone. "I can't."

"Give me a break. I'm your friend."

"What if it's stupid?"

"Then I'll laugh." Al snorted.

Zita smiled. "Yeah, I guess you will." She leaned toward the fire and spoke as if she were telling the fire a secret.

Al leaned closer to Zita.

Zita whispered, "We see the stone statues, so we assume they were humans turned into stone."

Al nodded.

"They talk to us, so we believe their bodies are inside the stone bodies."

"Right."

Zita paced back and forth in front of the fire. Great shadows moved across the walls and furniture as she paced.

"Remember Erik said all he saw was stone when he searched inside Dickerson? It's not like they have an outer covering of stone over a carbon-based body. Turning them to stone duplicated their bodies, but—" She paused in her steps and spoke as if she didn't believe what she was about to say. "The reason I thought about this was because of the secret chest Mom gave me. In fact, I stored your staff there when Kestrel wanted it back. The chest can hold things, but it disappears. It's sent to a new plane, where it hangs out undetected. I think King Haskell's spell sent their actual bodies to a different plane."

Al's skin tingled as he jerked his head back. "Brilliant! That explains it."

CHAPTER 43

Sherry held tight to a tree in the mountain forest as she surveyed a path for the aqueduct. In this area, the ground sloped at a fifteen-degree angle, which made it difficult to work. They had worked hard marking trees with whitewash, clearing brush, and mapping the path from Triponca to Crossroads.

It was already midafternoon when Sherry said, "We've only done one mile, and all we've done is examine the flow of the land." She wiped her brow of sweat and dirt. "How will we ever finish this project in three months?"

Paxton stood ten feet farther up the mountainside. "This is just like farming a large farm. In the early spring, you look at all the acreage and wonder, can you get the crop in the ground on time? And then in the fall the same question: how will we harvest it all before the snow falls? We do a little each day and see where it takes us."

Sherry smacked a mosquito feasting on her arm. "Another ten feet. Move to the next tree." They moved the tape measure, and Sherry marked whitewash on the tree. Some of these trees would have to be removed, while others would serve as a base for the wooden channel needed to run the water through.

A million thoughts raced through her mind: pine resin, clearing trees, footings, laborers, limestone, and time. The conversation in her brain always hinged on time.

Paxton yelled, "Okay, mark it."

She slapped whitewash on the tree and moved on to the next mark. Some of this was guesswork. They might end up building a section of the aqueduct and then having to rework it because the landscape didn't flow quite the way it appeared by eye.

"Mark." Paxton started to the next spot.

Sherry placed the brush in the leather bucket of whitewash, grabbed the cloth tape measure, and tried to wipe her brow as she repositioned to the next spot. Her foot caught on a tree root, and she tumbled forward. The curvature of the mountain prevented her from regaining balance, and her momentum carried her down. She held on to the tape measure, but her speed pulled it out of Paxton's hand as she lost balance and tumbled.

The bucket fell from her hands, and she used her forearm to prevent herself from crashing into a tree with her head. She fell to the ground. The bucket flipped in the air and landed on her back, and whitewash spilled over her tunic and into her hair.

"Argh," she yelled as spots floated before her. She lay crumpled on the forest floor, sucking in great gasping breaths to keep from screaming as the bucket tumbled on every open wound the whipping had left on her back. Tears formed in her eyes, but she would not give in to the pain.

Paxton laughed. "Great show, my lady. Nice landing."

Sherry checked for injuries, decided that she was fine, and slowly flipped over onto her back.

Paxton raced down to her location and helped her to her feet.

She brushed off her tunic and then tried to reach her back.

"Wait. Don't touch that."

"What's wrong?"

"You have half the bucket of paint on your back, and you've picked up every piece of leaf, bark, and dirt with the tunic and paint."

"Nooo." Sherry moaned. She went to wipe her brow with her sleeve.

Paxton grabbed her arm to stop her.

A quick glance at her arm showed paint and forest fragments on it too. Sherry grimaced.

"No one said it would be easy." Paxton laughed.

She enjoyed working with Paxton. He had a simple style about him. He wasn't bossy or objectionable. When she voiced concerns, he gave her feedback but would agree to her requests after a period of discussion or give solid reasons to use his ideas over hers.

He asked, "Are we done for the day?"

She picked up the bucket. "We still have paint, and we don't have enough time to waste an afternoon."

They recovered the tape measure and continued their surveying until dusk forced them to stop.

* * * *

The next day, they continued working their way down the mountainside. It took them an hour to reach the previous day's end point. The land topology and geology changed in this area as they encountered fewer trees and more boulders. The land flattened and then began a section of small rolling hills, which worried Sherry because water didn't flow uphill. If the ground contained rock, that would make it more difficult to run their aqueduct, and they might have to rethink some of the earlier sections.

She wondered if she should start in Crossroads and work up to Triponca. Didn't the engineers who built the train lines in the eighteen hundreds work from two separate points? What kind of survey equipment did they have?

Paxton cried out, "Hey, look at this."

Sherry hurried to his location. "What is it?"

Paxton pointed at a dry creek bed that ran across their proposed lane. "Can we incorporate this creek bed into our plans?"

"I think we have to since that represents a natural flow of water on this hill." Sherry studied the creek bed, which ran at an angle from their proposal. "Okay, we drop off our aqueduct structure into the creek bed. Do we lose some of the water as the soil absorbs it?"

"Only at first. Then the creek bed becomes saturated, and then you won't notice the loss. Plus, how long a stretch do we use?"

"I'm wondering how we pick it back up and force it in the direction we want it to go. A strong rain or a heavy snow melt, and the flood may eradicate any structure we create to divert only a little portion."

"Let's follow it and see where it leads. Maybe the landscape itself will tell us the answer." Paxton walked through the creek bed.

Sherry drew a white arrow on the boulder near the creek and followed him.

The land appeared to have sections where water had puddled over the years and contained a sandy flat bottom and a larger area of the creek.

"We might want to use this sand later." She dashed a slice of paint over nearby stones.

They walked another hundred yards, at which point the creek dropped in elevation over a short distance. It wouldn't be a waterfall, but water streaming across exposed limestone had worn a groove into the rock.

The creek angled off in the opposite direction than they wanted to go at that point. Out of curiosity, Sherry followed it another fifty yards and found where the winter snow runoff creek plummeted off the mountain as a waterfall.

She stared into the valley. Crossroads stood to their right, and the waterfall dropped at least fifty feet or more into a valley where the water ran left, and a hogback knoll prevented water from running toward Crossroads.

"That's the ridge Kestrel told us about." Paxton pointed at the hill separating the two meadows.

Sherry said, "If that wasn't there, it would make our lives easier."

"We could dig a trench or tunnel through it."

"And what if it's all granite? There's a reason the water has chosen the direction it has."

They retraced their steps back to the exposed limestone.

Sherry pointed at the limestone. "I think this is where we capture the water. We can dig under the limestone and build a small raceway to divert some of the water toward our structures, and it will withstand a heavy spring flood." She scanned the surroundings, looking for sections where the creek had escaped its bank.

"The area near the creek bed before the creek dips looks pretty flat. This might be a suitable spot to locate our operations center. We have limestone and trees, and once we get the previous section built, we run water down to this point with no concerns about letting it follow the creek bed until we're ready." Sherry walked up to a flat area above the creek. "How about here?"

Paxton examined the proposed area, commenting on trees and boulders in the area. "No, I think you want it over in this area. You'll have to drop fewer trees and have better access to our original water flow."

Sherry giggled and stood next to Paxton. "This is perfect." She went to move her hair out of her face. Her hand caught up in the paint and goo she couldn't get out of her hair the night before.

Paxton laughed.

She didn't care. They were making progress. The creek bed would keep them from having to build more aqueduct structures. There was a lot to do, but for the moment, she felt hopeful.

CHAPTER 44

Day three of the survey would have to wait until Sherry met with the mayor. She couldn't give him any reason to imprison her or prevent her from working on the project. Sherry and Paxton arrived at the mayor's office midmorning to find that he wasn't there, and they would have to wait.

They stood outside the village council building, studying the mountain as they waited.

Sherry said, "We can't afford to lose a whole day once a week to wait for the mayor."

"It's part of the bargain."

She knew that it was part of the bargain, and she mentally told herself to calm down. Getting agitated with the mayor would solve nothing. Sherry pointed at the mountains in the direction she thought Triponca was. "Look how much we have to do. It's been three days and we haven't even started."

Paxton took her hand and repositioned it to the left. "Triponca is actually there."

That didn't help Sherry feel better. The land between Triponca and Crossroads was filled with trees, hills, rocks, and valleys. "We'll never complete that distance in time."

The mayor walked up behind Sherry. "Yes, that's exactly what I'm counting on, at which point you'll receive the justice you deserve."

She crossed her arms and rolled her eyes as she turned to the mayor, "The prince gave me the proper justice. Why wouldn't you want to help us? Finishing the aqueduct will make you look good; you'll be a hero."

"Building an aqueduct between our villages"—he nodded to Paxton—"is a fool's errand. It's impossible and unnecessary. The rains will start in a month and refill the well, and the villagers will be happy."

"But you can have so much more." Sherry thought of running water—water coming into each home, providing everyone with a better waste system and a shower. She brushed her hand through her hair where the paint still clumped. "How many months out of the year do you run out of water or find the water reaches its dirty stage?"

"When will you bring the blonde girl in for her trial?"

"Never. Lily did nothing wrong, and I won't allow her to be harassed by your corrupt and abusive henchmen." Would she have to fight the battle over Lily's arrest every week? "I'm reporting to you for this week. Let's go, Paxton."

"I look forward to seeing you next week." He sneered. "We'll catch up with your blonde friend."

Sherry stepped back into Paxton's coach, her breathing quick and shallow as the heat built on her skin. Sweat formed on her cheeks, chin, and forehead. "We're going to build this aqueduct on time, and then I'm going to run for mayor of this village. That man infuriates me."

"I don't see Crossroads accepting a woman mayor."

"But Forest River Blossom runs her little village."

"She carries a lot of power in Tanuku, but they have their own mayor. A man."

"I don't care! It's time for this village to accept change. Women are so much more than this." Sherry waved her hand out the coach window as it picked up speed back to Triponca.

* * * *

It was midafternoon by the time they returned to their surveying work, where they had left off the day before. Sherry felt stressed. *How can we lose all this time every week?* They pushed back and forth down the mountainside, following the flow of the land as best they could.

Sometimes they had to back up as they encountered a granite boulder in the way. Those moments required reassessing the landscape and going back a quarter mile to rework the aqueduct run. This meant moving the path higher over the boulder or dropping the run lower. It didn't matter. Making these changes took time. Even with the surveying and analysis, she knew they were guessing. They might finish it all and find a critical dip or hill that would destroy everything.

Paxton said, "A couple more back and forth down this side and we'll end up in the meadow below. According to Kestrel, that will give us a run of a couple of miles."

Sherry knuckled her back and stretched her arms above her head. "We need that. Do you think we'll be able to dig a small ditch instead of using wood?"

"Once we get down there, we'll check it out."

As the shadows lengthened, Sherry felt the fatigue of the day catching up to her. They reached the mountain meadow, a fairly flat section where the water would run nicely. Paxton checked the flow of the land as Sherry continued painting trees and rocks in the path.

A twig cracked behind Sherry, causing her to stop. She had learned to check what animals might be behind her. She knew dangerous beasts might be in the forest.

A man said, "Hold it right there, little lady."

When she turned, she found the man twenty feet away with a bow and arrow pointed at her. She put the paint on the ground and raised her hands in surrender.

"Why are you painting trees on my property?" The man's long, scraggly gray beard bounced off his chest when he spoke. Long gray hair hung below his shoulders.

"Is this your property?"

"Go on, git."

"But sir, we need to run an aqueduct through here, to bring clean water to Crossroads."

"I don't know what an aqueduct is, but you aren't running anything through my property."

Sherry felt a tightness in her chest as she pinched her lips and rubbed the back of her neck. *This can't be happening. This land would be perfect for the aqueduct raceway.* It had a gentle slope, a place to set up another workstation, trees, and other needed resources easily available. They had spent the last two hours getting the path to work in this area. The man had to see reason.

"We don't need a lot of this land, just a path over by the mountain."

"Nope, been my family's property for hundreds of years. Can't use it. I know as soon as you and the mayor start using it, then he'll make up some excuse to steal the land from me."

She doubted this man had family at all. He looked like a hermit, just living off the land. He had three rabbits hanging from a belt.

"Is there some way we can get you to reconsider? Payment?" Sherry didn't have money and had no way to pay the man, but she had to think of something. "We'll work a split into the aqueduct. You can use it to irrigate your crops."

"My crops don't need a lot of irrigation."

Paxton came up behind her. "Hey, there's a hut down the way a bit."

The hermit said, "Stand over by the girl, young fella. You shouldn't be going through my things in the hut."

"I just saw your hut. I didn't go inside. Put the bow and arrow down. We aren't a danger to you."

"You're trespassing. Now git."

Paxton tried to reason with him. "We don't want to bother you, sir. If we could use a small portion of your property, over by the mountain there, you wouldn't even see the structure we build. It won't make noise, and you'll be able to use the fresh water we bring down from Triponca."

"I get fresh water when it rains."

"It might not rain again for a month. Imagine having fresh water flowing near you on those hot summer days."

"It's not a hardship to walk up the hill to one of the Triponca lakes. I got all day, and sometimes I can find game on the way back down. Now you two git." He let loose an arrow that thwacked into a tree behind Paxton.

Sherry looked at the arrow still bouncing on the tree and made eye contact with Paxton as they both raised their eyebrows. By the time her attention turned back to the hermit, he had another arrow nocked.

"Okay. We're leaving. Sorry to bother you." Paxton grabbed Sherry's arm.

She picked up the paint can, and they walked back up to a point in the mountain they hoped was off the hermit's property. "Is that really that man's property?"

Paxton said, "Doesn't matter, does it? Unless you think we should mount an army and force him off the land."

"No, we can't do that. It's not his fault we're running the aqueduct this way." Sherry looked at the dwindling sunlight. "We better head back home."

CHAPTER 45

The next day, they started at the point above the meadow and continued along the side of the mountain. The slope became steeper, and it would be dangerous working through here with large timber. Sherry wondered if she should try to reason with the hermit again.

Despite the rough terrain, they made significant progress, and by midmorning, they had reached a small canyon. The other side of the dry gorge stood eighty-five feet away. Sherry held onto a small tree as she caught her breath.

Paxton came up beside her. "How do we cross that expanse?"

"We'll have to build a bridge over the ravine."

"Do you think the other side is higher?"

"I can't tell from here. How come Kestrel didn't tell us about this?"

"The forest canopy is thick in this section."

"This is all limestone. Maybe we'll be able to use it."

Paxton wiped his face with a handkerchief. "I know you keep seeing all these resources, but how are you planning to mine the stone? Who's doing all this work? You and Lily?"

Sherry sighed. That was a question she hadn't the nerve to ask Paxton. She hoped he would lend some of his farmhands to help with the project. She knew that his time was valuable, and she probably had used too much of his generosity to get this far. They were only halfway done surveying and had taken most of the week to reach this point. He had been very generous with time and resources to care for Sherry and Lily. How much more would he be willing to part with?

Her chest muscles constricted, and she threw her hands up. "I. Don't. Know." She sat in the dirt with a heavy sigh.

Paxton sat next to her and gently stroked her arm. "It's okay. We'll figure it out together. I can spare some farmhands for the project for the next month to six weeks. Then the harvest season will start. We'll have to get them back for the harvest. When the crops are ready, we harvest, no matter what."

"I understand." The Anticletus moon headaches were beginning, and Sherry rubbed her temple. "Let's see if we can find a way to clear this canyon."

Without ropes and climbing equipment, the slope was impossible to climb. The landscape forced Sherry and Paxton to walk a quarter of a mile to a point where they could get into the gorge and back to the crossing point. Here, the ground appeared to be soft earth, and they thought they could build footings for posts to support the wooden aqueduct. Then they could bridge the distance. The walls stood thirty feet at the area's maximum point, and with the right size trees, they could support the water flowing over the gorge.

"Now let's see what's on the other side," Paxton said.

They walked back to the canyon entry point and climbed the opposite slope. The first sign of problems occurred when they ran into a boulder that required Sherry to stand on Paxton's shoulders to reach the top with the paint bucket. Paxton got a brief run up and somehow found a point on the wall where he could jump and reach Sherry's hands. She helped drag him up.

Paxton said, "That'll be inconvenient to work around."

Sherry surveyed the surrounding countryside. "We can find alternative paths to the top another day. For now, we can keep going."

They lined up with the paint marks on the other side and continued forward. A couple of boulders looked problematic, but Sherry and Paxton worked around them.

They measured and cleared twenty feet through thick brush—hard sweaty work that took time. They rested and ate lunch in a small clearing. Birds whistled to one another in the trees. Dragonflies buzzed overhead, and bumblebees checked out Sherry's lunch of bread, nuts, cheese, and water.

Paxton asked, "Why aren't you married?"

Sherry almost choked on the slice of cheese. She didn't know how to tell Paxton about Earth and its customs. "I'm not ready yet, and my boyfriend, Al, is off on a quest for something." She didn't know where Al was off to. Sherry was upset that Al hadn't stuck around until she returned. Why couldn't he wait a day or two?

"Oh, you're betrothed?"

Sherry snorted. "No." All kinds of questions churned in Sherry's mind. What if Al asked her to marry him? She would wait until the portal opened, and she reunited with her mother. Would they marry on Earth or Aloheno? "It's complicated."

"I see."

Sherry stared into his brown eyes that sparkled with spots that looked like pieces of gold. Paxton was a handsome man like his cousin, Kestrel, and she wondered why the man was asking these questions. Paxton had to be in his early thirties. His wife had died two years ago in a farming accident.

Sherry stood. "We better get back to work."

Paxton looked off into the distance with an empty stare. "Yeah," he mumbled.

CHAPTER 46

Day seven of the survey work dawned cloudy with a hint of rain and had brought them within two miles of Crossroads. The land was flattening. The aqueduct raceway would run along a narrow ridge, with a thirty-foot drop-off on either side. This wasn't land that anyone could farm or own, and it led to the meadows below, where the village of Crossroads sprawled.

Sherry thought they could finish the survey work today. Once they reached the meadow area, then it would be a straight shot to the village walls. She wanted to speak with Crossroad's blacksmith to see if he could make her some metal pipes. She didn't know what she could offer the man for the work if he had the capability. Maybe the village would pay the money for the pipes. It would help everyone, but she knew it would mean another argument with the mayor. For someone who claimed to work for the people, he found a lot of ways to be disagreeable.

Paxton cleared trees and bushes while Sherry brushed paint on boulders and trees.

When they stood within ninety yards of the meadow, Paxton called out, "Come here."

Sherry approached. "What?"

"Look."

Paxton stood in front of a twenty-foot-tall granite boulder that extended over both sides of the ridge.

Sherry's shoulders slumped, and she leaned her head against the boulder. "No. This was our best path to the meadow. This can't stop us. We'll have to build another mile around the mountain to get back here."

"Don't know of any way to get through this rock."

Sherry splashed the boulder with a quick dash of the paint bucket. "We go through it."

"It's granite, not limestone. You don't just go through granite."

She felt her chest stiffen as if someone pulled a corset too tight around her body. This close to the meadow, they couldn't go back up into the mountains. She screamed and kicked the boulder.

They examined the side of the ridge, but there was no way to divert the path along the edge. Its slope was too steep.

"Can Kestrel use magic to blast the granite to pieces?" Sherry asked.

"Maybe. I don't know how difficult a task that might be for a wizard."

"I say we continue as if Kestrel can blow this boulder to smithereens and our path is smooth before us."

"Okay."

"How do you and I get around the boulder?"

* * * *

The next day, they sat on the porch, planning strategy. They would work in one-mile sections. Lily, Kestrel, Paxton, and three of Paxton's farmhands would do the work. Not nearly enough people for the project but all they could afford. Kestrel sent a message to his father to see if he could spare a few people for the project.

The work involved felling trees as they worked toward Crossroads. They planned to split each tree into three lengthwise pieces. The two rough edges would be the sides, and the middle piece would be the bottom. They would create braces, small bridges, and structural parts as required. Topping the tree trunks would be part of the bracing.

After a tree was in place as part of the aqueduct, they would run a marble down the length to verify that water would flow. If the marble test failed, they had to rework it, even if it meant destroying everything they built for that section.

Sherry asked, "Can we use one of your horses?"

Paxton stared out over the lake and shook his head. "No, I'm sorry, but I can't allow that. If the horse gets injured, I won't be able to bring in the harvest."

"That means we would have to haul—by hand—one hundred and eighty logs for every mile we clear." Sherry knew horses were in short supply in Triponca and even in Crossroads. She didn't know why so few had been bred for riding or heavy farm work.

He rubbed his hand over his eye and face. "I understand how this will make the task more difficult, and I'm sorry, but I can't risk my animals. That's my livelihood, and the uneven terrain where you're building the aqueduct will make it too dangerous."

Kestrel said, "I'll move the logs with magic. We don't need horses."

Paxton said, "Don't you have to worry about magic sickness if you use your magic too much? You'll require extra rest. Are you willing to risk it?"

Lily smiled at Kestrel.

He nodded. "I can do it. I'm not worried. That's for old wizards, not us young guys."

"Okay, that'll help." Sherry wrote a comment on a piece of paper. "That leaves the resin needed to seal the transition points and the corners of the log structures. Lily and I will harvest resin from the trees and prepare it for the logs."

"Have you ever done that?" Lily asked.

"Nope, I'm hoping that's something that will work. I think it will. We'll need some metal buckets, I think."

"I can provide a few of those," Paxton volunteered.

"I have to warn you they might not be useable for the harvest after we experiment with them."

"I'll give you two. If your experiments work, maybe I will give you more."

After lunch, Sherry and Lily headed out into the forest where the aqueduct would begin. Adrenaline coursed through Sherry's body as they started the first part of the building process. They each had a short axe and a bucket. Sherry was eager to see if all the book learning she had in school would translate into useful skills.

They set up around a pine tree.

"Do we have to climb the tree?" Lily asked.

"No, we stay close to the ground. I think for our purposes, we should be able to work within three to five feet of the ground."

Sherry placed the bucket next to the tree and hacked into the tree above the bucket. She trimmed off the bark and cut deeper into the inner wood. She tried to cut a V shape to help the sap run out.

The task proved harder than she imagined, but after multiple strikes with the axe and some heavy breathing, liquid ran from the tree. It flowed down the bark but slowed and hardened as it neared the bucket.

She couldn't get the bucket close enough to the flow when it was on the ground, so she picked the bucket up and held it under the flowing resin.

"We can't hold the bucket under the sap all day," Lily said.

"We need to get the sap to run a few inches from the tree. Run back to the farm and see if they have a metal piece we can stick into the tree. It needs to be flat or V-shaped."

Kestrel and the farmhands stood a hundred yards away, and Sherry heard a saw working its way across a tree trunk.

They were making progress. She smiled and readjusted the bucket to catch more of the liquid. A small spider with a brown body and white and brown stripes across its legs ran across the flowing sap and was swept away into the bucket.

The bucket became heavy before Lily returned with two V-shaped metal pieces and a couple of large nails. Sherry used the back of the axe to hammer a nail into the tree. Then she pounded the wedge-shaped metal piece under the flowing liquid, getting a quantity of the sap between her fingers.

The contraption worked, and the girls almost hugged until Sherry realized she would get the sticky goop all over Lily's back.

A crash of a tree and a yell of satisfaction came from the forest.

Lily did the work on the second tree. The process took a little longer, and more of the goop ended on her hands, but she and Sherry cheered in satisfaction.

Sherry asked, "How's it going with Kestrel and you?"

Lily answered in a bubbly voice, "I liked him when we first met back on Earth, but now that I see him on his home planet and understand his powers… I'm in love."

Sherry didn't know how Lily could *love* the man that almost sacrificed her just a few months ago. She gave her head a slight shake. "Don't you want to go back to Earth?"

Lily was silent for almost a minute as she scooped a bug out of a half-full bucket of resin. "No. If it means leaving Kestrel here in this world, then I'm willing to stay here with him."

Sherry's eyes widened, and she tried to maintain a smile for her friend's benefit. *Will I have to make a choice to lose my friends if I go home when the portal opens?* She had never imagined that any of them would stay on Aloheno. If Lily stayed with Kestrel, she wondered if Zita and Erik's relationship would keep Erik on this world too.

"You and Al could stay with us at Kestrel's castle." Lily smiled at Sherry.

Even after being mistreated by King Haskell, Kestrel, and the mayor, Lily still wanted to remain on this planet. "I don't see Al talking me into staying. I want to go home. I want hot water, showers, cars, the internet, and air travel." She would not stay in this underdeveloped civilization.

"If we build this aqueduct thingy, then next you can create running water in the village, and we can have hot baths and showers. It's just a matter of time. You'll be remembered for centuries as the person who brought modern-day plumbing to Crossroads. You'll be famous." Lily laughed.

Sherry pursed her lips in thought. Was fame on this planet worth the cost? If the mayor and his cronies hated her for trying to teach their children, there would be *more* people working to prevent her from bringing other advanced technologies. She smirked and rolled her eyes. "That's fame I can do without."

It took a few hours, but Sherry collected a bucketful of pine resin. Bark, leaves, a couple of wasps, at least one spider, and a bumblebee were mixed into the substance. The bucket was heavy, and the sap had congealed into a dried gooey mixture. It wouldn't pour out into the corners of the raceway to act as a sealant in its present form, forcing Sherry to heat it before using it.

They created a fire with limbs they picked up from the ground. The cleared area provided protection from a forest fire, assuming the wind didn't strengthen. Four logs laid in a square pattern created a way to set the bucket on top of the fire.

"This should do," Sherry said. "Stand back in case I'm wrong."

Lily moved back a few steps.

Sherry had to use two hands to place the heavy bucket on the logs. She stepped back toward Lily.

"How long do you think it will take to heat it up?"

"A few minutes, I'm guessing, same as water."

"It'll be hot. You'll need something to grab the handle with."

Sherry thought about it. "We'll use a stick between us to pick it up and move it safely."

Lily clapped her hands. "Perfect."

Fire licked the top of the bucket, which then exploded into a flame seven feet high.

CHAPTER 47

Two weeks later, Sherry and Paxton entered Crossroads for her weekly visit with the mayor. Sherry knocked on the mayor's door.

"Come in."

They entered and found the mayor and former students Gabriella and Travis in the room. Mooney and Justin stood next to the students.

"I'm reporting for my weekly visit. I haven't run away."

The mayor sneered and leaned in closer to her. "Yeah? I want to keep a closer watch on you."

"Why?"

The mayor raised his chin and approached Sherry. "I have a vested interest in the outcome of this project."

"What do you plan to do? I won't accept Justin anywhere near the project. I'll shoot the arrow at the man myself if necessary."

He raised his voice and stood within a few feet of her. "Such anger and aggression. I would expect better behavior from a criminal that is doing community service and only because we allow it."

Sherry sighed.

"No, not Justin." He turned toward Travis and Gabriella. "Mr. Mooney and Travis's parents have allowed their children to help you."

Sherry smiled at Gabriella. This project would be significant for her. Gabriella would learn project management skills, math, and construction knowledge. Sherry welcomed her.

Travis asked, "Lily didn't come with you?"

"No, Lily is hard at work building the aqueduct. Are you going to listen to instructions and work hard?" Sherry raised her eyebrows at him.

"Yes, ma'am, I'm a hard worker."

Sherry doubted that.

The mayor said, "They will stay with you, and each week when you check in, bring them with you so their parents can make sure they're okay."

Sherry shook her head but said, "Okay."

When they came out of the mayor's office, a large crowd had gathered around the square. Sherry looked cautiously at the people milling about, and concerns of being imprisoned again flashed through her mind. Why did the mayor bring all these people to the village council building? She felt a slight quiver in her stomach as she evaluated the situation. With a quick grab of Paxton's arm, she pulled him toward her and whispered, "Watch out. This might be a trap."

"No, I don't think so." Paxton held her arm. "The priest must be in town."

They made their way toward Paxton's coach, stepping between men, women, and children jamming the square.

She opened the coach door and helped her two new helpers get into the carriage. Gabriella got in first, and Travis quickly stepped in and sat beside Gabriella. He should have waited for Sherry. The first thing she would do was teach the boy some manners.

With a glance at the crowd, she stepped into the coach. Sherry stared out the window at the people, feeling bad she couldn't do something for them.

Paxton banged his hand on the coach's side and directed the driver to go.

Travis said, "You must be rich to have a coach. My dad says only rich people have coaches."

Such an impertinent little boy. "Travis, it isn't polite to talk to people about their money."

"My dad told me only rich people own coaches." Travis rubbed his nose with his garment sleeve.

The coach nudged through the thronging people as the driver guided the horse and coach with care.

Sherry felt a lightness in her chest. *What did Paxton say? The priest is in town?* Sherry yelled, "Stop!"

The coach rumbled forward.

"Did you forget something?" Paxton asked.

Sherry fumbled the coach door's latch and opened it as the coach still moved. "Please stop."

"This isn't the best place to stop."

Sherry jumped out of the moving vehicle, almost falling on her face. She gained control and stood while studying the crowd.

Travis asked, "Where's she going?"

"I don't know." Paxton banged on the coach door. "Stop the coach."

Sherry examined the crowd to see if they were queuing in any manner. The smell of freshly baked bread filled the air. She trembled as she yelled out, "Cugbert!" The man was a giant compared to the villagers, and he should be easy to find in this crowd.

She ran through the crowd as adrenaline pulsed through her body. "Cugbert."

Paxton caught up to her. "Is everything okay?"

"You told me the priest was in town." She yelled, "Cugbert." Then she saw him. Not Cugbert but Erik, dipping a ladle into a giant pot and pouring hot soup into a bowl held by a young woman. Two young children, not even five years old, held on to the woman's skirt.

Erik said to the woman, "We have plenty of soup. You come back and make sure your children get some. There's bread at the next table."

Sherry ran to the table, bumping into people and dodging children. The whole time, she shouted and waved. "Erik. Erik. Erik."

Her friend from Earth focused on the people he served. He spoke to the men, women, and children as he ladled liquid nourishment into their bowls.

She skirted around the table and stood next to him. "Erik."

He looked at Sherry without recognition. Then something must have clicked because he dropped the ladle into the pot of soup, picked Sherry off the ground, and hugged her.

Warmth spread through her body as he continued the hug.

He put her down. "How are you?" He looked at Sherry for a moment and then turned his attention to the crowd as if searching for someone else.

"She's not here." Erik was thinner than when he left on his quest, but she could see muscles bulging in his arms and shoulders.

His shoulders drooped.

"Oh, cheer up. She isn't here with me, but she's at the farm. She'll be so excited to know we saw you," Sherry said.

Erik smiled, but it didn't reach his eyes. "Are you okay?"

"Yes and no. I have so much to tell you since you've been away. Where's Al?"

"Al isn't back yet? His task should have taken a week at most." He looked at her a moment longer.

Icy fingers touched her neck, and she felt an ache in her throat. "You let him go on his own?"

"I had to get back to my training with Cugbert. Didn't he stop to see you before he left?"

Sherry wanted to tell him so much, but here wasn't the place or time.

Paxton came up beside Sherry. "Can you and Cugbert visit us tonight? We'll make a feast, and we have beds for you."

Erik looked at Sherry and raised his eyebrows.

She patted his hand. "Please come see us. Lily is there, and so are. . . others you haven't seen in a while." Sherry hadn't forgotten that Kestrel and Lily were getting closer every day, spending time on the porch talking and kissing. She wondered if Erik would be okay with that.

"I'll talk with Cugbert."

Paxton said, "I'll send my coach for you."

Erik grabbed the ladle and returned to feeding the people, ladling soup while looking at Sherry with sad eyes.

What bad news does he have for me?

* * * *

At dinner that night, Erik listened while Sherry explained the aqueduct project. He couldn't believe she had taken on that endeavor. There must have been easier community service tasks she could have chosen. She could have joined him and Cugbert in feeding the homeless and jobless.

"Do you really think you can finish this in the next two months?" Erik concentrated on Sherry despite being distracted watching Lily, who sat on the opposite side of the table. He needed to talk with Lily alone and tell her that his heart belonged to Zita now.

Sherry said, "Erik and Cugbert, stay and help us. What could be more service oriented than bringing fresh water to a village?"

Cugbert took a bite of chicken and looked at Erik.

Erik could tell by the look that Cugbert planned to move on, and Erik would have to decide to continue his studies with Cugbert or help his friend. He couldn't let Sherry and Lily go back to prison, but he needed to keep up his training with Cugbert.

Cugbert said, "Fresh water diverted to the town is indeed important. Providing food to the poor and homeless is important too. We heal the minds, bodies, and spirits of those we help. We have to prepare these people for winter, which is coming on quickly."

Erik looked down at his plate of chicken, peas, and carrots. Paxton had a successful farm, and not everyone in Crossroads ate this well. Many were well past their pickled winter foods, surviving on bread and water until the next harvest. Erik received such a boost in confidence when he healed a child or an elderly woman with signs of arthritis. Would he be willing to give that up to help Sherry?

After dinner, Gabriella, Travis, Paxton, and Kestrel retired early, and Cugbert, Sherry, Lily, and Erik sat on the large farm porch, looking at the stars, and telling stories of what had happened the last few months. Erik showed them the Sword of Freedom.

Cugbert said, "It's a dangerous tool in the hands of a fool. You should toss it into the lake and be done with it."

"We want to use it to rescue the stone warriors."

"I know that you have killed one stone warrior with your foolish attempt at something you know nothing about."

"This is all about becoming a priest and nothing about the sword." Erik didn't know why Cugbert had steered the conversation in this direction. For the last month, they had worked side by side, and Cugbert had been silent about the sword.

"Shove it in a pit and bury it."

"I won't part with it until we try again. Plus, you know how powerful it is in healing people."

Cugbert stood and towered over Erik. "Decide your true calling. Is it to be a priest, a warrior, or with your friends? You can't be all things to all people. Specialization is difficult, but you have to trust your gut instinct."

Erik's gut instinct was pulling him in a dozen different directions. Right now, he felt a genuine need to help Sherry build the aqueduct. If he let Cugbert walk away again, would Cugbert ever offer to train him again? Was this his last chance?

"A sword is the tool of a warrior. I've carried a sword and killed enemies. I put down the sword and became a healer. As long as you carry the sword, people will not see you as a healer and priest. They will see you as a warrior."

Erik never won arguments with Cugbert. The priest worked from logic and caring for people, while it seemed Erik always let emotion choose his path for him. Was he working to rescue his father to gain respect or because of an altruistic desire to help others? Cugbert was one of the elite warriors. How did he make the switch to priest?

Cugbert headed to the door. "I'm leaving in the morning, and if you want to be a priest, you need to leave with me. We have work and training to do."

Erik looked out at the stars. *What should I do?*

After Cugbert left, Sherry pulled her chair next to Erik's. "We need you for this project. We are so shorthanded and will never finish this on time. Can't you stay and help? Talk to Cugbert and get him to stay too."

"He's already decided. Cugbert is committed to his cause the same way you're committed to yours. He likes to tell me, 'You don't help others to make yourself feel better. You help others to make the world feel better.'"

Sherry leaned close to Erik. "Building the aqueduct is the right thing to do. The water in the village is horrible. We"—she pointed at Lily—"are making the lives of the citizens of Crossroads better."

"I know you are. And based on your stories tonight, you're doing a great job and—"

"If we don't finish the project, then we'll have done nothing. If we get the water near Crossroads, that won't help anyone. It has to go all the way to the village in two months. Can't you spare two months from your training?"

CHAPTER 48

Moments after sunrise, a bell rang, which startled Erik awake. It took him a moment to remember where he was. Sleeping on straw mattresses at the farm was more comfortable than his normal sleeping arrangements on the ground under the stars.

He searched for Cugbert at breakfast, but the priest had already left. Cugbert didn't even bother to wake Erik. He must have known what Erik's decision would be. Was this Erik's last chance to become a priest, and had he failed?

Sherry showed Erik and the two kids, Travis and Gabriella, how the aqueduct would work. "When we open the gates at the lake, water will flow into the raceway. This occurs because of gravity, which drags the water downhill." She had to explain to the children what gravity was and how it worked. Then she placed a marble on the small portion of the completed raceway, and they watched it roll down the track.

Sherry's work crew had created a half-mile of raceway so far. That represented only one-sixteenth of the total distance, which meant they had to increase the pace of work to meet the goal date.

Erik teamed up with Kestrel, Travis, and the farm hands. Kestrel would use magic to cut down a tree. The others used saws to trim the branches off. Erik tasked Travis with cutting the branches down to use as stakes. Erik and the others used saws to trim the wood into three pieces. The work was backbreaking and repetitive.

As they ate lunch, Erik talked with the team. "You'll never finish this project at this rate. The milling of the wood into pieces is taking too long by hand. We need to automate this process."

Paxton asked, "How do you do that?"

"I'm thinking we can build a mill."

"Tell me more."

Erik explained how something like that would work. "Water turns a wheel, and the wheel's drive shaft drives a saw to go up and down or we could create a circular blade." He drew out the plans for a rough waterwheel-driven mill. He could conceptualize it, but could they build it?

"An enormous structure like that would take months to build. We don't have months."

"We don't need a building. The whole setup can be outdoors."

"How will you get the fallen logs you take down to your mill?"

"For our project, we'll find a place that has the wood we're looking for and take them down there. Then we're only hauling finished cut pieces instead of trying to cut this all by hand."

Paxton said, "I don't think it will work and will take too long to build. If we were going to build it, where would you locate it?"

Sherry looked at Paxton. "Where we planned to run the water in the dry creek bed. We're a week from reaching that point. Then we can start sending water down the raceway. Erik can use the lake water, and we can test our building methodology. Anything that runs off can flow through the creek bed."

Paxton didn't look convinced.

Erik knew it was possible, but could he create it?

"You have one week. If you don't finish in a week, then you're back to sawing by hand."

"Okay."

After lunch, Erik took Travis with him, and they walked to the dry creek bed. Trees abounded on the property.

Erik said, "The first step is to build a wheel for the water to spin." He explained to Travis how the process worked, but he didn't think Travis understood.

They took down a tree, and Erik cut off portions of the ends in equal sizes until they stacked twenty ends in a pile. The next step required Erik to attach the pieces onto a rounded frame. He needed something to pin the boards to the water wheel.

"Travis?" Erik yelled for the young man helping him.

No answer.

Did he lose Travis? Sherry had told Erik to keep an eye on the kid. Again, Erik yelled, "Travis."

He heard animals barking and growling in the forest, but Erik knew those sounds, and they wouldn't be a problem. Where was the boy? He must have gotten bored and wandered back to the others.

Erik called out the boy's name and walked along the area where they were working. How would he tell Sherry he lost one of her charges?

"Travis."

Erik saw a piece of clothing next to one of the downed trees. There was the boy, taking a nap. "Travis." He shook the boy awake.

"Wha. . . hey." Travis woke.

"I need you to run back to the others and bring back some nails. Can you do that?" The boy didn't seem to be awake. Erik joggled him some more. "Come on, boy. I have a job for you."

"Yeah." Travis opened his eyes partway.

"I need nails."

"What for?"

"To attach the paddle boards to the wheel."

"Can't we get them tomorrow?"

He clenched his jaw as he said in a strained voice, "We can't wait until tomorrow. We're in a time crunch, and it's midafternoon. There's a lot of work to be done yet." Erik dragged Travis to his feet. "Do you know where the farmhouse is?"

"Maybe."

"Not maybe. Be sure. We can't have you wandering in the forest. There are animals in the forest that'll eat you. Find the aqueduct and follow it back to Paxton or Sherry."

"What if I find Lily?"

"Yeah, find Lily. Ask her for some nails." Erik grabbed the boy's hand and pulled him over to the pieces of the waterwheel. "They need to be this long." He took Travis's index finger and measured out the size. "From here to here."

Erik didn't trust the kid to find his way to the raceway by himself, so he walked with the kid until they reached the section already built. "Stay next to this all the way back to the farmhouse. Find Lily and ask for nails."

"Okay."

Travis went walking back along the built structure. Erik didn't think he would see Travis again until dinnertime.

While Erik waited for the boy to return, he went back to where the others were prepping the logs. He watched as Kestrel brought down ten trees with his magic and moved them to a staging area. After the last log was moved, the wizard sat heavily on a log, his hands on his head like he was in pain.

Erik rushed over to Kestrel. "Are you okay?"

"Yeah, I'm fine."

"You don't look fine. You look like you're in pain. I'm a healer. Would you like me to look?"

Kestrel's face looked flush, and he clutched his body as if he was cold, but he shook his head.

"Give me a chance. I can help."

Kestrel stood. "Get out of the way. I need to fell another tree."

Erik said, "These guys can't finish these by the end of the day. Take a breather."

Kestrel walked over to Erik and poked him in the chest. "I'll rest when I think I need a rest."

"Okay." Erik raised his hands in surrender.

Erik helped the others with the logs already brought to the ground. Kestrel sent another five crashing to the forest floor. The wizard stood on shaky legs and then sat hard on the ground.

Travis didn't return with the nails.

* * * *

Erik found Travis that night at dinner, talking with Kestrel and Lily.

He pulled Travis aside. "Did you find some nails?"

"No."

"What do you mean, no?"

"I found Lily and Gabriella and helped them collect buckets of sap."

"Why didn't you bring the nails?"

"I forgot what I was supposed to get."

Erik's work that day had taken a toll on his body, which ached with sore muscles and dehydration. He rubbed his hand through his hair. "Do you understand how important this project is to the village?"

"I think so." Travis stared over at Lily and Gabriella.

Erik sighed. "Listen." He grabbed Travis's shoulder so the boy would look at him. "When I ask you to do a job, I expect you to do it. When I ask you for nails, I expect you to bring back nails. We lost half a day. I have only one week to build this mill."

"Okay." Travis turned his attention back to the girls.

Later in the evening, Erik sat with Sherry on the porch.

"Travis is a complete waste of time," Erik said. "First, I found him sleeping in the forest. Then I sent him for nails, and he never came back."

"I wondered why I saw him working with Lily and Gabriella. Can you handle him?"

"Maybe. I'll try to keep him more involved."

Then he leaned in closer to Sherry and whispered, "I'm worried about Kestrel."

"What do you mean?"

"He looked sick or in pain this afternoon."

"He was fine at dinner."

"Kestrel brought down fifteen trees with magic and then was so weak he fell on the ground."

Sherry jerked her head back. "Was he using magic all afternoon?"

"I assumed he was. They had a number of trees on the ground."

"Paxton told me wizards could become sick if they used their magic too much."

He frowned back at Sherry. Kestrel was obviously sick, but Erik couldn't force him to slow down or get healing. "I just thought you should know."

"I'll talk with Lily and see if she knows anything." Sherry looked toward the lakes and the night sky.

Erik loved the night sky in Triponca. The three moons and their dance each night made a spectacular presentation. When the moons weren't around, the stars were brilliant.

Sherry asked, "Has Lily talked with you yet?"

"About what?"

She rubbed her hands together as her hair fell over her eyes. "You know. Don't you?"

"Know what?"

"Don't make this harder than it has to be. You need to talk with her."

Erik gave his head a slight shake. He knew what Sherry wanted him to do—talk with Lily about their relationship. He saw the way Lily looked at Kestrel. Whatever thing Erik and Lily had was over, which was okay because he wanted to be with Zita. He wondered if Kestrel was reluctant to let Erik heal him because of Lily.

"Yeah, I'll talk with her tomorrow."

CHAPTER 49

Al sat in Finn's wizard training center library and raised his eyes from the scroll he had been reading. "I think this is the one we've been looking for. Apparently, there's something called the Phantasmal Moors. This document leads me to believe that we can enter the moors and find different planar doors."

Zita raised her head in disbelief. "The Phantasmal Moors are dangerous. My father told me to never go there."

Al, Finn, and Zita had studied many scrolls and manuscripts found in Finn's library, looking for a way to enter the plane where Zita thought King Haskell had sent the warriors. The scroll in Al's hands was the first to mention the moors.

"What are the Phantasmal Moors?" Al asked.

Cold fingers seemed to grip Zita as she thought about having to enter the moors. "A plane or portal to other worlds and other dimensions. It isn't the world itself, just a pathway. I only know a few details from my training. Every time you enter them, you risk getting lost forever, sucked into another plane, or even death."

"That doesn't make me feel better," Al said. "Any details?"

"Mom described it as a giant castle hallway with doors on either side. The hallway extends to eternity, and each doorway enters a different planar dimension."

Al leaned back from the scroll. "Then we look for a door and out pop the warriors?"

"My instructors cautioned me to never open the doors, and they told me if I got lost in the Phantasmal Moors, I should look for the moons and head toward Pantaleon."

"Do all the dimensions circle the planet Aloheno, or could some doorways open to Earth?"

"Maybe one of the doors opens to Earth." She came over to Al's side of the table and looked over his shoulder. "Does the scroll tell us how to enter the moors?"

He ran his fingers over the words as he read. "It talks about some dangers, animals trapped in the hallways, lost people, and…" Al looked up at Zita. "Some characters known as lesser gods."

Zita laughed. "You can ignore the lesser gods. That's a myth used to scare children to stay in their beds at night."

Finn cleared his throat. "That isn't a myth. They are considered the most dangerous creatures to be found in the moors."

Al stared at Finn. "Should we find another solution?"

Finn cracked the bones in his neck as he tilted his head from side to side. He came and stood on Al's other side. "There is a language that the lesser gods use. Confusing. Part riddle. Part nonsense. We'd have to study the language."

"So we aren't going into the moors?" Al asked.

Finn had that look on his face that always told Zita that he was thinking of Ursula. Then he said, "We *must* travel through the moors."

Zita felt a prickling at her neck. "How will we know which is the *right* door?"

Finn looked off into the distance, seemingly deep in thought.

Al studied the scroll some more. "Okay, we must wait for all three moons to be in the sky. Pantaleon must be at least a quarter-moon." He grabbed a chart that lay near him on the table. "Hmm. It looks like that won't happen for another couple of months."

Finn still had glazed eyes.

"That'll give us more time to research what we're doing, so we don't get ourselves killed." Zita grabbed a chair, sat next to Al, and grabbed the scroll. "Let me study that. Go check the shelves for more information about the moors."

Zita tensed her facial muscles, her teeth locking hard together. *We don't know what we're doing, and we're planning on going into this dangerous environment. There must be a different way to accomplish this task.*

* * * *

Three days later, Zita began running experiments on the stone students. The first experiment had her dripping water on Ursula's head while chanting words. Nonsense words, as far as she was concerned. She studied the scroll lying on the table in the conservatory as she ran the experiments.

The scroll said that if the water turned green as it flowed over a replica of the object that was sent to the moors, then you could find the hidden object behind a blue door.

"That doesn't make sense. Shouldn't you then find the object behind a green door?" Al asked.

She squinted, trying to determine the color running off the statue. Zita was tired of Al asking her questions at every step. He could read the documents just as well as her. "What color does that look like to you?"

Al leaned in close. "Maybe a pale pink."

"What does it say about pink?"

"Oh, you're not going to like this." Al peered up from the scroll. "A pink, light red, or light pink color means that a lesser god has taken an interest in the object."

Finn groaned from his position by the green beans, which he was busy harvesting for the group's next meal.

"That's only one experiment. Let me try this next one." She blew into one student's ears. Then she held a burning candle under his chin.

Al asked, "What is that supposed to do?"

"I'm searching for flaws in their structure. I want to determine the planar properties that were used to send off their spirits."

"And?" Al hurried over to the statue.

Zita shook her head. "I don't know what I'm doing. Read the passage where it talks about structure." As she said this, the flame increased in intensity.

Al held up the scroll. His gaze moved up and down the document. "Aha! If the flame burns bright, the object has landed in a new plane."

"The flame is burning an orangish hue," Zita said.

"The object can be found behind a purple door," Al yelled. "Zita, you did it."

She pressed her lips together. Even if they found the door, they shouldn't travel through the moors. They should use objects that were already attuned to the planar level they wanted to reach, like her music box. This wasn't a task for amateurs without a competent guide.

Al said, "So, we travel through the moors and search for a purple door. That doesn't sound too hard."

"Did you read the part about the passage of time?" Zita placed the flame under another student to see if they all landed in the same plane.

"Let me see. I remember reading something. Yeah, time in the moors can either stretch or shrink. That doesn't tell me anything."

Finn walked over to them. "To stretch time means that if you are in the moors for an hour, the time that actually passes in your original plane might only be fifteen minutes. And to shrink time is the opposite. Fifteen minutes might actually be a few hours."

Zita said, "Not a problem, then. We shouldn't be in there for very long."

"It also might mean many months."

Zita closed her eyes at the thought of being gone from Aloheno for months. "Let's hope time stretches, then."

She placed the candle under Ursula's chin. Nothing happened for a few minutes, and she saw Finn staring intently at her actions. Then the flame spiked. Zita expected an orangish hue again, but instead, the fire burned a forest green. "This can't be right. All the other students had the same color flame."

"Means she isn't with the others." Finn began pacing back and forth across the room, rubbing the back of his neck. "Like you said before, one of the lesser gods has taken an interest in her. That's the worst possible outcome."

A heaviness weighed on her chest as she watched Finn pace about the room. If Finn thought it was bad, then Ursula was in serious trouble.

Al looked up from the scroll. "There's a sixty percent chance she's behind a teal door."

Zita said, "That's encouraging. We can find a teal door. One purple door and one teal door, easy. We open the doors and rescue everyone."

Finn yelled, "No! We can't open the door. We can mark it, but we have to research how to extract those people trapped in the different plane. There's still more analysis needed."

"What happens if we open the doors?" Al held the scroll in front of him as if holding a shield to protect him from the answer.

"This is the potential for you to get sucked into that dimension and space," Finn said. "Very bad."

Zita watched Finn pacing back and forth. "How do we mark the doors?"

"You need to do more research." Finn stopped for a second then continued his pacing.

Al threw the scroll on the table. "We'll need another scroll, then, because this one doesn't tell us much about marking doors and extraction techniques."

Finn groaned.

CHAPTER 50

The Pantaleon Moon led the charge of the three moons across the sky this night. It was a white moon that, if closer, would light up the meadow, but the moon stood the farthest from the planet, and the light had to filter through some clouds.

Al held his staff in his hand. He didn't know what to expect, but he felt he should carry it into the moors. His stomach felt a little jittery as the sun went down. Al looked into the night sky and saw Velidred had entered the arena, causing a red glow to overpower the light from Pantaleon. *One more moon, and then we go into the Phantasmal Moors.* He sat for a moment, didn't feel comfortable, and then stood.

"Will you relax?" Zita asked. "You're making me nervous jumping up and down and moving your hands and staff around. Be still."

"I can't. All this talk about infinity and eternity and doors to other dimensions. I can only think of all the things that can go wrong."

Finn rubbed Ursula's cheek and gave her a kiss on the lips. "We'll find you, my love." A red-stoned necklace that hadn't been there previously encircled Ursula's neck.

Al hoped they would find her. Whoever the lesser gods were, they might have to engage them to actually find Ursula since it seemed to him that she wasn't with the students. Zita had studied the language of the lesser gods and he hoped she was fluent. If this experiment or foray into the unknown worked, he hoped they could replicate it with the stone warriors.

Anticletus, the fastest of the three moons, rose into the sky, its blue glow overpowered by Velidred's red.

"It's time. Come." Finn said. Zita and Al drew near. "Zita, put on the Helmet of Justice."

Zita pulled the helmet out of the box, took a deep breath, and placed it on her head.

Finn reached over to Ursula and removed the necklace.

Finn turned his attention to Al, appraised Al and the staff, then nodded his approval. He said, "The first step of this process is to open the gateway. Be prepared to fight monsters, soldiers, or other world gods. Anyone or anything can escape their dimension and be waiting at our door."

Al's mouth went dry as he worried about all the things that could go wrong. *Great, we open the door and then get vaporized.*

"Al, you'll stand before us and prepare a shield."

Why do I always get picked to make the shield? I'm like the guy who gets picked last on the playground. Nobody else to choose? Then we'll pick Al to create a shield.

Zita pushed Al in front of her.

"Relax, Al. You're way too nervous." Zita picked up a pinch of dirt and a medicine dropper full of some oil she had made from plants in Finn's greenhouse. "I will chant the opening sequence, and the doorway to the Phantasmal Moors will open. We'll enter the moors and turn right. Be prepared to fight or flee at my command. No matter what, don't split up."

Al's stomach churned bubbling acid and bile like a fiery volcano. He darted a glance at Zita. "How do we know what door to return to?"

"Follow me."

Yeah, and if you die, am I stuck here forever?

Finn looked at Al. "We'll be fine."

They faced the door to the conservatory, and Al wondered if they had to go through that physical door. Or would the door be virtual?

Zita closed her eyes, raised her hands, and raised her voice.

Moon of white and moors of purity,

Moon of red form rains of redemption,

New worlds, trapped spirits, guide our group.

Open doors to friends and family.

Find the virtuous, decent, and righteous.

Fight squalor, vileness, and wicked men.

Al stood on trembling legs. He didn't know what to expect, but he prepped the shield and guarded the group.

A bluish glow extended from Zita's right arm to Al's staff.

Honest students, loving wife,

Bring their bodies back to life.

The bluish glow reached the red necklace in Finn's hand. *What magic did that object contain?* A deep fog encompassed the group.

A partial door showed in front of Al. He strengthened his grip on the staff and faced the door.

Justice flow from our world on.

Strings of goodness fly before us.

Remove atrocities and iniquity.

He felt the flow from Finn stream toward the Helmet of Justice. A shock wave flowed into Zita. She flinched, and Al felt all she felt. A shiver ran down his spine.

Taboos, abominations, perversions acquit.

Decay and rot desist as we travel through your halls.

A golden glow formed around Zita like the first rays of the morning sun over a tree.

Friends abound, wholesome, near.

Open the gate to moors unknown.

Abysmal energy, unleash your flow.

The blue stream finished the connection around the circle, and the door became fully formed—a simple gray wooden door with a bronze lever handle.

Al eased the door open. Fog drifted through the space between their current world and the opening portal. He gripped his staff with both hands as he prepared for the onslaught of whatever evil creatures stood between him and the moors.

Through the foggy scene, Al saw what looked like an old London cobblestone street. Stones were missing from the street, giving it a pockmarked look. Light from the three moons filtered through the fog, mixing an eerie combination of red and bluish-white.

Zita took a deep breath and said, "Let's go. Stay close." She led them into the fog.

Cries of distress were uttered through the fog, and Al felt a slight change in the swirling fog as unseen creatures ran past the three humans from Aloheno. He followed the halo of yellow surrounding Zita.

Zita called the Phantasmal Moors a hallway with doors, but Al thought it a never-ending old village alley, tightly packed between stone buildings without windows. He and his companions walked as a group through the fog and passed closed wooden doors. Most of the doors showed as plain brown, but every once in a while, Al saw a yellow, green, or red door. No one in the group spoke.

Zita stopped next to a teal door on the left and knocked.

Al wondered if she expected a butler to come to the door. Would she ask if Ursula was available to visit?

A piercing scream echoed off the walls, and a bipedal monster stood before them. The creature stood twice as tall as Al and had a bird-shaped head with a foot-long, sharp, hooked beak.

The animal screeched and pecked at Zita. Its mouth could consume her with one bite.

Al's shield held as the birdlike creature pecked multiple times without reaching Zita.

Finn raised his arms and said, "Go away."

The creature ran off into the fog.

Al breathed again as his heart pounded in his chest. He didn't want to visit whatever dimension that creature came from. How did creatures enter the moors if they weren't wizards? Did they randomly stumble through a portal into this Phantasmal plane or did someone leave a door open? He thought about how he and his friends stumbled through the portal into Aloheno.

Nothing happened at the door Zita knocked at. No one answered. Al didn't know if that was good or bad.

They passed three more doors without incident. On the fourth door, Zita stopped and knocked. The wooden door showed inscriptions scratched into its surface, in a language that looked like Latin.

Zita took her vial of oil, squeezed a drop from it with a medicine dropper, and let it flow down the door. As the drop traveled down the door, the oil turned bloodred.

She made wide sweeping motions with her arms to move the three wizards away from the door. "Move, get away. We must be fast."

They hurried down the street.

"What was it?" Al asked.

"When I knock, I listen for the voices on the other side. They can be good, friendly voices, apathetic voices, or like that one, the sound of dread and madness."

"What if the students or warriors are in those dimensions?" Al asked.

"Then it's best we don't bring them back."

Could we be going through this whole exercise and decide not to even try to rescue the warriors? Erik wouldn't accept that.

Voices carried along the alley. "That last dimension was a slimy bit of meat, don't ya think, guvnor?"

Another fellow laughed. "Did you see the look on that mope's face when you took his pouch of gold and slashed your sword across his chest?"

"We'll have to avoid that door next. . . Whoa, what do we have here, gentlemen?" Four men came into focus within the fog. They were all dressed in black pants and jackets, and all carried swords.

A patch covered one man's eye, making him look like a pirate. "My, my. We have found a beautiful woman, don't ya think, mates?"

"The boy and old man look to be carrying coin too." A second man, smaller than the pirate, held his sword up. "It'll be nice getting women and coin without going through one of those wacky doors."

Finn said, "Why don't you boys scurry off into the woodwork?"

"Are you going to let that shrimp talk to us that way?"

A breeze picked up in the alley, making the fog swirl. The stench of decay carried on the wind.

"Should I blast them?" Al asked.

"Not yet," Zita said. "Put down the shield."

Al asked, "Are you crazy? They have weapons."

"This is the part I studied in the scrolls. It'll be fine." Zita clenched her fists, and a tight smile played across her lips. "Remove the shield."

Al bit the inside of his lip and looked at the strangers. Ha. Were these the lesser gods Zita and Finn talked about? Al hoped Zita knew what she was doing. She didn't seem too confident. And even if these guys were harmless, that didn't mean another one of the bird creatures wasn't roaming the alley. He glanced around them, looking for danger, and saw no one but the men. "I'm dropping the shield."

Zita moved closer to the man with the eyepatch. "Are you the leader of this fine group of soldiers?"

"Did you hear that, mates? A fine group of soldiers." He looked at Zita and smiled, showing a gold tooth as one of his incisors.

The men with the pirate laughed.

In a quick move, the pirate grabbed the back of Zita's helmet and pulled her toward him. Then he planted a long kiss on her lips.

CHAPTER 51

Zita didn't struggle. The pirate had nice full lips, and the kiss took her breath away. She thought the stories about the lesser gods were only fairy tales, but this was rather nice.

At last, the man disengaged and pushed her away.

Zita fanned her face with her hand, and her eyes sparkled. "That will cost you two answers."

"Ooh. Two answers." The lesser god with long sideburns and a handlebar mustache laughed.

The pirate held up his hand, and the others stopped laughing. "Go ahead."

Zita waited a moment, running her tongue over her lips as she continued to relish the kiss. *I need to find out if these are the lesser gods that took Ursula, and I hope I can get some answers about the students and the warriors.*

She took a deep breath and tried to think of the crazy vocabulary the lesser gods used. She had practiced what she was supposed to say and hoped she understood their answers. Zita said, "Trees are green, and skies are blue. What time did Ursula and the students eat at the zoo?"

The pirate looked at his fellows and smirked. "Never eat sardines with Ursula on the Coast of Twirlypad."

"Hmm, I see." Zita had to think back to the scroll she had read to interpret the answer. She needed to ensure that she responded appropriately. Yes, the lesser gods had seen the students but not Ursula. She looked at Finn, wondering if he understood the conversation.

Finn lowered his head and pressed his lips together in disappointment.

Zita stared into the pirate's eyes and lowered her voice. If the warriors were stuck behind a planar doorway, would the gods tell her? "If the spires fall, and the golden dome turns into a bowl, why did the warrior marry the fox?"

That question seemed to stump the pirate. He turned and whispered to his friends. The conversation lasted a few minutes, but Zita didn't interrupt. The men gestured at each other as they whispered, and one guy even drew his sword. The discussion looked to her like a heated argument.

At last, the pirate turned. "The ash fell on thirteen horned dragons. The fish lived, but the rabbit died." He stopped talking.

The mustached man waved his arms at the pirate. "Tell her everything. It's the bargain you set."

The pirate pinched his lips and rubbed his jaw with a dirty hand. "Are you sure it's stegox ribs and not fried bacon?"

The other three men nodded and waved for him to continue.

Al pointed at something in the distance. "Hey, should we be worried about the approaching red lights—"

"Quiet," Zita commanded.

"But. . ." Al pointed his staff behind the lesser gods.

"We have a bargain, Pirate. Finish the transaction."

"The stegox ribs broke the warrior's foot, and water gushed over the fallen redhead."

Al asked, "The shield?"

"Not yet." Zita wanted to go now, but the lesser gods required a question of their own. She saw the monster with two red eyes materializing in the fog. "Your question?"

The three men glanced back at the approaching monster, and all encouraged the pirate. "Go on."

"If the ship flies south, when will the dragon swim to the ocean floor?"

Zita gasped, but she didn't answer right away. She couldn't believe the lesser gods would ask about the dragon. In this language of the gods, the dragon could only mean one thing. They wanted to know where they could find her father.

The monster growled and continued toward the group of humans.

Al tensed his muscles and backed up a bit. "Uh, Zita."

The red-eyed monster was the size of a bus. It had four arms with three-inch claws extending from each hand.

Zita stood there, locked in thought. They had seen the warrior's door and confirmed the army had settled on a different plane. They had given her an answer. She had to answer their question, but she didn't dare give a false response. The lesser gods were a crafty bunch, and she doubted they played fair. *I have to tell them where to find my father.*

"Madam, do you respect the bargain?"

With a growl, the monster raised its arms to strike.

She felt pain in her jaw from clenching her teeth so tightly. *My dad can't survive a confrontation with the lesser gods in his weakened state.* Zita didn't know what they wanted with her father, but she knew it wouldn't bode well for him.

The angry, red-eyed monster came closer.

Zita closed her eyes. *I'm sorry, Dad.* She blurted, "The octopus speaks, but the golden bee is silent. Take the Effingham trail to the island of ice."

The pirate nodded. Then he embraced Zita, and they engaged in another long kiss.

Once the two disengaged, Zita felt a little disheveled. She stared at the pirate and yearned for another kiss.

The pirate smiled, and the man with the sideburns slapped him on the back.

Zita smiled. "Al, protect us. Now!"

The lesser gods disappeared.

Al threw up a shield as the monster raked its arms over them. The creature buffeted the shield despite numerous strikes. A small creature ran down the alley, and the monster chased after it.

"What was all that nonsense about?" Al asked.

"That wasn't nonsense," Zita said. That was a conversation with the lesser gods who roam the Phantasmal Moors and other planes and moors. If you want to journey through the moors, you have to learn how to communicate with them."

"They didn't look like gods to me."

"They are, and if you aren't nice to them, then they will eat you, throw you into another dimension, or turn you into a beast." Zita adjusted her tunic and continued through the alley.

Al asked, "Did they tell us where to go?"

"They knew things that confirmed our suspicions. They identified the door the warriors have been trapped behind—a door painted a twilight purple." Zita's head ached; she felt the familiar discomfort associated with wearing the helmet. The radiation poisoning was returning. They couldn't stop now. She didn't want to have to enter the moors again. They had some answers and needed to persist in their search.

"Is Ursula here?" Finn asked.

Nausea formed in her stomach because she wanted to give Finn good news, but she had none. "These lesser gods don't have her, which means there are others we have to find."

Al asked, "Are we done? Can we go home?"

"Not yet. We need to check two doors, and then we return to Finn's place."

The helmet itched, her headache got worse, and the nausea increased. *What do the lesser gods want with my father? I should find a way to warn him. Maybe if they see his current condition, they'll leave him alone.*

They traveled at least a mile without checking doors. They met small monsters that were more afraid of Zita than the foursome was afraid of the beasts.

The group reached a door painted in a deep purple, like the sky between the end of day and the start of night.

Al tapped the door with the staff. "Is this the one? Who painted it purple?"

Zita raised her hand. "Don't touch it. Quiet."

She stood in front of the door for five minutes waiting for a response. Then she knocked three times on the door and placed her ear close. Zita took out her vial and repeated placing a drop of oil on the door. The drop rolled six inches then defied logic and gravity and rolled into a circle. In the middle of the circle, a single eye formed.

Finn smiled and said, "Aha! The Sjonauka spell. You have learned well."

Zita stood close to the door and peered into it.

The eye changed colors, first brown then blue then green, and finished with a hazel color. Zita and the door entity stood eye to eye for many minutes, and the door's eye color repeated the sequence about once a minute.

She continued to look into the eye and then said, "This is it. We have marked it."

She waved her hand over the eye, and it disappeared.

Zita smiled and turned. "Follow me."

The alley was quiet of creatures, but the fog persisted.

Zita pointed at the sky. "Anticletus is about to set. We can't afford to be trapped in here after the moon sets."

Finn asked, "We can't leave without searching more for Ursula."

"Maybe the next door."

Al raised his eyebrows. "The next door? I thought we were leaving before the moon set."

"We owe it to Finn to look for Ursula and the students. The gods gave us one more door to search. It won't be long. Follow me."

In a few minutes, the group reached another door, which was plain like the others.

Zita took her pinch of dirt and threw it at the door.

Nothing happened.

She knocked on the door. Once. Sharp. The sound echoed off the walls of the Phantasmal Moors. Then she leaned in and placed her ear against the door.

After a moment, she stood and shook her head at Finn.

Finn's shoulders drooped, and he rubbed the palm of his hand against his chest. "Is there another door?"

"There might be, but we don't have time to search. I'm sorry. We must leave."

Finn asked, "Did they enter through the door and leave the vicinity of the portal?"

"They did not enter through this door. The door has no remembrance of their presence. Dirt from the student's statues sprinkled on the door informs us if they have entered."

A fireball roared down the alley and smacked into Al's shield in brilliant reds and yellows and an explosion of sound.

"We must leave. Now," Zita yelled.

A second and a third fireball caromed off Al's shield.

"Quick, place your hand on mine." Zita placed her hand between the wizards.

Al laid his hand on hers.

Finn looked longingly at the doors dotting the moors.

"Finn, we can't do this now. Your hand." Zita's head throbbed, and she wanted nothing more than to throw the helmet off, but it was needed to return to Finn's place.

"I want to keep looking."

Another fireball burst against the shield, noticeably weakening it, and Al started sweating. He yelled, "Hurry, we're losing our armor."

Zita struggled to maintain her concentration. "Finn."

He took a hard swallow, grimaced at the other doors in the alley, and then placed a shaking hand atop Zita's.

The fog thickened as the barrage continued to pummel the shield. Their attacker had magic stronger than Al's. Zita knew she must hurry to form a door to escape through.

A yellow door materialized near them. The bottom half was visible, but the top half struggled to form.

"Hold," Zita said as she watched the shield begin to buckle under the attack.

Two more fireballs hit the shield, but they didn't explode like before. They acted like the shield was jelly and dimpled the shield inward then bounced off in an explosion of color.

Another two inches of the door showed.

The door wasn't generating fast enough. The shield would collapse, and they would all die before saving the warriors. No one would know what happened to them.

Zita wanted to supply extra power to the shield, but she had to concentrate on forming the door. Her nausea almost overwhelmed her. "Finn, can you help Al with the shield?"

The next fireball exploded off the shield like before, and the shield weakened. Finn continued to stare at the adjacent doors in the moors without helping Al.

She concentrated on creating the door. Zita wanted to criticize Finn, but she knew it would be difficult to leave the moors without him knowing where Ursula and the students ended up and if they were together.

In a flash of yellow, the door solidified. Zita grabbed the handle and pushed the door open. She forced Finn through as he struggled to stay in the moors. Then she grabbed Al's arm and pulled him back inside Finn's conservatory. She slammed the door closed.

Al bent over, his hands on his thighs, gasping for air. He mouthed a thank-you to Zita.

Zita dropped to all fours and retched. After emptying her stomach, she said, "We must hurry to the warriors."

"Why?" Al asked.

"The marker only lasts a few days."

CHAPTER 52

Sherry was worried about Kestrel. Each night when he came back to camp, he looked tired, stressed, and sick.

"Can you do anything to help him?" Sherry asked.

Erik shook his head. "He won't let me touch him. Paxton thinks it might be magic sickness, but Kestrel won't talk to us about it."

"Did you know he hasn't flown in days?"

"Yeah, I've walked with him for miles, whereas before he would fly off and say he would meet us at the destination."

They had taken to camping in the forest, so they didn't have to spend too much time hiking to the job site each morning.

"Kestrel has started on the granite rock. I don't know what we'll do if he can't complete the hole."

Sherry rubbed the stress out of her stiff neck muscles. What could they do about Kestrel? She had talked with Lily to see if she could convince Kestrel not to work so hard. Instead, the conversation had angered him, and he was working even harder.

Erik laid his hand on Sherry's shoulder. "We start the bridge today. If we can get that built, then it's smooth sailing to connect to the village."

They had made significant progress once Erik got the lumber mill working. The process required a different blade than what the blacksmith originally delivered, and Erik had to add a couple of gears to get the speed he needed to slice through the trees. That allowed them to get three sections from each tree instead of just the one section they started with. Sherry hoped to go back the following summer and replace the other sections with the milled lumber.

Sherry felt tension in her shoulders. "We have two weeks to go. Do you think we will make it?"

"I think we can."

"Have you heard from Al? It's been months since he left to find Finn. What could take him so long?"

Erik shook his head.

"What are we doing today?" Travis asked.

"We're building a bridge."

"That's funny," Travis said.

"Why is that funny?"

"You're building a bridge to take water over a valley. Don't you think that's funny?"

Sherry shook her head at the boy. She had tried to get the mayor to take the boy back, but he persisted that they used him. The mayor said that Travis was an asset to the aqueduct-building project and that she mustn't complain about the help the mayor gave her. She considered just leaving the boy at his mom's house but knew the mayor would find out.

Dark clouds formed over the horizon, and thunder boomed.

"Is it going to rain?" Sherry asked.

"Do you want me to call off the work for today?" Erik pulled on a shoe.

"We don't have time to lose a day's work. We must get something done." Sherry felt pressure building in her chest. With every victory, nature and stupidity set them back. Like that day when Travis left the work site and warmed a bucket of sap over a fire. The same way Sherry experienced it before they had learned to use a double boiler for the process. They lost a whole bucket of pine resin when it erupted in flames.

They headed to the valley, dragging downed trees using two wagons created for pulling logs through the forest. The wagons were thinner, with higher walls and taller wheels, which allowed for easier movement. Sherry had mapped out the needed posts for the bridge, a design Paxton and Erik agreed would work.

The heavy rains started when they were within a half mile of the valley. Lightning pounded through the treetops, sending cracks of thunder so powerful Sherry could feel them through the ground.

When they reached the valley, water streamed through the completed sections of the aqueduct, flowing out and over the ledge into the valley, which was already two inches deep in water.

"Will this end soon?" Sherry yelled in the tumult of wind, rain, and lightning.

Erik shrugged. Wet hair hung from his head, and his soaked tunic clung to his body.

They would lose this day and maybe more if the valley didn't dry up quickly. Should she send the work crew back to the farm for safety?

Erik shouted, "We should unload the logs on the side of the hill. They'll wash down the valley in all this rain."

"Okay."

An explosion came from down the path. *That must be Kestrel blowing up the giant granite boulder.* She was happy he could still work, though she'd sent Lily with the wizard today.

The men pulled the foundation logs from the wagon and staged them on the side of the cliff.

Travis pulled on Sherry's sleeve as the rain pounded on them. "I want to go back to the farm. I'm scared."

She couldn't let Travis go anywhere by himself. He had proved himself incapable of making rational decisions.

Sherry pointed at a section of limestone where a natural cave had formed. "There's a small cave over there. That'll keep you dry." It wasn't deep but would provide safety and comfort for the boy.

Lightning struck nearby, and Sherry ducked at the noise. "That was close."

Travis ran to the cave.

She wondered if they should all shelter in the cave until this maelstrom weakened.

A log slipped out of Erik's hand, and she watched as he scooted his feet back to keep the log from landing on his foot.

Something exploded in Kestrel's work area.

Three strikes of lightning brightened the sky.

Then the sky turned green, and hail pounded from the clouds.

Sherry ran to the cave, where she found Travis shivering at the back.

She shook off the wet and pebbles of hail from her tunic, hoping Erik and the other men had found shelter.

Lightning came in a jagged line and struck a tree near the cave.

She watched in slow motion as the tree broke in half and came crashing toward her. For a second, she thought about running but remembered Travis, so she slid in beside him as the tree enclosed the cave rocks with its branches.

"No," Sherry screamed.

The limestone rocks creating the cave couldn't hold the tree's weight, and rocks toppled into the cave.

Sherry threw her body in front of Travis to protect him. A rock bounced off her head.

* * * *

The storm flashed and crashed around Erik and the farmhands. They pulled three of the six logs off the wagons before it hailed. Once the hail began, it was every man for himself, and they all ran, searching for shelter from the hail.

Erik ended up in the valley, plastered against the limestone wall, protected from the pounding hail. He stood in a half foot of water and asked himself if that was the right thing to do with lightning lashing out at them.

Thunder echoed off the cliff walls, and Erik heard a tree crash into the forest. *Good, we might be able to use that tree with less work than trying to take the tree down by hand.*

The hail didn't last long. The sky lightened to a dull gray instead of the bruised green from before, and the rain settled into a gentle downpour. Erik ventured out to check on the damage and see if they lost any men or resources.

Paxton yelled, "Erik, we're over here."

They were back to working the logs off the wagons.

An explosion occurred, and Erik figured Kestrel had returned to attacking the granite boulder.

Erik asked, "Can we roll these logs into the valley and use the water to move them near to position?"

"Good idea." Paxton nodded.

The water had risen to Erik's knees. With a little searching, he found a mostly dry area where they could stage the logs.

They rolled a log into the stream, and Erik guided it to the dry area. Two of Paxton's men helped stabilize the log on the dry land. As long as the water didn't rise in this area, the log would be okay.

A second log came down the stream, and the farmhand guiding it slipped and pushed the log forward to Erik. It struck just below his knee and forced him to the ground in pain. The log streamed past Erik as he struggled to his feet. He knew his leg wasn't broken, but he couldn't put pressure on it.

Erik reached out to the log, hobbled toward it, and reeled it into a safe position.

The workers continued rolling the logs down into the valley. The storm subsided, and the rain stopped, but the temporary stream rose. Erik worried about the staged logs. Had he made a tactical error? It was too late to reconsider.

After unloading the first batch of logs, they took the wagons back up the mountain to retrieve other logs for this portion of the project.

Each step Erik took caused pain, and when he examined his leg, he found it swollen and a round six-inch bruise that colored his skin.

They unloaded six of the ten logs into the stream, and Erik guided them to the safe area. The staging area became larger as the water slowed and the stream became shallower from the lack of additional rain.

The valley floor had become a base of muck and mud. They would need to dig a deep foundation for the support logs if they expected them to handle this much water running underneath it.

Erik needed to get feedback from Paxton and Sherry. This area was critical to the aqueduct bridge, and if it didn't work, they would be in trouble.

* * * *

"Miss Torkel, are you all right?"

Sherry came to, and her head felt horrible. She reached up and touched the back of her head and found it bloody. She didn't feel okay, but she didn't want to make Travis panic. "Yes, I'm fine. Are you okay?"

"Yes," he said in a shaky voice. "I thought you were dead. I shook you, and you didn't answer."

Sherry pushed rocks off her legs as she examined the cave. The rocks had cascaded into their space and built a wall around them. Light streamed through cracks in the fallen rocks.

"Have you seen the others?"

"No ma'am."

"That's okay. Relax, Travis. We'll get out." Sherry grabbed a rock high above their prison, and when it moved, several rocks above it slid down on top of her. She threw up her arms to protect her head.

"I guess we won't do that again." Sherry brushed debris off her tunic.

Will Erik and Paxton find us in this little tomb?

CHAPTER 53

The temporary stream petered out late in the day, leaving a bog of mud and gunk. It forced Erik and the farmhands to hand-carry a couple of logs to the staging area as their tree cart bogged down in the mud. As he worked, he wondered where Sherry was. It wasn't like her to quit early for the day, and even if she had taken Travis back to the farm during the storm, she would have left him there and returned to help with the work.

Erik dug a hole in the mountain's side, where rocks and other debris had fallen from the cliff over the years. They estimated how deeply to bury one end of the log, which was to become a foundation pole. He guessed five feet should do the trick but wanted to rethink that decision as they reached a layer of large stones and rubble instead of dirt.

"How much farther do we have to go?" Erik asked.

Paxton stared up at the top of the pole and the guideline strung across the expanse. "At least another two feet."

"I don't see it happening."

"You saw what the rainstorm did. We go that deep or the entire structure will float downstream after one of these storms."

"I'm digging through rock."

Paxton said, "You know what we decided and why. Find a way—here, let me try." Paxton took the shovel from Erik.

Erik took a drink of water from his waterskin and watched the farmhands on the other side of the valley running into a similar problem. They dug a hole and then worked the twenty-foot log into the hole. A rope ran from the Triponca side of the valley to the Crossroads' side. After they struggled to place the pole in the hole, it pushed the rope up at least a foot.

The guys grumbled and struggled to get the pole out so they could deepen the hole.

Paxton worked the hole for a half hour and made progress, but it wasn't enough.

Erik took over and sweated and toiled with the rocks.

A cheer rose from across the valley as the farmhands placed their pole in the hole and it fit. Erik grimaced. They had been racing, and Erik had bet them his night's dessert for the team that anchored their pole first.

Paxton laughed. "No dessert for you tonight, my friend."

* * * *

Sherry yelled through the holes in the rock until her throat was sore. She worried about her head and felt lightheaded when she yelled.

Travis shouted, "Help! We're over here."

Sherry covered her ears with her hands.

"We're never going to get out. We're going to die."

"Relax, Travis. We will not die." She tried to sound confident for the boy. She realized she was the adult in this cave, but she had only three or four years on Travis. The boy had no life skills to figure out how to escape from this.

"I'm never gonna see Mum again, and it's your fault."

"Why is it my fault?" Sherry wanted to tell him she didn't want him with her, anyway. If he had stayed home, she would have been happy.

"Mr. Mooney said I had to do it."

"Why?"

"I don't know why. He comes by to see my mum once a week, and they must have talked. They always kick us kids out of the house when Mr. Mooney comes over. Then one day when I came back home a couple of hours later, Mum told me I was to help you with the aqueduct."

"Have you learned anything?"

"I don't like Kestrel. He's too close to Lily."

"Yeah, they're dating. You're too young for Lily. Do you report back to Mr. Mooney or your mom what you're doing here?"

"Mum doesn't care. She's happy she doesn't have to feed me. Mr. Mooney wants to know what we're doing each week. I report to Mr. Mooney and Justin."

That did not surprise Sherry, but she wondered what Justin might be planning. She didn't trust him and was sure he would cause conflict when they drew closer to completion. He wouldn't be happy if Sherry and Paxton won this little war.

"What have you told Mr. Mooney and Justin?"

"Not much. They're pretty angry at me most of the time, wondering what I'm doing."

Sherry knew Travis didn't really understand or care to understand what Sherry's team was accomplishing with the aqueduct.

Travis yelled again, and Sherry covered her ears.

* * * *

Paxton and Erik had set their first pole and dug the hole for the second. This required the hole to be in the section where the water had been a foot high, and the ground was wet and mucky.

As Erik dug, Paxton asked, "Where's Sherry? Did she not come back?"

"I haven't seen her since the hailstorm. I'm assuming she went back to the farm."

"That's not like her."

Erik stuck the shovel into the mud and pulled up, but the mud slipped off the shovel and back into the hole. "She's probably checking on Kestrel or working with Gabriella on some more pine resin." He stopped digging the hole and gazed in the direction where Kestrel was making a hole in the granite boulder. He had heard no explosions in the last hour.

"Maybe. Kestrel's not that far away, but I think she would have stopped and checked on us before leaving to see Kestrel. I don't remember seeing her at lunch either."

"She's babysitting Travis today. That's always a handful. She probably took him back to the farm and tied him to one of the porch posts."

"Ha. You're funny, my friend," Paxton said.

Erik tried to pick up another shovelful of mud when he heard a woman shouting. Lily ran across the valley, struggling to stay upright in the mud.

"What does she want? Did Sherry get hurt?" Paxton asked.

Erik threw down the shovel and raced over to Lily. "What's wrong?"

"It's Kestrel. He fell, and he can't stand up. He's talking gibberish." Lily's eyes were red, and she sniffled over and over to keep her nose from running. "He can't move his left arm."

Erik didn't want to say anything out loud, but he wondered as they ran back to Kestrel's location if the wizard's magic sickness had finally caught up with him.

Paxton and Erik raced ahead of Lily since they knew the location of the granite rock. Erik hoped Kestrel hadn't fallen off the ridge. The rim didn't have much foot purchase space. Adding a broken bone to an already sickened body would not be good.

When they reached the rock, they found Kestrel on the ground. He said something when they reached him, but Erik didn't understand the words.

Erik asked, "Do you have pain anywhere?"

Kestrel gave an unintelligible answer.

Erik tried to move Kestrel's limbs, but one side didn't cooperate. Erik said, "Stick out your tongue." Erik stuck out his tongue in case Kestrel couldn't understand him.

Kestrel attempted to stick out his tongue, but it didn't go straight. Instead, his tongue came out halfway and wobbled to the side of his mouth.

"Can you smile?" Erik smiled for Kestrel.

Kestrel tried to stand, but Erik forced him down.

"Come on, fella. Smile for me."

Kestrel moved his face, but it drooped to one side.

"Can you move your arms?" Erik flapped his arms.

When Kestrel tried it, only the right side responded.

Paxton asked, "What do you think it is?"

"I'm guessing it's a stroke," Erik said. "But he's young, so I'm wondering if this is a symptom of magic poisoning or sickness."

"Can you heal him?" Lily asked when she reached their location. She was out of breath.

"I can try." Erik placed his hands on Kestrel's head.

Kestrel tried to move his head away, but Erik held it with both hands.

Paxton stood beside Lily. "Lily, has Sherry worked with you this afternoon?"

"No, I haven't seen her all day."

Lily's comments distracted Erik. They couldn't afford to lose Sherry and Kestrel when they were this close to the finish line.

The granite rock had a one-foot section carved out of it for a distance of about six feet. That wasn't enough, and doing the work without Kestrel would be impossible in the little time they had left. Where was Sherry?

Erik delved into Kestrel's brain, searching for a way to heal him.

CHAPTER 54

They used a cart to carry Kestrel back to the farm, losing many hours of work. Erik knew the lost day was monumental and wondered how Sherry would take the news when they reached the farm. She would be livid that she wasn't there to help, forced to babysit Travis the whole day.

They reached the farm and placed Kestrel in a bed and when given a blanket, he pulled it over his body with his good hand.

Erik decided he needed to heal Kestrel using the Sword of Freedom. He knew it enhanced healing power but still remembered the awful experience with Dickerson. His original diagnosis of Kestrel seemed correct, but he couldn't figure out how magic sickness could manifest as a stroke. His initial scan of Kestrel's brain showed nothing unusual, no blood blockages that Erik could tell. He'd never had a stroke patient before, and he felt unsure of what needed fixing.

Lily sat next to Kestrel, holding his limp hand. Redness ringed her eyes.

"Paxton, can you get me a wet rag or washcloth?"

"Sure."

Erik didn't really need a damp cloth but thought he could give it to Lily to dab at Kestrel's forehead so she would feel she was helping. He hated seeing her in this much pain.

He went to his room, grabbed the Sword of Freedom, and brought it into the bedroom.

Lily's face went white. "You're not going to kill him, are you?"

"No, it has healing powers. I hope to make him comfortable. I might not have the ability to help him."

"Make him feel better. You can't leave him like this."

"I will try to heal him, but I want to make sure I don't make the problem worse. He's a wizard. Cugbert told me once that magic sickness wasn't something we priests could heal, but I'll do everything I can for him."

Lily didn't look convinced but resumed holding Kestrel's hand and stroking the back of his wrist.

Kestrel stared at the ceiling, gritting his teeth. He had stopped trying to talk and didn't even respond to Lily's questions and ministrations.

Erik wondered where the center of magic originated. Was it in the brain, or did some other genetic transformation occur? Did the magical person have another organ that people born on Earth didn't have? He thought maybe Cugbert would have told him if that was true.

Paxton came into the room with a wet washcloth and handed it to Lily.

"Dab his head with the cloth. That'll make him feel better," Erik said.

Paxton whispered in Erik's ear, "Sherry's not here."

Erik sucked in his breath. He had a sour taste in his mouth about Sherry. "Where's Travis?"

"We can't find him either."

He imagined the worst. He worried Travis wanted to test gravity some more to see how it worked with a human body and threw Sherry off the cliff. Had the boy worked with Mooney and the mayor to capture her and put her back in the prison?

Erik shook his head and decided he could do only one thing at a time. "Let me heal Kestrel first. Then we can search for Sherry and Travis."

Lily gasped, "Sherry's not here?"

Paxton narrowed his eyes at Erik. "Everything's fine."

Lily returned to sobbing.

Erik had to concentrate. Before he used the sword, he wanted to do another examination of Kestrel's brain. He placed both hands on Kestrel's head. He wasn't like a spiritualist or wizard. There was no chant or magic spell to say. He placed his hands over a section of the body and delved into the patient to find the problem. Once the healer found it, then he decided on the best method to repair the injury. Broken bones were easy. Magic sickness looked to be more difficult.

Five more people crowded into the room, but they all remained quiet as Erik continued his examination. Erik followed veins through Kestrel's brain, looking for blockages or slowing of the blood. Twice he thought he'd found the problem, but then Kestrel's heart would pump, and the blood flowed unobstructed past that point.

Erik removed his hands from Kestrel's head.

Lily looked at Erik with her bloodshot blue eyes. He wanted to help Kestrel. He hoped the sword would make a significant difference. Would Lily still like Kestrel if he didn't heal from this sickness? Erik couldn't think about Lily that way. He knew he loved Zita now, but he would do everything he could to make Lily happy, including restoring Kestrel's health.

Erik grabbed the sword and placed the blade point on Kestrel's head.

Kestrel looked at Erik like he wondered if Erik planned to kill him.

Erik shook his head and ever so slightly touched the wizard's head. The effect of using the sword was immediate. Where Erik visualized the blood flowing through the veins in his earlier analysis, he now saw individual blood cells. There looked to be red blood cells, which he remembered from high school anatomy class. Also running through the plasma were white blood cells, as expected.

He examined the cells and looked for foreign antibodies attacking the cells or a cancerous growth. He didn't see signs of either.

Erik's chest grew tight. He wanted to solve this problem, and he ground his teeth as he searched Kestrel's brain. Then he saw something different. They were difficult to see, but tiny flecks of gold and silver flowed through the blood. The gold seemed to shine and shimmer, but the silver pieces looked like unpolished steel, dull, grey, and dead. Should he remove the silver pieces or change them into gold? Were the gold pieces the problem?

He couldn't risk Kestrel's life by removing the silver flecks only to find that he should have removed the others. Erik didn't know, and he thought back to Dickerson. It was better to do nothing instead of trying to fix the wrong thing.

With a slight pull on the sword, Erik disengaged from Kestrel, and a wave of energy lurched through him. He dropped the sword to the floor in defeat.

Paxton asked. "Are you okay?"

"Yes."

Lily asked, "Did you fix him? He doesn't look any better."

Erik's shoulders sagged, and he dropped his gaze. "I did nothing. I analyzed his blood vessels. They looked fine, and then I examined the blood. I have questions about a wizard's blood compared to non-wizards. Cugbert should be here to help." He grabbed Paxton's arm. "Are there wizards in Triponca?"

CHAPTER 55

Erik went to search for the wizard in Triponca that might help with Kestrel's magic sickness. The wizard's cabin stood dark and quiet when Erik arrived. It squatted in the woods a hundred yards off a little path. The time was late, and he felt bad having to interrupt these people, but he knocked on the cottage door.

A candle brightened a window, and someone moved in the room.

A male voice in the cabin said, "What do you want?"

"I'm looking for a wizard."

"Come see me tomorrow."

"There's a medical emergency."

"Go see a healer."

"I am a healer."

A loud sigh followed, and the door opened a crack. "What do you want?"

Erik said, "I have a wizard friend that might have magic sickness, and I need information. My friend Paxton said you could help."

The man looked behind Erik as if checking for a gang of criminals. "Come on in."

Kenneth Brown

The cabin smelled of cooked cabbage. The room consisted of a small kitchen area, a fireplace, and a mattress in the opposite corner. A woman sat on the mattress, the covers pulled up to her chin with trembling fingers.

"I'm sorry to interrupt your sleep. If it wasn't an emergency, I wouldn't be here."

A short man in his late fifties with a little balding on his forehead invited Erik to sit at the table. "Can I get you some tea?"

"No. That won't be necessary." Erik sat on a stool.

The man sat across the table from Erik. "I'm sorry about your friend, but magic sickness isn't healable. Once you have it, then you will die within six months to a year."

"I understand, but as a healer, I came across an irregularity, and I want to examine you and determine if you have the same irregularity as my friend."

"How old is your friend?"

"My age."

"Few wizards his age would experience burnout, and in my experience, that only happens to wizards in their twenties and thirties who are attempting to do too much without the proper rest."

"Yes, I understand. My friend is helping with the aqueduct, and he tried to do too much with magic."

"I see. What can I tell you?"

"Not tell me. Let me examine you. . . with my sword." Erik touched the sword hilt.

The wizard jumped from his stool and fired a slight shock at Erik's hand. "Don't touch that in my home."

"Ouch." Erik brought his hand to his mouth and sucked on a finger. "I don't want to hurt you. I want to examine you. This is the

Sword of Freedom and has healing power." *I guess I could have explained this part of the process better.*

"The Sword of Freedom is a myth."

"What would it take to convince you otherwise?"

"Take your sword and go. We don't need your foolishness."

"Please, I beg you. It's important and could save his life." Erik stayed seated so as not to threaten the man. "Pull the sword and examine it. If it isn't what I say, then I'll leave."

"I have no desire to touch the sword or any weapon. I'm a peaceful wizard." He looked over at his wife. "We don't want trouble."

His wife shook her head and pulled the covers farther up her chin.

What could Erik say to this man and his wife that would allow him to stay? Erik knew he had an answer for magic sickness but wanted to prove it. He had to get more information. He was too afraid to solve the problem blindly. "I promise you, I'm also a peaceful man. The sword is a tool of healing."

The wizard opened the door.

Erik stayed seated.

"I can force you to go with magic."

"And I won't fight you. I'm doing this for a fellow wizard and friend. I'm not your enemy."

The door stayed open.

Erik said, "Touch the sword and see for yourself. I'm Cugbert's student."

The man looked at his wife again.

She shook her head and continued to hold tight to the blanket.

What had happened to this couple that would make them so afraid? Now Erik wished he had taken Paxton up on his request to come with him. Maybe Paxton could have helped them see Erik was no danger to them.

"Cugbert is a friend of mine. I've known him a long time. Is he in the village?"

"No, I'm sorry, but he left recently to help more people."

"As his student, wouldn't you go with him?"

Erik didn't want to go through a long conversation with this man to explain his situation and why he had to stay with Sherry and help her complete the aqueduct. "Normally I would, but I needed to help a friend who's been staying at Paxton's farm."

The wizard rubbed his chin and looked at his wife.

She wobbled her head as if she was unsure.

The man swallowed hard and closed the door. "Stay where you are. I will slide the sword out with magic and examine it. If it isn't what you say, I will forcibly remove you from my home."

"I agree." Erik bowed his head to the wizard and pressed his hand to his heart in gratitude.

The sword slid out of its scabbard and floated to the wizard. It lay flat in the air while the wizard inspected it.

Even after examining the sword, will the wizard still let me perform my experiments?

The sword glowed crimson as if the handle burned, but the metal didn't change its shape. The man turned it over and checked the handle, blade, and blocker.

"Okay, I agree. The sword has properties I'm unfamiliar with. I cannot determine if it is the Sword of Freedom, but I agree its purpose is for healing and not for battle."

"Thank you." Erik took a deep breath and raised his eyebrows. "Now, would you be willing to let me test your blood?"

The wizard pressed his lips together as he sent the sword flying back into its sheath.

"It will be totally safe. I'm looking for flecks of gold and silver in your blood. All that's needed is a touch of the sword. You won't experience any pain or damage."

The man pulled his ear, ran his hand down his chin, and then scratched the back of his neck.

Then it hit Erik. He didn't need to put the sword against the man and examine his entire body and brain. If it was something in the blood, then he could do it like a scientist on Earth and draw a little blood and examine a small sample. "Sir, if you're uncomfortable letting me touch the sword to your body, then I could also do the experiment with a sample of your blood."

The wizard's wife said, "No, you can't take his blood. I knew it. You're a charlatan conjurer, and we don't want any part of you or your cursed magic."

Where did this come from?

"You want my husband's blood so you can ruin him with a blood curse. Get out of my house."

Erik looked at the woman. He looked at the wizard.

The wizard dropped his gaze to the floor.

So close to getting the information that he needed. Erik couldn't let this end. "I won't take his blood, and I surely won't curse your husband. I need a quick examination. Please. It might save a fellow wizard's life."

"No. Get out!"

The wizard opened the door and nodded in the door's direction.

Erik's chest tightened, and he thought about Kestrel and Lily. How could he let them down? This planet had so many social rules that Erik didn't know or understand. He heaved a long, inaudible sigh. The day's trials and work had left Erik exhausted.

He stood and questioned the wizard once more, "Please, sir? My friend's life depends on it."

The wizard shrugged and looked at the door.

Erik walked out of the cabin and trudged back toward the farm as his heart thudded in his chest. How could he tell his friends that he had failed?

He had scared the old couple, of course. He should wait until morning and then try again. If Paxton could talk to the wizard and get him to come into the woods, then Erik could do a quick analysis.

Erik heard a sound behind him and turned. There stood the old wizard.

"I can't let you have my blood, but you can do a quick examination with the sword."

Adrenaline rushed through Erik's tired body, rejuvenating him. "Yes! It'll take just a minute." Erik pulled out the sword and gently touched it to the wizard's brain.

As he delved into the old wizard's body, he encountered old physical injuries the wizard had incurred. Erik ignored the injuries for now. He could return to heal them if he had time. First, he needed to answer the original question.

He entered the blood-stream and evaluated its attributes. The old man had both silver and gold flecks, but the majority were gold. He had the answer. Erik took a couple of minutes and healed the man's other physical injuries.

When he was done, Erik felt a warmth tingle through his body. He had the ability to heal Kestrel now. He thanked the old wizard and squeezed his forearm in thanks.

The wizard nodded at Erik and returned to the cabin.

Kestrel had too many silver flecks. There were still many questions that needed answering but first, he had to change the percentage of silver compared to gold within Kestrel's system.

What would happen if Erik removed some of the silver flecks from Kestrel's blood? Not all of them, maybe ten or twenty percent. Then Erik could watch Kestrel's status for a couple of days. If Kestrel improved, then Erik could remove more, but still not all of them. Erik was sure the silver flecks harbored the illness. The gold flecks were bright and must be the good flecks. He believed he could remove the ones that caused the sickness, and he hoped he wasn't supposed to be turning them to gold.

When Erik returned, Paxton greeted him at the door. "Kestrel's getting worse. Is there anything you can do? His family will never forgive me for letting him get sick like this."

"I have a plan that I think will work." Erik followed Paxton into the bedroom where Kestrel lay.

The young wizard's face looked paler than before. Lily sat on the floor, holding his hand while Kestrel slept.

Erik touched Lily's shoulder, and she turned her puffy face and red eyes toward him, giving him a questioning look.

He nodded and gave a half smile. "I think I can heal your Kestrel, but it will still be trial and error until I learn what I'm doing."

Paxton took Lily's hand. "Come with me. I'll make you some hot tea."

CHAPTER 56

Erik pulled his sword from the scabbard as his stomach quivered. He closed his eyes and took a calming breath, thinking of Kestrel lying on the bed. Would this work or would it make Kestrel die faster? Maybe the young wizard needed to rest. A couple of months in bed and a little physical or mental therapy, and Kestrel might be fine, though the old wizard said magic sickness was always fatal.

Kestrel's breath changed to a raspy knock.

Erik placed the pointed end of the sword against the young sick wizard. He wondered who had made a tool of destruction into an instrument of healing.

Using the power of the sword, Erik delved into Kestrel's body. As the blood raced past Erik's examination, silver flecks had increased in number from the previous analysis. What caused them to increase? What was the source of the silver flecks, and if he eliminated several of them now, would Kestrel still die because his body kept making the silver specks?

There were so many things Erik didn't know. He hoped wizards weren't given a fixed number of gold specks that changed to silver, at which point the wizards lost their magic and died. Here he was, a teenager from Earth, trying to solve a centuries-old problem with magic sickness.

Erik decided to remove a few silver specks and then check on Kestrel's health as the night wore on. He captured a handful of the silver specks by creating a tiny sieve in Kestrel's vein. The silver ones were larger than the gold, so the filter allowed the gold specks through and captured the silver.

He didn't understand how it all worked, but once he collected a few, he could analyze them. He tried blasting them with mind energy to see if they were gold specks that had somehow become coated with silver. Maybe that was how magic sickness worked, like a dirty carburetor. Erik poked at the specks, sandblasted them, and even tried to mutilate the tiny things, but nothing changed their makeup.

As the night lengthened, Erik went to the simple strategy of removing the silver specks from the blood. He decided Kestrel would rather be alive with some magic than to be dead.

Kestrel tossed and turned. When it looked like the wizard was cold, Erik placed a blanket on him. When sweat formed on the wizard's forehead, Erik removed the blanket. Every couple of hours, he re-examined the veins. At first, despite his efforts, the silver specks multiplied and outnumbered the gold. Then six hours later, the gold and silver were at the same level. A sample of one hundred specks showed half gold and half silver.

Erik stopped at that point and let Kestrel rest.

Lily came into the room before sunrise. "How is he?"

"Stable."

Lily placed her hands on her stomach as if in pain. "Were you able to help?"

"We have to wait and see."

Lily touched his shoulder. "You need to rest."

Erik rubbed his bleary eyes. "No, I'm joining the team to look for Sherry. Paxton is rousing a group for the search."

"Should I do anything with Kestrel?"

"No, keep him comfortable. If he wants food, give him some. Make sure he drinks a lot of water."

Lily gave Erik a big hug.

Paxton stuck his head in the doorway. "Are you ready?"

Erik grabbed one of Lily's hands in both of his. He stared into her eyes. "If you see him getting worse, send somebody to get me."

He held her hand for a few ticks then let go.

The sun tried to show its face, but low clouds hung in the mountains, and fog blanketed the forest. The day felt dreary and full of failure.

They had a team of six prepared for the search for Sherry and Travis.

"Where should we start?" Paxton asked.

"Let's start at the camp," Erik said. "Maybe when it got dark, Sherry was forced to hole up there instead of coming to the farm. She might not know about Kestrel."

* * * *

Sherry woke with a start. Lying on the wet, damp ground had chilled her core temperature, and her whole body felt wet and cold. She checked on Travis by shaking him awake. "Wake up. It's morning." They would have to get their core temperatures back to normal.

"I'm hungry and cold."

"Yeah, me too."

"Did anyone come to rescue us?"

"Not yet. Today, they'll search for us." A shiver buzzed down her back as she thought about the consequences of not being found. They might eventually reach a point of being unable to yell. Then animals might come in looking for them. She chewed on a fingernail, which she hadn't done since breaking the habit back in junior high school.

"They don't care about us. They're just going to let us die. I want to go home to Mum."

I bet you do. She looked through the slit in the rocks, but the tree limbs and leaves blocked her view of the area. She yelled, "Help!"

Travis started yelling and screaming, "Help! Get us out." Over and over, he yelled.

Finally, Sherry had to stop him. "Stop it. They'll come looking for us and find us. Save your energy."

Travis scowled and jutted out his chin. "When? I want out now."

"So do I, but we have to wait."

"I'm not waiting any longer." He reached for a rock near the top of the pile and pushed it out.

"No, don't do that!" Sherry screamed in pain as rocks tumbled down on top of her.

CHAPTER 57

Erik and Paxton walked past the fallen tree and searched down the hill. The farmhands had already covered this ground, but Erik yelled out Sherry's name anyway.

Paxton stopped. "Did you hear that?"

"What?"

"It sounded like rocks tumbling and a woman screaming." Paxton turned back toward the tree.

They waited for another sound.

"I hear nothing." Erik slowly shook his head and pinched his lips.

"It came from the fallen tree. I'm sure of it." Paxton walked back up toward the tree and yelled Sherry's name.

Erik searched under the tree and in the limbs but didn't find Sherry or Travis. He yelled, "Sherry."

A muffled sound came from the hill or behind the hill. Erik couldn't tell for sure.

"Are they stuck in the rocks?" Paxton asked.

"Like a cave? And the tree knocked the cave roof in?" Erik ran to the rock pile and pulled on one at the top. The rocks shifted down into the cave.

"Hey, be careful. You don't want to cause the entire roof to collapse on them."

Erik shouted, "Can you hear us?"

A faint, "Help," came from the rocks.

Heat radiated through Erik's chest. With a bubbly voice, he said, "At least one of them is in there."

It took careful choosing of rocks to open the space to peer down into the cave. Sherry lay unconscious under a pile of rocks, and Travis had his leg pinched between two fallen rocks.

Paxton and Erik moved the rocks to the point that it was safe to extract Travis, and then they stepped into the cave and pulled the rocks off Sherry. Erik checked her vitals. "She's alive, but she has a concussion." He went to his knees, and the tension in his shoulders released.

They took Travis and Sherry back to the farm. Paxton had his staff prepare food for her, and Erik re-examined her and healed additional wounds and bruises. He then healed Travis.

Sherry looked at the calendar lying on the kitchen table. She pointed at the date the aqueduct project needed to be finished. "Eight days. Can we complete the work in eight days?"

Erik shook his head. "No way. Kestrel is down, and he cannot use magic until he heals. I'm sorry, Sherry. I want you to succeed, but Kestrel is in danger. I can't guarantee he's completely out of the woods."

Sherry asked, "What can we complete? Can we complete the bridge?"

"I think so," Erik said.

Paxton and the farmhands all nodded.

"Then we concentrate on the bridge."

* * * *

Kestrel was supposed to help to blast a hole through the granite rock. Eight days to finish the bridge and tunnel through the granite. Without the hole through the granite, they couldn't get the water into the valley. We still have so many things left to do. Sherry looked at the ceiling and felt like her body was falling off the bridge into an endless abyss.

Despite still being cold and tired from her time in the cave, Sherry followed the workers back to the bridge.

They reached the work area by noon and began digging post holes. They took the displaced dirt and piled it upstream in the meadow, planning to divert the rain and winter-melt water through a single area that would avoid taking down the bridge foundation. The teams worked hard, and by the end of the day, they had placed four more posts.

As they ate dinner that night at a campsite near the bridge, Erik expounded on an idea he had about getting around the granite rock. "How far up the mountain would we have to go to be above the granite rock Kestrel was working on?"

Paxton shook his head. "We can't build a bridge from that point. That will take as long as digging through the granite with crude tools."

"Agreed, but hear me out. Sherry, how do water towers work on Earth?"

Sherry thought. "I don't know exactly, but I think they just use gravity."

Erik picked up a stick next to the fire. "That's the way I understand it, too, though there might be another factor in the amount of pressure in the pipe."

He took the stick and drew a diagram on the ground. "Imagine we work our way back up the mountain and find a point higher than the rock. Then we enclose the aqueduct from that point up to the top of the rock. We might need methods to provide additional pressure to force the water to travel up."

Sherry felt a moment of breathlessness and heightened senses. A wide grin spread across her lips. *This plan of Erik's could work. We can still beat the mayor and his bullies.*

* * * *

Two days later, Sherry and Paxton visited with the mayor. They brought Gabriella and Travis to see their parents.

The mayor asked, "How's the project? I don't see any water flowing across the meadow, and time is running out."

Mr. Mooney stood with his arms around Gabriella's shoulders. Gabriella said, "Dad, we're making significant progress. We're building a bridge and forcing water to rise. I'm learning so much about gravity and math. Miss Torkel is really smart."

Justin, standing in a corner of the mayor's office, asked, "Will you finish on time?"

Sherry wasn't happy that Gabriella had revealed information about the bridge and the modified water tower. She didn't like that Justin asked the question and not the mayor. It didn't matter. They were proceeding. She looked at the mayor. "I guarantee water will flow into Crossroads next Tuesday." Four days away. Sherry shook her head and closed her eyes, trying to tap down the fluttery, empty feeling in her stomach.

"I see." The mayor and Justin exchanged glances.

"We plan to have it flow into the well. We have a team working on that solution right now." Paxton had contracted with three village men and a blacksmith to connect the aqueduct to the village well. She knew they were almost done. After the meeting with the mayor, they would check on the blacksmith's progress.

The mayor smirked. "I'm sure my people will be happy to get fresh mountain water into the village."

Sherry thought of several rude comments she could make about the mayor's people, but she held her tongue. She couldn't get the mayor or Mooney angry now, this close to the project's completion and her freedom.

On the journey back to the work site, Paxton filled her in. "The contractors finished the work on the pipe. It extends two hundred yards to the low point in the meadow. I asked them to build an enclosed box we could flow the water into, and then the piping will take it the rest of the way to the well."

Sherry gave Paxton a kiss on the cheek. "Thank you for using your time, farmhands, and other resources for this project. We couldn't have finished without your help."

He licked his lips and placed his hand on Sherry's.

She thought about pulling her hand away. She hoped the peck on the cheek didn't bring other connotations to the relationship. Sherry only wanted to let him know how grateful she felt for his service to her project. They could have a conversation about it later since the next day's work would keep them too busy for romance.

CHAPTER 58

Erik slept poorly as he dreamed of goblins chasing him through the Pit of Wretchedness where he had gained the Sword of Freedom. This dream had troubled him many nights since his and Al's last adventure, and he woke long before daybreak. As he lay thinking about the aqueduct, he wondered about Al and Zita. He knew Al went to search for Finn, but where had Zita gone? Why hadn't they returned?

The team of laborers was sleeping in the forest, and at this time of night, sounds traveled great distances in the forest.

Something thumped in the night. A steady beat. *Kerthump. Kerthump. Kerthump.* Not rapid but regular.

Erik sat up, intrigued by the sound. He thought he heard a voice bark a command, but he couldn't make out the words.

Kerthump, kerthump, kerthump. The beat grew faster.

Erik crawled over to Paxton and shook him.

Paxton came to. "Wha—"

"Quiet," Erik said. "Listen."

Kerthump, kerthump, kerthump.

Then a yell, "Timberrrr."

Paxton sat up. "The bridge is under attack."

Erik ran to the sleeping workers and grabbed at ankles, arms, and legs. "Wake up. Move! Now."

The workers were so tired, they didn't respond as fast as Erik wanted.

Paxton woke more of the crew.

Once they realized what was happening, they snapped awake.

"Grab a tool for a weapon. We have to stop them. Hurry to the bridge." Erik picked up a shovel and ran through the dark forest, following the aqueduct down the mountain. He sped up in a steep downhill section, and his arms windmilled to keep from falling.

As he neared the bridge, a red glow encapsulated the mountain area. What was that, he wondered? Erik stopped at the side of the cliff where the bridge started, and it leaned at an angle. Twelve men stood below with torches as others chopped the foundation logs.

"Hey! Stop!" Erik shouted.

One man yelled, "Light them up."

The men with the torches placed the flames at the base of the bridge support poles. A pile of brush surrounded each foundation. The brush quickly caught fire, and the men backed away from the roaring conflagration.

Erik commanded the farm hands. "Half of you go that way and the other half the other side. Be prepared to fight."

They raced down the hill and into the valley.

A cry of triumph rose as the foundations started burning.

The attackers had chopped four of the bridge poles, and the bridge leaned to one side. The only thing keeping the logs from falling was their attachment to the bridge. Men pushed on the foundation logs to get them to fall.

"Whoa, they're coming. Scatter, men." The men ran toward the village, away from Erik.

Erik and the workers chased after them. The sound of metal hitting metal reverberated in the darkness. By the time Erik reached the bridge, the bridge support logs burned, and there was no way to stop the fire. He hoped it didn't travel far up the aqueduct. When the fire reached the part of the bridge treated with pine resin, flames raced along the edges.

He ran under the burning bridge.

CHAPTER 59

They did what they could to control the fire. Sherry sent Erik back along the aqueduct to open the flow gate about a mile from the bridge. The water cascaded down the aqueduct and kept the aqueduct from burning ten feet from the bridge. Sherry watched the water flow into the meadow.

Sherry had difficulty swallowing as she assessed the damage from the night's raid. She clenched her jaw and rubbed her arms as if she were cold. The morning light brought the reality of the damage.

"Travis, run up to Erik and tell him to turn off the flow."

"Yes, ma'am."

Gabriella wailed.

Sherry put an arm around Gabriella's shoulder. "It's okay, honey. Everything will be okay."

"How can you say that? We can't rebuild this in a day. The mayor will put you back in prison. Why did they do this?"

"I can't teach you everything, but learn this. There are bad people who are envious of others' success, and rather than work for their own success, they prefer to destroy people who are succeeding. We will rebuild."

"There isn't time," Gabriella cried.

The girl was right, of course. The mayor's thugs had chopped four foundational posts, and the fire had charred others, and those would need to be re-evaluated for replacement. If the team had to replace all of them, it meant more than a week's work.

"Who did this?" Gabriella asked.

Sherry wanted to tell Gabriella that her father and the mayor were responsible, but she didn't. She picked up a charred piece of the bridge and threw it at the water dripping down the cliff face. Sherry huddled with Paxton and Erik when he returned, and they strategized a way to rebuild the bridge.

Erik said, "Paxton can get the team chopping trees down. Let's get the foundation up first. Then we can build the bridge portion again. We can work through the night, and maybe we can still finish on time."

Paxton said, "Even working through the night won't be enough."

Sherry's muscles quivered, and a vein pulsed in her neck. "Erik, you work with the farmhands. Paxton, I need you to take me into the village. I need to have a conversation with the mayor."

"Is that wise?"

"No, it's not wise, but he will hear me."

"Let's work your anger out rebuilding."

Her body tensed as she raised her voice. "We're going to the village."

* * * *

Paxton's coach rolled to a stop at the council building, where the mayor and Mr. Mooney stood, their arms crossed and their chins upturned in a pose of superiority.

Sherry crawled out of the coach in the early morning light.

The mayor asked, "Did you come to tell us you finished the project?" He clapped Mooney on the back, and they both laughed.

"You know we haven't finished the project because you and your henchmen sabotaged the aqueduct. How petty are you that you have to win by ruining others' work?"

"We don't know what you're talking about, do we, Mooney?"

"No, sir." He crouched with his hands on his knees and laughed.

"Did you come to surrender so we don't have to chase after you?"

"I still have a day to finish the project. I can't believe you hate your village so much that you would destroy their only chance for fresh water."

Two women from the village stood on the village green, watching the exchange between Sherry and the mayor.

"Mooney, bring out the member of their project who surrendered to us." The mayor nodded at Mooney.

Mooney went inside the building and returned with Justin, who held Lily in chains with a gag across her mouth.

Lily's body trembled, and her eyes seemed to bulge.

What had they done to her? Sherry couldn't leave the village without Lily. "Let her go."

"She's a criminal that escaped from prison. She needs to be prosecuted and sentenced for her crimes."

Sherry moved toward the men, and Paxton held her back. "It won't work. They're baiting you."

"We can't let Justin have her. They will beat her to death because of me. It's not her fault. She had nothing to do with the school."

"You can't. They want nothing more than for you to attack them. Then the deal is off, and they will imprison you. I know how these people work." Paxton held Sherry tight to keep her from bolting for the mayor.

A crowd formed around the building.

Two women stood watching the action between the mayor and Sherry. She pointed at the women and shouted, "Do you like the dirty, stinking water the mayor has provided for you?"

They looked at each other and shook their heads.

"Did you know you were one day from getting fresh water straight from winter snowmelt?"

They shook their heads.

"That man." She pointed at the mayor. "Your mayor destroyed a project that I worked on that would have supplied fresh water to you. Your mayor"—she paused, her body shaking with anger—"your mayor kidnapped one of my workers, chopped down part of the aqueduct I was building, and burned the rest."

"Now don't be telling lies, Miss Torkel." The mayor walked over toward her.

Her nails bit into the palms of her hands. She stomped her foot on the ground. "Lies? You're holding my friend that you kidnapped in the night from our campsite, and you're calling me a liar?"

"I had nothing to do with that. Justin is a trained bounty hunter, and he was bringing a criminal to justice."

"There are three criminals here, and Lily isn't one of them. Justin is a deranged man that should be locked up."

Justin smirked and flashed malformed teeth. He pulled on Lily's chains, causing her to wobble.

The crowd grew.

Sherry had trouble swallowing as her neck tensed. She clenched her hands into fists. "Your mayor doesn't want you to have fresh water. How do you feel about the mayor now? Are your children sick, and is it because of the water?"

A murmur rose in the crowd.

"How many times did the mayor stop one of your projects?" Sherry realized it now. *This was probably a repeatable strategy by the mayor. People started a project, the mayor destroyed it, and then they found the mayor's cronies taking over the project and taking credit for it.* "Did you find he took credit for the project after he forced you off of it?"

A few men nodded.

"How long will you accept the mayor putting your breadwinners in prison or killing them so he could take your source of income and enrich his own pocket?"

"Come on, folks. She's just rousing you up. Go on home." The mayor waved to men standing behind the crowd.

Men carrying swords and clubs pushed into the town square.

Sherry shouted to the bystanders, "You're letting these thugs win again. Bullies that have never had a creative thought in their lives. If they say they're here to help you, you can bet you'll be out of money and homeless before the day is over. I want you all to know that I was the one who gave you fresh water!"

The thugs swung their clubs, and the crowd scattered.

Sherry pushed Paxton toward the coach and looked back at Lily. She hoped Lily survived.

CHAPTER 60

The men were hard at work rebuilding the bridge when Sherry returned from the village. Midday had arrived, and three men toiled over one of the chopped and burned foundation poles as they wriggled it free of the mud holding it in place. Two replacement poles lay in the meadow, ready to slide into the vacated spot.

Kestrel stood in the meadow, watching the work.

"What are you doing here? Erik told you to rest," Sherry said.

"I'm looking for Lily."

Sherry took a deep breath. "Where's Erik?"

Kestrel walked closer to Sherry. "Milling more lumber for the bridge. Have you seen Lily?"

Sherry took Kestrel aside. She had to be delicate. The magic sickness limited Kestrel's magic despite Erik's healing. Erik had told her that he needed to continue the healing treatments for Kestrel. Sherry had to keep him under control.

"Listen." She took a deep breath. "Justin and the mayor have Lily."

His nostrils flared, and he ground his teeth. "What do you mean, they have her?"

"During the raid, they kidnapped her. We were putting out the fire and didn't know they had planned to capture Lily."

Kestrel turned to leave, and Sherry grabbed his arm.

"Let me go."

"I can't let you run off and try to rescue her. They want you as much as they want her."

"They'll kill her."

Sherry rubbed the back of her neck. Kestrel was right, but they needed a plan. There was too much to do and too little time left. "We'll go for her at night. They have a bully force that expects a rescue. We need a plan."

"I have a plan. I blast anyone who gets in my way."

"Erik says you can't use your magic for a while. It's dangerous." He pulled his arm, but Sherry held tight.

"I have to rescue her."

"We will. Can you wait for tonight? I promise we'll go for her."

An engorged vein in Kestrel's neck pulsed, and his voice deepened. "If they hurt her. . ."

"We'll rescue her."

Kestrel stared at Sherry with cold, hard, flinty eyes and shook Sherry's grip off his arm.

"Get that pole out of the ground. Come on," Kestrel yelled at the farmhands wriggling the next foundation pole.

Sherry's heart thudded. She stood on a powder keg—the months of hard labor, the tight deadline, and the stress now of losing Lily to the mayor's henchmen. It would be difficult keeping these men from acting on their own to rescue her.

* * * *

The work crew sat on rocks, eating their dinner, as Sherry munched on a carrot. She wasn't hungry. In fact, she wanted to find a bed and sleep. After all the months of work to complete this project, she saw defeat written in the workers' postures. It took hours to remove a foundation pole and then drop a new pole into the hole.

The workers had lost sleep last night putting out the fire and worked all day today. They all knew they had to work all night tonight. Paxton's men were good workers who didn't complain. They did what needed to be done, but now their shoulders slumped, and they wouldn't look Sherry in the eye. The men acted like they had failed, but she knew they couldn't have worked any better, harder, or faster. They did everything she had asked.

Paxton sat next to Sherry, eating the jerky that he and his men enjoyed.

Sherry said, "We won't make it."

"Don't say that. There's still hope. We only have five more foundation poles to pull and replace."

"I'll let the men go home tonight. They deserve time with their families. They should all be resting."

"We can still work overnight. Maybe we won't finish tomorrow, but we can ask for an extension from the mayor. Surely, he wants to see this completed. And if not the mayor, I'll ride to see Prince Krunal. We'll get that extension and keep you out of prison."

She sneered. "He can't have me complete this project. He wants me in prison as a lesson to anybody else that might have an opinion of their own."

"I will keep working on the aqueduct until it's complete." Paxton pointed his beef jerky at the bridge.

"Anybody who works on this project after I'm imprisoned will find their lives and their family's lives in danger. It's not worth it. He beat me."

"My men will work all night for you, and we can defend the bridge until we complete it. I want to do this for you."

Sherry placed her hand on top of Paxton's. "You've been a great friend and have given us all these resources to use. I can't thank you enough, but it's time to go back and live your life. The mayor can have the aqueduct."

He took her hand in his. "Come back to the farm with me. I can hide you and keep you safe."

She looked into his eyes. He was very different from Al, who was still a boy. Paxton was a mature man and not the type that would wander off on an exciting quest for the thrill of adventure. Paxton was a stable and down-to-earth man with the resources and lifestyle that Sherry could enjoy on this backward planet.

"I would like that, I really would, but. . ." She withdrew her hand as moisture welled in her eyes, and she thought of Al. Where was the tall lug? She stood and walked to the men.

"We'll work an hour after sunset, and then you can all return to your families. Thank you for your hard work." She saw the mixed emotions on the men's faces—their desire to go home and their determination to finish the project.

"We don't mind working all night," one man said.

"I know you don't, but it won't matter. We can't complete the entire project tonight. There's no reason to be away from your families any longer. Thank you for your help."

Each of the men expressed his disappointment differently. One man dropped his head and closed his eyes, while another looked at his coworkers and slowly shook his head. A third stared at Sherry with a stony expression while he chewed at his bottom lip. A fourth took the knife he was using to carve off pieces of jerky and jammed it hard into the log he sat on.

Sherry couldn't look at them like this. She left to find Erik, Gabriella, and Travis.

CHAPTER 61

Sherry found Erik milling wood needed for the bridge. Gabriella and Travis stood near a fire heating pine resin to seal the joints to keep the structure watertight. Sherry hoped to show Gabriella how to be a strong woman, but here she had to tell the child that she had failed. She explained to Erik and the children what she had decided.

Sherry's stomach tightened, and she squeezed her fists so tight the fingernails bit into her palms.

Erik hugged her and stopped his work. They walked back to the camp, where she expected to see the others packing up their gear.

When they reached the bridge, the workers had set up another foundation pole. They hadn't left for home yet, even though the darkness was only minutes away. Several torches burned brightly, lighting up the area so much the night looked like day.

Paxton stood next to Sherry. "I couldn't convince them to leave. They want to stay and finish the project."

They all continued working, but soon they saw a light bouncing across the meadow.

Sherry gasped in a breath and yelled, "Grab a weapon! They're coming back."

They didn't have proper weapons—no bows and arrows, no magic—but the men hoisted shovels and pickaxes to their shoulders.

Sherry knew the men wouldn't go down without a fight. They had worked as a unit and built a magnificent structure that wouldn't even benefit themselves or their families. A selfless act to help Sherry.

As the light got closer, it changed from a single point of light to multiple torches. She couldn't make out how many people were in the gang, but there were more than the twelve sent the night before.

Erik stood beside her, an axe in his hands.

"I can't believe they would come back again." *The mayor is an unbelievable bully and thug. This village isn't worth all the backbreaking effort Paxton's men had accomplished.* She wanted to tell the farmhands to run, but she knew they wouldn't. They were willing to defend their work with their lives.

"Do you have a weapon?" Erik asked.

Sherry pulled out a long knife she had used to harvest the pine resin. The knife reflected the red glow from the torches.

The group of people continued to approach, and Sherry could make out individuals. It included women and even some older children. There had to be over a hundred people in the group. They all carried shovels, axes, hammers, hoes, and picks.

At the front of the crowd of people stood Ciara, the mayor's wife.

Sherry's stomach tightened, and her mouth slackened. *What does that lying woman want?*

The farmhands all moved to protect Sherry.

None of the crowd tried to attack.

Ciara called out, "Can we talk?"

An intuitive feeling flushed through Sherry's body; a prickling of skin rushed down her back. She furrowed her brow and gritted her teeth. Sherry had suffered all the pain she could take from this village, and the mayor's wife wasn't on her list of friends. "What do you want?"

"I just want to talk."

Sherry started toward Ciara, but Paxton held her back. Sherry didn't care. She wasn't afraid of these people anymore. She struggled forward until he loosened his grip on her.

Erik and Paxton walked with Sherry to face the crowd.

"What?" Sherry crossed her arms and stood before them.

Ciara took in a deep breath and looked at the crowd behind her.

A woman standing nearby poked her in the side. "Go ahead. Your husband caused this mess."

Ciara said, "We're here to help you."

Sherry stiffened. She expected the mayor to jump out of the crowd and shout, "Just kidding."

Ciara continued. "I was wrong, and these villagers have convinced me we should all help you. We want fresh water for the village. We brought horses and men and whatever you need. The village is here to help."

Adrenaline tingled through Sherry's body as she took in the crowd. She looked at Paxton and Erik, who both nodded. *Is this help too late?*

CHAPTER 62

Paxton led a group of men into the meadow between the rock and the village. The aqueduct had been roughed out in that area but still needed to be finished. Erik led a group up the hill to the lumber mill, where he developed a quick system to move sawed lumber from the mill to the sections of the aqueduct that needed lumber. A farmhand worked with a team of men and horses to retrieve additional lumber for the foundation poles, and Sherry managed the section at the bridge with a horse, pulling the burnt poles out of the ground and hauling new poles into position.

She couldn't believe how fast the project took shape. Within two hours, the workers had stripped all the foundation poles and set the new ones. A group of men passed lumber across the tops of the poles to set the base for the bridge. The villagers helped rebuild the enclosed portion that traveled over the top of the granite boulder and attached to the bridge portion.

Teenagers walked over the top of the bridge, applying generous amounts of pine resin to seal the boards. At two AM, Sherry sent a runner to Erik to start a test to see if they could get the water to go uphill.

Fifteen minutes later, Sherry heard water flow through the aqueduct. A teenager sat at the top of the granite boulder to watch the water spill out through the aqueduct bridge's up portion and onward to the meadow and the village.

Sherry yelled up at the girl. "Do you see any water?"

The girl held a torch over the aqueduct spillway. "No, but I can hear it."

Water gurgled. In some places, the seal could have been better since water leaked, but the flow didn't come over the peak.

Sherry directed a woman standing near the bridge. "I'm going up to Erik to see if I can help. Send a message to Erik if the water flows over the boulder." *We have to solve this issue. Otherwise, we fail.*

She trudged up the mountainside to Erik's position, checking the aqueduct for major leaks or structural issues, but she didn't find any. This section was critical to the success or failure of the aqueduct.

"Is it working?" Erik asked.

"No," Sherry said.

Erik said, "I don't know what's wrong."

"Where's the point where you cover up the aqueduct? I think there isn't enough pressure"

Erik led her a hundred yards farther up the mountain. "At this point here."

"Do we need a basin?"

"What do you mean?" Erik asked.

"Like a water tower, you need a body of water pressing down to create the pressure needed."

"Shouldn't the enclosed section work like that?"

Sherry shook her head. "There's not enough pressure in the system. There are many little holes in our structure where water leaks out. Build a little reservoir and make the walls higher than your entry point."

Erik yelled out, "We need lumber and pine resin. Hurry, people."

Sherry didn't know where the people came from, but within an hour, Erik and his team were constructing a wide pool to capture the flow from the lakes. When they had it built and sealed, Erik released the gate that prevented the water from going into his reservoir.

Sherry watched Erik and his team work. Then she glanced at the rising sun, turning the sky from dark to light blue and making the clouds on the horizon a pale red. *Work faster, Erik.*

The reservoir filled with water from the Triponca lake. The highest point of the makeshift water tower reservoir stood five feet over the top of the aqueduct, and Sherry and Erik hoped that would be enough.

It took an hour for the water to fill most of the aqueduct entry point. With fifteen percent of the reservoir left to fill, the water quit rising. Erik and Sherry looked at each other. The sun had broken the horizon. Day was upon them.

"Do you think it's working?" Erik asked.

Adrenaline rushed through Sherry's body. She grabbed Erik's arm and stared into his eyes. "It's gotta. We're out of time."

They both scampered down the mountain to the bridge.

Sherry was running too fast, and she plummeted headfirst onto the forest floor and slid two feet through the brush.

In the distance, a scream pierced the sky.

"What was that?" Sherry asked.

Erik helped her to her feet, a worried look digging deep ridges in his tired face.

Sherry stood, brushed off her tunic, and then increased her pace to the bridge.

They reached the bridge. Everyone stared at a teenager watching the point where the water was supposed to flow over the large granite rock.

She had her hands lowered to her side.

Sherry bit her lip. *It didn't work. We aren't done.*

The teenage girl stared intently at the makeshift aqueduct, then she raised her hands and cried out, "The water is flowing." She danced on top of the granite rock, screaming, "It works. Water is flowing."

Then a cheer rose from the countryside.

Erik shouted, "You did it!"

She hugged Erik, and her eyes sparkled. "*We* did it."

By the time Sherry reached the valley, the townspeople were dancing around the foundation poles, cheering, shouting, whooping, and yelling.

Sherry and Erik continued their journey to the other side of the granite boulder. She smiled and congratulated everyone she passed. They found the point where water flowed into the meadow section of the aqueduct. It cascaded fast and furious through the structure toward the village. They didn't have to check further because they heard shouting and whooping near the village.

Sherry said, "We need to stop the water until later. We can check the systems in the morning since the villagers already know it works and everyone will be excited to see the well fill with clean water."

Paxton met up with them. "The water is flowing into the basin at the point where we have the pipe to the well."

"Woohoo." A great weight lifted from Sherry's chest. She wanted to run to the bridge and join in the dancing and celebration, but she and her companions still had a task to complete.

Kestrel reached them. "Do you have a plan to rescue Lily?"

CHAPTER 63

It took an hour to get everyone together. They had closed off the water at the lumber mill. It would run off the side of the mountain until they were ready, and then they could reopen at the appropriate time.

Sherry stood among the villagers. "Thank you all for your work and service tonight. We could not have finished without your help." She touched her hand to her chest and almost came to tears, but they still had to rescue Lily.

The villagers slapped one another on the back.

"We still have a task to do, but it's dangerous, and you don't have to help us if you don't want to."

A cheer rose from the crowd. "Sherry. Sherry. Sherry."

She raised her hands. "Please, we have little time. Justin has kidnapped my friend Lily." She had almost said "evil people" but didn't want to implicate Ciara. "We have to rescue her."

A cheer rose from the crowd. "Let's go. I'm ready."

Forty-seven men and women volunteered to help. Sherry sent the rest of the villagers home. Ciara stayed with the volunteers. Sherry was unsure if she wanted Ciara as a member of the rescue team. She might leak vital information to her husband, preventing Lily's rescue.

They strategized for a while, and then a plan developed. Then they left for the village square.

Sherry, Paxton, Kestrel, Ciara, and Erik hid behind a building near the village square.

Paxton said, "The guards are on the square, just as we expected. The mayor's men are surrounding the outside of the council building."

Sherry asked, "How are we going to get into the building?"

Ciara answered, "The wives and I have already discussed that. Give us a minute." She placed two fingers into her mouth and whistled.

"You'll have to show me how you do that." Sherry giggled.

In a moment, several women walked up individually to guards and whispered in their ears.

Two of the guards vehemently denounced what their wives told them. "I'm not doing that."

The others seemed to understand the need for the plan, and Sherry wondered if the guards might lose privileges at home if they didn't comply. Sherry knew the general plan but not what the guards' wives were telling their husbands.

The guards formed up on either side of the council building and charged it, rounding up the mayor's thugs. There was some contact of metal to metal and a thud or two as village soldiers struck the men, but it happened fast, and then another whistle sounded in the square.

"That's for us," Ciara said.

All the women formed in the square with Sherry and her friends.

Sherry knocked on the council doors.

"Who is it?" a voice yelled out from inside.

Gabriella said, "It's me, Daddy."

The door opened an inch, and Gabriella waved at her father. He opened it farther, and all the women in the square squeezed through the door into the council hall.

Sherry found the mayor standing in the hallway outside his personal office. "Where's Lily?"

"She's in prison until we can try her for crimes against the village. Have you come to turn yourself in for your prison sentence?"

A twinkle of mischief formed in Sherry's eyes. She smirked. "No, I'm here to invite you to an event. At eleven this morning, we open the sluicegates, and fresh mountain water fills your cesspool of a village well."

The mayor's face turned the color of eggplant, and he blustered. "That's impossible."

Ciara asked, "Why is that impossible, dear?"

Sherry thought the mayor's eyes would pop out of his head.

"What are you doing here?"

Ciara's nostrils flared, and she spread her arms wide, pointing at all the women in the corridor. "We're here for Sherry's friend Lily. Where is she, dear?"

"You can't have her."

Ciara walked up to her husband and bunched his tunic in her hands.

"Let me go," the mayor stammered.

"Where's Sherry's friend?"

The mayor looked like he wanted to say something, but instead, he opened the door to his office.

Sherry burst into the room. Justin looked surprised to see her. Lily was tied to a table, and Justin held a whip in his hands.

Justin cracked his leather strap at Sherry.

Sherry tried to grab it, but it slapped across her wrist, drawing blood. Pain blossomed on her arm.

Justin whipped it again, and Sherry pulled back.

"You're not getting the blonde." He held the whip ready to strike at Sherry.

She stepped back.

He relaxed.

Then she raced at him.

He wasn't expecting the move and was slow in responding.

She caught the strap on its downward movement and pulled it toward her.

Justin held it tight, and they struggled with it.

They pulled like two people in a tug of war, but Sherry's adrenaline and anger won out, and she captured control of the whip. Women came into the room and stood with Sherry.

Justin hid behind Lily.

Kestrel, Paxton, and Erik entered the room and quickly wrestled him to the floor. They tied his arms and legs with rope.

"What's going on?" the mayor asked.

Paxton said, "The citizens of Triponca are taking Justin to stand trial for kidnapping, trespassing, property damage, and crimes against our citizens."

"But you. . . can't—" The mayor couldn't finish his sentence.

Ciara looked at him. "I have bargained for your amnesty, dear, but only if you don't make a big deal of it."

The mayor's face turned ashen white, and he moved into the hallway.

* * * *

At eleven o'clock, everyone stood in the village green. They had arranged for the farmhands on the mountain to open the gates at ten.

Sherry stood on a little raised platform the mayor had carted into the square. The mayor was on one side, and Lily was on the other. Lily looked tired, but after Erik had healed her, she seemed in good spirits.

Sherry shouted to the people on the village green. "It is with great pleasure I announce that we have built an aqueduct to bring fresh spring-fed lake water from Triponca to Crossroads."

The villagers cheered.

"I want to thank the people of Crossroads for your help in the project. You can be proud and know that you built it. It is yours. Not mine. And not the mayor's. It's a public works project built for the people of Crossroads."

A flutist and a man with a lute played a song, while the villagers danced in the square and cheered. Children danced around with their parents, siblings, and friends.

Erik brought a bucket of water to Sherry. She raised her hands.

The crowd quieted.

"This is the first bucket pulled from the well. Let's see if it is fresh mountain water." She poured the clear, cold liquid over the mayor's head.

CHAPTER 64

Al led the way as Finn and Zita followed on the path away from Finn's training center. He hadn't bothered to eat breakfast in the morning for his fear of traversing the two-hundred-rung ladder to reach the mountain trail to take them back to Velidred. Finn had made it so difficult for people to get up to see him Al was surprised he even had students.

They reached the point in the trail where it intersected with the path to the pond and in the opposite direction the cave with the creepy-crawly wall.

Al stopped and looked at Finn. "Do we go over the dome or around it to get to the ladders?"

Finn stared at Al for a moment and then burst out laughing. "Is that what you've been so worried about this morning? I forgot about your fear of heights." He chuckled for a moment and then pointed to the right. "We go to the cave over there."

Zita said, "No, you're not trapping us in there again."

"Aren't you two powerful wizards? One is afraid of heights and the other has a fear of bugs." Finn picked up a stick as he turned toward the cave.

Zita crossed her arms. "It's not just the bugs. Scorpions and spiders can be dangerous. I'm surprised you didn't add snakes into the mix just for fun."

"Don't worry, I promise not to trigger the magic wall. There's a back way into the meadow that leads to a trail down the mountain."

Finn took the lead, and Al assumed there was a hidden door along the cliff face that helped create the cave. But the elder wizard didn't look for other doors, he kept walking right into the cave.

Al heard Zita take a sharp breath before stepping into the space.

Finn walked to the back wall.

Al pointed at the rocks. "We looked for a hidden door. There isn't anything back there."

Finn touched the stick in his hands to the wall, threw dust against it, and said, "Open to the world. Use wind. Use earth. Use fire." A flame shot from his fingers and ignited the stick. He used magic to splash water from the pool onto the wall. "Volcano to metal, wood to ash. Open this door without a crash."

Then Al felt the magic. Powerful magic, elemental magic, something an old mage would think of, while a young pup like Al would look for fancy solutions. Nicely done, Finn.

The stones moved and a door just barely five feet tall and two feet wide opened to reveal a narrow shaft less than ten feet deep. Sunlight shone through the tunnel and Finn bowed his head and walked through the tight rocky passage.

Al exited onto a small meadow, and he followed Finn onto a pathway through flowers of brilliant reds and yellows. In less than a minute they reached the edge of the mountain and the landscape changed to rough rocks.

The route spiraled down the mountain, five-feet wide in some sections and narrowed to barely a foot at its smallest. Al looked over the edge and cringed as he moved closer to the mountain wall. An hour later they reached the stone bridge where Al had battled the ghost of Kroft Kyrtill. No defender challenged them as Zita and Jackson led the trio across the bridge.

They walked and talked about how to rescue the warriors now that they had marked the door.

* * * *

A few hours later they reached the little village of Svero Garden. The same village where Al had met Ylfa and had been chased by Clive. Al asked, "Do I need to hide my staff?"

Finn gave a funny snort. "Did Jolene tell you that? And my sister, Ylfa, she asked if you could do magic and…" He watched Al's expression and began laughing. "Ylfa knows magic herself, and probably used it on you without you knowing."

"What?" Al sputtered. "I could have used magic to protect myself against Clive and his friend?"

Finn was laughing so hard he had his hands on his knees. "The people on this mountain love to play pranks on visitors."

Al felt the heat rise in his face as he realized he'd been fooled by just about everyone he met on his trip to Finn's place.

They stopped at Ylfa's arrow shop, and Finn invited her to dinner with them at the local tavern.

Ylfa said, "You know when Clive was firing his arrows at you, I put a spell on the arrows. They would never hit you, but it was exciting watching you run." She started laughing. Then she took a swig of ale. "Now the stegox, she was real. Turns out Clive and his buddy stood between her and the twins. Not a good combination for Clive. He's probably limping now unless he found a good healer."

Finn studied a scroll as they ate. After studying the document Finn murmured, "We don't have everything we need."

"Did we leave something at the training center? Should we go back?" Zita looked up from her dinner.

"It's not something I own or have even seen. To my knowledge, the item is a myth. To harness the amount of energy we need to keep the connection open with the Phantasmal Moors requires us to tap into the power of one of the moons."

Al raised a mug of ale to his lips, then stopped. "How do you tap into a moon?"

Ylfa responded, "There are specialized magical objects that have historically been used to make a connection with the moons. There are three of them that I'm aware of, one for each moon."

Oh brother, another magical object we have to search for before we can rescue the warriors.

She raised her index finger. "One is the Velidred Imperium Wand."

Zita placed a piece of fried anouora onto her plate and wiped a napkin across her lips. "The wand isn't a real item. I've heard it mentioned by my father and some of the wizards at the castle and the general consensus is it isn't real."

Finn said, "I had a discussion with Gadiel once and he assured me that it is real. I thought maybe he held possession of it, but he implied it required a wizard with great magic to use it. We all know that Gadiel didn't have the skills."

"We killed him," Zita said. "I searched through all his things for any useful magic items and found nothing."

"He had a manor out in the country, did you search that too?" Finn asked.

"I thought he got rid of that when my father became king. They both moved into the Velidred Castle."

Ylfa pointed a kabob of stegox, anouora, peppers, onions, and other vegetables at Zita. "There's a chance your father had control of it. That might explain how he managed to acquire so much power."

Zita shrugged. "Maybe. I never saw it."

Al brought the conversation back to the problem at hand. "What other magic items can we use?"

Ylfa held up a second finger. "The second is the Crystal of Zaraboth—"

Al interrupted, "Yeah, that's what killed my grandfather."

Finn said, "The crystal didn't kill him but his attempt to capture it did. It's my understanding that he could have captured it if he had brought the third moon charm, the Crown of Anticletus."

Al's pulse increased and a big grin spread across his face. He grabbed Finn's forearm from across the table. "Sherry is my girlfriend. She *is* the Crown of Anticletus."

"Is she now?" Finn and Ylfa exchanged glances, and a smile rose across Finn's face. "And do you know where to find her?"

Al ran a hand through his beard. "Well, I'm not sure, but I think I can find her." *She has to be back in Crossroads after all these many months. She's probably been bored for months and is looking for something exciting to do.*

Zita said, "We don't have time to tramp all over the mountains looking for your friends. When we get to Oakwood, I'll send out messages to my network and get them to meet us at the Village of the Stone Warriors."

* * * *

The next day they reached Oakwood and had to stop so Zita could send off her messages. Zita disappeared into a small building to send out her messages. Al saw Clive and the bouncer from the

Hound and Chicken standing at the tavern's doorway together watching the three wizards walk through the village.

Clive yelled at Al. "Hey, wizard boy. Blackstone wants that staff you carry."

Al shouted back. "He can't have it."

Clive pushed the bouncer on the shoulder. "Get Blackstone, while I grab my bow and arrows. I'm going hunting. Stop right there, wizard."

Al rolled his eyes. *Why can't these guys just leave me alone? This is just like high school where the bullies always pick on the odd person.* He looked over at Finn. "Are these guys just having fun? I was told I can't shield against nonwizards."

Finn said, "Who told you that?"

Al stared at them and shook his head.

The bouncer came out of the tavern with the man wearing the faded blue felt hat.

Al snorted in disbelief. Blackstone was Tice, the man that had helped Al leave town.

Finn seemed happy at seeing the man and said, "Blackstone how's the magical objects business?"

"Pretty slow since you don't have students and council members coming up to see you all summer."

They met in the middle of the street and shook hands. The bouncer stayed close to Blackstone.

"How much can I offer you for the boy's staff?"

Blackstone is bargaining with Finn for my staff?

Al held the staff tighter and pulled it nearer his body. "Not for sale."

Clive hobbled toward the rest of them trying to nock an arrow as he walked. "You don't have to buy it from the wizard. I'm gonna kill him, and I'll sell it to you."

Blackstone looked at Clive and pointed back at the tavern. "You had your chance at grabbing the staff a few months ago. You failed."

"The wizard sent a stegox after me."

Al smiled and stiffened his back. "Bad things happen when you mess with a wizard."

"Watch your back. I'm coming for you."

Blackstone moved toward Clive and the archer retreated back into the tavern.

"I can get a good price for that magical item. What's it worth to you?"

Al looked at the staff. He didn't even know how to fully use it yet. He examined his grandfather's image carved into the top, rubbing his fingers across the image's beard. "Not for sale."

"I see." Blackstone's attitude seemed to soften as he moved closer to Al and the staff.

Al backed up.

Blackstone came up to Al and placed his hand on the staff.

Al jerked it out of the man's hands. "Not for sale."

The man just stood there and smiled. He looked longingly at Al's magical object.

When Zita returned, she said, "I've sent out messages to friends in Crossroads, Velidred, and a couple of mountain villages. I asked for Sherry, Erik, Kestrel, and Cugbert."

"And how do we know if the messages get delivered?" Al asked.

"The people we messaged show up at the Village of the Stone Warriors."

Al rubbed a hand over his eyes and forehead. They had limited time to open the marked door in the Phantasmal Moors where he hoped the warriors waited. If they were a day late, then they would need to find the door again. He yearned for the speed of communication on Earth.

CHAPTER 65

Zita stood next to the stone warriors with Jackson by her side. Finn, Cugbert, and Alpherge the Mighty with his staff stood off to her left. Today would be the day they attempted to rescue the stone warriors, and her stomach was doing flips.

A crowd of people formed near the village. Somehow, word had spread that the wizards were rescuing the warriors this day. Several family members were in the field with their stone-warrior fathers, brothers, or sons. Would Finn kick these people out of the area when the portal opened? Many of the people on the hill brought a picnic dinner and were making it a celebration in the perfect fall weather.

"Where's Erik?" Zita asked.

"He hasn't arrived yet," Al said.

"Wasn't he with you, Cugbert?"

Cugbert answered, "No, he was helping Sherry."

"Did he get the message to come here?" Zita searched the crowd for the umpteenth time.

Could they perform the task without Erik and the Sword of Freedom? The scroll Zita and Al found at Finn's said the Helmet of Justice and Sword of Freedom had to work together. They had sent a messenger to notify Erik, but if he didn't show, they would have to cancel.

Al asked, "Are we supposed to stand by the portal entrance to Earth? That was where King Haskell stood when he turned them to stone."

Zita continued to scan the crowd for Erik. "I think we should stand on the hilltop with a view of what's going on. We don't want to be down by the portal and miss what's happening in the meadow."

Finn said, "Sherry has to be in the center of the action so she can direct the warriors through the portal."

Sherry hadn't shown up yet. Their research indicated they needed the Crown of Anticletus for the magical energy from the Anticletus moon to reach into the moors and intersect with the marked door.

"No, I appreciate what you all are saying, but we need to space ourselves and the artifacts out over the entire battlefield." Al pointed in three directions. "Zita, you stand on top of the hill as one point of a triangle. Erik will be down by the portal. I will be on the other side of the warriors at the third point."

Zita shook her head. "How will we know what to do and if it's all over or if something went wrong if we're so far from each other? Shouldn't we all be together?"

Finn fingered the red necklace he had removed from Ursula before they left the mountain. "Al is right. You will need to center the energy from your magical objects over the center of the warriors."

"Where will you be?" Al pinched his lips.

"I'll be near Zita in case she runs into trouble."

"What kind of trouble are you expecting?" Zita asked.

"I've heard from my Velidred contacts that Kang, a wizard from the Council of Nine, has planned to disrupt our rescue. He lost a brother during the wars with King Haskell, and he always envied the warriors that were encased in stone. He's an angry man. Don't worry. I'll control him."

Zita's radiation poisoning had returned after their trip into the moors. She already felt queasy, and she hadn't even put on the Helmet of Justice yet. She ran her fingers through her hair, and a clump of tangled hair dragged out. More than anything, she wanted to hold Erik and kiss him; but she didn't want him to see her like this. She tried to cover up bald spots on her head by brushing her long hair over those spots, but that strategy grew useless.

"Do you see Erik?" Zita asked for the hundredth time.

"Not Erik, but I see Sherry." Al took off running up the hill.

"Where?" Zita looked, but she wasn't as tall as Al and couldn't see over the people. Had Erik arrived with Sherry? Her heart pounded. She dropped to her knees and vomited.

"Zita, are you okay?" Erik asked.

Really, he shows up now? Could I look any worse? My hair is falling out, and I'm emptying the last meal I had in the grass. She looked up at Erik. He looked wonderful, but she felt horrible. "Hi?"

He lifted her up in his arms and spun her around. "I'm so happy to see you."

"Please, easy on the spins."

"Sorry." He set her on the ground. "I missed you. Is the radiation poisoning back?"

"I had to use the helmet for a trip through the Phantasmal Moors."

"That sounds dangerous. Will you be able to control the helmet and the magic?"

"I don't know. I think part of my problem this morning is I've been worried about you."

Erik smiled that lovely smile. She didn't know what he had done these last two months, but his muscles bulged beneath his tunic. He was so beautiful.

"We can finish this task, bury that helmet and the box in the ground, and then never touch them again."

Jackson barked and ran around Erik and Zita.

"We won't bury you, Jackson. You're a good boy."

Finn approached. "Okay, he's here. We'll get started in about thirty minutes when the Anticletus moon is in the sky."

"How will we know when to add our part of the magic?" Zita hoped all the stone warriors didn't explode like Dickerson. Could she handle all the pressure of this becoming an event rather than wizards experimenting and seeing what they could do?

"Watch me. I'll point at you when it's your turn."

Sherry turned to Finn. "What are we supposed to be doing?"

Finn took a deep breath. "You'll start in the middle of the warriors. You'll have to initiate the Crown of Anticletus."

Sherry shook her head. "I don't have that kind of control over it. It just kind of happens when my friends are in danger."

Finn made a noise in his throat. "The whole process hinges on you and your power to keep the gate opened while the warriors are rescued."

I knew we should have met in someone's house before coming here to the warrior field. We're going to fail before we start. Zita said, "I should be in the middle of the field, directing the flows to the moors. How can you have Sherry doing this task?"

Finn replied, "We aren't opening a door. We're doing what is known as a cascading planar promise. You will direct the flows through Sherry."

"What does that mean?" Sherry stood next to Finn with her hands on her hips. "Will I be in danger while all this is happening?"

Finn raised his hands in a calming motion. "When the warriors were first sent into the moors, they weren't escorted through the moors into the planar dimension. Instead, King Haskell transferred them through a virtual door and set them in the dimension. All in one action. Then he replicated their existence here on Aloheno as stone statues."

Cugbert towered over Finn. Strands of gray hair intertwined with his red beard. "Have you considered the corruption of evil that was encased in the sword? This process could send it out over all these people."

Zita's eyes widened. *Is that a possibility? Al, Erik, and I entombed the evil in the sword. There is no way it could be released.*

Sherry said, "I still don't know what I'm supposed to do."

Finn handed her a small golden ring. "This ring is the portal transference focus key. After you become the Crown of Anticletus, you will place this in your palm and spin it." He showed her what he meant.

"I'm not a wizard, so if it requires magic—"

"That's what Al, Zita, and Erik will supply."

"Wait, I don't have magic either." Erik stepped up close to Finn.

"That doesn't matter. The magic from Al and Zita will be enough to fill the portal trough, and your object will act like a mirror, reflecting the energy back into the arena. Sherry's connection with the Anticletus moon will multiply all your magical energy."

Sherry raised her eyebrows and shook her head.

"I assumed Sherry would have more control over her powers." Finn pointed at Al, Erik, and Zita. "You three will need to start out close to Sherry surrounding her with your magical objects. As she gets the hang of what she's supposed to do, you will slowly retreat to a spot outside of the perimeter of the warriors."

Zita looked at her friends one by one. They all had confused expressions. *We are so going to fail in front of all the warriors' families and friends.*

"Erik, as you back away from Sherry, you head to the portal entrance where you arrived from Earth. Al, move past the point where Dickerson once stood. Zita, your position will be at the top of the hill."

"That wasn't how we talked about it back in the mountains. Why are you changing it now?"

"It's been a long time since I've seen the warriors. Now that I've seen the battleground, this is the way it should work." Finn took a piece of paper from his pocket.

Another wave of nausea burbled inside Zita, and she fought to keep from emptying her stomach. "Don't you think we should talk about it some more?"

"Time is running short. We need to get started, and I don't know how long it'll take to retrieve all the warriors from the planar dimension. Go to your positions. Cugbert, chase those people out of the meadow."

CHAPTER 66

E rik stopped to see his dad before heading to his position. "Dad, we're going to bring you all back to your normal self."

"Do you promise not to kill my warriors and me?"

"I can't promise anything, Dad. Finn and Zita are leading the procedure, and I'm just lending a hand and the Sword of Freedom." Erik waved the sword three revolutions in the air. He realized just then that he didn't know what he was bringing to this event.

"Who can I talk to in order to stop this travesty?"

Erik's jaw tightened. "We're trying to help you." The words rushed out of his mouth.

"At what cost to the lives of my warriors? Do you know how hard they have lived to follow our fight against the mountain king? They are here because of decisions I made. It was hard enough to see them become statues, but if you plan to blast them into a million pieces, then I want no part of it."

"Dad."

"Enough."

Erik hardened his stomach as he looked at his father. A hard man indeed. What would it have been like to have grown up with him in the house? Or would it have mattered because as a soldier, he probably never came home? Today, they would save these warriors, and Erik would see what his father said then.

Will Zita have the strength to stand up under the pressure of working her magic with the Helmet of Justice and the radiation poisoning?

* * * *

Zita walked with her teenage friends and Finn to the center of the stone warriors. She wondered if she had strength enough to do her portion of the spell. The Helmet of Justice had a role, but she felt reluctant to wear it one more time.

At the hilltop, children ran around playing tag or kicking and tossing an air-filled pig's bladder back and forth. Their parents stood in groups of five, seven, or more, talking as if they were at another summer picnic. *What is wrong with these people? Don't they see all the things that can go wrong?*

Cugbert strolled through the stone warriors, yelling at people to vacate the area.

Zita dropped to her knees next to Jackson and shape-shifted the animal back into a lead box. She manipulated the clasp and opened the box lid. The Helmet of Justice rested on the bottom of the box, just like always. It felt like a vise gripped her stomach. Could she take another two hours of radiation poisoning to help Erik's father and the other stone warriors? She lifted the helmet from the box, took a deep breath, and adjusted it on her head.

A group of children ran through a line of stone warriors and then returned immediately as Cugbert waved his hands up and down and forced them back to the top of the hill.

Finn positioned Sherry facing the entrance to the portal to Earth. "Try to always face the portal. I believe it might provide resonance as we perform the ceremony, and we need to minimize the reflection of the magic."

Zita noticed Sherry's fingers trembling. The redhead hugged her body as if she was cold.

Finn gently touched Sherry's shoulders. "Don't worry. Everything will be fine."

Sherry said, "You don't understand. My control is minimal. Even now, before becoming the Crown of Anticletus, I'm feeling vibrations all around this area. I may not be able to do what you request."

"That's why Erik will be stationed near the cave entrance. The Sword of Freedom will prevent the vibrations you're feeling from causing a problem."

Sherry looked at Erik.

Erik shrugged.

In a few minutes, Finn had set up Zita, Al, and Erik ten feet apart in a triangle facing Sherry.

Finn looked at the small scrap of paper in his hands and handed it to Zita. "Read this when you are ready to begin the process."

"What is this?"

"I found a scroll in my chambers. A scroll I was reluctant to open after the students were turned to stone. It reminded me of the ring. You must read it to make the portal open."

She looked down at the chant found on the paper. Finn had been holding out on them. He did know how to rescue the warriors. He should have shown them this earlier. Had he forgotten the scroll when he had lost Ursula?

Zita looked with pity at Finn as she saw the strains of sadness etched across his face.

She nodded at Cugbert.

Cugbert's booming voice asked for silence from the crowd of spectators.

Finn and Cugbert walked to the top of the hill. Then Zita began chanting using magic to enhance the volume.

Peace by day, trials by night.

Struggles in darkness, restore in light.

Twilight flinches, daylight struggles.

Terrors of shadows, darkness snuggles.

The wind began to blow, and Erik raised his sword high into the sky. He tilted the sword point to face Sherry. Zita noticed Erik's hair stand on end and saw energy forming around him. Then a stray lightning bolt from a cloudless sky struck the sword, knocking Erik to the ground. The sword fell from his hands. He rushed to the sword and lifted it back to the sky, a look of grim determination lining his face.

Al jumped at the sound of thunder and ducked his head. Then he raised his staff tentatively into the sky.

Zita continued.

Doors and pathways to new dimensions.

Moors of darkness with evil intentions.

Guards of obscurity, search and find

Levels of gloom, warriors confined.

Planes of existence, open to sight—

Planar doorways cast with lunar highlight.

Storm clouds built over the portal to Earth.

The clouds rose from the mountain, starting white, and circled over the mountain top, turning darker and darker through their rotation.

Sherry rubbed her fingers back and forth over the ring Finn had given her. She glanced at Finn then looked at Al with her lips pressed tight. Sparkles of gold floated around the ring like strikes of a blacksmith's hammer hitting red-hot metal.

Another lightning bolt struck near the portal.

The rotating cloud built lower, blocking out the sun.

Sherry's body began to turn a hazy pale blue.

Zita could barely stand as winds gusted around her. Tablecloths and blankets tried to fly in the strengthening storm as their owners held them to the ground. Children stopped playing and ran to their parents. Why couldn't someone have foreseen this happening and told the families to stay home? A dangerous mix of safety, curiosity, and potential danger rushed through the air.

Electrical discharges bounced near the Earth portal, and she wondered if the tempest might open the portal. Would Erik choose to stay on Aloheno or go back to Earth without her if it opened? She worried about his safety while he held the metal sword.

Zita raised her voice to counteract the storm's fury. She read the next lines from the paper.

Lightning, thunder, storms of despair,
The Torch of Lareez ignites and flares.

The Crown of Anticletus formed over Sherry's head. Her body glowed a bright blue, forcing Zita to avert her eyes.

Paths, streets, ways of yore.

Cobblestone broken, marked doors of war.

Find our men tried in the furnace of battle,

Warriors alive despite death's rattle.

Sherry fingered the ring in her hand and tried to spin it. The ring circled once, shot out little golden sparks, but then fell over. She looked at Zita with feverish eyes.

Zita nodded, and with a confident smile, signaled her to keep trying.

Sherry spun the ring again, and it flopped after two revolutions. The third time, the ring rose slightly from Sherry's hand and rotated on its own. Golden sparks flew off its metal.

The storm encircled the camp in a rotation of wind and energy.

A current of electricity flew from the top of Al's staff to a point two feet over Sherry's head, which joined with a similar volt from the Sword of Freedom. Erik seemed to struggle to hold the sword steady as the stream increased in power.

Am I supposed to do something? Zita assumed the helmet would tell her what to do and when. *Why isn't the Helmet of Justice talking to me?*

Zita felt a tightness in her chest as a spike of adrenaline raced through her body. *I've never done anything to initiate the helmet. I don't know how. My sickness has left me too weak to interact with the helmet.*

She stood confused; her head tilted at an angle as she shrugged at Erik and the others. She tried to slow the rising tension forming in her shoulders. Zita closed her eyes and recited a mantra her mother had taught her. "Calming blue, calming green. Calming blue, calming green." She repeated the words and took long soothing breaths. The panic and confusion reigning in her mind dissipated.

Something happened within Zita, a spiritual connection made or a mental block removed. She didn't know, but with a bright flash and enough power to almost knock her over, a contact formed. A spark flew from the Helmet of Justice in an arc above the ring and met with a lightning bolt from the Staff of Ishwa, which joined with a stream of energy from the Sword of Freedom. Sherry and the Crown of Anticletus were now enclosed in a giant bowl of energy.

The storm's intensity kept Zita from moving as if a giant magnet held her in place, requiring every ounce of power she could muster to keep from perishing.

The ring Sherry held in her hand grew until it had a three-foot diameter.

Zita didn't know what Sherry saw, but from her vantage point, the ring's center became opaque. Zita believed she saw the cobblestone paths in the moors.

Her hands shook as she tried to read the next words.

Unblemished promise from Sword of Healing,

Hear the call from rescue pealing.

Staff of Knowledge shrewd and true,

Helmet of Justice see through.

The marked door with oil of magic,

Find the warriors from lands pelagic.

The ring had grown to have a ten-foot diameter. Sherry manipulated the ring, and it rotated on a single point, not quite touching the ground, going faster and faster. Doors in the Phantasmal Moors flashed by as the ring rotated.

Wizard Kang shouted over the tumult of wind, lightning, and pandemonium. "Stop. Stop it now." He ran toward Sherry.

Sherry either didn't hear him or ignored him as she sent the ring spinning faster and faster. Zita saw visions of purple as the ring spun. *The purple door. We found the door.*

Kang shot a fireball at the top of the triangle dome the three teens held, and energy from the blast shot out along Zita's connection.

Zita collapsed, and she gasped as the blast knocked her to the ground. Her helmet secured tight to her head, held firm. The magical connection remained stable. Zita wobbled to a standing position.

"What are you doing?" Finn raced after Kang and shot a firebolt at him.

They exchanged blasts, each wizard throwing up shields.

The stone warriors' friends and families ran back toward the Village of the Stone Warriors, dragging their children but leaving their belongings on the ground. The spinning dervish snatched blankets and linen tablecloths and whipped them into the sky.

"These warriors shouldn't be able to return to their families if my son can't return to me," Kang shouted over the tumult.

Finn stood close to Zita, and she worried about being hit by a stray blast from Kang or a ricochet from a shield. Finn needed to engage in battle with Kang away from the teens.

The blankets and tablecloths blew around the charged atmosphere as if dancing around the dome.

Sweat and fever encapsulated Zita. She wasn't well, and the extra power needed to hold the energy spewing from the ring weighed heavily on her body. *I need to open the purple door before it's too late.* She raised the paper more closely as her eyes became irritated with blowing dust and debris.

Al held firm to the staff of Ishwa. Zita could see and feel the streams of magic flowing through the dome. The ring drew massive amounts of energy into it. A single stream came from the point where the three flows linked at the dome's top down to the spinning ring.

A blue light of energy rushed from Erik. A green light came from Zita, and Al's yellow light connected at the top of the dome and swirled its way to the ring like a kid's top spinning on a bedroom floor.

A fireball flew over Al's head and bounced off the electrical connection with the ring. Sparks of golden light radiated off the ring and caromed off the stone warrior closest to it. Dust blasted off the stone warrior where the sparks hit it.

Zita froze as a fireball nicked the leather helmet over her right ear.

Kestrel came over and raised a shield between her and the fighting.

She mouthed a thank-you and raised a hand to her heart but noticed a weak shield. *What is wrong with Kestrel?*

Finn yelled at Zita as he continued to fight Kang. "Finish the incantation and then move back to your positions."

Despite the blasting of fireballs, electrical discharge from the dome, and the fury of the deafening storm, Zita held control through the Helmet of Justice. She shouted the final lines on her paper.

The crown defeated from justice postponed,

Ring remove the bodies of stone.

Free the warriors from the moor,

Warriors unfasten the bolt secure.

The ring seemed to spin faster to the point that Zita could no longer see inside it. Golden sparks flashed along the ring's edges. She struggled to move to her position at the top of the hill. The surge of current from their connection to the ring ebbed and swelled as the three held their connections. They moved off to their assigned areas.

When the three had reached their positions, Zita finished the incantation.

Return to family from him who harmed,

King and father, I reverse the charm.

The battle between Finn and Kang still raged beneath the dome. Kestrel stayed in the center, protecting Sherry and the ring.

Every few seconds, a lightning bolt broke free from Earth's portal behind Erik and bounced off the sword. Zita could sense with her helmet that Erik struggled to maintain control of the sword when the lightning struck the dome.

She searched the battlefield for some sign their magic was working. Was that how it would work? The warriors would enter the portal door from another dimension and walk onto the battlefield?

CHAPTER 67

Zita saw a sword extended through the spinning ring. A heavy fog blurred what was happening on the other side of the portal. A warrior stepped through the ring into the battlefield. One of the stone statues turned to dust and blew in the wind.

As the first warrior breached the other side, Kang sent his own electrical charge into the dome. Bolts of lightning flashed in the sky. Zita fell to the ground as thunder boomed across the field.

Lily rushed over and helped her to her feet.

Zita felt so tired. Only one warrior had escaped his prison, and they had thousands to go. She worked against pain from the helmet, radiation poisoning, and exhaustion to control the current of magic to the gateway.

Golden sparks from the spinning ring scattered over the stone warriors. As a warrior stepped through the doorway, his duplicate statue turned to dust. The sparks increased the distance of their path with each spin. Earlier, the ring rescued one or two warriors from the Phantasmal Moors each minute, but now she saw twenty to thirty warriors walk through the ring as their prisons of stone returned to dust every few seconds.

Kang threw a burst of power at the dome, causing something to change in the energy flows. A discordant sound shook the dome.

The ring slowed its spin.

What is wrong with this man? He is so petty that if he can't have what he wants, then no one can have happiness. It's too soon to stop. At least half the warriors are still stone. I need to stop him now.

Zita reached out through the helmet, searching for Kang.

* * * *

Headaches had plagued Sherry all day from the Anticletus moon. Forest River Blossom had promised Sherry comfort, but so far, the headaches persisted. The fight between the wizards had waged through the afternoon.

The blue glow of the Crown of Anticletus blazed about her body, and she felt the energy expending from the wizards and artifacts. A discordant resonance sounded through the meadow as if two discordant chords played simultaneously on a piano. She realized she had to work fast to resolve this problem before the ring stopped spinning and ruined everything.

She used the Crown of Anticletus's power to delve into Kang's mind, which was a feeble one despite his attempt to look powerful. Sherry probed for a weak point in the wizard's brain, but he blocked her.

Interesting. She had never seen that before. How did he do it, and how could she counteract his actions? The good thing about her attack was he couldn't defend against Finn, throw fireballs at Finn, Kestrel, and the dome, and block Sherry at the same time.

Kang stopped his assault on the dome and worked on holding his shield against Finn's attacks and Sherry's mind attack.

Next to Sherry, an image of Zita formed, and the green-eyed wizard held out her hand to Sherry. "Take my hand."

Sherry sucked in a quick breath, surprised at Zita's presence this close to her.

Zita said, "We need to work together to defeat Kang."

"I can't get through to manage his mind."

Sherry reached and took Zita's hand, and she almost collapsed from the power being emitted. How could Zita stand there while this energy blasted her very soul? Then Sherry felt it filling her whole body. She felt the source of the girl's drive and passion.

Zita smiled at nothing but thought of a man. Sherry could understand Zita's passions, her longing to be held, to be wanted and loved. She could handle the force and power of this process because of her love for Erik.

With power from Zita and the Helmet of Justice, Sherry broke through Kang's defenses.

When the barrier in his brain broke, Kang's magic shield disintegrated. Finn's next fireball blasted Kang and set the wizard on fire.

Kestrel collapsed to the ground, and Lily rushed to his aid.

Zita squeezed Sherry's hand and disappeared.

* * * *

As more and more of the warriors returned to Aloheno and the present dimension, a celebration began. The celebrating warriors were no longer stone statues but moving, feeling, and loving human beings. They danced and shouted on the former battlefield.

Zita knew they weren't finished. She saw at least two hundred stone warriors still needed to transition from the Phantasmal Moors. Erik's dad hadn't returned, and she wouldn't quit without knowing the man lived. Fatigue racked her body, and she struggled to hold the tide connecting the dome.

Sherry's focus had returned and seemed transfixed on the spinning ring, despite the commotion within the dome.

Zita checked the moons in the sky. The clouds had been blown away from the spinning winds around the battlefield. Anticletus slowly dropped toward the horizon. What would happen to Sherry and the ring when she could no longer form the Crown of Anticletus?

More men transitioned, and their stone statues on the battlefield disappeared.

Sherry collapsed to her knees, and the ring's spin decreased.

The ring slowed as twenty-five warriors escaped from their stone prison.

The strands of yellow, green, and blue slowed their rotation. The golden sparks no longer drifted over large sections of the meadow.

Zita's stomach tightened as she watched Lily race toward the Sherry in slow motion. *We can't fail now. We're so close, just a handful of warriors left to rescue. Erik will be devastated if we don't rescue his father.*

Lily reached Sherry and helped her to her feet, sharing water from her water skin. Sherry seemed to catch her breath then gave the ring a spin, renewing its power.

A lightning bolt from the portal to Earth struck Erik, knocking him to the ground, and he lost control of his sword. The energy field broke for a moment between Erik and the dome. As the sword fell, it peaked with intensity, forcing a jolt toward Zita. Then the voltage resumed and reconnected with the others.

A magic spell slammed into Zita, causing her to stumble. Magic smashed into her from the portal to Earth. Icy fingers of despair raced down her spine as she clutched her arms about her chest, and her shoulders curved forward.

She shook her head as if that might make her feel better. *What just happened?* She checked behind her for a wizard but found no one. After the initial impact of the blast of magic, she didn't feel any different.

Zita saw a person transition from stone to human on the battlefield and thought it was the last one. No other stone warriors stood on the field. All had turned to dust as their counterparts had transitioned through the ring. It was time to shut the process down.

Then another person walked through the ring, despite the absence of remaining stone warriors. This man walked through the moors onto the battlefield. He looked familiar somehow, but she couldn't make out who it was.

Sherry touched her finger to the top of the ring and slowed its spin.

Many of the warriors walked over to the man who had walked out of the ring and clapped him on the back, and a chorus of cheers roared across the meadow.

Then a chant picked up. "Dickerson. Dickerson. Dickerson."

Anticletus set, and the stream of energy between the ring and the top of the dome winked out. Zita detached her connection to the source as she saw Al and Erik's discharges trickle to a stop. She ripped the helmet off her head and threw it into the lead box. Then she dropped to all fours and retched. Never again would she wear the Helmet of Justice. She hoped she lived through the night.

Villagers still hiding in the Village of the Stone Warriors returned to the battlefield to greet their returned family members.

CHAPTER 68

Five days later, Erik took in the huge Velidred Castle banquet hall, enjoying the feast thrown by Prince Krunal for the returned warriors. He held Zita's hand as they talked with Erik's father.

Erik asked his father, "What do you plan to do now that you're free?"

"I've fought my entire life, and you tell me there is peace in the land. I don't believe that, but I will relax for a few days before bringing warriors back together to prepare and train." The commander wore a tunic borrowed from the prince since the commander's tunic was war-torn and dirty. He had no home to go to since his wife and child had escaped to Earth.

That's all he knows, how to fight wars. That wasn't the path for Erik. He enjoyed healing people and needed to convince Cugbert to take him back as a student. He doubted that he could ever be friends with his father. They had too many differences. Even now the man seemed aloof.

Commander Anderson had an unfocused gaze, and Erik wondered if he was thinking of Mom.

A group of six people came up to Erik and Zita. A warrior stuck out his hand and gripped Erik's wrist. "I am fortunate and thankful for your help in releasing me"—he waved his arm around his friends—"us from the portal."

"Hear. Hear." the men said as they downed their vessels of wine.

The women with them hugged Zita. "We thought they were gone forever. How can we ever thank you?"

"Just to see you back among the living is enough," Erik said.

Erik had asked his dad what his plans were, but Erik wondered about his own plans. He wanted to spend more time with Zita and hoped that could occur, but he also wanted to become a Third Braid priest like Cugbert. He hoped it would be possible to achieve both goals. He needed more conversations with Zita and Cugbert, but he enjoyed being next to Zita here and now.

* * * *

Champagne bubbles tickled Zita's nose as she enjoyed the music from the lyrist, harpist, and flutist who sat in the corner of the banquet hall. She was familiar with grand parties like this one and did her best to welcome guests and make them feel comfortable.

Zita's health had improved with help from Cugbert and Erik. She had lost a lot of hair the first two days after wearing the helmet on the mountain and was happy the current style at the castle included headwear. The style was silly, a conical hat with a veil, but she refused to show off her ragged scalp. She had shaved her long black hair and hoped to see it grow back. Erik assured her, once she quit wearing the helmet, she would heal completely, and her hair would return.

What direction would her life take now with Erik by her side? She knew his desire to become a full-fledged healer, but would that leave her journeying across the countryside and helping people? She would love to stay at the castle, host parties, and talk with friends, but she sensed Prince Krunal might not approve. They needed to talk after the party.

Zita watched Kestrel and Lily dance to the music. They were a beautiful couple, and Lily's feet seemed to float across the floor. Zita had to verify that Kestrel wasn't using magic to make her glide so effortlessly.

Finn walked over to her. "I will leave in the morning." They had talked Finn into taking the Helmet of Justice in the lead-lined box back to the mountaintop with him.

Zita said, "I saw you speaking with the Grand Wizard. Are you two friends again?"

Finn shook his head and grimaced. "The Grand Master asked me to rejoin the Council of Nine after Kang's death."

"That would be a great opportunity for you."

"An opportunity I'm not interested in pursuing. I want to pursue science and knowledge, and I can't do that here. I have no passion for the political games played in the Velidred Tower. I think it's time for me to open the wizard school again."

She nodded her head. "Do we know why Kang attacked us?"

"We found documents of a study he did on the dangers of the moors. He feared we would open a permanent portal to the Phantasmal Moors and leave everyone open to attacks by beasts, gods, and wizards."

"It was more likely all the havoc he caused on the battlefield that would have caused the problem rather than preventing it."

Finn said, "Promise me you two and Al will visit me, and maybe we can visit the Phantasmal Moors once more to find Ursula and the students."

She gripped his hands. "Of course. We'd love to." She touched her mother's necklace and looked at the floor. Zita knew how much Finn loved Ursula, and she would help to find her in the moors. However, she didn't know if she could ever wear the helmet again, even if that was needed to rescue Ursula. "Will it be okay if we use the back entrance? I don't think I can talk Al into climbing the iron rungs again."

They laughed.

* * * *

Sherry enjoyed the party atmosphere at the castle. Al danced with her in an awkward box step that pitted her skills at keeping her feet out of the way of his giant shoes. She did her best to guide him from running into other guests as they danced.

The mayor of Crossroads and his wife, Ciara, had come to the party, and they made polite smiles at Sherry when their paths crossed. She wondered if the people of Crossroads would accept a woman as mayor.

Forest River Blossom roamed about the room, chatting with people in power. She came to Sherry and Al, and they stopped dancing.

Forest River Blossom asked, "Will you visit me in the next few weeks?"

"None of your herbs have helped."

"We have to test. Maybe it isn't a single herb but multiple herbs blended into the right formula that will solve your headaches."

"I won't have much time. The townspeople convinced the mayor we should start up a school. I will contact you to allow you to experiment with your formulas."

"Wonderful."

Warmth spread through Sherry's body as she contemplated her life on Aloheno. She stood on tiptoes and gave Al a kiss. She had helped a community become better not by political posturing but by hard work, planning, and great friends. Could she make a difference on Aloheno? Maybe she could work with Alpherge, and they would bring some of the modern conveniences of Earth to this underdeveloped planet. She released a deep, satisfying sigh.

The End

Thank you for reading my book. If you enjoyed it, won't you please take a moment to leave me a review at your favorite retailer?

Thanks!

Kenneth Brown

More from the Series

The Mountain King Series by Kenneth Brown

Haskell – Orphan to King – Prequel to the Mountain King Series

Eclipse of the Triple Moons

Zita's Revenge

Rescue of the Stone Warriors

Go to https://kenbrownauthor.com/ for more details

.

About the Author

This is Kenneth Brown's third book in the Mountain King Series. He has been writing professionally since the release of his first book in 2018.

He loves to hike, spend time with his family and sings in the church choir. Even though he started writing later in life, he loves to create worlds, creatures and characters to have exciting adventures in those fantastical worlds.

Check out https://kenbrownauthor.com/ for novel release dates and details about the author.

Acknowledgements

I want to give special thanks to the people that helped make this book the best it can be.

Editors: Red Adept Editing

Sara N Gardiner – Developmental Editor

Virge B – Copy Edit

Alyssa B – Proofreader

Members of the Poplar Creek Library writing group:

Mary-Megan Kalvig

Thank you all for your willingness to educate me on word usage, story flow and grammar.

The cover artwork was created by Kenneth Brown using images from FXQuadro and backUp from Shutterstock. Kenneth's creative director, Mary Brown, was instrumental in getting the final image into a format worth presenting to the world. We hope you like it.

Bonus Material

Thank you for purchasing this book. We hope you enjoyed Rescue of the Stone Warriors. Please take the time to write a review of this book on your favorite book buying website.

To find out more about the author, Kenneth Brown, and get advance notification about future books, check out the website, Ken Brown Author, https://kenbrownauthor.com/. Join the Kenneth Brown Author Readers Group to receive these great benefits.

- Get the latest information on New Releases
- Insider Looks at Outlines, Plots, Characters, Deleted Scenes and Exclusive behind the Scenes Glimpses at Kenneth Brown's Writing
- Sneak Peeks of Upcoming Chapters
- Ask the Author Questions
- Exclusive Offers
- And MORE

Find out more about the exciting prequel to The Mountain King Series, Haskell – Orphan to King. Read the fantasy story of how orphan, Haskell, lost his parents, and rose from orphan thief to become King Haskell, the Mountain King. An exciting tale of intrigue, fear and magic.